David,

All the best in 2024.

[signature]

SHADOW TIER 2

SHADOW SANCTION

CLEARED AS AMENDED
For Open Publication

Jan 24, 2023

Department of Defense
OFFICE OF PREPUBLICATION AND SECURITY REVIEW

Also by Steve Stratton

Shadow Tier

SHADOW TIER 2

SHADOW SANCTION

A LANCE BEAR WOLF NOVEL

STEVE STRATTON

FORCE POSEIDON

DETROIT

FORCE POSEIDON

Published in the United States of America by Force Poseidon
forceposeidon.com

Library of Congress Control Number: 2023934577

Force Poseidon hardcover edition – August 2023 ISBN-13 978-1-7375200-4-7

Force Poseidon trade paperback – August 2023 ISBN-13 978-1-7375200-3-0

Force Poseidon ebook – August 2023 ISBN-13 978-1-7375200-5-4

This book was produced in Adobe InDesign CC 2023 using LHF Tallington for titles, Literata Medium 10/17 for body copy and Cooper Black for chapter headings.

Manufactured in the United States of America

🐦 @ForcePoseidon · ForcePoseidon.com

To know your enemy, you must become your enemy.

—Sun Tzu

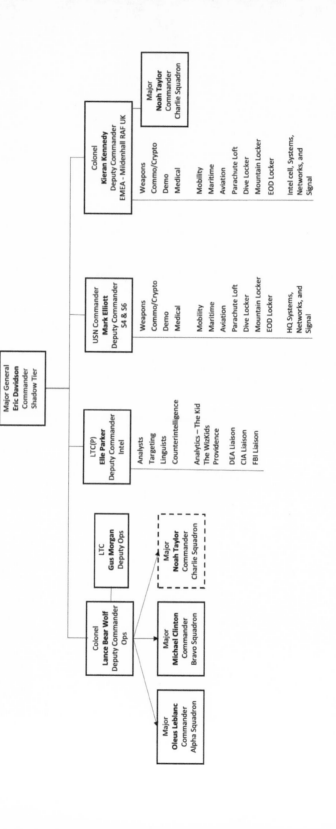

SHADOW TIER 2
SHADOW SANCTION

For Danny, the best of us.

Chapter 1

A re you sure you want to do this?" Elle Parker asked.

"Yes. We agreed we wouldn't let threats keep us from living our lives. It's important for us to be there, and Chayton's final service isn't until one this afternoon."

Lance Bear Wolf, a Native American Crow, smiled as he drove to one of his favorite places on the Crow Indian reservation, the park and trailhead leading into the area they had been elk hunting on 9/11. The date and place held special meaning for both, as it marked another turn in the unlikely story of Shadow Tier, a new and unconventional warfare group with only one rule of engagement: Win.

Chartered by the president of the United States to fight the drug war on America's southern border, Shadow Tier had expanded its reach and punch to operate clandestinely against middle eastern extremists alongside CIA. It had been six years since its creation in 1998, and Wolf had to admit they were doing better stopping terror groups than the Sinaloa cartel. But there was a growing sentiment in Washington that it was time to bring war back to the war on drugs. Shadow Tier was to be the tip of that spear.

Wolf pushed it all away to focus on honoring his uncle. He backed the Suburban in until he felt the rocks marking the parking area boundary. He stopped for a moment and smiled at Parker as the sun accentuated the red in her auburn hair and green in her eyes. He was amazed that she was in his life.

He pushed the button to pop open the rear hatch. Parker was about to speak when the air was filled with angry murder hornets of a different kind. The rounds banged against the truck's steel body as windows shattered from rifle fire.

Parker reacted without hesitation, sliding down in the seat and reaching for her pistol. Wolf grabbed his pack and rolled out of the Suburban to a position behind the front tire and engine block for cover. At a glance, he saw four men split into two elements, each taking a side of the road and entering the trail head. Wolf dropped a shooter on the right and heard Parker firing. When the second shooter took cover, Wolf used the break to move to the back of the Suburban.

"Covering fire!" Wolf yelled as he unloaded six rounds in rapid succession. Parker slid over the center console away from the shooters and joined Wolf, now at the back of the SUV. She pointed as two more men joined the fight.

"We're outgunned," Wolf said. "Let's see if they'll come into the house, where we'll have even odds," Wolf said.

Parker nodded, slipping her pack on and cinching the chest and waist straps.

Wolf fired again, dropping the attackers behind cover. "Go!"

Parker leaped over the rock barrier and sprinted into the woods. Wolf fired two shots left and then two right before following her. The shooters cursed, filling the air with a salvo of returning fire.

Wolf heard three of them run dry. He stopped and used a tree for support, hitting one of the shooters on the left side low in the gut. Not dead, but out of the fight. Wolf fired again, the rock chips showering the hiding shooters.

He sprinted after Parker, reloading on the run, stopping next to Parker a quarter mile later. She had taken cover behind a large cluster of deadfalls and leaned in to Wolf, whispering.

"What is our bounty up to now? Two million?"

Wolf shook his head. "I don't know, three, maybe. This is getting old. I want to make an example of these guys, but I don't want to desecrate the land or my uncle's memory."

Parker asked, "What would a Crow warrior do?"

Wolf nodded and took the Randall Model 18 knife from his pack, inserted it into his waistband, and accepted a small, pistol-sized crossbow Parker held out to him. They had planned to use it to hunt grouse. Wolf would have to be close for it to be effective, but it would do the job.

"How many mags do you have left?" he asked.

"Two mags, plus—" Parker dropped the mag from her pistol to check it. She double-tapped it back to make sure it was reseated. "—six rounds."

"Let's guide them to the Widows Peak, through the notch," Wolf said. "There are some good places up there where we can even the fight."

"When we get near the bear cave, I'll draw them in where we can ambush 'em like we did that team during selection."

He nodded and watched his wife run down the trail in a combat crouch, and his face grew dark. Gauging the enemy shooter's slow and unsure advance, Wolf sang his death song in his head. Sung by his mother before her death—and by thousands of Crow warriors stretching back into time—the song asked his spirit guide for bravery if it was his time to die. As those Crow ancestors did,

Wolf asked for an honorable death. He opened his eyes, thanked his mother, and went hunting.

The shooters moved in loose formation, the men in the back sweeping their rifle barrels over their teammates' backs. Right on time, Parker yelped and cursed slightly aloud, as if she had fallen against a tree, ripping her shirt. Ninety seconds later, Wolf watched as the enemy leader pointed to the shirt swatch Parker had planted, and the men gripped their weapons and followed the trail into the notch.

Wolf let them go and then dropped in behind the last man. Similar in size and weight to Wolf's five-foot eleven-inches and one hundred seventy-five pounds, it was an easy last step and reach around to cover the man's mouth.

In a move he'd practiced a thousand times, he buried his knife between the shooter's collarbone and trapezius. Wolf dragged him backward while rocking the blade in the man's flesh to sever his carotid artery.

Off the trail and hidden behind some brush, Wolf stood and whistled. The shooters spun and fired, but Wolf was already gone. Parker fired from down the path, hitting one man in the shoulder and spinning him to the ground.

He tried to rise with his good arm and Parker shot him twice more in the chest. The three remaining men began shooting on fully automatic, spraying wildly until their AK-74s ran dry. Wolf ran by to their front, disappearing into the woods. They cursed while reloading.

From down the trail came a loud gasp.

"Wolf, I can't walk. Help me. I need help."

Wolf watched from up a tree only thirty feet away as the leader sent one man to circle from the left. The other backtracked, taking a wide route back toward Parker's distress call. After they passed

Wolf, he followed as the group closed up because of the rock's funneling effect on their movement.

A beat later, Wolf stuck his knife in the back of the trailing gunman, letting him scream. His partner spun and, seeing Wolf, fired his machine gun. Wolf held the stabbed man in front of him as the bullets made the dead gunman dance. When the shooter's AK jammed, Wolf dropped to a knee and let loose a bolt from the crossbow. It pierced the man's throat, exiting behind his carotid. He dropped his rifle, clutching at the bolt, gasping for air and coughing bright red blood from his carotid artery.

The shooter fell to his knees, drowning in his own lifeblood. Wolf scaled the notch, stood on the rim and screamed a war cry. The last shooter called out for his teammates but none responded. Wolf climbed down and saw the last attack run for his life.

Parker came from behind the bushes hiding the entrance to the bear's den with a tight-lipped smile and nod to Wolf. She spun the suppressor off her pistol barrel and dropped it into her pants cargo pocket, and pushed the pistol under her shirt in the small of her back.

"One of these times, they will be ex-Mexican Marines," she said. "They won't scare so easily."

"I'm not so sure. I think El Chapo sends his second tier after us just for show, to keep his lieutenants in line. After we destroyed his Antrax team, he's not wasting top resources on low-probability missions."

"Let's hope El Chapo continues to be that thoughtful."

"You know what they say about hope."

"Yeah," Parker said, grinning. "I do. Let's head back. We need to call Chief Hogan if we're to make it to the service in time."

Wolf parked at the church, several folks giving the shot-up

SUV a double-take. Wolf held Parker's hand as they strolled to the church, his quiet reflections on the azure blue sky and bright white clouds. They reminded him of paintings about buffalo hunts with warriors swarming the colossal beasts to provide for their tribe. The sky contrasted with the plains, now empty like the souls of many living on the tribal stipend.

Wolf and Parker entered to greetings from his extended family. His gaze took in the simple one-room church with ropes hanging behind the pulpit from the bell tower. The smells inside spoke to Wolf of the Crow converted to Christianity from one hundred and thirty years ago when the church was first built.

He saw the coffin and pointed out the Pendleton blankets hung on either side. "It's a family tradition to repay the pall bearers for their time."

Parker said, "He left this earth a genuine warrior. Fighting for his people."

"Agreed, but the cost was too high. He should have called the Tribal Police instead of trying to stop a drug deal himself." Wolf paused. "They used to call him 'old school.' He taught me many lessons, but none I considered more important than being one with nature. He was a gentle soul with a warrior's heart."

Elle Parker appreciated this side of her husband. She saw the beauty inherent in the Crow way of life, more spiritual than religious, respecting family and the tranquil connection to the land.

She was about to learn tranquility was not always a given. An aggressive threat was fermenting—not just to Elle and her husband, but to the entire Crow reservation.

Chapter 2

L ater that evening, the lights in the simple ranch-style house were low, befitting the somber mood after Chayton's funeral. The furniture was a collection of comfortable Seventies country plaids and light woods. Warmth flowed from the families crowding the front as Wolf and Elle joined them in front of the fire. One man, a cousin, mentioned the Tribal Police chief wanted Wolf and Parker back at the police station to continue his investigation into the ambush.

"He can wait," Wolf said.

Aunt Winona brought them bowls of elk stew and bread. Eating in silence, Wolf stared at his food. He winced at seeing his dead mother in his aunt's face. Alma Nighthawk Anderson, Wolf's mother, had died on the order of a Sinaloa cartel lieutenant six years ago, but the memory remained fresh.

The restaurant gunfight that had quickly boiled over to include Wolf and his family had started his hunt for revenge. It had also claimed his stepfather, Andy Anderson, and the lives of several innocent Mexicans. Thinking back, he was sure he couldn't count all the lives touched and changed by his attempt to protect the innocent that day.

Wolf gripped the spoon as if it was his last hold on life, darkness surging through his soul. Parker's soft touch brought him back to the present. Wolf stuffed the memory and his hatred for El Chapo and his Sinaloa cartel back in the cage where he would unleash it when the time was right. El Chapo could wait, now was the time to connect with family. Wolf forced a tight-lipped smile and complimented his aunt on the stew.

Aunt Winona sat at the table and said, "I can see I remind you of your mother. Stay in the light, Lance Bear Wolf. Your demons have no power here. We need you here, and the Crow need you here."

Wolf looked up at her. "The Crow need me?"

Wolf watched Winona use her wrinkled hands to smooth the tablecloth. She was four years older than her sister and, as she looked up, the wrinkles in her face deepened a look Wolf took as concern and empathy.

She said, "Before your uncle was killed, he told me many things I was blind to. Drugs and the demons they cause are eating at the soul and future of the Crow. He said the drug problem on our reservation and those of the other tribes in Montana had grown worse in the last year. He talked of gangs from Michigan and California using tribal lands to make and distribute drugs. He thought the casinos were involved in distribution, too. Now my eyes are open, and I have seen hard-looking men who are not tourists. Chayton said to tell you. That you would know what to do."

They sat silently for a minute until Parker broke the silence. "Did Chayton tell you how he came to know these things?"

"He said talk with Billy Red Fish."

"We will go see him tomorrow." Wolf got up and took his bowl to the sink. "It's getting late, and we should go." *I need time to think,* Wolf thought.

Wolf and Parker said their goodbyes, careful to speak with everyone. An elderly man pulled Wolf close and whispered, telling him they needed a warrior. Wolf nodded and turned to find Winona smiling.

"You two come see me before you leave."

"Yes, ma'am. Thank you for the stew," Wolf said, hugging her.

Parker leaned in for her own hug, and they headed for the SUV.

As they drove off, Parker said, "I thought it was interesting that she didn't point us to the tribal police."

"No, she didn't. They aren't held in high regard. No telling what Billy is up to. Andy knew him, a Vietnam vet. They kept an eye out for illegal activities like drugs and poaching when I was a kid."

Wolf took the southern route to Billy's house in Pryor the next morning. On the way, they stopped in at the town of St. Xavier to ask if anyone had seen Billy. Two people who remembered Wolf's mother said Billy and his Reservation Rangers, as they called themselves, hadn't been seen for weeks.

What are they doing now? Playing at being a military style neighborhood watch? Wolf thought.

As they drove to Billy's house, Parker rolled down the window and inhaled deeply.

"I didn't realize there was so much ranching on the reservation. The cut fields and hay bales look so peaceful," Parker said.

"It looks beautiful from here," Wolf said, "but it's much hard work. Ranching and farming are declining ways of life. It's a struggle to make a living in it anymore. You really have to love it."

As they rounded a bend in the road, Wolf slammed the brakes and steered into the skid, stopping the truck at an angle to the SUV and four men armed with rifles in the road in front of them. Parker dove out her door and took a position at the backside rear tire. Wolf took a position at the front tire. Peering over the hood, Wolf saw the man's eyes as he came forward, hands raised.

It took a second for Wolf to register. The man had gained thirty pounds or more and was much older looking than Wolf expected.

"Wolf, it's me, man—it's Billy. Don't shoot me, okay?"

Wolf flashed a grin at Elle and nodded.

"We're good," he said, holstering his pistol.

Wolf strode around the front of the truck and took the offered hand, pulling Billy in for a bro-hug and slapping him on the shoulder—which at Billy's six foot two inches was a reach around his pot belly. He looked to be maybe two-hundred and sixty pounds, and the reddish complexion he was known for still evident.

"What's with the roadblock?" Wolf asked. "Something less threatening might have been a better welcoming party, Billy."

Red Fish laughed. "Well, yeah, but we weren't expecting you. We thought we had some intel on a vehicle using the reservation to get around a highway patrol checkpoint." He gestured toward a small cutoff into a field. "Let's park down by the creek and talk." Two men and a pickup truck were left at the tribal checkpoint and the rest followed Red Fish.

The air was cool under the shade trees. The burbling of the creek settled Wolf, the gift a moment's peace.

Turning to Billy and his guys, Wolf saw a determination in their eyes. Billy introduced the men and said a sentence or two about their military service. Vietnam, the Gulf War, and one young guy just back from Afghanistan. All of them infantry, airborne, or Ranger. They had seen combat, death, and were kitted for war.

For the next twenty minutes plus, Billy talked of the growing use of the Montana reservations by gangs to produce meth and get around known Highway Patrol checkpoints. The low density of Tribal Police meant they rarely visited many areas of the reservations.

"I have scouts out on the east-west highways who report when anyone tries to get around Highway Patrol or Tribal Police checkpoints by diverting through the res, but we're spread thin out here, brother. We catch a few, but we think most slip through."

Wolf listened and nodded his understanding. What Billy described was disturbing to the core. And it had the potential to change the fabric and future of the tribes.

"This all has cartel fingerprints. Keep a low profile, make war in the shadows," Wolf said. He handed Billy a card with his last name and his Shadow Tier voicemail number. "We'll have some of our folks look into what you've found. Anything big happens, leave a message at this service. I get them immediately."

The group exchanged farewells and departed.

As they headed to the truck, Wolf turned to Elle and said, "Get the Kid on Billy's claim right away."

The Kid, as he was known, but Jack Wayne his name. He'd been conned by Kennedy into helping during Wolf's unsanctioned war against the Sinaloa cartel and subsequently full time at Shadow Tier.

"The ramifications are making me sick. Just when I think that evil son of a bitch El Chapo can't take it any further, he surprises me again."

Chapter 3

Wolf talked little on the flights he and Elle had taken back to Tampa. What he'd seen and heard scared him. The Crow nation was in more danger than it understood.

After dumping their bags at home, they drove to Shadow Tier headquarters on MacDill AFB to reconnect with current operations, including Bravo Squadron's new focus on an Islamic extremist group called Ummah Tameer-e-Nau.

Operating out of Pakistan, UTN's stated purpose was to rebuild Afghanistan's infrastructure and raise money to develop Taliban-held areas. The group had been formed by former members of the Pakistan Atomic Energy Commission and former Pak Air Force and Army officers, they had access to the biggest foundry in Pakistan and help from a leading engineering firm.

Shadow Tier's second in command, Kieran Kennedy, and the intel team, had used all-source intel and some new software the Kid found to see interesting new patterns that had been missed.

Parker and Wolf walked into the Secure Compartmented Information Facility, where the level of excitement in the SCIF was palpable.

Kennedy stood looking every bit the football defensive tackle he'd played in school and said, "Okay, quiet down." He paused for a dramatic moment and said, "We've found what the big guys didn't—a connection between UTN's 'relief efforts' and what they're really after." He nodded to the Kid, the youngest member of the team.

The Kid smiled. "Using the new link analysis software, we've uncovered that the locations UTN visits with high regularity in southern Helmand province are within easy reach of uranium deposits."

Wolf shook his head. "You're kidding me, right? Helmand province, where most of the opium is grown?"

"Yeah, that Helmand," Kid said.

Parker sighed. "We're headed to Afghanistan, aren't we?"

Kennedy nodded. "We need eyes-on to assess if they've started mining operations."

The secure phone in front of Wolf flashed and rang its synthetic electronic tone. He grabbed the handset and said, "Wolf here. Yes, sir—zero-six, with you. Roger that. Out." Wolf replaced the handset. "That was General Davidson." Colonel Eric Davidson had gotten his first star when he'd been elevated to command of Shadow Tier. He normally operated out of the teams small DC headquarters and dealt with the absurd politics. "The vice president wants the general and me in the Oval Office tomorrow morning to talk with the president about Afghanistan and opium."

Vice President Kathleen Singerton was a prickly, hard-fighting politician who'd earned her stripes in Washington the hard way, first in the House, then the Senate, and now the White House. She was a tough old bird, but she supported Shadow Tier and its goals. For now.

Major Michael Clinton, the Bravo Squadron commander, said, "Without objection, I'll start spinning up my team for deployment to Afghanistan."

Wolf nodded. "Good idea. Seems we are going for uranium or opium. Probably both. Either way, Helmand is the hot spot."

Update complete, Wolf, Parker, Kennedy, and the Kid waited for the rest of the team to leave the SCIF and the door was closed

The Kid asked, "Why not have the DEA and state department pitch in? They have a leadership role on international narcotics."

Wolf chuckled. "I'm sure you've seen their reports. Neither agency has a winning scorecard."

"Scorecard?"

"The administration has implemented scorecards to assess if an agency is meeting its stated goals," Kennedy said. "Like reducing the amount of opium cultivated in Afghanistan."

Wolf smiled. "Novel idea, accountability. It's shaking up government and its leadership. But back to the task you have for me?"

Kennedy pointed to the large digital screen on the wall with a laptop cursor. "For the last six months, we've been working a side project to extend our knowledge of the routes and players involved in the movement of processed opium out of Afghanistan, through Europe, and into the United States. Here is what we have so far."

Wolf moved closer, tracing the routes, talking to himself. In their new world of analytics, the thickness of the line showed the value of the route.

While there were comparatively few low-risk routes out of Afghanistan, there were still hundreds of routes and connections throughout western Europe and Russia. Wolf glanced at the Kid and Kennedy, then back to the map. There was almost nothing in three of the thinnest lines from Europe to Canada. And very little between Canada and the United States.

Wolf said, "It makes no sense. Heroin doesn't just disappear."

Kennedy smiled. "Exactly. What you're seeing are the gaps in our data. Afghan opium, heroin, whatever form it's in, never runs dry here ..."

Kennedy double-clicked the icon and France jumped out on the screen.

"... Marseille."

"Interesting nexus of activity. Given its history," the Kid said.

"Yep," Kennedy said. "The French Connection, about which the movie was made. I believe someone is trying to revive the Marseille mafia. The thin line you see from Marseille to Canada is extrapolation, not confirmed data."

The Kid said, "DEA and state department believe ninety-eight percent of the heroin in the United States comes from the Southeast Asia Golden Triangle. It transits through Vancouver, Canada, San Francisco, and Los Angeles. And we have unconfirmed rumors that the Sinaloa cartel is going to grow a lot more opium. I'm tracking indications of new plantings that will push production past the modeled consumption level in Mexico."

Wolf stared at the screen. "So, what you're telling me is Afghan opium is reaching America, but we don't know for sure how or who is pushing it. And you're also telling me El Chapo is seeing heroin as a growth market and is adjusting his cultivation model in order to compete better?"

"Yes, for sure," Kennedy said. "Cocaine usage is falling off, and a new young, white affluent demographic wants heroin."

Wolf shook his head. "Afghanistan, with its terrorist drug business, a fresh wave of French mobsters wanting to recreate its past into New York, and the Triads protecting their single-sourced monopoly. Not to mention the shit going down on my reservation. Have I missed anything?"

Kennedy grinned. "No. But stay focused on the Afghan Europe-to-America connection in your briefing tomorrow. That's what the vice president wants to hear. Speak to her interests."

Wolf said, "I know, I know—it's how we get our funding. We're going to need another whole squadron to prosecute these new threats. So, where can we find new talent, with the National Guard and Reserves holding down Afghanistan and active troops fighting in Iraq?"

It was a long minute of silence before Wolf smiled.

"I know this seems trite, but Clancy had the right idea in his novel *Rainbow* Six. And ah, Kid? You're coming with me."

Chapter 4

They had just made the left off Connecticut Avenue when Wolf glanced up at the sky. It was wispy blue, the air crisp and full of the sounds of commuters flooding into the District of Columbia. Their perimeter ID checks complete, the government driver took a visitor spot near the entrance to the West Wing. Stepping out of the black Suburban, Wolf habitually scanned the area and then smiled at the nervous Kid.

"Never been here before," the Kid said. "Pretty cool, though."

"Deep breaths, and just relax," Wolf said. "You know this data cold. Answer the questions you're asked, but don't free-associate. Elaborate only if asked to do so."

General Davidson came around from his side of the vehicle and clapped the Kid on his shoulder. "You'll be fine, mister."

Bringing the Kid with him and Shadow Tier's commander to the White House was a risky choice, even though Wolf had thought the Kid and vice president would get along well. The wait outside the Oval Office was short. Once inside, Vice President Kathleen Singerton greeted them, asking polite questions about their trip and yes, DC traffic is always terrible. Please have some coffee, the president will return in a minute.

Wolf was doctoring his coffee when President Gerald Dent walked in and shook hands. He sat in a chair between the two sofas. The three Shadow Tier teammates took one couch and the vice president took the other.

The president began. "I need you boys to connect some dots for us. Do those drugs from Afghanistan do more than provide funding for the Taliban? Do they reach America?"

The vice president cleared her throat. "I've briefed the president on Shadow Tier and what you've done. No need for background."

General Davidson nodded to Wolf. Wolf briefed the situation for the next twenty-four minutes, what they knew, what they believed, and what gaps they still needed to fill. The president was animated and questioning.

When the president asked about the Marseille connection, Wolf nodded to the Kid. He presented the developing French Connection details and linkage to Afghanistan. When the vice president asked who Shadow Tier was coordinating within Europe, Wolf pointed out there wasn't a presence yet, but to that it made good sense to position a full-time squadron in the region to provide intel gathering—and, if necessary, a quick reaction force.

Davidson said that with the British taking over counter-drug leadership for Southwest Asia, plus the Taliban narco-terrorist mission, it would be a smart move to place an operational squadron in the United Kingdom as well.

The president, ever insightful, didn't ask about cost—he asked how Wolf expected to staff it.

"That's a lot of people" Dent said. "Operators, loggies, support elements. Plus all their equipment. Weapons. Aircraft. That's going to take some time." Wolf suppressed a smile.

"Mister President, I already have NATO-member special operations and counter-narcotics personnel assigned in Shadow Tier. I'm confident we can broaden our staffing and training pipeline with personnel from other nations as impacted as we are."

The president thought for a moment, then rapped his knuckles twice on the arm of his chair and stood, signaling the end of the meeting. Singerton and the teammates stood as well.

"Good. Let's make that happen then. The Joint Chiefs tell me dope isn't their fight. For them, Iraq and Afghanistan are about stopping terrorism. I need Shadow Tier to disrupt the Taliban's drug funding." He extended his hand and shook with the teammates.

"Yes, sir," they replied in unison.

"Thank you for coming," the president said, as if it had been optional. The vice president escorted them out.

Outside in the hallway, Singerton pasted on one of her simulated friendly faces and looked almost earnest.

"Okay, that went well, but you'll need stuff, and a lot of it. Send your budget request directly to my office. I will approve it and let the Agency director know." She leaned in for emphasis. "Hurt them, Wolf. Hurt them like they're hurting us."

The growing base next to Kandahar Airport had become a jumbled mess of coalition partners in the Global War On Terrorism. Clinton wrinkled his nose at the stench coming from the nearby porta-potties so early in the morning. Now that the US had invaded Iraq, the base had become a NATO and coalition point of entry prior to joining the stabilization operations.

Clinton pushed a speed-dial button on his satellite phone to call Wolf's Shadow Tier headquarters office. When he heard Wolf answer he said, "Sorry for the time difference, colonel."

"No worries. What's up?"

"Moving forward was a good idea. There is a shit-hot intel unit here, and we've got targets for days."

"Nice. The Kabul embassy is no place for Bravo Squadron."

"Roger that. We have indicators pointing to a large processing lab. Taking the team in tonight to confirm."

"Good. The president wants the opium in all its forms shut down. And our buddy the vice president is in whatever-it-takes mode. The UN estimate is the Taliban are making $400 million a year from opium alone. Parker believes the vice president will see moving Bravo Squadron to Afghanistan as a positive, but she will also jump directly to demanding results. So, work this lab up and provide Joint Special Missions Command with a target package."

"Yep, can do," Clinton said, "but you know we need to disrupt the supply chain at many points along the route to the US"

"Yeah, agreed. I've got some ideas I'm just working up to disrupt the flow from Europe to America. If you have ideas, send them to my top-secret email address."

"Will do. Out here." Clinton smiled as he ended the call. Being assigned command of Shadow Tier Bravo Squadron meant Clinton had full command authority. Bravo was Clinton's sandbox, with his assaulters and support troops

Clinton surveyed his teammates sitting along the web seating of the Air Force Special Operations MC-130 Talon and nodded. It was Wolf's directive that all Shadow Tier operations personnel be proficient at High Altitude-Low Opening and High Altitude-High Opening parachute operations. It had paid off when more traditional options for infiltration didn't support the mission profile. This mission profile was all about undetected surveillance and intelligence gathering. The four-man team would open their ram-air parachutes at six thousand feet offset by a ridgeline to conceal their entry into the Taliban-controlled area.

Under the cover of darkness at twenty-two hundred, Clinton and his three teammates had left their living quarters in the "other government agencies" compound at Kandahar International Airport. Clinton purposely had not notified the State Department Bureau of International Narcotics and Law Enforcement Affairs back at their desks in the American Embassy. He was determined not to suffer the same fate that a series of Afghan-led missions had via leaks from their police partners.

The team boarded the dark MC-130 Talon from the back. Ramp closed, the red lights activated, and only then did Clinton expose his face to talk with the pilots. After a quick conversation confirming the flight plan, their drop altitude, and its GPS coordinates, Clinton said his thanks and took a seat.

The forty-five-minute ride to jump altitude of ten thousand feet went by fast. At ten minutes out, Clinton stood and started the jumpmaster commands to check that the team and aircraft was ready for the jump. Once the team completed gear self-checks and checked each other, Clinton took control of the door. He checked their location via his wrist GPS and made sure there was nothing loose around the door that would impede their exit. He stuck his head out of the door looking for other aircraft in the airspace and pulled himself back in, giving the team a thumbs-up high in the air for those at the end of the stick.

The team stacked behind him, the red light glowing in the dark. When the light switched to green, Clinton launched himself from the aircraft and the team flowed out after him. They quickly flew their bodies into position in a stacked diamond formation, the infrared chemical lights on their parachute packs glowing in their night vision googles and identifying who was who. Free-falling to six thousand feet, Clinton waved off and deployed his chute first. The team followed, and Clinton watched them correct left and head into the landing zone.

Good canopy above him, Clinton said, "Radio check One."

The team responded. "Two check. Three check, Four check."

"Copy all," Clinton responded. "Lead us in, Four."

The team landed within twenty-five feet of each other, then took turns hiding their parachute gear in some nearby scrub brush so they'd have maximum guns available if discovered. Clinton checked his GPS, passed *Olympia*, the beer-based code word confirming successful infil, back to the Shadow Tier Ops Center, and squeezed Two's shoulder. The team moved out, the only sound a whisper of gusting wind.

One mile in on their three-mile patrol to their surveillance location, their track took them up a steep climb. The mountains on either side bracketed an avalanche chute gratefully bereft of snow and ice. Fifty-five minutes later, they stopped on the military crest of a saddle, just short of the top. Clinton joined Two on the north side and scanned the area through the spotting scope, finding six men. One on close perimeter patrol, the others huddled around a small fire.

He lowered himself from the crest and whispered, "We are a Go. Plan Alpha." Then he passed they had achieved the *Coors* way-point to the Ops Center over the satellite radio.

Plan Alpha was a hide site on a side of the mountain boulder field providing cover and concealment, with a clear line of sight to the opium processing lab six hundred meters to the east. Tonight's number one priority to get to the hide site undetected and prepare to stay in place for twenty-four hours.

But like every other mission in Afghanistan or back in Mexico against the Sinaloa cartel, Murphy's Law decided it was time to clock in. Four rounded a boulder to find a lone fighter sitting between the team and its objective. He stopped quietly, hand raised, the infrared micro chem stick attached to his glove glowing in the team's night vision. He dropped to a knee behind a boulder as the team followed suit, moving to supporting positions.

Four radioed, "He doesn't seem on guard."

"Hold position," Clinton said. "Let's see what he's up to."

Four watched as the fighter fiddled with his AK, then ambled over to a rock and relieved himself. Four wrinkled his nose and whispered.

"This guy smells like a dumpster on a hot Florida day. If he takes a deuce, I'm shooting him." Clinton suppressed a chuckle.

Six minutes later, Four reported hearing noises getting louder. Then he saw donkeys huffing with exertion their heavy packs, scraping as their worked around the boulders. The donkeys appeared to know the path, their herder pushing them forward from behind. The lead donkey stopped, its head up, pointing toward Four. The fighter cursed, smacking the donkey on the ass to get it moving. When the herder reached the fighter, they shared some words and laughter, then headed down the hill together oblivious to their enemy mere feet away. Four radioed a vinegary trash-like smell as the donkey's passed, not unlike the guard.

"That's a common smell for black tar heroin," he said.

Clinton radioed to hold for another ten minutes in case anyone arrived late to the party.

When Clinton gave the okay, Four made to step over the donkey trail when he heard a clinking sound. The rattle came from two men who appeared from the darkness, their weapons slung around their backs. Instead of seeking cover until the threat passed, Four spun and put two suppressed rounds into the lead fighter's chest and he fell to the rocky ground. He saw Clinton flanking the second fighter as he ran into the boulders. One loud AK round fired in the crisp morning air and the mission would be over before it started. Four heard two suppressed shots before Clinton came on the radio.

"Second tango down. Four and Three, get your dead guy over here and cover our tracks. Two, help me dig. We've got twenty minutes to get these guys buried."

Forty-five minutes later, the team slowed as they got within a hundred meters of the hide site. Four went forward with Three in support and radioed all clear. Clinton and Two joined them, and the team began building out their hide, half working while the other half kept security. Clinton passed *Budweiser* and ninety minutes later took the first security watch with Two as Three and Four drank, ate, and rested.

The breeze flowing down the mountain caressed Clinton's back and his gaze softened, taking in the scene before him. The slightest flicker of light from a fire leaking through what he expected would be a rough-cut wood door on a hut near the lab.

Looking up at the beauty of the clear night sky, the stars littering the view with their twinkling white, blue, red, and strangely orange ones that probably were planets. To be so close to danger yet feel a peace.

Two hours later, they switched out with Three and Four. Clinton had gotten about an hour of shuteye when shaken awake by Three. Clinton moved to Three's side where his outstretched arm pointed into the darkness.

They watched as headlights bounced along the road. The first time Clinton saw it, he thought he was mistaken and turned to Three with a confused look on his face.

"Why's a United Nations Land Cruiser in an opium convoy?"

Chapter 5

Clinton cursed under his breath. The six trucks, bracketing the single UN vehicle three and three, very likely were delivering opium for processing. Four rested a Nikon D2H Digital SLR and 80-400mm lens on his ruck to steady it. Deep breathing as if behind a sniper rifle, he exhaled. In his stillness, he started clicking off pictures as headlights illuminated the Land Cruiser.

Three said, "Got it."

"Looks like they're stopping. Can you see whose getting out?" Clinton asked.

Four said, "Gun monkeys are out on our side. Whoever they brought with them got out on the other side."

"Let's hope whoever it is stays until daylight."

Nautical daylight—when the sun is twelve degrees below the horizon—came at 0504 at this location in Helmand Province. Full sunrise arrived at 0541. Clinton smiled. The UN Land Cruiser had not departed, so Clinton designated its occupants Priority One—the team would always have one set of eyes on the UN vehicle while the rest of the team would document the site, its security, and activities, like the row of trucks now being loaded in a flurry of activity. Clinton woke Two and had everyone watching a sector of the site.

A lone farm tractor huffed black smoke as it struggled to pull a rickety trailer loaded with wrapped items over the uneven terrain. Men with carts and wheelbarrows of additional product followed it. The trucks were loaded, but they didn't leave.

The rest of the team spent the morning mapping out the lab and truck repair buildings along with the generously labeled "houses." Two used a laser designator to plot the target down to ten-digit coordinates with a one-meter accuracy. Four scanned for patrols and observation posts in rings starting at ten meters and working out to two hundred.

The processing of raw opium and coca takes only a few precursor chemicals that anyone can get. They had seen it on operations in Mexico, Chile, and Columbia, to name a few. No chemistry degree is needed to process drugs. And since it's an illegal trade, no one cared about the rules and regulations followed by the big corporate drugmakers. If some contaminant affects the product's purity or kills a few users, so what? All part of life's rich pageant.

From what the team had seen and captured via camera, this place was just another processing lab. But its scale was the key to its importance. Six long buildings were arranged in pairs. A mere fifty meters to the north of the buildings, the ground rose steeply. It was at the foot of Afghanistan's the Koh-e-Malik Do Kand mountain, near the southern border with Pakistan. It provided a natural barrier to the north and two observation points manned by teams of three fighters, one to the west and another to the east.

The opium processing station included labs, housing, offices, and even caves. What Clinton designated as Main Street stretched toward the team south from the center of two processing buildings. A blacksmith and a maintenance shop were the first of several huts that were smaller structures, maybe one-third the size of the processing labs. From there, the drab houses became mud and tin for the workers. Women were visible with armloads of wood as they stoked fires to bake the day's bread.

Four commented that he saw children headed to the processing labs. The comment sent a shiver up Clinton's spine. He'd seen children as young as five forced to work in places like this. He hoped it wasn't the case here.

The outer layer of security included several man-made bunkers, and trench lines in a horseshoe around the station. The team counted thirty-seven military-age males with weapons and other forty-three unarmed men, likely the opium processors.

Three saw the woman first and said the bodyguards were making it impossible to get a clear picture of her to determine her status. She was wearing a scarf to cover her head and most of her face. The bodyguards escorted her to the far side of the UN Land Cruiser. When two guards came around the SUV to the team side, Clinton radioed that they both had vests showing they were part of a UN medical team.

"Anyone ever see armed UN docs making house calls?" Clinton asked over the team channel.

Negative was the unanimous response.

Three radioed, "I think the protective detail looks to be former Legionnaires."

"How do you know?" Clinton responded.

"I recognize the distinctive way they move—and I served with the gun monkey who got in the driver's side rear door. He's not someone who would sign up for anything drug related. His brother and girlfriend overdosed partying in Marseille."

"Four, shoot a SITREP back to *Brewmaster*. Give them every-thing we have so far. Tell them imagery follows."

They watched as the convoy and UN vehicle drove off. Just before disappearing, the UN vehicle broke off and headed south.

More questions, Clinton thought.

The rest of the day had been slow, the heat intense, desiccating everything without water. At 1700, another convoy came in from the east. This time they offloaded and moved the trucks under the cover of old Russian-pattern camouflage without reloading them. The drivers went to their huts, greeting their women.

So far, the array of convoys made no sense. It was harvest time for opium crops, and the team expected near round-the-clock transportation from fields to the processing station. At 1920 the sensor alert flashed on the receiver Three had established. What Clinton expected but dreaded was now taking place just two hundred and fifty meters away from where they had crossed the trail and killed the Taliban fighters.

Three put an earpiece in and closed his eyes. He nodded and leaned forward, concentrating. "They're talking about the missing fighters," Three whispered. "When they get to the processing station, they are going to report them missing. I'd say we need to be out of here in ninety minutes. Two hours, tops."

"Everyone be ready to go in an hour. For now, eat and hydrate," Clinton ordered over the team channel.

An hour later, Two led them out. Clinton couldn't help but think they were coming away from their surveillance mission with more questions than answers.

Chapter 6

Two weeks later, what Wolf and Kennedy thought was an odd request for support came through General Davidson. Wolf and Parker drove the five miles to the US Special Operations Command headquarters on MacDill and General Davidson's office in the SCIF. The general got right to the point.

"Wolf, the Brit Special Air Service are going to prosecute the target package Bravo developed on the opium lab at Koh-e Malik Do Kand. They asked for you and Parker by name."

"Any idea who made the request, sir?"

"No. It has the SAS regiment commander's signature and I can't read that scrawl. Our liaison officer suspects someone you have worked with in the past is wanting a known operator."

Parker asked, "When do they need us, sir?"

"ASAP, natch. There's an Agency G4 taxiing to our ramp as we speak. Grab your kit and report in when you get to Kandahar."

"Roger that, sir," Wolf acknowledged.

"Two more things before you go. Please give Colonel Sinclair my regards, and make your own luck."

Driving back to Shadow Tier and their lockers to grab their gear, Parker called Kennedy on the car speaker, relayed the update, and asked if he wouldn't mind watering her plants once every five days.

Wolf chuckled and said, "I keep saying we should just buy silk plants and stop worrying about watering."

"That's not a very in-tune-with-nature mindset," Parker said, grinning. "That's more like 'Florida retiree cover the yard with Astro grass.'"

Wolf laughed. "True! What do you think about pea gravel, zero-scaping, and a couple of cacti for biodiversity?"

"Stop. We have friends because of me, and they like us—well, at least me—so let's trade chores until we retire, and then you can handle it full time."

Wolf hung his head. "Yes, ma'am. You're right again, as always."

Parker laughed. "See? I knew you'd get it, eventually."

The stop at Rhein-Main Air Base in Germany was too short, leaving not even enough time for a Starbucks run. When they finally touched down on Kandahar International six and a half hours later, the sun was rising, pushing the temperature on its relentless march to more than a hundred degrees. The air around the coalition base had a tan tint from the dust. The topspin of barely controlled sewage and trash didn't help the ambiance.

Parker squinted as she exited the plane and slipped her sunglasses on. At the bottom of the stairs, she peeked over her shoulder and grimaced. "Sweet Jesus. Same smell, different place."

Wolf said, "Something about the Middle East. It's not like this in South America."

A US Army MP met them on the tarmac in a golf cart to take them to the Other Government Agency compound about seven hundred meters away. Expressing thanks and waving off the cart, Wolf and Parker walked at a leisurely pace, working out the kinks from seventeen hours of flights. They entered the small OGA quarter within the larger compound and found Shadow Tier's Bravo Squadron.

The OGA compound seemed to have a pecking order with the Agency leading the way, followed by other intelligence agencies. Law enforcement, even the FBI, operated out of a worn set of air-conditioned construction-site trailers. The Shadow Tier counter-narcotics team was clearly at the bottom of this roster.

At least the tents the team was assigned were the so-called TEMPER tents—Tent Extendable Modular Personnel units designed for the desert to manage heat and dust.

Entering the air-conditioned Shadow Tier tent, Parker dropped her bag and hugged herself, stamping her feet. "Brrr! What do you knuckleheads have the AC set to—crushed ice?"

Clinton gave her a light welcoming hug then pulled Wolf in for a backslap. "Wait till this afternoon. You will wish it was still this temperature."

After greeting the rest of the team, Wolf, Parker, Clinton, and Taylor sat down to talk about ongoing operations, and relations with DEA and Joint Strike Force elements assigned to the mission.

"We can get the simple stuff out of the way quickly," Clinton said. "Our relationship with the JSF is ten of ten. If they see something for us, they let us know ASAP. If we need anything, they provide it if not already tasked. Their objectives are dead terrorists, so there's no conflict with us. There is a new DEA agent in place named Higgins, and he's pushing hard on the nexus of drugs and terrorism. He says there is another agent joining him soon, but that's it for them. State has pulled out the old playbook and we're seeing a replay of what they did in Columbia and, back in the day, in the Golden Triangle during Vietnam. Programs that didn't work, but look good in reporting to headquarters and Congress. There are a few folks who get it, but they're managed from DC and toe the political line."

"Local police, even the counter-drug unit, are flat perforated with leaks," Taylor said. "Infiltrated by Taliban-aligned assets focused on protecting opium production. Higgins is building from scratch essentially everything a normal DEA field office would have. His partner will focus on creating an Afghan counter-drug super unit that will investigate and vet to a much deeper level."

Parker said, "My assets say your cover is working so far. They haven't identified any movement against our team. Getting out of the embassy helps in the short term, but I think you might be targeted just by operating out of the OGA compound."

"You could go mobile if needed," Wolf said. "But you'd need some leave-behind assets for coordination."

"We're good for now." Clinton nodded. "But it won't last long unless DEA can create the super unit they're talking about. At some point, we will have to come out of the shadows to prosecute a target and our profile will be a lot bigger."

Wolf nodded and crossed his arms. "Right now we fill a void DEA can't and the military won't. The politics go all the way back to the White House, but I see us working with Higgins once he gets rolling. Change of subject, tell me about this new operation."

Taylor said, "Speaking of politics, *Operation Blast* is just that. The British Prime Minister was complaining the SAS unit sent to Afghanistan late last year was not given any useful tasking, so they went home. Now the president has ordered the US Task Force Commander to give intelligence to the SAS, along with the full authority to strike any target they see fit—and they want to strike the lab Bravo surveilled. They requested the four of us, by name, to provide tripwire reconnaissance for the primary force. We leave for Qatar at 1130."

Wolf looked at Parker, who nodded almost imperceptibly.

"Any sign who asked for Parker and me?" Wolf asked.

"No." Taylor shook his head. "But a contact of mine told me the UK prime minister is posturing to take leadership of the UN Southwest Asia counter-narcotics program. Has the UN ever been briefed on Shadow Tier?"

Wolf said, "Not to my knowledge, but we're about as secret as the JSF guys. Why are we flying back to Qatar?"

"While you were en route, the SAS decided it's better suited to handle readying their large force," Clinton said.

Parker said, "Speaking of the UN, do we have any leads on the female seen at the processing station or her Legion bodyguards?"

"The UN is being tight-lipped," Clinton said. "Kennedy and the Kid are working it, but nothing so far. We have alerted JSF and the Marines."

Wolf said, "Okay, copy that. Let's take a break. How are we fixed for chow?"

"All set, boss." Clinton nodded. "We know you get hangry when you don't eat."

Parker smiled. "I have never seen Wolf pass up a meal when he's not on a mission."

"It's true. So, let's go eat before a fight breaks out," Wolf said, grinning.

Clinton handed Wolf and Parker their Agency badges. A short walk later they entered the cooled dining facility, hospital-clean and smelling of breakfast joy reminiscent of a busy Denny's.

Clinton and Taylor nodded and shook hands with friends and

former battle buddies as they found seats. Wolf mentioned how impressed he was with their networking.

"It's a small community, for sure," Clinton said, "not unlike high school in some ways. The table over in the corner is known as the JSF table. We could sit there with the cool kids, but we prefer to eat with the analysts and support personnel. We feed them and the Army military intelligence battalion information when we can, and they reciprocate. Win-win."

Clinton and Taylor made a great team, Wolf mused. Taylor was ready to lead his own squadron, and Wolf had plans to make it happen. The British prime minister's push to take over operations would provide the rationale to stand up another squadron.

After breakfast, a large black coffee in hand, Wolf and Parker sat down in Bravo's ops center to learn their target. The team and support staff spent the next two hours walking through every element of the objective and the estimate of the processing station's volume. Clinton stopped the briefing at 1100, saying it was time to head to the ramp and their two-and-a-half-hour flight to Al Udeid in Qatar.

On the flight to the US air base southwest of Doha, Clinton caught Wolf and Parker up on regional politics, and the State Department efforts develop alternative crops for the opium farmers like had been tried in Columbia and Chile. Parker asked for Clinton's thoughts on their ability to protect the women and children at the lab. Little did Parker or Clinton know, Wolf was already developing a rescue plan.

A SAS squadron sergeant major and his driver met them on the Al Udeid Air Base ramp next to the aircraft.

"Crikey, will you look who it is!" the sergeant major said, rising and bear-hugging Wolf.

Wolf laughed and hugged back. "Peter McDonald himself!

What are you doing here, mate? What happened to making the world's best chocolate?"

"The regiment called up some of the territorial army lads at the start of operations, and I thought it a good time for a chocolate sabbatical. Since I saw you last, I've trained a younger generation at MARS to make honest chocolate." McDonald chuckled.

Parker extended her hand. "Elle Parker."

McDonald bowed slightly, shook her hand, and smiled. "Sergeant Major Peter McDonald at your every service." McDonald lowered his voice. "I trust this is not too impertinent of me, but rumor has it you could call yourself Mrs. Wolf."

Wolf turned to McDonald and shrugged.

Parker tilted her head and tapped her nose. "Yes, but I've kept my maiden name so some chairborne ranger doesn't object to Wolf and I being on the same mission in a war zone."

Clinton laughed. "I'm still trying to recover the IQ points I lost at your reception."

Taylor said, "Wasn't it Regar the security police had to drag out of the F-16 he was trying to start?"

Wolf smiled. "Holding the wedding and reception on MacDill Air Force Base may have not been my best idea. But getting back to business, Peter, this is Major Mike Clinton, Commander of Bravo Squadron, and you know Major Noah Taylor," Wolf said.

"Glad to make your acquittance, Clinton. Major Taylor, these lads treating you well, then?"

"Indeed they are, Sarnt Major. You should join us."

"If Wolf is involved, it's well worth consideration," McDonald said. "But let's get on to the planning cell, shall we? You lot play an important role in this mission."

The drive around the familiar but continuously growing base took longer than Wolf expected. The heat, wind, and smells of JP-4 jet fuel combined with the roar of aircraft brought back memories of the last time he had been at the base. That mission had nearly cost him his life. His brother and Colonel Neil Gates plucking him from a cliff face as a platoon of Spetsnaz closed in had saved his bacon that day.

The blue US Air Force Suburban stopped before a large trailer, snapping Wolf from his reverie. *Get your head in the game,* he thought, stepping from the Suburban and into the planning cell.

Wolf's quick scan of the room lingered on a logistics listing on a whiteboard to his left that rostered an impressive armada of machinery. The list included eight Air Force MC-130H Combat Talons—one-third of the entire Air Force inventory—thirty-eight Land Rover Desert Patrol vehicles, two logistics vehicles, and eight Kawasaki dirt bikes fitted with advanced noise reduction.

A quick calculation came to one hundred and twenty-six SAS and support personnel for the assault. It would take four to six men to mark the landing strip, and with Shadow Tier's four, Wolf got one hundred and thirty-six SAS and Shadow Tier personnel planned to achieve mission success.

Wolf trailed the team as Sergeant Major McDonald brought them forward to meet mission commander Colonel Alister Sinclair. After the introductions, Sinclair got right to the point, explaining the need for a tripwire element to ensure the SAS G-Squadron's air troop wasn't compromised while it laid out the C-130 landing strip for the primary force.

The secondary mission was to gather more intel on the mysterious UN team if it made another appearance.

The MC-130H HALO drops would take place at twenty thousand feet, and that was briefed in detail. The commander thanked the Bravo team for their support and bid them fair winds and soft landing before directing Peter to coordinate comms frequencies, call signs, and other essential details.

After the comms briefing and equipment tests, Wolf pulled the team aside.

"Thoughts?" Wolf asked.

"Lots of moving parts and people," Clinton said.

Taylor said, "A daylight assault in Helmand Province is pretty bold, boss."

"Limited close air support," Parker added.

Wolf said, "Yeah, agreed. Sinclair seems to have a voracious hunger to get in the fight."

"Yes, and in true SAS fashion, it will probably turn into a slugfest," Taylor said.

"We could end up becoming a diversion for the primary force," Clinton said. "We need multiple exfil options in case we gotta bug out in one big hurry."

Wolf stared at Parker for long seconds. He had ultimate confidence in her professional abilities, but his emotional side screamed to sit her out on this one. His logical side knew suggesting she stay behind could be damaging, not just to his marriage, but also to the concept he and his leadership team held gender didn't determine who could be an operator.

Teammate Lizzy Armstrong was already a squadron legend, and he would go to war with her tomorrow. So why not Parker, his wife? She had the skills. Why was his spirit guide so agitated? Was it telling him something he couldn't recognize?

Wolf focused on preparing for the mission but kept his subconscious tuned to the darkness flowing through his spirit guide. A darkness he couldn't shake. A darkness with meaning he didn't understand.

Chapter 7

The night air was frigid at altitude when the loadmaster lowered the ramp on the unevenly heated MC-130H Combat Talon. Beyond the glow of the red interior lights, Wolf saw the night sky beset with stars, the dusty band of the Milky Way bright against the dark empty spaces. Wolf finished his death song and gave the signal to switch from the floor-mounted oxygen system to their bailout bottles.

Nods from his three teammates indicated they were breathing normally, the first critical checkpoint at the jump altitude of twenty-three thousand feet. With practiced efficiency, Wolf took them through the pre-jump checks ensuring their Cypres automatic chute openers were set. If all else failed, their activation device would automatically open the reserve parachute at thirty-five-hundred feet.

Wolf had been hard on Parker when she demanded HALO and HAHO training, and probably too harsh a taskmaster. He was trying to discourage her, but failing that, he needed her—and himself—confident in her skills. Her reasoning was that Shadow Tier needed her competent in all forms of infiltration techniques.

Like the rest of the leadership at the unit, she was not content to ride a desk. She knew her best value was at the pointy end of the spear, in the field doing the intel work she trained for. Wolf's resistance had been futile.

He finally agreed to put her through hours of training on the ground and in the Tampa iFly indoor skydiving tunnel before her first static line jump. She had left the training helicopter on command without a moment's hesitation. Even her landing was decent, as were the five more she did that day at the Brooksville airport with the help of Wolf's old Florida National Guard unit, 20th Special Forces.

Her final jumps were in her own jump gear with Wolf and Gus Morgan. She had deployed her parachute right on time and landed standing up. Her progression was rapid, getting the hang of flying her body much quicker than Wolf had.

Wolf put his wife as far out of his mind as possible. On this mission, she was Four. He was Three. Taylor was Two, and Clinton was One, as mission commander. They stood at the edge of the ramp lined up in twos, all eyes riveted to the lights. When they flashed green, the four jumpers left as a single pod.

Stacked in an offset V, they flew down to six-thousand five-hundred and deployed their chutes. The infrared chem lights on Clinton's reserve parachute pack showed the way to the *wadi* landing site in their night vision goggles.

Parker flared her canopy a beat too soon and sat back on her ruck at landing. The team collected parachute gear and closed in facing out, holding position for what seemed a long three minutes before One radioed clear. Two found a place to hide the jump gear in some brush just out of the *wadi*.

"Coach, this is Striker, I pass *Chelsea*," Clinton radioed the first of the soccer-based code names and waypoints to the operations center.

The radio transmission bounced to the new module inside the US Air Force Predator MQ-1 drone patrolling overhead. The recent addition of a communications relay pod sending comms to a satellite gave teams and units of all kinds of better coverage if you could keep the drone on station.

Clinton had suggested a different hide location, one with more elevation and a better view into the processing station and the ridgeline beyond which the SAS was to lay out their landing strip. Two led out, taking a route that kept the team hidden from view.

Thirty-five minutes into their movement, Clinton called a halt over the team channel. He whispered that the Predator's infrared camera was offline. Clinton had expected its continuous operation to ensure their route was clear, but now they would have to slow down for safety. They had built extra time into the plan, but any other deviation and they wouldn't report target status to the main force at the next comms window.

At their hide, Clinton radioed the Operations Center. "Coach, Stryker. I pass *Liverpool*, I say again *Liverpool*. Copy?

"Roger Stryker, Coach copies *Liverpool*, out."

The team spent the next hour camouflaging the hide site overlooking the opium lab. Wolf tuned to the main force satellite radio channel and heard the positive report from the SAS element that had jumped in to prepare the expeditionary runway for the C-130s. The runway was to be ringed by the IR lights, and the C-130s were on their way.

He wouldn't overtly disagree with a coalition partner mission plan, but Wolf still thought the mission was ill conceived with its many constraints. With the war in Iraq consuming most resources in the region, there was limited close air support and it was only available during daylight hours. The SAS operations order demanded a daylight raid when it had been proven that the US and British forces owned the night. They were lucky to have the partially operational Predator overhead.

The mission was to destroy the opium processing station. The houses with non-combatants on either side of the main street were designated no-fire zones. Smart move to limit collateral damage, but the Taliban were not above using women and children as human shields.

Wolf voiced his concerns for the safety of the women and children. Parker agreed. During Wolf's one-man war against the Sinaloa cartel, he had confided in her some of his actions after the assassination of Colonel Gates, his team leader, on a classified mission. It involved a botched attempt to terminate a bio-weapons scientist.

The target had been unharmed, but his wife and daughter had been killed. Wolf had marked the target with his laser designator that day. It wasn't until years later Wolf learned the truth. And she knew it drove his focus on stopping what he thought the planners so callously called collateral damage.

Wolf told the team he had a plan to protect the women and children. "It's pretty simple. Once the attack kicks off, I'll gather all the women and children I can and hustle them to the caves. It's likely the attack will draw any Taliban out to fight, so I'll flank them, clear a cave, and hold until the SAS ends the fight. I don't need you to agree, or even to join me, but that's my plan."

Wolf was surprised when Parker appeared upset. Clinton's wide eyes and open mouth said without words that he too thought the plan was about the dumbest thing Wolf had ever said.

Taylor was first to voice his thoughts.

"What do you mean, 'we don't have to agree or join'? Bloody hell, why not?"

Parker shook her head. "I don't think so, Lone Wolf McQuade. We're a team here."

As the sun cracked the horizon, Clinton radioed their final situation report. "Coach, Striker Actual. Be advised *Penalty Kick*, I say again, *Penalty Kick*. Copy?"

Clinton listened for a beat, his call was acknowledged, and he switched to the team channel. "The raid is a go."

Parker heard them first. "Here comes the close air support."

Four fast movers roared into view, US Navy F/A-18 Hornets. The pre-raid bombing was underway, and when they cleared the target, the primary force would launch from their holding area. The first pair rolled in parallel to the mountains and dropped their bombs two at a time, walking them into an along the length of the lab buildings.

As the aircraft climbed out, the bombs set off secondary explosions as the chemicals used to wash the opium detonated. The next pair of Hornets focused on the buildings around the lab and the truck parking area. Equipment and trucks lifted into the air on billowing tongues dark yellow and black fire.

Explosions followed by zinging noises from shrapnel filled the air. As the second pair of fighters climbed out, the first pair came back and used their twenty-millimeter guns to tear up the trenches. Wolf noted they had gotten much lower than any jet he'd ever seen besides an A-10. Two minutes later, after firing on the trenches, the last jet roared vertically into the dark blue sky and wagged its wings in a farewell gesture.

Taylor pointed to the west. The SAS in their "pinkies," as their

Land Rovers were nicknamed, came roaring across the desert, dodging Taliban defenders firing RPGs and machine guns within meters of the trenches. Shadow Tier teammates scrambled out and joined the fight in the trenches and assaulted the bunkers, while the support force poured machine gun fire and anti-tank rounds into what remained of the processing station.

Clinton switched to the command channel, telling the main force and support element commanders the Shadow Tier element was advancing on the houses.

Clinton shook his head. "Colonel Sinclair is pissed you didn't brief your plan. He called you a cowboy but said 'have at it.' The support commander just said 'good hunting.'"

"This is our chance. The Taliban is focused on repelling the main force. We have to save the women and children," Wolf said, looking at Parker.

Parker nodded. "You go, I go."

Wolf led the way through the firefight toward what was left of the lab buildings.

Chapter 8

Wolf took a zigzag route into the housing area that minimized their exposure to the friendly fire coming in from the east and south. Between the Navy's bombardment and the Milan anti-tank missiles the SAS had fired, the processing buildings were destroyed.

Wolf watched as a technical—a truck with a heavy machine gun mounted in the back—loaded with fighters, tried to make a run for it. It got only a quarter mile away before an anti-tank missile caught it in the middle of the cab, splitting the truck in half in a fiery explosion when the fuel tank erupted.

He heard the barks of .50-caliber sniper rifles and the burps of the light machine guns from his five o'clock, the sound giving him confidence that the support element had seen his team and shifted fire. The Taliban's distinctive AK and machine gun fires to his eleven o'clock signaled they hadn't been seen.

Parker and Wolf took the west side of Main Street, Clinton and

Taylor took the east. To their advantage, most of the women and children were hiding in the west-side houses.

Using the remaining wall of the blacksmith shop as a holding area, Parker picked up a wounded young girl and asked in English, "Where are the rest of the women?" The girl spoke back in Dari, while pointing to the bombed-out labs. Parker understood enough to know her mother was dead there.

One of the older women touched Parker's arm and said "No, bad, no," motioning to the caves. Taylor ran up and said, "Is she saying there are Taliban in those caves?"

"I think so," Parker said, pointing to the opening in the hillside behind the destroyed processing building. The women also pointed west, indicating there was another cave. Suddenly, the zipping sound of rounds shot in their direction from the cave caused Parker and Taylor to push the women and children to the dirt and cover them.

Wolf ran up to the group and emptied a magazine at the cave opening, moved left and yelled, "Reloading!" Clinton sprinted up and launched a 40mm grenade into the mouth of the cave.

Clinton radioed the support element commander and gave him the intel on the caves. Within seconds, two Milan missiles flew by. One exploded just inside the mouth of a cave, the other penetrating much deeper. A series of secondary explosions followed as munitions stored in the cave detonated and coughed up a huge plume of dust and dirt from the mouth of the cave.

Wolf yelled, "Let's move."

Clinton radioed their plan to the support commander and asked for covering fire. Moving in two-person teams with the women and children behind them, they leapfrogged each other's positions until they got the group to the edge of the western-most lab. Safe behind the four-foot-high remains of a wall, Wolf scanned for threats. He was about to make the final push to the cave when a young woman came running up from behind. Wolf rotated to see her running as she screamed and waved.

Parker stood, adjusting the little girl held in her arms, and ran toward the running child to provide her with cover. The young woman gazed into the sky and was mumbling as she slowed to a trot and Parker neared.

Wolf recognized what was about to happen but couldn't fire at the approaching girl because Parker was in the way. All he could do was yell as loud as he could.

"*Bomb-bomb-bomb!*"

The girl's suicide vest exploded, and the nuts and bolts embedded in it ripped through the air.

When Wolf rolled over and opened his eyes he saw that the explosive shock wave had flung Parker a dozen feet into a heap of the women hiding against the wall. He instantly forgot everything else, struggled to his feet and ran to his wife.

No, no, no!

The dirt kicked up around Parker's body with fires from enemy Taliban. Wolf dropped two, spun his rifle around to his back, and checked the rescued girl laying on top of Parker. Her blouse bloomed with bright red blood. Wolf applied direct pressure while he checked for a pulse, finding none, and was about to start compressions when he noticed blood above her right ear. Pulling back her *hijab*, he saw the hole in her skull about the size of a .22-caliber round, and the rest of her youthful body was peppered with dozens of other impacts.

No resuscitation was available here after all.

He gently pulled her *hijab* over lifeless brown eyes and laid her to the side. He put her hands together, straightened her dress and closed her eyes, then rotated back to an unconscious Parker and checked her for life-threatening wounds. She had a graze on her hip, an L-shaped hole in her forearm, and a piece of shrapnel in her right shoulder. The child Parker had been holding had taken the brunt of the blast, and Parker's chest plate most of the rest.

Both Clinton and Taylor had eaten dirt, but they had triaged each other and were treating the wounded and attempting to keep the survivors calm, as they had been trained.

They weren't out of the woods yet. Wolf flinched as mortar rounds started landing—but these belonged to Wolf's team. The concealing smoke a welcome sight.

Wolf stood. "Let's go."

Wolf carried Parker in a fireman's carry as the survivors shuffled across the open ground to the cave. Wolf held at the entrance as Taylor reconned. A minute later, Taylor called clear.

Wolf was sitting Parker up when she came to, fighting and scrambling for her rifle. Wolf held her tightly in his arms and repeated her name. "Elle, Elle—you're safe, honey. You're safe."

Parker groaned and squirmed against the pain of her wounds. She stared at Wolf for a moment, tears streaming down her face.

"Where is she? The child?"

Wolf inhaled deeply. "She didn't make it."

Parker twisted away, her left hand reaching for her rifle. She started to get up, but Wolf held her down.

"She's safe now. No one can hurt her anymore."

Parker struggled, but her injuries and blood loss had left her weakened and ineffective. "Let me go, damn it! They're going to pay for this. Who gets a young woman to blow herself up and kill other women and children? *Let me go*, I said!"

Wolf held her down by her shoulders. "Elle, please! Don't give in to darkness like I did." Wolf stared into her eyes until he thought she saw him. "It isn't you—and nothing you can do will bring her back. Your job now is to stay here with us and help protect the survivors."

She glared at him fiercely for a moment, fat tears streaking her dirty face. Then, anger and adrenalin spent, she slumped against the dirt wall.

Parker grunted as Wolf bent to removing the shrapnel. He packed and bandaged the wounds to her shoulder and arm. He started a saline IV and gave Parker a fentanyl lozenge for the pain. She took several deep breaths that seemed to help her relax, and the painkiller did the rest.

Seconds later, radio traffic brought the welcome report that the SAS had gained control of what was left of the processing station, and the teams were in mop-up mode. As the SAS support team moved forward, Wolf had Taylor handed off rescued women and children to the support element commander and had Clinton radio for their ride back to the compound.

Eight minutes later, a MH-60 Black Hawk that had been waiting at a Forward Arming and Refueling Point settled onto the LZ in a large brown bloom of dust and debris. Wolf helped Parker aboard followed by Clinton and Taylor.

Wolf buckled Parker into her seat and the helo clawed into the sky. As the bird circled the processing station, Wolf scanned the wrecked building knowing today's attack was only the beginning.

Chapter 9

The forward-based field hospital tent reeked of antiseptic smell just short of nauseating. A Marine Corps Humvee had struck an improvised explosive device and the seriously wounded were being triaged ahead of Parker. Between cries from the wounded and doctors shouting orders, the yelling in the overloaded temporary emergency department was overwhelming.

Stopping at the Air Force hospital on Kandahar Airport had been quick but not painless, as the physician's assistant and nurses had to re-clean, stitch, and dress Parker's field-engineered medical treatment. At Wolf's insistence, they had given her some pain meds and cleared her for travel, with her promise to check in at MacDill Regional when they got back.

Twenty-four hours later, Wolf was nearly certain that the fallout from his last-minute decision to help the non-combatants would end in disciplinary action. But as he was now a technical civilian, Wolf wasn't sure what form discipline could take. The action had caused transatlantic messages to be shared between the Commander SAS and Commander JSF, and that's never good.

Cowboy, dangerous, out of control, led the negative public messaging. But the SAS mission commander's personal message to General Davidson, Director Shadow Tier, was more supportive.

In fact, the SAS message stated bluntly that Wolf's actions and those of the Shadow Tier team justified awarding of the British Conspicuous Gallantry Cross—second only to the Victoria Cross, and the equivalent of the US military's Medal of Honor.

This was even possible because Shadow Tier was a hybrid military unit—part civilian, part DOD, and part Agency—with its people coming from the Army National Guard and Army Reserve. As such, it remained within General Davidson's purview to award military medals for valor.

With the JSF and SOCOM commanding general's concurrence, he signed off on a Silver Star for Wolf, a Bronze Star with V device for valor in combat for Clinton, and a Bronze Star with V device and a Purple Heart for Parker. For his part in the mission, the SAS mission commander awarded Taylor the Conspicuous Gallantry Cross.

Davidson stared at the files for a long take, lost in reverie.

Afghanistan, and now Iraq. Awards, letters of condolences, men and women changed forever. He stared out the window. *What will be the toll this time?*

Now Shadow Tier had new tasking that Wolf would have to complete without Parker. Inside the Secure Compartmented Information Facility, Wolf walked up to Kieran Kennedy's desk.

Wolf's old friend had been assigned Shadow Tier's deputy director of intelligence position, operating in an Agency-funded billet. He had been active Army when recruited by Wolf for the war against the Sinaloa cartel. But Kennedy's world had flipped upside down when he, Wolf, Parker, and Gus Morgan, the operations deputy, had their world rocked.

Two years ago they had attended a four-day meeting at DEA EPIC—the El Paso Intelligence Center. After a third long day of droning presentations from PowerPoint commandos and hard discussions about the effectiveness of current operations, Wolf took his teammates out for a working dinner. Wolf's skill in locating small, hole-in-the-wall places with authentic regional food found them in a little place behind a truck stop off I-10, south of town. After all, it was a Green Beret's fundamental training to blend seamlessly into new surroundings and become one with the locality. Wolf had done his homework on El Paso.

"Always read the local papers," Wolf had said, "and drink the local beer."

The incessant wind had whipped up the dust, and the resulting odor from nearby livestock pens assaulted their senses. The place looked abandoned except for din light leaking through incredibly dirty windows. Parker grimaced when Kennedy asked if Wolf had gotten lost.

Inside the blue cinder block building, all was forgotten as the aromas from freshly cooked food took over. Wolf put away all the concerns of the day to enjoy a great meal with his wife and friends. It was muscle memory that had Wolf leading the team to the corner table next to the kitchen.

They would learn later that a well-placed network of cartel informants had already identified Wolf and the team as they departed the Air Force C-37 they'd flown in from Tampa. By the time the team had gotten across Fort Bliss to the EPIC facility, the Sinaloa cartel was planning ambush options.

And they were taking no chances of failure.

The unassuming restaurant table had been full of tacos, carne asada, chili relleno, filete tilapia, chips, salsa, and many beers from a loaded rolling cooler cart brought tableside.

"We're eating like kings!" a tipsy Parker exclaimed, her grin bright with joy and face flushed with alcohol. The love and warm friendship infused them with happiness. Warriors often know so little of such things, and this occasion would be one for the record books.

Just not in the way they'd hoped.

Morgan was in the middle of a funny war story about Nicaragua, Sandinistas, Contras, and leading a CIA-trained hit team into the capital city of Managua, when a vehicle-borne improvised explosive device—a car bomb—exploded with inconceivably deadly force directly next to the ramshackle restaurant.

A large section of the left-side wall, and the eight people eating dinner on that side of the dining room, just disappeared in the powerful blast. The shockwave threw four other diners, their tables, and the Shadow Tier team into the wall at Wolf's back.

When he woke, the kitchen was on fire and he couldn't see Parker. Morgan was staggering in the swirling gloom, his arms slightly out from his sides, covered in dust and debris, and he had a fork jammed into his upper back. He was saying something, but Wolf's hearing was gone, and all he could concentrate on was the fork sticking out of Morgan's back.

Wolf saw Kennedy lying across an overturned table and he heard the cries of the wounded as he shook the dirt from his hair. He was emerging from his stupor when he saw Morgan regain his senses and slowly bend to help Kennedy. A beat later, he remembered Parker.

He flipped the table over to find her regaining consciousness and covered with food. Wolf didn't know how much time had passed, and he knew his team wasn't armed tonight for a dinner on the economy, so he clapped his hands for attention.

"Morgan, listen up! We don't know if anyone's coming to finish the job and we gotta roll outta here. See if you can get Kennedy out and I'll get Parker—we gotta go right now."

In the distance, police, fire, and ambulance sirens filled the cloudless night.

At the University Medical Center's Level 1 trauma center, Wolf and Parker were treated for concussions, scrapes, and minor cuts. Morgan had a Grade 2 concussion and also needed stitches from being forked, which, once the urgency had passed, would likely generate jokes for forty-four years.

Kennedy was being treated for a blast-induced Grade 3 concussion when a junior nurse swabbing blood and dust from his face observed blood leaking from his right eye. On further examination, the attending ophthalmologist and neurosurgeon located a tiny metal splinter that had neatly penetrated the frontal lobe of his brain through the tear duct of his right eye.

In Wolf's estimation, the ensuing two years of physical and psychological therapy had helped Kennedy to an impressive but incomplete recovery. He was one hundred and twenty-five percent smarter than anyone at Shadow Tier, but it was Kennedy's inability to focus and concentrate over time that drove Wolf to advance a recovered Parker, the unit's former counterintelligence specialist, into Kennedy's leadership position while he mended. But Kennedy was still a formidable analyst, especially with his protégé, known as the Kid, at his side.

Kennedy said, "It was too close, Wolf. You could have lost her over there."

Wolf's tone was somber. "Yeah, it was a tough one. Still is.

Parker's not talking about it, but I see it in her eyes. She's haunted by the little girl who saved her."

Kennedy said, "Processing and learning to live with loss takes time. She's strong, and it's not her first rodeo. She'll be back."

After his meeting with Wolf, Kennedy sat in his office and thought about his UK cousin, Andrew Cavendish. He'd been promoted to his first star in the British Army, and to a new command stood up for him that could make him an important partner for Shadow Tier.

Cavendish had been assigned as the director of the newly created Joint Narcotics Analysis Center, focused on Southwest Asia and Taliban opium that was ravaging the UK. The JNAC was so new that even its public phone numbers weren't yet listed, so Kennedy called Cavendish at his home in Radlett, a quaint little town in Hertfordshire just inside the M25 near St. Albans, where the Magna Carta had been drafted.

The call was picked up on the third ring. "Cavendish."

"Andrew, it's Kieran calling from the colonies, squire. Jungle drums say you finally blackmailed someone for your brigadier, mate. Well done! How are you and the family?"

"Well, thanks very much, Kieran. So thoughtful of you to call. We're all very well, cousin. How are you and Maya? Getting on well, I trust?"

"We're well, thank you. I'm on the mend every day, but I still have my 'slow days,' as we call them."

"Yes, you had a bit of hard luck, but I knew you wouldn't let it keep you down for long."

"The reason I called is to congratulate you on your selection for the directorship at the JNAC. I know it's early days, but I and my group would like to spend some time via the appropriate secure connection toward possibly coordinating activities."

"Interesting. Are you finally coming to your senses and basing a squadron here?"

"Looks like it. It will be quite the mix of NATO partners."

"Excellent. I'm working out of the Joint Analysis Center until they complete our secure facilities. I'll call you from the high side tomorrow, and we can discuss our partnership. Does 1100 Eastern work for you?"

"Yes, thank you, that's great. Talk to you then, and best to your lovely wife."

"She will be excited to hear we're working together. Cheers, mate. Out here."

Kennedy squinted at the large paper wall map showing the port of Marseille. Slowly rising from behind his desk, he moved to the display and pointed.

"Marseille will be the key to the fight, Kid. This is where we will ... we will break ... the Taliban ..." Kennedy's voice trailed off. He sank back into his chair in slow motion and gripped hard the armrests until his knuckles showed white.

Sergeant Jack Wayne—the Kid, because his first name was actually John but he couldn't tolerate it being used—went to the breakroom to get fresh tea for his friend and boss.

Chapter 10

The dark gray sky, swirling winds, and tall, swaying grasses matched her mood. There was a storm brewing, and it matched the conflict in Eliana Cortes's mind against Kennedy's control.

Eliana was the west coast lieutenant for El Chapo's Sinaloa cartel. Astride her favorite stallion, she gave him a sense of freedom through a light touch on the bit as the horse galloped up the hillside west of the new ranch house she'd built on the family compound. The horse surprised her by stopping short and bucking, nearly throwing her off. Eliana laughed, because riding the stallion in the lightest of English-style saddle, bit, and reins was madness. But she wasn't in the mood for his antics and spurred the stallion back into a gallop that she didn't attempt to control.

Instead, she rose out of the saddle and leaned forward over the stallion's neck, grabbing some mane for stability in the stirrups and letting the horse run as fast as he wished. The speed and wind in her face was as exhilarating as powering through a hundred miles an hour in one of her convertible sports cars.

Just prior to cresting the hill, she sat back and fought the wild-eyed stallion to a standstill. The stallion snapped its head back and forth, frothing at the mouth until it bent to Eliana's will. She rubbed its neck and dismounted, pulling two sugar cubes from her pants pocket for the horse's reward.

The combination of wind in her face, danger, and the energies of a wild animal had helped Eliana name what had been eating at her soul for the last three weeks. Like her stallion had, she had grown tired of being controlled. As light a touch as it was, the control combined with the sense she owed Shadow Tier, her life, and that of her baby, weighed on her.

After six years as Shadow Tier's asset inside the Sinaloa cartel, she was done. It was time for an exit plan, one so airtight neither El Chapo nor Shadow Tier could track her. She remounted the horse, gazed out over the town of Los Mochis in the hazy distance, and headed back to the ranch and headquarters of the Cortes operations.

Six years ago, El Chapo had used her brother Alejandro as a bargaining chip with Wolf and his newly formed Shadow Tier unit. Then, in a last-minute change of heart—she laughed, El Chapo did not have a heart—he left her for a Tijuana cartel sniper. Wolf had saved her and her unborn child from being murdered by El Chapo and kept them on ice for a few days, debriefing her on cartel operations and securing her agreement to trade confinement for life in a US prison for a life as a spy in the cartel.

Wolf devised a plan that permitted Eliana to "escape" American custody and return to the cartel as the head of Sinaloa's US West Coast operations. El Chapo's skepticism of her escape was quickly forgotten as she took the position and brought predictability to operations while her peers continued to have problems moving cartel product. With her brother Alejandro off the field in witness protection, Wolf and Kennedy could spread their attacks around to include Eliana's operations, hiding her collaboration.

Back in her office, Eliana reviewed her plan to make millions of legitimate dollars from the US government and a few non-governmental organizations. Her new Global Air Services was a joint venture with an Alaskan Native American "super 8A"—a federal designation that meant a contractor could be awarded a sole-source government contract of up to a hundred million dollars. Offering use of her aircraft to several super 8As at once would speed up her exit plan.

Her first bold move via her cutouts was to hire a firm full of former senior leadership from the special operations community and land a spot as a subcontractor on the five-year contract for worldwide special operations logistics, focusing on Southwest Asia. The most lucrative task orders were for flights into and out of Iraq and Afghanistan.

Just as the legions of small businesses throughout the world extend the corporate reach of UPS, DHL, and FedEx, Global Air Services quickly became a trusted transportation partner of the US and UK air forces.

The flights out of Afghanistan were quickly profitable as she used her considerable expertise in shipping illegal drugs to move opium through Ramstein, Germany, and on to the United States. With a cadre of loyal soldiers sprinkled through all the key route aircrews, she was counting her exit time—six months, max.

The timing of her exit was right. Recent leaks leading to intercepted shipments and an attack on El Chapo himself had the drug lord in a paranoid state. He had yet again replaced his intelligence lead, this time with officers recruited from the Cuban *Direccion de Inteligencia*, the Cuban version of a combined CIA and FBI. El Chapo placed particular importance on counterintelligence, hoping to stop the leaks and root out moles that were bleeding him in the millions. The DINTEL operators would try to improve profitability by reducing losses, no different from Walmart or Target.

A squinty accountant-looking man named Sartorio had visited Eliana three times in the past two months, seeking clarity on her expenses and revenues. He was unkempt and greasy looking. She didn't trust him and believed he was a cover masquerading a highly intelligent investigator. Her source confirmed her read on the man with connections to the DINTEL.

He was El Chapo's spy.

And there was El Chapo's long-cultivated relationship with Cuba. While she didn't know for sure, she suspected El Chapo had struck a deal to switch to a higher percentage of opium cultivation in Mexico while arranging for new locations to grow the very profitable drug, making Cuba a logical choice. She vowed to learn more. A Cuban misdirect to Shadow Tier could be helpful at the right time.

Her satellite phone buzzed and she read the text. It immediately superseded Cuba in her plan. It said *Pacific Northwest distribution - think Indian casinos.*

Chapter 11

A cool breeze in the waning darkness of another Tampa morning gave relief to the usual humid air as Wolf pushed through the one hundred yards of loose sand. Keeping his knees high and his upper body relaxed, Wolf sprinted toward the MacDill Air Force Base beach. At the beach, he stripped off his shoes and pulled on his swim goggles. He wedged his phone in a shoe and headed for the water as Alpha Squadron's assaulters ran on the beach.

Wolf laughed as a former SEAL on the team joked about getting the old man a lifeguard's float. He heard Alpha Squadron Commander Oleus LeBlanc put five dollars on him, and the betting started. Money, beers, and barbecue bets were placed. While the Alphas were making their bets and joking, Wolf slipped into the water. Wolf flashed LeBlanc three fingers for three miles and started his watch, diving into Tampa Bay.

Swim completed and rinsed off, Wolf retrieved his items and

ran off base, headed up Shoreline Drive toward home. He was weaving his way up the sidewalk overlooking the bay as he dodged the regular people beginning their day when his cell buzzed. Glancing at the screen, he saw a text message. He picked up his tempo, finished the last half mile to the house and took off his shoes at the sliding door to the patio.

Inside, Parker was sitting in the kitchen.

She handed Wolf a coffee. "What is it?" she asked.

"I have a feeling I know who it is," Wolf said, taking a drink and punching up his personal voicemail. He sat the phone on the large marble kitchen island and touched the speaker button. It announced, "One new message."

"Wolf—Billy Red Fish, man. They burned the church down last night and killed a tribal police officer and shit's outta control here. We need help, man—we need *you*. Call me ASAP, brother. Out here."

Parker stared at Wolf for several quiet seconds before making a reply she was sure wouldn't sit well with him.

"You know reservation crime is not part of our charter. What are you going to do?"

"I need to help my people any way I can," Wolf said. "But I'm not sure what that looks like right now. Maybe a task force with tribal and state resources."

"We're covered up with 'task forces' already!" Parker instantly thought her statement might have been too abrupt. "Lance, listen, I'm sorry. I didn't mean that like it sounded. But we gotta prioritize. We're already fighting the drug war on two fronts, in Mexico and Afghanistan. You and the vice president want to open another front in Europe. How are you going to do all that? No, let me rephrase—how are *we* going to do all that? And fight an unknown force on the Crow reservation?"

Wolf stared out the window, his eyes unfocused, seemingly in a meditative state, and smiled.

"I appreciate the reality check. I do. You know my weaknesses better than me. So, back to the question: My answer is to keep doing what we already do. If you think of it from a special forces mindset, each team has its regional assignment. They're designed to be autonomous and organically complete minus air-lift, water-craft, subs, etc. It will take some time to bring a new squadron up to speed, but with Taylor and a few key personnel from the existing squadrons, we can accelerate their training and actually reduce our workload. While you and I make sure Taylor has everything he needs, I can spend time figuring out what to do about the res-ervation problem."

"The president and vice president expect your undivided atten-tion on the Taliban opium and terrorist funding issue. You can't be in three places at once. Something or things will suffer."

Wolf smiled. "Agreed, so let's give the UK squadron standup to Kennedy. He's ready, and his cousin is the new commander of the Joint Narcotics Analysis Center. Brigadier Cavendish. It will be good for him, physically and mentally."

"Okay, that's a smart move. He and the Kid are working already to make sure the squadron hits the ground running when they're stood up. But it still leaves you split between Afghanistan and Montana. You can't just boot the expectations of the White House."

"But I will if it means saving my people on the reservation and the rest of the tribes. Subverting sovereign tribal lands and casi-nos is actually a smart operational move. Using legal gambling as a cover for drug distribution will work if we don't stop it."

Wolf paused for a beat, lost in thought, then started again.

"Please don't take this the wrong way, but no one at the state or federal level is looking out for our best interests. I know some of it is blowback from tribes trying to keep some level of sovereignty by pushing the states and feds away. But they need our help before it's too late, and the feds use rampant drug problems as an excuse to take what little sovereignty we have away."

His gaze hardened.

"I will make it work. The fight for my people starts today."

Chapter 12

Wolf paid for the ticket to Montana himself. This wasn't a Shadow Tier mission yet and might never be. The four-hour flight from Tampa to Denver gave Wolf time to be amazed anew by the beauty of America as he crossed it at thirty-six thousand feet. The word idyllic came to mind.

Wolf allowed himself a few minutes to enjoy the view knowing all the while back on the Crow reservation, crime, neglect, poverty, and disease clawed at the people—his people.

Wolf's mother had focused his early learning on the value of tribe and team, and his time in the Ranger regiment and in special forces had reinforced his mother's lessons. Building his tribe, his team, was the key to winning.

A "coalition of the willing," Wolf thought, as he assembled his coalition list. FBI, DEA, Montana Division of Criminal Investigations Narcotics Bureau, Highway Patrol, National Guard, Department of Health and Human Services, Fish and Wildlife and

Parks. Last but in fact most important, was the real key to success—the tribal councils. He'd have to balance a potential positive outcome with a combination of real and perceived control exerted by the tribal councils. If the plan worked on the Crow reservation, Wolf was certain it would at the rest of the Montana tribes.

Before he had left, he got thirty minutes with the director of Shadow Tier, General Davidson. He was of the same concerned mindset as Parker, but he was willing to give Wolf the latitude to pursue the issue on his own time. It came with the warning of getting pulled back if anyone in the chain of command noted Wolf's lack of focus on Afghanistan.

Sitting in the Denver airport United Club between flights, it crossed Wolf's mind that the simple solution to the growing drug problem on the Crow reservation would be to make it too costly to do business there. Wolf, with Billy Red Fish's help, could wage a guerrilla-style war like he had done on the Sinaloa cartel and drive the drug problem off the reservation. That only made the issue someone else's problem, but first things first.

Before Shadow Tier, Wolf and his brother had impacted the Cortes's Los Angeles drug business by contaminating the product and then creating a turf war between the Sinaloa and Tijuana cartels. Both had been temporary adjustments, not permanent fixes. In the reservation's case, Wolf thought, if he interdicted enough dope in transport and destroyed enough in production, and the smart ones would move elsewhere.

The stupid would die or go to jail.

Wolf saw a tidy ninety-day mission in his mind's eye. But the constraints of federal, state, and tribal law would limit any useful effect. Flooding the area with law enforcement would work in the short term, but the smart drug gangs would just wait them out. Some high-ranking officials would declare victory, and the resources would be reassigned. The drug lords would take their time but, in the end, business would return to normal. Maybe reduced, but not stopped. A temporary setback at worst.

Onboard the short hop to Montana, Wolf tapped his seat arm rest as he studied the Wyoming landscape. The clear blue sky gave him a spirit guide's view of the world and the truth he had learned from years of fighting the drug wars.

Pain in the form of lost product, profits—and people—is what changes a drug lord's thinking.

Wolf spent two days pitching the coalition idea as a pilot project to the agencies on his list. Fortunately, their offices were all in the state government area of downtown Billings, and General Davidson's adjutant had quickly arranged meetings. To a person, the special agents in charge, directors, and administrators all agreed success was predicated on the willingness of the tribal council to let non-Indian personnel operate on the reservation without restrictions.

Several noted they could, of course, investigate and prosecute their findings on reservation land, but tribal pushback and politics had kept them focused elsewhere in Montana. It was time to take the concept to the tribal councils, but first Wolf needed feedback from his people.

The four-hour drive to the reservation would give Wolf time to check in with Parker, read her in on the plan, and enjoy some of the familiar ancestral countryside he missed being at Shadow Tier headquarters on MacDill AFB in Florida.

Wolf sat in his rental truck and hit the speed-dial button for Parker's office, then drove out of the parking garage. He took Interstate 90 South and listened as Parker filled him in on Kennedy's coordination with Brigadier Cavendish. She suggested a replacement for Taylor on Bravo—an SAS captain named Devon

Lancaster, who Taylor had been recruiting. Wolf approved and suggested giving Taylor two weeks' leave to prepare for his new assignment and report to the Joint Analysis Center. He agreed with Parker that she and the Kid should meet and brief Taylor if Kennedy wasn't up for the travel.

Wolf had concerns about his friend and battle buddy, second in importance only after his wife. Kennedy was the first person Wolf had asked to join him in his original revenge-fueled fight against the Sinaloa cartel—they were plankowners in Shadow Tier. Wolf wanted Kennedy back in action, and Shadow Tier needed him.

"Is he ready, though?" Wolf asked. "Physically, mentally?"

Parker said, "Yes, he's getting stronger every day. He's pushing himself to get back in the fight. Too hard, sometimes, I think."

"I'll call him later. I'm headed to Aunt Winona's to meet some of her friends and Billy. Hey, uh, wait one ..."

About a quarter mile ahead along the shoulder, a Chrysler minivan with emergency flashers blinking sat low on the left rear and its spare tire out. A young woman in blue jeans, boots, and a short-sleeved top stood at the back of the van, holding a baby.

"Sorry, need to go." Wolf signaled right and started scrubbing off speed on the pavement before slipping off the roadway to the gravelly shoulder. "I'm stopping to help a young lady with a baby and a flat tire. Call you later?"

"Okay, Good Sam. Be careful. 'k?"

"Roger that," Wolf said, and disconnected.

Wolf stopped about thirty feet behind the van with his vehicle's nose pointed slightly left to provide some shield against oncoming traffic. He shut the truck down and engaged his own flashers, then exited the truck and walked up to the minivan, taking in every detail.

"Hey there!" he said with a smile and an upraised hand as he approached. "My name is Lance. Can I help you with that?"

"Yes, please. I, I don't know what to do, really, and my baby ..." the girl said, falsetto voice cracking.

"I understand. I'd want someone to help my wife if she needed it." Parker wouldn't want such help, but the point was valid.

Wolf smiled to ease the tension while watching her eyes dance and her hands shake.

Is it alcohol—or just roadside anxiety? She seems quite young.

He went to the back of the van and was relieved to find a breakdown kit. He grabbed flares and three reflective triangles from the kit and walked back about a hundred feet behind his truck as several tractor-trailer rigs went by. One of them was a dual trailer system and its second trailer was swaying back and forth enough for Wolf to shake his head at the potential for disaster there.

Wolf started the first flare, then stepped back several paces and started the second. He put the reflective sign down next, using a rock to hold it in place. Wolf glanced back to the mom and saw her clutch her baby to her chest. He repeated the triangle/flare drops in measured lengths as he walked back to the van.

"Not to worry, ma'am. I should have you on your way in twenty minutes or so," Wolf said, forcing a smile.

He took out the spare and went to work loosening the lug nuts on the flat before jacking up the vehicle just enough to take off the wheel. He was rolling it around to the back of the van when he saw the woman turn and sprint off the shoulder toward the grassy median.

Wolf instinctively ran, too, but he wasn't sure why—and then the screeching wail of an eighteen-wheeler's worn-out metal-on-metal brakes reached his ears.

In his peripheral vision, he saw the trailer headed their way at an ever-increasing angle of attack. It had jackknifed and was about to swat Wolf, his truck, and the minivan from the face of the Earth.

Wolf caught up to the mom and baby and dropped into a depression, shielding her and the child as the trailer tipped over and slid toward them on the grass. The mom kicked and screamed, rising from the grass and dropping the baby to get away.

"I'm not here for this!" she screamed and turned to flee.

Wolf embraced the bundled-up baby in his muscular arms and hunched down into the depression, tucking in his head and trying to get as small as he possibly could. The mom only got a few feet away before the trailer slid over them.

Wolf closed his eyes and waited for the cacophony of the dying eighteen-wheel to stop. When it did, he found himself and the baby under the trailer and, miraculously, unharmed.

The child hadn't uttered a single peep, and Wolf lived to sing his death song another day.

Wolf panicked at the thought that he might have crushed the baby. He crawled backward out from under the overturned trailer and cursed as he realized he'd been protecting only a heavily bundled-up doll. On his knees, he scanned the area and found the "mom." A tennis shoe and a bloody ankle showing exposed bone stuck out from under the trailer. It was not moving.

Wolf switched from loathing to combat mode as rounds cracked past, tearing into the overturned trailer with metallic thumps and kicking up tufts of grass from the median. Wolf reached for his pistol to return fire as he ran along the trailer for cover, only to find his holster empty. The damned pistol must have been shaken loose in the scramble to save the "baby."

Another burst of automatic fire and shouted commands made up Wolf's mind. He sprinted in a zigzag for the safety of the treeline. He could see gunmen leaving the cover of their SUV and lined up abreast, working around the trailer.

Win the fight, Wolf thought. He took stock of his weapons. He had a folding SOG Escape knife and a flare that had somehow stayed in his pocket. He had an extra magazine for his Browning High Power, but without the pistol, it wouldn't be useful for the fight he was planning.

From just inside the treeline, he watched the men advance, focusing on a younger man on the far left. He had to still be in his late teens and clearly he hadn't patrolled to contact before.

Wolf ran deeper into the woods and started circling left.

Chapter 13

Wolf hummed his death song again to himself as he dropped deeper into the woods, angling left to flank his target. The sounds of heavy breathing overshadowed the distant sounds of the highway and cracking branches from the men sent to kill him. Wolf drew his knife, gripping it backhanded so the blade faced out from his wrist. As he got to within twenty feet, he saw the closest shooter, rifle ready, looking for him.

They brought a kid to a gunfight.

Wolf closed the blade and stalked forward, matching the rifleman's steps. Then the young man responded to a radio call—the volume stupidly at maximum.

"Hartmann, keep your damned eyes open! We swingin' around right. We gotta get this fuckin' guy or it's your ass!"

The leader was angry that his team hadn't found Wolf yet.

"Ro-roger, that," Hartmann said, nervous. Inexperience radiated from him like heat waves. "Will do."

Hartmann's rapid and loud breathing, combined with his tunnel vision, made the next part easy. Wolf slammed the tungsten window-breaker end of the knife into the side of Hartmann's head and he dropped, out cold. Wolf caught him and dragged him behind a tree. A small trickle of blood ran down Hartmann's head from where the metal tip had broken his scalp.

Wolf tied Hartmann's hands with his own belt and then used strips of his shirt to tie his feet. Another strip of shirt was stuffed in his mouth and Wolf was sure Hartmann wouldn't be a problem.

Looking over Hartmann's rifle, Wolf was pleasantly surprised to find an old but serviceable full-auto M-16A2. Wolf hadn't held one since his first days in Army basic training. There was one full thirty-round magazine in the rifle and two spares on Hartmann's belt, which Wolf collected. The kid's pistol was also ancient—a well-used fifteen-round 9mm Beretta M9. Both were shabby, as if someone had stolen them from a National Guard armory in the Nineties.

Wolf checked the pistol was loaded and pulled back on the charging handle of the M-16 to confirm a round in the chamber. He left the rifle on automatic and sent up a quick prayer to Samuel Colt for smooth operation. Wolf turned down the volume on Hartmann's radio and listened to a request for an update.

He responded by keying the mic and rubbing the radio against his shirt. He didn't know what they would make of the result, but it would sound like poor transmission quality and probably keep them thinking something happened to their teammate.

Wolf turned the volume back up to maximum and opened the squelch on the radio so the speaker filled the air with the sound of radio static. Then he lit the flare, setting it on a nearby rock. The red glow illuminated the tied-up Hartmann. Moving toward the other shooters, Wolf set himself up as a one-man ambush.

To their credit, they came in quietly. Two of them, staggered formation, muzzle control, the last shooter was checking their six. Wolf wanted all three at once, but he would take two, so he raked their legs with automatic rifle fire, splintering leg bones between the knees and ankles.

They probably wouldn't die from the injuries, but that was going to hurt for a long time.

They screamed and dropped heavily to the ground, writhing and clutching at their wounds. Wolf stayed hidden, scanning for the last shooter. Fifteen seconds, thirty seconds, a minute, and no sign of him.

Two rifle shots rang out from Wolf's right, and the wounded shooters stopped moving. The static on Hartmann's radio stopped and a voice cold as ice called out.

"Wolf, they call me Amaru. It is an honor to kill you, a worthy man of great skill and cunning. I am coming for you, Wolf." Amaru paused. "Prepare."

Wolf rubbed the dark, rich dirt onto his face, hands, and arms. He took off his shoes and covered his bare feet in dirt, then backed out of his hide and ran deeper into the woods, flowing silently like a deer.

When he was sure he had put the assassin between himself and the highway, he stopped and lowered his heart rate and breathing. He sat with his back to a tree in near meditation, listening to the sounds of the forest, becoming one with its flow. In his quiet, he heard Amaru.

He might be good, Wolf thought, but he was out of his element.

This guy thinks he's an Inca dragon. We are in the land of my people. This is where I hunt, not him.

Wolf stretched, deep breathing through his mouth to oxygenate his senses. Rising with care to not make sounds, he moved to flank his target. A couple of long minutes later, Wolf realized Amaru was attempting to do the same. Then Wolf froze mid-step, detecting the faintest of tripwire threads spread across his path. Wolf moved left and saw the grenade booby trap. Then he heard the snick of an M-16 being switched to auto-fire mode. It might as well have been a fire truck siren for its ability to move Wolf's muscles without thought.

Gunfire ripped through the air from an elevated position at Wolf's two o'clock and he returned fire. A round creased his shoulder as he dove for cover—right across the tripwires. Amaru was smarter than Wolf had given him credit for, and he kept shooting until the booby trap grenade released and exploded.

Razor-sharp shards of hot metal peppered Wolf's shoulders and embedded in trees. He sprinted from the kill zone, vowing not to underestimate his foe again. In the distance, sirens grew louder in response to the truck crash that had been reported to 911 by people on cellphones.

Wolf radioed, "Looks like your window to kill me is closing, Amaru. These woods will soon be crawling with cops." He forced a laugh into the radio. "You have failed."

"I don't fail, Wolf. Time is the variable. If not this time, next time. I have all the time in the world." Amaru chuckled. "You do not. See you soon."

Wolf marched out of the woods and cleared the rifle, holding it aloft over his head as he emerged from the treeline. A highway patrol officer ordered Wolf to stop and identify himself, which he did with custom-made FBI credentials from a cargo pocket.

Wolf asked the officer to radio a BOLO for an armed and dangerous Hispanic male, giving the officer a description of Amaru.

"He's five-seven, about one hundred thirty-five pounds, wiry frame, black hair, gray-blue eyes, tats on the back of his hands, and missing most of his right pinky finger. He's wearing jeans, hiking boots and a long-sleeve black T-shirt."

"You've done this before, Marine?" the trooper asked.

"Yeah, Army though. Back in the day," Wolf said. "There are two other dead shooters in the woods, and a kid I tied-up." The officer stared into the woods and back at the accident scene.

Wolf said, "Oh, yeah, I think you will find an accomplice under the trailer."

The office grimaced. "EMS can handle it. Let's go find the kid."

"Follow me," Wolf said, re-chambering a round into the M-16.

When they got to where Wolf had left the kid, there was a dark blood stain next to his motionless body. Wolf didn't need to get any closer to know Amaru had stopped him from talking.

The officer stared at Wolf for a long moment. "I thought you said he was alive when you left him."

"He was. Amaru did this."

"Who's that?" the officer asked.

"The man leading the assault on me. It's what he called himself—Amaru. It's the name of an Inca dragon." Wolf said.

Professional soldier against professional assassin. Crow warrior versus Inca Dragon.

The officer voiced Wolf's thoughts.

"What the hell is going on that someone would try to take you out with an eighteen-wheeler—and then send an assassin after you to make sure you're dead?"

Chapter 14

The sun was clawing its way into the sky as the sounds of a working ranch filled the air. Just back from another early morning ride, Eliana Cortes stopped in the courtyard, its ornate stone fountain burbling behind her. The horse ride across the property hadn't helped her decide.

She had made deals with two devils—Joaquin "El Chapo" Guzman Loera, the leader of the Sinaloa cartel, and Lance Bear Wolf, leader of the Shadow Tier counter-drug unit. Wolf had saved Eliana and her unborn baby from certain death at the hands of a sniper. Then he placed her back in the cartel as their informant.

She owed debts to both powerful men.

She strode into the building. Large double doors were open as she peered into her office, once the domain of her brother Alejandro. The same office her father had worked from to build the Cortes's drug empire under the protection and guidance of El Chapo. But her father was dead now and her brother was in the American witness protection program, so Eliana now led one of the Sinaloa cartel's best-producing franchises by herself. Her reach and responsibility stretched from Sinaloa up through the western states into Canada.

In the office restroom space, Eliana blotted the dust of her ride from her face with a warm washcloth and washed her hands. She pulled up her shirt sleeve to stare at the brand her brother had given her. It read, PENSAR—THINK, in recognition of her former propensity to be impulsive. Often with violence.

Readjusting her sleeve, she returned to the desk and pondered the timing of her plan to leave the cartel and Shadow Tier behind.

Today is the day I begin my walk to freedom. From Wolf and El Chapo. For good.

The handset radio on her desk crackled alive with a sentry announcing visitors—two black Chevy Suburbans and a pickup truck of uniformed, heavily armed men. It could only be El Chapo, descended from his mountain hiding place with a protective entourage. Something must be important to him because he would never risk a social visit.

"Let them in, fool!" she barked back into the radio. It wasn't smart to make El Chapo wait.

Eliana sat still and meditated for a few moments, centering. Any attempt to divine why he was there was a waste of time. The best plan, roll with what you get. She pulled open the top right drawer of the desk to find her brother's gold-plated .50-caliber Desert Eagle Mark VII automatic pistol.

Eliana rose and came around the front of her desk as El Chapo strode in wearing shorts, worn leather sandals, and a loud Hawaiian shirt like he was working from one of his beach houses. He was all smiles as his security team swarmed the office, posting to the doors and windows and standing on either side of Eliana while El Chapo sat down across the expansive wooden desk.

El Chapo ordered his security out.

"Déjanos. Close the doors behind you."

When the doors closed, he left the desk and dropped into an overstuffed leather chair, motioning Eliana to join him across the little table as he poured himself a tequila from a booze cart.

El Chapo leaned in.

"We are now partners with the Mountain Rain Triad. They own eighty percent of the heroin business in America, and we are their newest distributor and supplier for meth precursors. I want you to convert twenty-five percent of your land to opium production."

"Si, *jefe*," Eliana responded. "I have seen the growth in heroin use reported by the DEA. But you know it will take time to switch. A month to harvest the last crop and then at least one hundred and twenty days for the fastest growing poppy to produce opium. Four months, at least, more like six while the fields are not producing profits."

EL Chapo smirked and waved her comment off with a flick of his hand. "Rotate through the crops so you are not taking out all twenty-five percent at once. Even then, we will soon make up the loss and ten times more."

What idiot is he listening to now? Eliana wondered.

She nodded. "An ambitious plan. To get ten times your return, you would have to own the business." She smiled knowingly and nodded. "Your plan reveals itself."

El Chapo relaxed against the overstuffed back of the leather chair. He raised his heavy glass of tequila and sipped it.

"This is why you are one of my best lieutenants, Eliana. You understand our business, and our need to grow our share. The rich Americans are tired of marijuana and cocaine. I read the same DEA reports as you. We will grow like the early days of cocaine and be rich as kings."

Eliana nodded. "Two hundred and ten days from now, maybe less, you will have the new opium. Do you want heroin as the final product or a shipment of paste to another location?"

El Chapo stood and said, "*Seguridad*."

His detail rushed back in at the ready but relaxed slightly to see no threat existed.

"Refined heroin, *el amado*. Do your finest work. I will have Jesus send you the information on the drop points and communication codes when we are closer to the transfer time. I've become aware of an opportunity to use Indian casinos to strengthen and expand our distribution network. And Eliana, report your successes every two weeks. Make it your number one priority. *Estoy claro?*"

"Yes, of course. Understood. Every two weeks."

El Chapo abruptly spun without another word and headed for his SUV within a formation of security detail.

Eliana watched El Chapo and his easy-to-target gaggle roar away in their black Suburbans, trailed by the truck of soldiers.

Reporting every two weeks. What a stupid idea. Where is a military drone when you need one? She smiled, tight-lipped at the imagery of El Chapo's convoy being destroyed by those nasty Hellfire missiles Wolf and his kind liked.

Eliana snapped back to the present. It would take a lot of bodies to take the business from the Triad, and a lot of El Chapo's money to create the labs necessary to process the new deluge of raw opium. These would be enormous sums of money from which a cut for her escape plan wouldn't be missed.

Eliana wandered into the courtyard and stared into the fountain. She wondered what her brother and his former operations lieutenant, Martin Amaro, would think if they saw her now. In just over six months, she would become one of the ten largest producers and distributors of heroin in the world. Yes, it would be the

Sinaloa cartel, aka El Chapo heroin, but everyone would know it was her genius who had made it work.

Yes, *everyone will know, and eventually, someone will talk.*

Chapter 15

Five thousand, four hundred miles to the east, in Marseille, France, six well-dressed men in their twenties and thirties sat around a table in the warehouse district of the Port of Marseille. The rough-hewn area had seen many a meeting and plan agreed to here by the former leadership of *Unione Corsa*.

This smoke-filled room had been stripped of its storied history, the walls painted royal blue. The lights had been replaced with tracks of mini spotlights, focusing light where needed and leaving moody pools of shadow that enhanced the mood and seriousness of discussions taken in the room.

A young man of twenty-nine mixed a drink at the bar and all eyes were focused on him. Jean Paul Croce finished making his drink, glided to the head of the table, and smiled. At six-two and two hundred and twenty pounds, his movie-star good looks and a seemingly sincere smile belied his cruel streak when dealing with those who impeded his rebuilding of *Unione Corsa*.

"Our struggle is about to pay off. We are *mafia numero un* in Marseille. Four months from now, we will be the largest distributor of heroin in Europe and the United States. We will solidify our position in the Eastern United States and continue to push West. The Triads cannot keep up with demand, and we will replace them. Our reach will rival Sinaloa. 'The French Connection,' as they famously called us in America, is back—and back to stay."

Croce raised his glass and toasted. "À la *nôtre!*"

The men in the room responded as one.

"To the new *Union Corsa!*"

Chapter 16

Wolf had passed on treatment by the EMS crew at the highway crash site and declined a ride to Billings Memorial Hospital, instead using some of their water and a towel to clean up. He downed a Vicodin and drove his new rental SUV to the reservation.

His aunt offered Wolf the use of the sweat lodge and an EMT friend by the nickname of Topper, who used herbal medicines and a pair of tweezers to address Wolf's wounds.

The sweat lodge was ancient and, according to his aunt, his biological father and uncles had all used it. The scents were hard to describe, old but not stale, with notes of sage and bear root, and hints of others, including tobacco and what Wolf imagined was peyote and marijuana. Stones around the fire were dark inside the ring and stained from water on the outside.

Running shorts was all Wolf wore as seventeen fragments of steel shrapnel were removed from his back, butt, and legs. Once there was no more shrapnel to find, Wolf thanked Topper and the medic departed.

In the sweat lodge, Wolf prepared the process of ritual cleaning and second sight. It was during the last pour of water on the hot stones that clarity came to him.

It was a war of the worlds in its scope of destruction, a swirling vision of heroin, cocaine, and methamphetamine destroying the world, sucking dry the souls of all who used. As he left the sweat lodge, his new understanding consumed Wolf—and provided his new direction.

I've got to talk to the tribal council.

On Wolf's behalf, his Aunt Winona had asked for twenty minutes of the council's time. Out of deference to Wolf and respect for all his mother had given to Crow children, they had granted ten. Wolf would speak at 11:50, right before the council's lunch break. Winona broke the news to Wolf during dinner.

"I hope this will work for you, nephew," Winona said.

He kissed the top of her head.

"Thank you, Auntie. Hope is not a strategy, but if I can get them talking during lunch, we will have a chance."

After dinner, they talked about his childhood and his mother. It was a good evening, full of the pain of loss and gratitude for the love of family and place. The laughs left no place in his heart for the ache of losing his mother or Andy, his beloved stepfather. Wolf went to bed embracing his heritage, his family, and renewed focus on ensuring the cartel's stain would not mark the Crow people.

Wolf rose before dawn and drove the half-hour south to his favorite lookout. Looking east, he watched as the vista unfolded before him, the sunrise creeping over the peaks in slow-motion reds, yellows, and oranges. The mountains cast low shadows where the land had yet to greet the new day.

Wolf watched a pack of wolves playing as they moved through an open area, and a pair of eagles soaring on the rising warm air. He felt alive and part of the land. Yet he understood being one with the land would not win the day by itself. He was about to enter the realm of men and women who had other spirits they worshiped, like money and power.

There were three elements to his argument for increased policing of the reservations—mind, body, and spirit. And all three needed to be in alignment to win against the forces of the cartel.

In the council chambers, the scene reminded Wolf of a military courtroom, with the members sitting before him in a semi-circle with the chairman in the center and stenographer off to his left. His aunt had warned him about the chairman. His partnership with and granting of exclusive rights to various businesses had gone beyond his position and authority. His lifestyle, according to Billy, was well above his pay.

Rumors abounded, but they had not investigated him as his business deals provided value to the tribe. Wolf had asked Parker to find out if there was any past or present focus on him by the Montana Department of Justice and its Division of Criminal Investigation and still awaited that report.

At his appointed time during public comment time, Wolf strode to the podium, grabbed the wireless microphone from its stand, and moved closer to the members seated on the slightly higher dais. Wolf was dressed plainly, only his coup belt visible to show his status in the tribe and the seriousness of his request to speak.

At the center of the council table, the chairman nodded at Wolf, signaling him to begin.

"Brothers and sisters of the Crow nation," Wolf began. "I come to you with a concern for us all."

For the next four minutes, Wolf warned the council about the

Sinaloa cartel. He used examples of drug activity and unclassified intelligence pointing to more cartel depredation to come. He was going to leave out the beheadings and other gruesome details of the cartel's and triad's enforcement actions, but his people had seen much the same in their history and needed the truth.

There were gasps from the packed room when he described things he and Shadow Tier had seen and combated.

"The fight is upon us, like it or not. To protect our people and way of life, we must resist these forces using every resource at our disposal, including those from the federal and state agencies we normally shun."

Wolf stopped to let what he'd said sink in. His brow furrowed as he saw head shakes and frowns on the council members' faces. It did not fill him with hope. There was small talk among the council and in the gallery, and then, as if of one mind, all talking stopped and the people stared at Wolf.

"I have a plan to combat this threat—and I have permission from my agency to work it on behalf of the Crow people," Wolf said.

The Chairman leaned forward. His face was unreadable, but his words were plain.

"The view from the outside is always more dire, and you are an outsider to your own tribe, Lance Bear Wolf. You live in their world and follow their ways, and you have become one of them." He paused without blinking. "But we will consider your warning. We will adjourn for lunch and respond when we return."

Stung by the outsider label, Wolf stared at the Chairman as he rose and left the room. Wolf replaced the microphone in its stand and went with Winona to the cafeteria in silence. After ordering, they found a corner table by themselves and spoke in whispers.

"What was that about? I'm an *outsider* now?" Wolf said, the anger clear in his tone.

Winona shook her head. "The Chairman is a weak man, always trying to put people below him to make himself look higher. He is a child, but you made a convincing argument. One that a logical person would appreciate, but we know the council is not always logical when it comes to working with federal and state agencies, even when there are clear benefits for our people."

"Nor with one of its own sons, evidently. It's as if their distrust of governments and their oversight is bred into their DNA. Sins of the father-type fixing of blame. It hinders moving forward."

Winona said, "It may look that way from the outside, but remember, until recently, all the government did for us was take. Ours is a natural defense mechanism."

Wolf nodded and ate. All he could do was all he could do, and he had done his part. One of the hardest lessons he had learned since leaving the reservation to make his way in the world was sometimes people do not want to be helped. Living in denial was more common than Wolf had ever imagined. Wolf let go of his negative thoughts and texted Parker an update. Her response was positive, but short.

Be strong but humble, warrior but diplomat. They will see the way.

When the council returned, they made Wolf's plan their first order of business.

The Chairman said, "Lance Bear Wolf, we will consider your plan in chambers. Follow us."

Winona squeezed Wolf's arm and smiled. Wolf followed the council into a side room and waited for the council to sit before beginning. The plan was a simple one in Wolf's mind, with as much political risk as physical. The tribal police would be the command element coordinating the on-reservation activities of DEA, FBI, and Montana Highway Patrol. Wolf would support the tribal police chief while Shadow Tier's Alpha Squadron would act as the quick reaction force. Together, they would push the cartel to take its business elsewhere.

A member asked why the desired outcome was pushing drugs out versus stopping them from doing business. Wolf gave some drug war history and the amount of money and personnel devoted to the effort. His admission that you don't stop the top-level cartels that you disrupt made him pause and question his own value to this endeavor.

Wolf said, "Let's focus on saving our people and way of life. Hopefully, others can follow our example."

The council voted to accept the plan by a single vote, giving Wolf approval to coordinate the effort. The Chairman had voted no. *He's going to continue to be a tough sell,* Wolf thought, but that didn't matter now.

Except for his ideas about upgrading communications and walking through the plan with the tribal police chief, everything else was already in place.

As they drove back to his aunt's house, Wolf thought about his stark admission. *You don't stop the cartels you disrupt.*

Wolf called LeBlanc, his Alpha Squadron commander, and left a message.

"Need you up here. If we act now, we have a chance—maybe our only one."

Chapter 17

Noah Taylor, the Shadow Tier Charlie Squadron commander, stood outside the hangar at RAF Mildenhall and inspected the formation of fifteen men and women forwarded by their governments for selection. Hard and arrogant looks were returned without a word, not a hint of trepidation, all perfect alpha males and females who were used to giving no quarter nor taking one.

Let's see who really wants to be here.

The three weeks of selection he had planned would determine the makeup of the assault team. Phase 1, physical hell; phase 2, combatives; phase 3, intelligence, surveillance, and recon.

The ultimate test would be a target surveillance and assault mission.

There were two Norwegians, three Brits, two Spaniards, two Germans, two Israelis, three French, and one Swede. All had arrived highly recommended, and all with meaningful law enforcement or combat experience. Many had both.

Phase 1 was a tough infiltration exercise comprised a five-hour flight and static line jump into the South Wales Breacon Beacons SAS training area. The five candidates who were not jump qualified were briefed on the training plan, tossed with their gear into the back of a military truck, and driven off to the training site five hours to the west.

Those who were jump qualified got their briefing and four hours of static-line jump refresher training and tower falls. Thirty minutes before heading to the aircraft, three candidates were given heavy, inoperable sniper rifles. Two more were given large radios with dead batteries, all intended to test their adaptability.

As they boarded an unmarked C-130J for the flight west, Taylor smiled. Hell Week, as those who survived would call it, was about to begin.

In the intelligence cell, Kennedy had been sorting through support personnel and standing up their sections. He'd brought along the Kid, and a few select senior members from MacDill AFB to accelerate the process. In the UK at RAF Mildenhall, the US Air Force Special Operations Command building, with its connectivity to the Joint Analysis Center RAF Molesworth and European Command, was the perfect place for the Charlie Squadron base of operations.

A large element of the Air Force's Mildenhall staff supporting the Afghanistan and Iraq wars had moved forward to Al Udeid Air Base in Qatar. This freed valuable space at the UK base for facilities, communications, housing, and runways that Shadow Tier needed to execute operations in Europe and the Middle East.

Kennedy had come to the United Kingdom with a secondary tasking directly from the secretary of defense: to support the chief of staff of the Air Force in his military drug smuggling investigation.

Kennedy's coordination with Cavendish and his Joint Narcotics Analysis Centre was paying off by providing important clues to the military dope angle. And somebody was gaining real control of the operations. Police in the port city of Marseille were seeing a significant drop in gang-related violence.

What piqued Kennedy and the Kid's interest was an effort to consolidate several gangs. A confidential informant had reported the *Unione Corse* gang of 1970s "French Connection" fame was making a comeback. The same gang had once tried to coerce a US Army sergeant into smuggling two hundred forty pounds of heroin into the United States.

Marcel Francisci's grandson, Paul, was mentioned. The Kid had found Paul Francisci and several other names from the Air Force drug investigations at RAF Mildenhall, Ramstein Air Base in Germany, and Naval Support Activity Naples into PROVIDENCE, the Shadow Tier data analytics system.

Prior to arriving at RAF Mildenhall, the Kid had developed an extract, load, and transform program to ingest Interpol's massive trove of data related to drug smuggling and distribution. Now included in the data warehouse, PROVIDENCE's artificial intelligence ran against the data, looking for connections too disparate and faint to connect otherwise. Kennedy and the Kid planned the first run to be a learning job. Their role was to help PROVIDENCE understand the important needles found in the haystack of data.

Two hours later, they ran a new job called DARK ART. When the job finished, the Kid selected a network view of the data. The connections spanned the globe, with nodes of interest in Alaska, France, Germany, Afghanistan, Russia, Iran, and China. It was plain to see Afghanistan was the nexus of the network.

Kennedy asked the Kid to expand the Marseille and Landstuhl nodes. Landstuhl, home to the US Army's premier medical facility in Europe, was also next to Ramstein Air Base.

"What's your take on the network, Kid?"

He pushed a few keys and threw a presentation on the wall screen.

"Simple stuff first. Afghanistan is the nexus of activity, as it should be, considering it is the number one producer of opium in this part of the world. We also know from our friends at the JNAC and others there are well-used routes from Afghanistan through Iran to Turkey, and then into France and Spain by ship. We also know the overland routes through Iran, then Turkey into the Balkans, where it bifurcates to Western Europe and Russia. But the first node I'm surprised by is Mashhad, Iran. It's a lot of traffic for a country that supposedly bans drug use. The second is the level of traffic between Marseille and Landstuhl. Goes to what the Air Force chief of staff is worried about."

He rose from his seat and gestured to the display of information. "And third, because of the oddity of connections, I'm concerned about the Alaskan contract airline and its subnetwork through Ramstein, RAF Akrotiri, and Al Udeid into Afghanistan. Why are the people we are interested in mentioning their names?"

"Agreed—why?" Kennedy said. "I'll contact Air Force OSI at Ramstein and coordinate a meeting. You call Army Criminal Investigative Division at Landstuhl for the same. I'm not sure what we'll find, but I have a feeling we'll find more than local users."

Chapter 18

Wolf made sure the new superteam of investigators, special agents, and other enforcers didn't overwhelm the tribal police chief and his crew, who were frankly impressed with the full-court press Wolf had brought to bear.

The pallets of gear Wolf had borrowed from his friend Mitch Jankowski included the latest in satellite phones, cellphone jammers, long-range surveillance cameras, night vision optics, infrared scopes, and GPS tracking pucks so task force asset locations were known at all times.

Wolf ensured the superteam elements were introduced slowly and methodically, always reinforcing that the tribal police chief was in charge and that the superteam was in support. As the FBI, DEA, and state assets became available, they joined the team and uncharacteristically took up the support role, too.

Wolf was sure this was a first in the tribe's history with outside agencies. In a move that surprised Wolf, the chairman of the tribal council claimed it was his goal to make this a model for tribal interactions with federal and state law enforcement across the United States. He sat in on every meeting and demanded a satellite phone for himself.

The first operation was a coordinated set of strategic "health and safety" checkpoints. Montana Highway Patrol set up two staggered blockades at the north and south ends of the Crow reservation, one in each direction. They stopped all the trucks and made the cars drive slowly through a different lane to be examined by drug-trained canine units.

While those were the visible checkpoints, the tribal police, with FBI and DEA support, covered the alternate routes a drug runner would take through the reservation to avoid the checkpoints. LeBlanc and his Alpha Squadron assaulters were assigned the QRF mission, complete with the 160th Special Operations Aviation Regiment and a Nightstalker Pave Hawk helicopter on standby.

Wolf stood next to Joe Hogan and pointed out the blue icons showing the different enforcement locations.

"Once the cartel's spotters locate the Highway Patrol checkpoints, they will instruct their driver to take an alternate route through the reservation. When we intercept them the spotters will have to find still more routes. They will push the dope runners north of Billings and possibly even south into Utah and Salt Lake. If we don't catch them outright, we will certainly disrupt their business. A good day's work."

The chief shook his head. "This operation is much bigger than I ever saw in the Marine Corps. As a staff sergeant in charge of the heavy weapons platoon, my scope of responsibility was at the company level," Hogan said. "This is like battalion-level stuff."

"Nothing you won't get with a little time." Wolf chuckled. "I remember feeling the same way my first time in a battalion tactical operations center. Don't let the scope of operations fool you. All action still happens at the fire-team level. It's coordinating the efforts of all the teams to achieve our desired result. Use your combat experience and intuition. I've even asked my spirit guide for help."

"Thanks for all this, Wolf," Hogan said. "Drugs are a plague that will ravage this tribe if we don't take a stand."

Thirty-seven minutes late the first suspect vehicle was identified. One of Billy's scouts reported an unmarked tractor-trailer rig exiting the highway before the Highway Patrol checkpoint. It came in from the north and headed south right through the reservation's center. The tribal officer and his DEA support element blocked the road and placed flares out seventy-five yards to their front.

Out of sight around a right-handed turn, the driver had no alternatives when the flares suddenly came into view. He braked hard enough to cause the trailer to get squirrelly and the semi stopped barely twenty feet from the flares.

Tribal officers rushed to both sides of the cab, weapons raised. The driver's side window rolled down and a tribal officer with his pistol raised shouted, "Put your hands out the window and keep them there!"

The officer pulled open the door to the cab and backed away.

"Climb down slowly, turn around, hands where I can see them—do it now!"

As the driver dropped to the ground with his back to the officer, he reached to his belt. A DEA agent standing at the end of the trailer saw the driver's move and yelled *gun!* The drug agent dropped the truck driver with a single shot that entered the driver's neck and exited out the other side. The driver's gun clattered across the tarmac as he fell, his body turning toward the tribal officer as he did.

Blood splattered the tribal officer's face and chest rig as he too responded automatically, putting four .45-caliber pistol rounds into the driver before he hit the cracked asphalt pavement.

DEA agents and tribal police rushed to the scene as the seemingly endless silence became chaotic. The drug dogs had to be led away to calm them down.

The tribal officer used a handkerchief to wipe blood from his face and muttered, "What the hell's in this rig worth dying for?"

Agents climbed through the tractor's doors on both sides and disassembled the cab over the bed area. When the agent on the driver's side came back into view, his smile and a kilo bag of brown heroin in each hand vindicated the reservation plan.

In the command center, Wolf and Hogan high-fived. The tractor-trailer rig was brought to police headquarters and inspected to the last bolt. At the end of the vehicle search, the DEA reported six kilos of heroin, confirmed by test kit field test.

An hour and fourteen minutes later, dogs at the south highway patrol checkpoint alerted to a pickup truck that drove up. Instead of pulling over, the driver blew through the checkpoint at full throttle and officers took pursuit, radioing for help.

LeBlanc and his assaulters had not been happy at being designated the QRF, so when the request for help came over the net, LeBlanc volunteered the QRF to respond and Hogan cleared them to assist the tribal police.

Once airborne in the Pave Low helo, LeBlanc checked in and was given a mileage marker location as his spot to intercept the truck. As they closed on the highway, they saw the truck shadowed at a discrete distance by two Montana Highway Patrol cruisers, lights and sirens wailing. The helo vectored right to the location and came to a hover sideways in the road, LeBlanc and his two snipers in the door, weapons ready.

As the truck powered over the rise, LeBlanc could see the driver's eyes widen in his scope. Snipers shot first, putting many holes in the radiator and engine block. The driver skidded to a stop and headed off-road, only traveling fifty yards before the engine overheated and seized up solid.

The driver clambered out, tripping over the door sill as he exited and face-planting in the soft dirt. He scrambled to his feet to run, but LeBlanc's rounds skittering across the ground stopped him. He raised his hands and dropped back to his knees.

LeBlanc and his medic, Kurt Duffy, leaped from the helo and moved toward the driver, weapons up.

"Lay forward, face down on the ground, *now*," LeBlanc shouted over the roar of the Black Hawk.

The driver complied. LeBlanc searched him and stood over him as Duffy bent to the man's ear and asked, "Are you hurt? Do you need medical attention?"

"No. I need my lawyer."

LeBlanc lowered his rifle and said, "In due time, sweetheart. For now, you're mine."

A smug grin creased the driver's face. "You're cops. Read me my rights and then fuck off."

LeBlanc tapped his shoulder patch. "Do I even look like a cop, dumbass? I'm not, and you *have* no rights here."

One of the snipers popped open one of many plastic bins in the back of the truck. "Just pot, but a friggin shit-ton."

"If this keeps up, it's going to be a busy day," LeBlanc said.

Chapter 19

The last four hours and thirty-eight minutes had been quiet in the command center if you didn't consider a few cars with personal-use amounts of pot.

Wolf had been on the phone with Parker and the intel team at MacDill AFB headquarters, working backward from the capture of the tractor-trailer rig through each of its stops. The truck driver's cross-country run had started in Maine with a seafood pickup and delivery to a New York Indian casino. From there, it stopped for fuel and to exchange cargo in Joliet, Illinois, and Minneapolis. It traveled north to Interstate 94, stopping in Bismarck, North Dakota, and Billings, Montana, before attempting to skirt the checkpoint headed south on Interstate 90.

Parker told Wolf she passed the data to DEA to make sure their local field offices would have the information for their investigations. The FBI liaison told Wolf their focus was on gaining access, via warrant, to the driver's digital logbook. Once acquired, Wolf was told he would get a copy of the data. He'd have the Kid load it into PROVIDENCE and use the power of the analytics to connect the driver's stops to drug activity.

Wolf's wanted any data related to an Indian reservation. The driver's stop at the New York casino appeared legit, but it felt wrong. Why not buy from a local supplier? Do they have a direct connection to a distributor in Maine? He didn't have any data to support his thoughts, just a feeling.

In the years since Shadow Tier's formation, Wolf had seen dope transported by every enterprising means possible. People with balloons of drugs in their stomachs and other body cavities. The post office, UPS, FedEx, boats of all sizes, trains, planes, helicopters, automobiles, eighteen-wheelers, semi-submersible drug subs, radio-controlled planes, dogs, horses, and donkeys. He expected drones next.

Wolf stepped to the edge of the light and into the darkness. Squatting, he grabbed a handful of pine needles and dirt, rubbing the material between his hands. His memories of missions and friends gone from the Earth but not forgotten were crisp. The reverie was broken by a yell.

"Wolf, we have another target."

He jogged back to the command center and listened to highway patrol radio chatter. They were in pursuit of a box van and someone had fired shots at officers.

Across the room, LeBlanc turned to face Wolf, who nodded.

LeBlanc said, "On it." And immediately radioed the helicopter to spin up as he headed for the team room.

Joe Hogan, tribal police chief, came out of his office, scanning the electronic display. An FBI agent used a laser pointer to highlight the path and last reported location of the officers in pursuit.

"Has Team Three been alerted?" the chief asked.

The FBI agent said, "Yes, sir. Nine minutes until contact."

Wolf knew better than to watch the clock. The command center fell quiet. The hum of the computers and an occasional cough broke the silence. Wolf heard the helo take off and felt better.

He closed his eyes and slowed his breathing to visualize the Team Three location and terrain. Set in a draw cutting through a ridgeline, there were no other routes the box van could take. Trees and steep terrain on either side of the road created a funnel ending in a natural choke point. A perfect spot for an ambush from a military perspective.

But tonight, it was the ideal location for a controlled takedown of a fleeing suspect with potentially dangerous cargo.

That's sooner than expected, Wolf thought. The radio crackled to life, automatic gunfire almost drowning out the voice.

"Command, Three-Actual. Heavy contact, seven, no eight tangos. Need QRF *right now.*"

Wolf sensed hesitation in the command center and grabbed the microphone. "Three-Actual, roger. QRF inbound four mikes. Hang tough."

"Copy. Out here."

In the background, Wolf heard a frantic call. "*Officer down...*"

Chief Hogan spun to leave and respond to the emergency call. Those were his officers out there. Wolf grabbed his arm and Hogan stopped mid-stride.

"No, Joe—you can't lead from your patrol car."

The chief growled and reluctantly nodded. "Get EMS headed to the Team Three location but have them hold a mile out until we clear them in."

"Command, Three-Actual. We are totally defensive. We are one KIA and two WIA. Two tangos down. We need the QRF now!"

The sound of a heavy machine gun in the background made

Wolf's blood run cold because he couldn't tell if the sound was from attackers or defenders.

LeBlanc broke in the net. "Three-Actual, QRF arriving now."

The pilot held the helicopter steady as the team kicked out the fast ropes. Bullet impacts striking the helicopter pushed the team to fast-rope right on top of each other. LeBlanc slid the forty feet as if in a freefall, clamping down with his feet and hands at the last second. Then he released his grip on the rope and dropped the last three feet, rolling left out of the way and up into to a tactical crouch, acquiring targets and firing.

Two and Three joined him and they moved left as LeBlanc yelled to the pinned-down highway patrolmen they were coming through. Halting his fire for a beat to check on the officer hidden behind his shot-up cruiser, he got an in-the-fight response.

LeBlanc said, "Three-Actual, Quebec-Actual. Flanking left. Covering fire in three, two, one."

The team's headsets adjusted for the roar of Team Three's 7.62mm Mk 48 machine gun, its red tracer rounds lighting the night. For a mad minute, Team Three fired all they had, forcing the attackers to eat dirt.

Quebec slipped into the tree line and quickly came abeam of attackers huddled around the box van. As Three's fire lifted, the bad guys popped back up and returned controlled fire.

These guys have serious training, LeBlanc thought. He radioed, "Team Three, keep those heads down when we execute. Break. Bravo element, time for some big love. Give 'em hell, rocket man," LeBlanc said, his grin visible in Quebec Two's night vision.

Two unpacked an M72 Lightweight Anti-tank Weapon. As he raised the LAW to his shoulder, LeBlanc and Quebec Three each squeezed an arm to let him know they were clear of the dangerous backblast area.

Two radioed, "Going hot."

The missile streaked across the seventy-five yards of open ground, just missing the van's tire, penetrating the sheet metal fender without even slowing and slamming into the engine block. The plasma jet of molten metal from the warhead transformed the engine and bodywork on the far side of the truck into a massive spray of hot shrapnel, killing everyone within twenty feet.

An attacker on the near side staggered to his feet, weapon by his side, and fell face first into the road, riddled with shrapnel. LeBlanc and his team were already on their feet and advancing, weapons up, ready to shoot anyone posing a threat. On the far side of the truck, Three engaged a shooter and dropped him with two shots to the chest. The team found one wounded shooter who had smartly laid face down and spread-eagled, his weapon pushed out of reach. As Two flex-cuffed him and checked his wounds, the team channel popped.

"Squirter headed north, got him on infrared," the co-pilot of the helicopter said on the command net.

LeBlanc radioed on the team net. "Quebec Five & Six, squirter headed north."

Five radioed, "On it, Quebec One."

Four minutes later, Quebec Six radioed, "Tango is down and secured. Need pickup on the road five hundred meters your east."

LeBlanc radioed the command center.

"Command, Quebec-Actual, copy over."

"Quebec-Actual, Command."

"Command, we have one KIA, three WIA. Wounded are stable and ambulatory. Eight enemy killed in action, two enemy wounded in action. One critical, send medevac. Copy?"

"Good copy Quebec-Actual. Medevac inbound."

Chapter 20

Wolf watched the command center staff process the cost of winning. A few of the staff stood together in prayer. Others sat quietly at their stations. Chief Hogan announced he was going to update the tribal chairman and headed to the tribal offices. Wolf got the team settled back down, letting them know the mission wasn't over yet.

A few minutes later the tribal chairman stormed into the command center, his face in a scowl and hands clenched in fists. He strode into the chief's office slamming the door shut behind him. The muffled sounds of an argument had the people in the command center looking to the chief's office. When the chief and chairman exited, the conversation was heated. Wolf signaled the men and women from the other agencies to take a break.

"Frank, listen. You are off base here," Chief Hogan said, pointing a knife hand at the tribal council chairman. "Wolf didn't start a war on the reservation. The Sinaloa cartel did. They sent a van full of soldiers with one thought in mind—to kill our people."

Wolf said, "Chairman White Horse. We're all saddened by the loss of Officer Lassiter and we pray for the quick recovery of the wounded. But you need to understand who and what we are dealing with. I know them well. They killed my parents and have killed hundreds of other innocent people. They will not stop. What is concerning is they normally don't respond like this unless something big is at stake. Usually, they consider the losses we inflicted in the last twenty-four hours as the cost of doing business. There is more going on in the reservation than we know."

White Horse narrowed his eyes and stared at Wolf for a long couple of seconds.

"You took the council's approval and militarized it. Instead of a low-profile set of apprehensions, you created an opening that the FBI and DEA will use to supersede tribal sovereignty—he very thing each of the council members warned against. You betrayed us to the federal government. We lost a valued member of the tribe, and we could lose more of our rights if I cannot contain this shit-storm you've created."

Chief Hogan got in White Horse's face.

"*Wrong.* We did good work out there tonight. We showed the cartel we aren't letting them use our people or our land. If we want to keep the scourge of drugs off the reservation, then we need to— *we must*—fight back!"

"I'll talk to you later, Hogan. You are part of this problem, too. This operation is over—right *now*, damn it." Chairman White Horse marched out of the room.

Chief Hogan shook his head and stared at Wolf as if to ask, *what can I do?* "You heard the man. Shut it down."

Wolf gathered the command center team, moved to the front of the room, and held up a hand. "Team, I'm sorry to say we need to shut down this operation. But before you do, know you did fantastic work. We've taken six kilos of heroin and two hundred-plus pounds of marijuana off the street. The cartel knows we aren't giving them a free ride. We fight for Montana and our people."

Wolf stepped outside and felt the helicopter's vibrations before he heard them. He had been here before, that odd place when his words described a win but his heart was heavy with loss. He recognized his sense of loss was tied to the fallen Lassiter, the tribal police officer killed in action.

Wolf had always had a tough time with the loss of teammates and those close to him. Though he knew it was his cost of doing business, every injured teammate, and especially every fallen battle buddy, hit him hard. He was the tip of this spear. He was responsible for bringing everyone home safe. He blamed himself for such losses, as proof that he had failed to plan effectively.

The hurt and killed were his fault.

In the six years since the start of his war against the Sinaloa cartel, Wolf had definitely sustained losses. That the cartel had lost significantly more didn't enter the equation. He was a protector, a guardian—a leader—and he hid his pain of loss and failure.

As he got to his SUV, LeBlanc and Alpha Squadron emerged from the darkness and encircled their leader.

LeBlanc said, "Boss, this isn't your fault. It just isn't. This is the outcome of operating with civilians. They don't understand this is a war—a shooting war no different than Afghanistan or Syria, just fought on the home front against a different sort of enemy. It's on the news sometimes, but not in the average Joe's face. When we play to win, it assaults their sense of right and fairness."

"Have we become them to fight them?" Wolf said, turning to look at the six men and two women of the squadron.

"Not even close, brother, and you know it," LeBlanc said. "We've all been there, and we have pulled back before, when it would have been easy to lose our humanity."

Wolf considered that. "True. You all saved lives tonight. Be proud of that." They shook hands. "I'll see you back at MacDill."

Wolf's satellite phone rang. He nodded to the team and got in behind the wheel of his SUV.

"General, how can I help you, sir?"

"You can't, Wolf, but I'm going to help you keep your job and not go to Leavenworth for the long course."

"Sir? I don't understand."

"I crossed the base to speak with Ms. Parker about an intelligence matter and what did I see on the Ops board but a C-17 mission to Billings, Montana? Its load out was a MH-60 Pave Hawk and crew. I also see Alpha has decided to train in the Bighorn Canyon area. So, I do some checking, and the FBI and DEA are talking up a successful drug interdiction mission this evening in coordination with the Montana Highway Patrol and the Crow Nation. An amazing coincidence, don't you think?"

"Sir, I can explain ..."

"No, you cannot. Your 'training mission' could very well be seen as misappropriation of government equipment and funds. If some inspector general gets a burr in his saddle, it would be bad for you, Shadow Tier—and the president. I don't have to tell you who the primary concern is for, do I?"

Wolf was silent for a moment. "No, sir. You do not."

"The agencies are reporting it as a huge win and commending the actions of Alpha Squadron, who saved lives. A piece of advice, and a direct order: Get your happy ass back to MacDill and focus on the president's priorities, and do it in one quick hurry. If you want to help your people, be a leader, not an outlaw. Out here."

He disconnected without waiting for Wolf to acknowledge.

Chapter 21

Wolf took a 0730 flight from Billings through Denver to Tampa. Driving home from the airport he left a message with Parker that he was on the ground. He was happy to be back home. Especially in one piece.

Parker wasn't home, so he dumped his bag inside the front door, threw on some running clothes, and filled his camelback before heading out for a restorative run. The traffic, heat, and humidity all fell away as he sorted through his actions and General Davidson's admonitions. After showing his badge at the Bayshore gate, he continued his run around the eastern side of MacDill AFB to the southern edge of the Bay Palms golf course.

Checking the road, he crossed and laughed. He was getting his stride now, and it made him feel good again. The first sprint through the one hundred yards of loose sand was work but fun. The second hundred was work and just okay. By the third, his legs and lungs burned with the righteous feel of lactic acid. By the fourth, everything but his breathing was gone, the pain intensified, and his motor skills were deteriorating.

Twenty-five yards from the end he tripped, but he turned the fall into an elegant roll back to his feet, completing the sprint as if the trip had been intentional gymnastic move. The sand stuck to his sweat and he laughed again, this time at himself, the human sugar cookie. He scanned the area and took a Great Blue Heron staring his way.

"Better now, bud," Wolf said, with a two-finger salute.

Wolf paused for a long drink from his camelback and took off again, pushing through the deadness in his legs and working easily into a mileage-eating lope that took him back to his house. He was out back showering off the sand when Parker came through the sliding glass door.

"You playing with your SEAL buddies again, hot dog?" she asked with a sly grin.

Wolf smiled back. "Nope, just getting my head right."

"Burning away the old to expose the new?"

"As Seneca said, 'Every new beginning comes from some other beginning's end.'"

"What other beginning did you just end, Wolf?"

"On the reservation, I felt this intense need to push the cartel off our land and out of our tribe's life in one fell swoop. My fear of their impact was so deep that, for a time, I became *them*. My only thought was to kill as many of them as possible. Seizing as much dope as possible. All without regard for decency." He shook the water from his head and droplets reflected in the sunlight like tiny diamonds. "Or for my soul."

"I've read the after-action reports and talked with LeBlanc," Parker said, tight-lipped. "What I see is a man who was feeling irrational but who kept it separate from his actions. Minus the misappropriation of government equipment and a potential long stay in Leavenworth, you did well."

"You talked with Davidson?"

"Yes, I did, my frustrated outlaw of a husband."

"You're right on both counts."

"I get it," Parker said. She unconsciously reached up to massage the scar left by cartel bullets. "Maybe sometimes it looks like we aren't winning, but then I look around and compare to where we were before. One of the many things which brings us all together is we hold ourselves to a higher standard than our peers or bosses do. I love that about you but don't let it lie to you. We must play the long game. And how do we win?"

"We win by never quitting."

"Right. Now finish your shower and get dressed. You are taking me to La Teresita's for dinner."

Chapter 22

Boss, you've run the data eight times now. PROVIDENCE cannot come up with the result you are looking for if it doesn't have the data to correlate. We have all the New York state, DEA, and FBI data there is to ingest. It's time to rely on people power to close the gap in our coverage."

Kennedy looked at the Kid across the desk littered with empty paper coffee cups and a pile of discarded tea bags on a plate with a few stale cookies.

"You're right. Tomorrow we're going to Germany. We'll stop in the clothing store before heading over. Ever wanted to be a FBI agent, Kid?"

"Uh, no. In my short time at Shadow Tier, they Feds don't impress me. Buncha note-takers and wanna-be deep thinkers. Give me the E-4 Mafia anytime."

Kennedy choked on his cold tea, tears of laughter rolling down his cheeks. "There are a few knuckleheads, like anywhere. Most are hardworking enough, if not brilliant." He wiped a fat tear from his cheek. "But yeah, I'd take a squad of Army Specialists for most things, I think."

The Kid smiled. His boss and mentor was back, had something to prove, and the Kid was happy for him and Shadow Tier. But the connections to Landstuhl and Ramstein Air Base were disconcerting.

Kennedy mused, "Have the Taliban or Marseille mafia found a way onto Air Force's Military Airlift Command flights? Hundreds of flights to and from Iraq and Afghanistan occur weekly, not to mention aircraft passing through those waypoints for fuel, and all those headed to other parts of Europe and the United States. That's a *helluva* gravy train that could well afford to corrupt a few carefully placed active-duty loadmasters and logistics people."

The Kid nodded and thought about a new solution that seemed obvious to him.

To catch criminals, we have to think like them. To stop the drugs ... we need to create our own cartel.

Chapter 23

The sky was a low gray overcast that seemed to compress the European humidity into solid matter. Kennedy and the Kid stepped off a C-130J-30 configured for passenger transport onto the tarmac at Ramstein Air Base, eighty-four miles southwest of Frankfurt, Germany, and into a scene of controlled chaos.

They carried soft athletic bags full of clothing and their personal items. No suitcases, as they weren't tourists, though a large man and his wife, both Army retirees on a free military hop to Germany, each deplaned with two large Samsonite roller hard cases.

The ramp area reminded Kennedy of Chicago's O'Hare International Airport, frantically busy and elbow to elbow with planes, forklifts, utility vehicles and tractors, and people. Lots and lots of people.

The glaring difference was here there were more ambulances than Kennedy had ever seen in one place at a time. The Kid grabbed

Kennedy's arm and nodded across the ramp as they walked into the military terminal.

"Wounded from Iraq and Afghanistan?"

"Iraq would be my guess. That's where the heaviest fighting is these days," Kennedy said, scanning the terminal for the contact meeting them.

The Kid pointed to their left. A young man in khaki cargo pants and an Air Force blue polo shirt right off the post exchange rack approached with his hand in the air, waving to get their attention.

"Special Agents Pope and Hubler? Lieutenant Carson, Air Force OSI."

Kennedy and the Kid held out their fake FBI credentials, which Carson scanned before shaking hands. Then he displayed his own Office of Special Investigations creds with a gold badge in a basketweave folder.

Kennedy smiled. A basketweave cred folder was a bold choice for someone not, say, a highway patrol trooper.

"Follow me, please," Carson said as he spun, heading out the terminal's exit for a blue sedan in the distance.

The ride to the OSI offices took longer than expected. The air base was teaming with people and traffic. "Pope" and "Hubler" signed in at the front desk and were given badges permitting full access to the base and facility short of the Sensitive Compartmented Information Facility areas.

They grabbed coffee from the mess area and were escorted by Carson into a SCIF. Inside, they found a fourteen-year-old looking airman and two grizzled veteran investigators sitting around a table. Carson locked the door behind them and pushed a binder across the table.

"Sign these, please," Carson said, and waited for them to finish. "Per United States Air Force Regulation—"

One of the investigators interrupted. "Lieutenant," the veteran on the left said. "They know where they are." He turned to the Kennedy and the Kid. "You have signed this non-disclosure and shall consider yourselves read into the *Hidden Treasure* program, gentlemen. Welcome aboard. I'm Air Force Chief Master Sergeant Geoff Grimes." He shook hands with them and gestured to his teammates. "This is Master Sergeant Ed Darden and Staff Sergeant Jerry Johannsen."

"Call me Jones. My cover name," the youthful Johannsen said.

Kennedy and the Kid slid the NDAs back across the table.

Kennedy nodded, and the Kid spoke. "Gentlemen, you have been briefed in on our mission." He looked down at the ring binder Shadow Tier had forwarded to the Ramstein OSI team. "We're seeing indicators of an opium ratline pointing to Landstuhl, and by association, this base."

Carson was confused. "Ratline?"

The Kid suppressed a laugh. "A route of travel with waypoints followed by trusted cartel agents moving the product out of Afghanistan all the way here to Germany."

"Ever heard of the Pony Express, Carson?" Grimes asked.

"Yep, got it," Carson said sheepishly.

Darden said, "We don't see much hard drugs here on the military side anymore, but the civilians, it's a different story."

"Our friends in the German *Bundesnachrichtendienst* intelligence service said the same. And it's why we suspect *Hidden Treasure*. No pun intended," Kennedy said. "It's worse. We suspect Ramstein and its MAC flights are unknowing participants in an opium ratline to the United States."

No one spoke for moments. Grimes started to speak and stopped, his brow furrowing, eyes burning. Carson pushed back from the table and stood. Darden shook his head. Only Jones seemed nonplussed. Carson started to speak, but Grimes shut him down with a side-eye and a shake of his head.

If dope was being transported to the States on military aircraft out of Ramstein, that meant OSI had failed to detect it.

Kennedy nodded to the Kid. "Go ahead. Tell them."

"Guys, we're here at the direction of the SECDEF to support the Air Force Chief of Staff and OSI. Your bosses are rightfully scared out of their boxers that the Taliban, or their partners, have infiltrated your logistics systems and processes. We're here to work with you to investigate the possibilities and put them to bed or, as necessary, take action to stop the flow of Taliban opium. Terrorist dope contributes about four hundred million bucks a year to terrorist coffers."

Jones smirked. "Thank you, 'Agent Hubler,' if that's your real name. I'm just a dumbass PJ assigned to work undercover for these guys." He glared at Carson. "What did I tell you?"

"Watch your tone, sergeant. You do not have any proof. At all."

"No, sir. I don't have proof—because we can't get the manpower we need to prosecute this investigation properly."

Grimes said, "Sir, I agree with Johannsen."

"Gentlemen," Kennedy offered, "we do have resources. Agents and analysts. We know the focus of *Hidden Treasure* is on arms traffic, and it's important to track and seize contraband weapons, but the SECDEF and the president are laser-focused on stopping the Taliban from cashing in from their opium harvests. Let's put together a plan that we will maximize the use of our analytics software and our combined deep-cover agents to uncover the ratline."

Kennedy stood as Carson and Grimes moved around the table.

"I don't want to know how you have the details on our code word project," Carson said, "but I'm happy you're here and look forward to working with you."

The three of them shook hands, and as Kennedy glanced across the table, he smiled. The Kid was bonding with Jones. He thought he heard a comment about dinosaurs being hard of hearing and suppressed a chuckle. It was all good.

Leaving the building, Kennedy said to the Kid. "I need Charlie Squadron here, ready or not."

Chapter 24

It pleased Charlie Squadron commander Noah Taylor that the multi-national joint-service team's Phase 1 assessment was going as well as expected. The mountainous Breacon Beacons terrain in South Wales was doing its best to weed out unsuitable candidates. One of the French lieutenants had demonstrated a complete lack of directional awareness and map reading.

A Brit who Taylor had thought was an easy pass had sustained an unfortunate fall in a night exercise and had been sent back for medical screening. If his back injury didn't disqualify him, he would return to the team as soon as he was medically released.

The women candidates especially impressed him. They were not loud, they followed orders, and they got their tasks done with efficiency and skill. He'd seen a good many female SWAT-type operators work the streets, but few who could also move at speed over long distances in rugged terrain laden with full kit. Not the fastest, not the slowest, but perhaps the most reliable.

Taylor stopped reading the evaluators' notes and smiled as he scanned the sky.

It *was shaping up to be an SAS kind of day*, he thought, stepping out of his Range Rover into the sleet and snow.

The radio squawked. "Charlie One, Four."

"Go for One."

"One, our Spaniard has rung the bell."

The team had no tap-out bell, but the term was universally understood to describe someone dropping out of a tough volunteer training program on request. No disrespect, because such units are designed to not be for everyone. Better to know now who was best equipped for arduous duty before they started out.

"Okay, copy that. Let's get him off the mountain soonest and out-process him back to his unit as soon as possible, with our gratitude for his attempt."

Assessment was about to ramp up harder and weeding out the weak of body or mind was what Phase 1 did. The next test would determine who had the heart and never-give-up mindset Wolf demanded from his operators. Taylor had been on missions with Wolf and had seen his calm but fierce warrior mindset. He had also seen Wolf let adversaries live when killing was unnecessary.

Taylor knew Wolf didn't think of himself as a model of excellence—Wolf would say he was more of a journeyman of the craft and just too stupid to quit. Taylor knew better. Operating in deep cover or on direct-action missions against Europe's mafias and drug cartels would take the best people the team could muster. The one percent who were willing to fight the scourge of illegal drugs had to be led by the best of the best.

Shadow Tier, and Lance Bear Wolf.

Tonight, the assessment team would use the largest mortar and grenade simulators available in tandem with light machine guns, firing live ammunition and tracer rounds in a mock defense of an objective against the assaulting Charlie Squadron nominees. The idea was to force them to respond to contact, to reason clearly while mentally and physically depleted, and still safely make their waypoints on the longest overland movement to date.

His evaluators would track candidates electronically and visually, and harass them at different times throughout the test—not only kinetically. They would offer them soothing words, extreme praise, hot coffee, soup, and hot food at the waypoints … if only they would figuratively ring the bell.

Losing three or four more candidates would fit the statistical average for this sort of torture test. Beating the average would make Taylor extremely happy. He climbed back into his Range Rover and headed for the starting point. They would drop the candidates off in an hour.

The exercise kicked off strong when a proctor triggered an airhorn. As they often will, the herd of male and female candidates alike struck off hard and tried to elbow past the man or woman next to them. This was wasteful of energy and teamwork. Soon the stragglers would present themselves and the demons would pounce on them.

"Just say you quit, bro," the exercise proctors would coo. "Stop beating yourself up, man. You know you won't make the next waypoint in time, so why bother? You do not need this crap. Let's bag this shit and call it a day. There is heat, hot coffee, and hot food waiting for you in the back of the truck." They would smile a devious, Cheshire smile full of hearts and flowers. "Waddaya say, sport?"

During the night, a missing Norwegian candidate, separated from his exercise buddy, was found via his electronic tracker. He was delirious and hypothermic, and wandering along a road. So disconnected from reality was the candidate that he didn't know where his weapon was. He had dropped it.

Lucky enough for him, he and his exercise buddy had each fashioned security lanyards with parachute cord for their weapons, and it dragged his FN Herstal FN40GL Mk2 grenade launcher muzzle first in the mud and snow behind him. After some IV fluids, hot food, a long nap—and two hours in the squadron arms room cleaning his weapon—he was on his way home with a letter of commendation for his effort.

A few had succumbed to the allure of relief and took the bait. Most had not. Twenty-four hours later, the finishers would comprise the core of Charlie Squadron's assault team. In classic assessment-completion style, the members who had completed the course were ordered into the back of a canvas covered truck, handed hot coffee, and told to wait. Since the time limit for the test had not been provided, the finishers sat in silence, wondering whether they had been forgotten. They all checked their watches; there was still almost an hour until the end of the test.

Two more candidates remained to cross the finish line. Their GPS trackers highlighted their positions. They could make it with a last push to the final point. Taylor was deep in remembrance of the test during his assessment. He'd used a common tactic—pain—to focus his intentions. He had made it, still unsure to this day how close he might have been to failing. He hadn't thought of it since. His only focus was moving forward.

His satcom phone rang, pulling him from his thoughts.

"Taylor."

"It's Kennedy. I need Charlie Squadron in K-town tomorrow."

"You cannot be serious. They've never worked together. We haven't even finished the assessment yet—two of them are still out on the damned course. And Kaiserslautern ain't in the neighborhood."

"I need you here now. We'll find a place for you to train."

"I need a day for recovery and three days to run them through the shoot house."

"I will see you tomorrow. Am I making myself clear, squadron commander?"

"Yes, sir. Very clear." *Very late tomorrow,* Taylor thought.

The call disconnected. So taken aback was he by the call, Taylor hadn't noticed the last of the stragglers had crossed the finish line under the deadline and was in the truck.

He dismounted his Range Rover and went to the back. The tailgate was down on the old US Army deuce-and-a-half they'd pressed into service and when Taylor stepped into the light, the candidates to a person sat up straight and listened intently.

Have we passed? Failed? Are there more tasks, dear God, no? The tension was thick, and no one was breathing much.

Taylor took a deep breath. "Welcome to Shadow Tier."

The truck full of depleted men and women couldn't hold their glee and roared their success, stamping their muddy boots, shouting, and clapping their hands on each other's backs.

After just a few seconds, Taylor said, "Listen up." The revelry stopped in an instant. "There is a situation. Get some food and sleep. We deploy tomorrow." He placed his hands on his hips and smiled. "Well done, all. Damned well done."

Happy to see the nods from the candidates, he briefed the cadre and ordered everyone back to Mildenhall.

Taylor replayed Kennedy's call to Stewart Portes, his number two, as he drove back to Mildenhall.

"This is daft. It must be big—big enough to take this kind of risk. What the hell are we rushing into?" Portes wondered.

Chapter 25

Wolf opened the door to La Teresita's for Parker and stopped to breathe in deeply. The dinnertime aromas of onions, garlic, pork, and beef on the grill filled the air, and Wolf smiled. Parker sat on her red swivel stool at the corner of the Formica-topped counter, its colors and metal trim a nod to the Fifties.

Wolf nodded as a waitress set down their waters and opened her pad.

"Tostones, frijoles negros for appetizers. Filete de tilapia espalda with camarones al ajillo for my wife. I'll have puerco asado. Two Modelo beers, please."

The food came quickly, which Wolf appreciated, since he was not in the mood for Parker's questions that were sure to come. She would pepper her husband with questions, and he felt it was right for her to ask them, just not here in the restaurant. He kept the subjects light, working hard to keep his normal situational awareness under control so as not to alarm Parker.

On the way home, she broke the stalemate in the truck. "How are you feeling after getting shut down? Essentially, kicked off the reservation?"

"Angry, sad, and focused."

Parker didn't reply for a long minute. "So, would you care to elaborate?"

"I'll start with angry. I haven't told you all the details because I am still trying to process them. First, I got conned into helping a young mom with a 'baby' and a fake flat tire. It was an ambush, and she died for it, but she was part of the deception, so. Mixed about that. The baby I protected with my life was a damned doll."

Wolf huffed and shook his head. *This life I lead*, he thought.

"Then I nearly got dead with a rookie move. The guy attacking me calls himself Amaru—an Inca dragon—and he was scary good, to be honest. For the first time in a long time, I wasn't sure I was going to live through the day. Then the highway patrol showed up and he bugged out, but he had me. He had me. He taunted me on the radio."

Parker leaned in. "I'm sure you didn't egg him on, right?"

Wolf's brow furrowed. "It started well at the reservation. Our setup worked as planned, funneling vehicles into checkpoints and finding illegal loads trying to slip by the highway patrol. We led them into capture zones we'd set up with FBI and DEA teams supporting tribal police. Intercepted two large loads, one heroin and the other marijuana. Both ended in positive outcomes. The third major intercept was a cartel attack with the only goal to kill law enforcement.

"Alpha Squadron defended and we limited our losses to one dead and three wounded, but the ante is officially raised. These people were a well-trained and heavily armed team of former soldiers. But the tribal executive was looking for any way to close us down. The idea that Feds on tribal land erodes sovereignty is a bullshit, out-of-date view. There is something else going on. I can feel it."

Wolf pulled into the garage. As they walked into the house, Parker said, "I can tell you're not done with this. I can see it in your clenched fists and hear it in your voice. Your energy screams, 'I have to fix this.' Before you say anything, know that I'm with you. It might mean our careers, but it's important to you. That makes it important to me."

Wolf hugged the love of his life, thinking about the tightrope they would need to walk moving forward. At the back door, he scanned the alley for threats. Amaru had gotten under his skin and in his head.

Thirty-five minutes later, Wolf and Parker were about to start a movie when the phone rang. Caller ID said Billy. Wolf sighed as he accepted the call and said, "Has White Horse rethought his position, Billy?"

"Wolf, it's Joe Hogan. Billy is in intensive care up in Billings. There was another attack, this time targeting the reservation rangers. Billy saved the rest of the team by assaulting into the ambush."

Wolf sat upright on the couch. "Will he live?"

"Yeah, but it will be a long recovery."

"What's White Horse saying now?"

"He's telling people this is all your fault. That you've poked the bear we were living with in harmony. He says you incited Billy and his rangers toward violence, and now there is a dead tribal officer whose family has no father and three wounded. And none of it needed to happen."

"Is that what you think, chief?"

"No, of course not. But we *have* poked the bear, and it's impacting White Horse. I have a bad feeling he's tied up with this somehow. We can't ignore this and expect it to go away."

Joe Hogan sighed heavily.

"You *warned* us about all this, and now it's happening."

"Our hands are tied right now. We will have to prove a clear and present threat before I can get my team back in the area, much less on the reservation. We're going to have to be creative. Let me get back to you. I'm not giving up on our people."

Hogan paused. He didn't want to sound alarmist, but things were moving faster now.

"You better hurry, brother. You know we're just seeing the tip of the iceberg. We won't even be a nation if this infiltration keeps up. Oh, and how 'bout this? Two of our graduating high school girls just got married here last week, and their husbands are Mexican. On a hunch, I had the wedding photos analyzed. The husbands' tattoos are from the Sinaloa cartel."

Wolf sighed. "Damn it. Tell Billy's guys to stand by. I'll be back soon with a plan."

Hogan said, "Copy that. Thanks. We'll be waiting, brother."

Parker slid up next to Wolf. "Don't tell me—it's gotten worse since you left."

"It has. Billy is in ICU. His team was ambushed, and Chief Hogan has found evidence the Sinaloa cartel is marrying into the tribe."

"How are we going to stop the cartel?"

"We're facing so many new threats, I'm not sure. I need to meet with LeBlanc and call Kennedy in the morning."

Chapter 26

Michael Clinton, Bravo Squadron commander, sat at the picnic table reading Dan Brown's *The Da Vinci Code*. The sun baked his tired back and relaxed his thick shoulders from the previous night's raid. The five-man team had interdicted a big dope load high in the mountains along the Pakistani border, and were forced to move the captured opium on their backs three and a half miles over rough terrain to a landing zone.

It still made him sad thinking about having to put down two horses injured coming down the mountain, plus it then added as much as one hundred pounds to their thirty-pound Mystery Ranch patrol packs. Not designed to carry the weight, it had been a struggle to keep the dope onboard. Clinton smirked.

Next time some idiot bureaucrat wants to show off the haul from a raid, create a sling load so we don't have to carry it.

Clinton was reading a paragraph when movement at the checkpoint into the compound caught his eye. He did a double take as an armed Pashtun was admitted inside the compound with no visible pass. Clinton placed his book face down on the table, preserving his place in it, and strode over and intercepted the second man. He held his left hand out in the universal signal for stop, his right on his pistol.

In his best Pashtun, Clinton said, "Stop. I need to see your pass."

The Afghani canted his head and replied in Pashtun. "You want to see my pass? Please is the proper word you are looking for." Then he switched to English. "Bloody yanks."

Clinton's eyes narrowed. "So, you speak English. Good for you. Now show me your pass."

The man chuckled and replied in perfect English.

"Sure, mate. I was told to look for a large, strong, and handsome black man," he said, handing over his pass. "I did not expect him also to be pig-headed."

Clinton scrutinized the man's pass—Devon Lancaster, SAS.

"Shit, dude. Why didn't you just tell me who you are?" he asked, shaking his head and extending his hand. "A man can get shot for less around here."

"Not nearly as much fun, brother."

"Just what we need, another damn prankster. Glad you're here, though. You've come to a target-rich operation, and we need you. Where's your kit?"

"No telling. Could be on the way to Germany or the Antarctic, but I imagine it will catch up. If I may ask, sir, why so tight? Is there an imminent threat?"

"If I'm acting a little squirrelly, it's because there was a green-on-green incident outside the checkpoint four days ago. The Afghan checkpoint soldiers and the border police disagreed over the border cops extorting money from refugees passing through. Push came literally to shove, and the matter got settled with machine guns.

Two border cops were killed. Now the Afghans are expecting reprisals, and thus so are we."

"My God. Is nothing sacred when corrupt cops can no longer get *baksheesh* from an innocent traveler?"

Clinton said, "Yeah, it's crazy." He clapped Lancaster on the back. "Let's go meet the team."

"Brilliant."

Bravo Squadron had moved up in the compound pecking order and now had a double-wide expandable office trailer for its command center and headquarters. In classic military style, the air conditioner built by the lowest bidder had two temperature settings, off and crushed ice.

Clinton saw Lancaster shiver in the sudden climate change and reached to a nearby coat rack.

"Here, we keep these handy for the uninitiated." Clinton handed him a bright blue Patagonia pile jacket.

"Hey, Bravo," Clinton called to the room. Everyone stopped what they were doing and turned to their commander.

"This is Devon Lancaster, SAS. He'll be our replacement for Captain Taylor. Devon, sitting in front of the pile of radios, crypto, and who knows what else, is Robert Baskin, our communications and all-things-tech nerd." Baskin smiled and waved. "Over at the map display is Ernst Mallard, our medic, and Mark Conklin, one of our snipers. Our team intel lead Stuart Hoffman and demo guy, Jeff Nash, are over at the Agency compound. Where's Jocko?"

The door flew open behind them. All eyes moved to the motion and fixed on a mountain of a man entering the trailer. He was covered head to toe in desert moondust and his T-shirt was stained was in sweat. He noticed Lancaster, wiped his brow, and laughed.

"Devi, don't you look the Pashtun warlord," Jocko Woods said, striding across the room to shake hands and bro-hug.

Lancaster said, "Have you been wrestling a bear, Jocko?"

"No, mate. Making sure our Humvees get proper maintenance. I've modified them into proper SAS-style gun trucks. Breaking down out there is a bloody nightmare."

"Why don't you introduce Devon to our intel and support cells? Get him squared away with some kit." Clinton glanced at his watch. "I have to be on a command call in five."

Jocko nodded and led Lancaster into the second section of the trailer system.

Clinton punched in a six-digit key sequence for the SCIF's door lock. The light changed from red to green and heard the electronic mechanism opened and simultaneously shut off the alarm system and countermeasures. Clinton thought it overkill to implement the sticky foam and the CO2 area denial systems, but they had come with the package at no extra cost.

He glanced at his watch, made the mental adjustment for Eastern time, and picked up the handset on the encrypted phone. He dialed an eight-digit code, then punched the speaker button, replacing the handset in the cradle. The system made its odd collection of noises as the phones in Afghanistan, the United Kingdom, and the United States all synced up and connected.

"Clinton here."

"Kennedy & the Kid here."

"Wolf and Parker here. Go ahead, Kennedy."

"First, congratulations to Clinton and Bravo Squadron. Your idea to spike the opium we reinserted back into the flow has paid off. The teams we deployed to the target locations PROVIDENCE gave us have had a high hit rate. Unfortunately, the rate of decay from the isotope has made any additional tracking impossible. The good news is we now have identified six waypoints leading to Marseille, four to Barcelona, and six more to Paris. I must admit surprise that the first three waypoints are shared amongst all the known destinations."

Wolf interrupted. "Can we spike the opium in Europe and track where it goes from our known locations?"

"Possibly," Kennedy said. "But we believe the opium is further processed into heroin at these sites, so we would have to get inside the organizations, which would be very dangerous and might take a year or more."

Wolf asked, "What if we offer high-end chemistry services? We build a lab and tout our new highly addictive heroin compound. Guaranteed to drive up sales."

"That is a great idea," the Kid said. "But why not go all the way and enter the business? Cartel, mafia, whatever we call ourselves. As a supplier of raw opium, the opium Bravo has access to will get us kick-started. We can create an organization with assets in Afghanistan and throughout Europe made up of former law enforcement and military types who have less than stellar reputations and histories. Not only will we get an integrated picture of the people behind what PROVIDENCE has identified, but also the possibility of understanding if and how any of the heroin gets to America."

The silence stretched on. Clinton was the first to break it. "Damn, Kid, it's a bold plan. Count me in. DEA in Afghanistan is focused on finding and destroying labs. We, as in the United States and our partners, are going to spend millions here and have nothing to show for it. This can change all that."

Parker asked, "Is Charlie Squadron mission ready yet? We will need them."

"Close," Kennedy said. "I'm pushing our new squadron commander to be deployable by the end of the week.

Wolf chuckled. "I think audacious is the correct term here. I love it. I want a business plan for setting up our new enterprise so we can make sure we have no gaps that might get someone dead. Let's include all the physical assets we will need. This is going to cost a ton and I'll need to sell it to General Davidson."

Kennedy said, "What makes this work is our understanding of the business and our adversaries. I think it was Sun Tzu who said, 'All warfare is deception.'"

"Agreed. We have work to do to prepare the deception. Kennedy and the Kid have point on this. Call if you need anything. Parker and I will brief the general."

"Kennedy, I'll call you back after I get the team working the idea from the supply side," Clinton said. "I've got just the right person to pull this off. Give some thought to introducing a Pakistani middleman into the plan."

"Anything to strengthen our story and make it airtight. We're about to play on the big stage where we can't misspeak our lines or stumble in our choreography. If we do, it will play out with all the elements of a Greek tragedy, but with a very tragic ending."

Chapter 27

Later, Parker watched Wolf end another call. She saw his frown and heard his sigh, and his cursing under his breath.

"News from the reservation?"

"Yes, and it isn't good. Sinaloa is exerting its dominance just shy of all out violence. Intimidation, threats, and arson."

"Do you believe the situation can return to what White Horse described as stable?"

"It's possible. I'm not there agitating for more pushback against the cartel, disrupting their business. What do we know about this crew? Do they report to Eliana?"

Parker said, "Not much about this specific group. They call themselves *Puma Grande*. Looks like maybe contractors outside of Eliana's organization."

"What makes you think that?"

"One, they only operate out of the big three, San Francisco, Portland, and Seattle. I called Fransisca and she says they've been tied to Pacific rim terrorism, Abu Sayyaf, and others. They're suspected of providing product security out of the Golden Triangle. In the US, they're into meth and heroin, with the predominance of their profits coming from meth. It's just a feeling at this point, but I do not see an Eliana signature here. I see El Chapo."

"Really?"

Parker nodded. "Yes. We know El Chapo is like a commercial business incubator, trying out new ideas all the time in his lieutenant's territories. I think he's contracted these Puma Grande people to test using the Crow reservation and others for transportation routes and production. Eliana must know what's happening, but I suspect El Chapo doesn't care if she does."

"What about Interpol?"

"Limited to liaison offices in key cities like Hong Kong and Singapore. I've already asked the FBI for a data dump. Same with the police departments in San Francisco, Portland, and Seattle."

"Good. Check in over the border with the Canadians at the RCMP, and Vancouver police, too. I'll read this and get back with questions."

Parker nodded, left the office, and headed back to her SCIF. On the way she stopped to check in with the cyber team and their ongoing support for Kennedy and the Kid. A half-hour later, she was in the SCIF, deep in thought.

She appreciated this side of Wolf. So focused and determined to get it right. She had seen Wolf risk his life to help others. It was a positive trait the cartel had mistaken for a weakness that nearly got him killed. First by a semi-trailer, then by a very good assassin. Parker started as the thing that had been pinging her subconscious brain from its farthest recesses bloomed into view.

They're profiling us.

She ran the rest of the way to her office, slammed the door

closed, and rushed for her phone. Wolf would go for his long run today. Her fingers trembled as she mis-dialed his number and hung up to call him again. "Damn, damn!"

She dialed again and the call went straight to voicemail. She disconnected and hit the speed dial button for Morgan. He picked up on the second ring.

"What's up?"

"Have you seen Wolf?"

"Nope. I'm headed out for the obstacle course with LeBlanc and Alpha."

Parker shouted. "Morgan! I think a new crew working for El Chapo has been following us, profiling Wolf. It's his long-run day and they're probably out there waiting for him."

"Shit. Which route does he take?"

"Just one. Up Bayshore over the bridge to Davis Island down to the airport and back."

"On it."

Parker was lost in thought when she finally registered the dial tone and, a beat later, placed the handset in the cradle. Then she did something she rarely did. She prayed for her husband and soulmate.

Ten minutes later a black Suburban left Shadow Tier head-quarters at a high rate of speed. When they picked up a base police tail, they flipped on their lights and siren. The patrol car followed them off base as they raced down Bayshore nose to tail.

They were about halfway to the Davis Island bridge when a Pave Hawk helicopter raced overhead and broke right over the bay, taking a direct route to the island. Morgan had experienced Wolf's ability to run forever at a six-minute-mile pace and expected him to be at or near the airport. The helo was three-quarters of a mile out when Morgan, strapped in the open doorway behind twin M240 door guns, spotted flashes from automatic weapons fire at the beach across from the Davis Island yacht club.

The helo pilots saw the flashes at the same time and rolled the Pave Hawk left like an F-18 Super Hornet fighter pilot, the security strap keeping Morgan from a brief and deadly free-fall experience.

What Morgan saw didn't make sense. Attackers in a fast boat were firing at Wolf from the water. He crouched behind sand dunes, shooting back with a small black submachine gun. The chaotic scene was confusing: No powerboat was fast enough to outrun a radio that would be used to call for help. Sense or not, they had to be stopped. The yacht club in the boat basin would be filled with the lunchtime elite, Tampa's power players, who Morgan was sure Wolf would try to protect at all costs.

The attackers had beached the fast boat and were sprinting across the beach to the club like sand crabs. Keying the crew channel, Morgan ordered, "I want a west-to-east strafing run. Put us between the club and the tangos."

The pilot acknowledged his request and dove toward the beach, pulling up at the last moment and nearly pushing Morgan and Harris to the floor with deceleration G-force. Having cut his airspeed to five knots, the pilot pushed the nose over as the helo's crew chief manning a GAU-19 mini-gun, Morgan the twin M240s, and Sergeant First Class Harry Harris with a grenade launcher, all fired on the attackers at once and knocked down tangos like bowling pins.

Morgan yelled for the crew gunner to shift to the fast boat, which had pushed back into the water and turned south to flee. The mini-gun howled as the crew chief walked the rounds through the water and chewed up the stern of the cigarette boat and its engines, which failed immediately with concussive explosions that blew engine and transmission parts into the air like bottle rockets.

The boat, no longer fast, coasted to a stop only a hundred yards offshore and began to sink stern first. Between the drilling of about eight hundred high-speed 7.62mm minigun rounds and the boat transmission exploding downward, the entire aft hull had been blown into the water. In the distance, dim sirens sounded as police, fire, and the Suburban all came into view, the Shadow Tier team dismounting from the SUV in a well-practiced set of two shooters per side.

Morgan switched to the other side of the Pave Hawk in time to see Wolf, MP5 in hand, now standing in the club's doorway waving and not obviously perforated.

The Florida Army National Guard helo pilot was good. He backed the Pave Hawk up to the end of the road turnaround by the yacht club and landed in a wide grass area in combat mode, power up, cyclic pushing the helicopter into the asphalt. *The pilot is showing off for the cameras,* Morgan thought, *and good for him.* All around the boat basin were witnesses holding aloft cellphone cameras that captured videos about which they would later tell huge lies when they appeared on cable news channels.

Morgan shook his head as he approached his boss and best friend at the same time as LeBlanc, who trotted over from the team's Suburban while police and fire personnel rushed to the flaming boat just offshore.

Morgan grinned and slapped palms with Wolf. "That's another fifth you owe me for saving your sorry ass now *three times.* One more save and I get a toaster oven."

"Saving *me*? Man, you got in the way. I had 'em right where I wanted 'em." Wolf safed his MP5 and loaded it into his backpack that was made to look like a Camelbak water reservoir.

"Yep, I saw that. You with your cute Swiss pea shooter against eight trained professionals with AKs, what we in the business call real battle rifles." Morgan tilted his head toward the yacht club restaurant. "Anyone hurt inside?"

"Thanks, brother. No, we got lucky. There are three grazing wounds, and a couple hits from flying glass, but nothing life threatening. Big war story opportunity for them, though, for that next lull in party conversation." Just as Wolf finished his statement, paramedics from the fire department rushed past the Shadow Tier teammates with gear bags over their shoulders.

Morgan asked, "How did you come by the peashooter?"

"Ever since the cartel started taking shots at us on this side of the border, I have battle packs stashed at a few points along my run. Here; where I stop for water; the hospital; and at a vacant house along Bayshore. I even have one in a dry bag over the seawall if I need it."

LeBlanc said, "No kidding? I need to keep that in mind next time one of my dates goes bad."

Wolf shook his head and laughed.

"Dude, when was the last time one went good?"

"Just when I think I know your tricks," Morgan said with a chuckle.

"I'm glad I'm still here to amuse you, to be honest," Wolf said. "You guys head back in the Pave Hawk and leave me the Suburban. I'll let the police know you and the team will be available later for statements and questions."

Morgan handed Wolf his work cellphone and said, "Before we leave, do yourself a favor and call Parker."

Wolf nodded. "Yep. Thanks, bro."

Morgan, LeBlanc, and the Alpha teammates who'd arrived in the Suburban boarded the helo with waves to Wolf as he dialed Parker's office. She picked up on less than the first ring.

"Hey baby—yep, all good—nope, not a scratch—yes, thanks

to Morgan, LeBlanc, and Alpha—yes, I'm driving back in the Suburban. I have some things to finish up and then I'll see you in a couple of hours."

Wolf flashed thumbs up to the team as the Pave Hawk rose into the bright blue sky, banking south toward home at MacDill AFB. Then his smile dropped as his countenance darkened. The volume of attempts on his life had risen exponentially since he had battled the cartel on the reservation. It had to mean he was close to something big—so big it was worth dead *sicarios*.

What are you hiding? What is it you don't want me to find?

Chapter 28

In the early morning light filtering through a copse of trees, Kennedy stood hidden southeast of Ramstein Air Force Base and east of the hospital complex at Landstuhl. He liked that it was hard to get line-of-sight on the former cross-shaped farmhouse from just twenty yards inside the tree line.

After scouting a dozen sites, he concluded this was the first-best option for a quick defensive setup. It had multiple routes of ingress and egress, which would be easily defended behind some strategic tree falls by a few sharpshooters.

Between the main house and staff quarters, there was lots of sleeping room for the team and support staff. There was good line of sight to all the satellites overhead, and with its elevation, radio coverage back into the air base and hospital area would be good.

Thirty minutes later, when Taylor arrived with Charlie Squadron, Kennedy put them to work. Demolitions personnel were sent to survey routes into the site for abatis—a defensive method where trees are dropped across a road or trail, and sometimes the branches facing outward were sharpened. The survey squad would also identify choke points if the site was under attack.

The communications personnel were sent out to test cellphone coverage. When they returned, they announced it would be five by five—strong and clear—with the installation of a private mini tower that would also be used with the cellphone spoofing system to crack any bad-guy phones.

At the same time, the support team cabled the house network and secured the doors with multiple magnetic locks on the inside. The doors could be opened with a card, specialty ring, or token worn almost anywhere on the body.

The weapons squad did a quick test of the indoor riding arena, demonstrating the team could shoot suppressed weapons with the doors closed with almost no sound detectable outside the facility. A random hiker could walk by at the wrong time and Kennedy didn't want to spook anyone, but he thought the suppressors would manage any overpressure issue.

The logistics cell was set up in the garage. In reverence for a rare and spectacularly valuable 1953 Porsche 550 Spyder race car they found on jack stands, they quickly built a stout platform over the car on which team boxes could be placed and closed in the sides so as not to damage the classic beauty.

The two-story house itself was classic German design and architecture. The stags head mounted over the handmade wall-to-wall wood cabinets suggested the property had become an upscale hobby farm or hunting destination. Kennedy kept the entryway and reception area just as it was in case they had visitors.

Behind the reception area, the rest of the squads were assigned rooms in standard cells by component. Operations in the main saloon; Intel in the library and reading rooms; Communications in the upstairs front bedroom; and Logistics in the garage.

In their first test of covert movement, teams of two assaulters from Taylor's Charlie Squadron took off in different directions to rendezvous with the bus taking them to a classified GSG 9 training facility. GSG 9 was the renowned counterterror unit of highly trained *Bundespolizei*, the German Federal Police, and its training facility was state of the art. Each team member carried pistols, their rifle in a backpack and wore their low-visibility body armor.

Train like you fight and you'll fight like you train, Kennedy thought, watching them take off via the wireless camera system deployed around the compound and surrounding land.

The liaison officer meeting them at the GSG 9 facility dropped a box on the floor and spoke in English.

"Welcome, warriors, to the best training facility in the world. This one-hundred-hectare training complex has parachute ranges and helicopter landing zones, firing ranges of all lengths and types, an Olympic pool, and two configurable shooting houses. We also have four urban terrain environments. There is no training that you cannot do here. You and everything you do is tracked. In this box—" He touched the container on the floor with the steel toe of his combat boot. "—are your heart-rate monitors and radio frequency tags. They permit the monitoring of your stress level, and the tags enable us to slew cameras to each team member. This has proved extremely helpful in the shoot houses."

"You received my training request?" Taylor asked.

"Yes. Range three and shoot house two are reserved and ready for your use. There is paperwork we need signed first. Yes, I know, we are German. It is what we do," he laughed and smiled. "Then I will assign you the tracking devices."

The team initialed and signed the non-disclosure agreement and waiver of liability and then stood to collect their tracking devices. They loaded into a SWAT-type van and were driven to range three.

Most started with pistols and transitioned to M4 carbines. Everyone but Joss, short for Joslin Vikander. She considered herself a sniper first, an assaulter second. From the standing position two hundred and fifty meters from the most distant target, she punched holes around the target's black silhouetted head and then put four in its heart, which could be covered by an American quarter.

After an hour, Taylor closed the range and they moved to the shoot house. It was large enough to hold three separate multi-level configurations.

Taylor smiled. The squadron was enjoying its day, but the excitement would soon wear off as he pushed them to stressful levels of frustration with themselves and each other. Given the short time to become operational, this was the crucible from which he would form Charlie Squadron.

"Scenario One," Taylor announced. The trainees gathered round him. "Mission: Apprehend Tango One. Protect non-combatants and secure intelligence. Situation: Single-level house, two armed men, one armed woman. One girlfriend with a small child. Meth lab in the kitchen. Task-organize and prepare to assault in fifteen minutes." Then Taylor moved off to find coffee.

Moments later, he entered the control room, coffee in hand. The techs shook their heads, they had seen this tactic before. But with established teams, not newly forming. Over the team channel, Taylor said, "Charlie One, Command One, copy?"

The response was quick and confident. "Command One, Charlie One. Good copy, standing by to execute."

Taylor scanned the radio assignments and smiled. The team had organized well and was ready to execute its task. Vikander had taken charge.

Is the rest of the team happy to just be shooters?

"Execute," Taylor radioed.

The team later watched the video replay together. The groans and laughs were good to hear as they took the review as professionals. As expected, the assault was slow and clumsy, but Taylor was happy to see no one endangered their teammates and no one shot the non-combatants.

On the negative side, he tagged the two team members who would have been shot by a tango. Fired up to do better, Taylor had them go again, and again—and again—until they got it right.

Then he changed it up using an in-floor device to trip Charlie Three in the middle of the stack to see how they adjusted and completed the mission. While the playback had gotten some laughs and the team had learned some new French swear words, they were also supportive in pointing out Three's quick recovery and adjustment to the last-man assignment. Taylor forced an inversion of the stack and made Three the team leader. The run-through was roughly an eighty percent successful.

The next was perfect.

Chapter 29

El Gato, the leader of the *Puma Grande*, sat in the shadows of the corner table on the second floor of a one-hundred-year-old restaurant in San Francisco's Mission district.

"You've failed me twice. Why should I expect this time to be any different?"

Amaru nodded. He understood and would have thought the same had one of his men brought the idea after two failed attempts to kill Wolf—his first failures since his apprenticeship started twenty-six years ago. He needed to redeem himself.

"Boss, your people tell me our reservation production and distribution are once again operating as designed. This is good, but temporary. My Sinaloa contact says Wolf will return to stop us. Let me kill him before he comes back. Send me alone," he said trying to keep the pleading from his voice.

El Gato drained his Tears of Llorona Extra Añejo tequila and stared at him. A moment later, he said, "You get one more chance.

One. Success or death, do you understand? There is nothing in between."

"Yes, boss," he said. "*Entiendo.*"

Amaru sat in his car steaming. Losing face angered him, making it hard to concentrate. He drove to the gym and his boxing workout to fight with three different sparring partners until he was too tired to punch or kick one more time. His anger exhausted, a plan came into view. It was indirect but personal at a level sure to cause a mental breakdown. At its conclusion, Wolf would beg him to take his life.

He slept fitfully during the flight from San Francisco to Tampa International, his brain refusing to settle down. His contact picked him up at the airport and briefed him on the setup before dropping him off at a Sinaloa safehouse. The contact concluded by saying, "Good luck. Call if you need men, or a woman."

The safehouse backed up to a wooded area and was the only residence on East 112th Street, just south of the University of South Florida. It had good access to I-75 and I-275 going north and south, and Fowler boulevard heading east and west. Amaru took the time to familiarize himself with the grounds and the house. The scrub trees and bushes hid the house from casual view.

He entered the house from the back door and immediately shivered. *The AC must be set to meat locker.* He located the thermostat in the living room and changed the setting from 65 to 70, then headed upstairs to the master bedroom. It had a combination of shades and thick blackout curtains that stopped light from entering, forcing him to use his cellphone light to navigate the room.

The living room was evidently used for storage, with boxes, card tables, and folding chairs stacked against the walls. The other two bedrooms were set up with futons and sleeping bags.

He went straight to the weapons cache above the plumbing access door in the master bathroom. He turned on the light in the fan and function-checked the Glock and AK-74 left for him. Each had come with ten preloaded magazines and there was an inside-the-waistband holster for the pistol and a mag.

Back on the first floor he found the kitchen stocked with food, water, and alcohol. The cabinets had paper plates and plastic utensils along with a note saying to drop anything he used into an acid vat near the garage door, destroying all traces of DNA.

The front room had an old fabric couch, a television, and a water-stained coffee table. The inside of the front door was covered with a thick steel sheet that locked top and bottom with manual bolts, and it had a large crossbar and an industrial lock to go with heavier-than-normal hinges. A *standard breaching charge isn't going to do this in.* Unlocking and opening a back door built like the front door, Amaru stepped through to the detached garage.

In the gravel driveway, he saw an unremarkable white work van his contact had said was prepped and ready to go. He used a six-digit code to unlock the door to the garage and heard the electro-mechanical locks disengage along with a small whoosh of air.

He flipped on the light switch next to the door and stepped inside, closing the door behind him. His ears popped slightly when the garage door closed. Looking around, he realized the garage had been soundproofed and was slightly pressurized, probably to keep out contaminants.

Along the walls, numbered stainless steel vats of acid denied investigators, should they ever stumble upon the location, of any hope of harvesting DNA. HEPA and charcoal filters on the vents eliminated scents from the air pushed outside.

The contact had said they had tested the system against bomb, drug, and cadaver dogs, and fooled them every time. On the wall opposite the vats, the cabinets reminded him of a medical clinic with its glass door refrigerator, providing a generous stocking of drugs to be used during his upcoming discussions. The dental tool set caused him to smile. *The classic.*

The tidy drawers included every kind of medical tool, including a full set of heavy equipment such as a drill, saws, machete, and a massive cleaver. And most important to his near-term plan, a CO_2-powered pistol sat on the bench with a note pointing to the four Propofol-filled sedative darts inside the refrigerator.

The weapon was an Olympic-quality pistol modified to accept a red dot aiming optic. According to his contact, it was highly accurate to twenty-five feet in a crosswind up to five miles an hour.

Content with his inspection, Amaru left the garage, locking the door behind him, and jumped into the van, the smile on his face flashing by the mirror. He started the vehicle, adjusted the seat and mirrors, and examined the registration and insurance documents left on the passenger seat in a brown envelope. Shifting into Reverse, he headed for Wolf's neighborhood.

The drive let him see his planned routes and adjust approaches around construction sites at Bayshore and the Platt Street bridge. Amaru drove to the west side of the Hyde Park area and hiked a random pattern meant to reveal any surveillance, all the while headed to Wolf's home. Tonight, he would make use of his map recon and get no closer than a tight diagonal view afforded at the corner of the alleyway into the back of Wolf's house.

Onsite as night fell at eight p.m., there was no one on the deck or in the hot tub. A light shone through the sliding glass door blinds. Satisfied with his ability to move to and from the back of Wolf's house, Amaru departed, taking yet another route back to the van. Tomorrow, he would apply the plumbing company magnetic signs to the van and park at the end of the street facing the front of the house. Then the proper work of learning the pattern of life would start.

Amaru had already requested an additional vehicle, but realized three more would be needed for close-in surveillance. As he got back to his van, the faint warning signal that had been pinging his mind finally broke through. His hand went to the Glock 19 pistol in his waistband as he cautiously scanned the immediate area, then widened his view to as far as he could see up and down the street. The hair on the back of his neck stood up and the warning signal yelled at him, but he still wasn't decoding the message. He jumped into the van and focused on maintaining the speed limit as he left the area and headed north.

Three miles later, after applying the training in surveillance detection taught to him by the FBI, he relaxed his white-knuckle grip on the steering wheel when no shadowing vehicles were detected. He hadn't seen whoever it was surveilling him near Wolf's house, but he had felt a hidden presence. It was there, he was sure of it: The eyes of another killer on him. Had El Gato sent someone to watch him and kill him if he failed?

This felt different, like he was surveilling himself.

He shook his head.

It *can't be.*

Chapter 30

Eliana was high over the Atlantic in her twin-engine Embraer Legacy 600 business jet, recently upgraded at a crushingly high cost for long distance and transforming it from a good cross-country aircraft to a solid intercontinental aircraft. Leaned back in a wide, leather-covered seat, she sipped a whiskey and thought back to how her fascination with the doctor had started.

In the planning stages for Global Air Services, she had come across a BBC story out of Helmand province about Doctor Sima Siddiqi. Eliana saw all three necessary vectors converge with her work—desire, need, and commitment. A deep-seated desire to help her people, particularly women, children, and young girls. A need for supplies delivered to remote and often dangerous areas in Afghanistan. And the commitment to do whatever it took to achieve her goals—including turning a blind eye to activities outside UN and World Health Organization programs.

Eliana felt a powerful attraction to the cause of women's rights, nowhere more so than in Afghanistan and Iraq. *Why don't I feel the same about women in Mexico?* she thought. In the Middle East, male domination was on a magnitude that she hadn't experienced, but thought she understood. Eliana had no illusions about her first goal to get logistics contracts inside the opium-growing provinces of Afghanistan. But if it also helped Doctor Siddiqi and the women of Helmand, all the better.

Four hours into what would be twenty-plus hours of travel time, Eliana closed her eyes and let her imagination build a world where her Global Air Services and Janus Logistics would operate in and profit from. Unseen by her security team behind her, Eliana smiled before drifting off to sleep. Worried about advancements in facial recognition the US government was employing in Afghanistan, Eliana requested the meeting take place in Chaman, Pakistan, just across the border. Doctor Siddiqi had said no.

"You need to meet me at one of my stops. See my work firsthand," she insisted.

The argument was brief, Siddiqi persevered, and Eliana relented, taking the GPS coordinates for the village just outside Najibullahkhan Kalay, Afghanistan. Two hours before landing, Eliana applied false teeth, a prosthetic nose, and cheek pads using the glue and makeup supplied by her makeup artist friend, Lacy, who she kept supplied with high-quality coke.

As the aircraft landed and taxied to a designated parking spot, she sat at the window and scanned the tarmac. She found the logo for the Italian company she had contracted. They flew Russian MI-8 helicopters throughout Afghanistan and were more than eager to take Eliana's last-minute business at three times the going contractor pilot rate.

The helicopter's VIP configuration was similar to the executive versions of high-end American helos. As Eliana and her security boarded the helicopter, the crew chief told them in passable Spanish not to worry. The MI-8 had been upgraded with the latest Kevlar bullet-resistant blankets and armor plating around the VIP sitting area.

Eliana's fear of being shot down spiked when her security lead asked about countermeasures against shoulder-fired missiles like the RPG and the Russian anti-aircraft Igla series. The crew chief held his hands palm up, mumbling something, which Eliana took to mean *we do what we can*. Not the comforting answer she was hoping for.

The hour and twenty-minute flight turned out to be a non-event. Eliana spent the time glued to the window, scanning the desert's broad expanse. The reddish brown earth below contrasted with the azure blue sky above. A pair of contrails high above headed north.

Bombers or transports—death or life?

Suddenly, a swash of green and red cut through the brown haze. It grew ever larger as she sped toward the meeting. The blue-green of the Helmand River was visible across the farmlands crowded around its life-giving banks. She grabbed binoculars from the pouch on the bulkhead. Her hands trembled as she focused on the poppy fields.

"Take us up another thousand feet and slow down," she said to her security lead, who passed the request on to the flight deck. The pilot acknowledged the request and increased the MI-8's lift, sacrificing forward speed. After her initial awe, Eliana's business brain took over calculating the value of the crop based on the data El Chapo had provided.

Tens of millions in opium, even more once processed into street-level heroin, she thought, exhaling the breath she just realized she'd been holding.

Eliana took the binoculars from her face and gazed upon the sea of poppies. She felt as if she was looking at bags of money.

"All right," she said, reverie over. "We can land now." A moment later, the engine sounds changed and the helo descended. Her confidence soared and an uncharacteristic smile spread across her face. She had made the right decision to come to this place to meet with Doctor Siddiqi.

Wheels down, the crew chief said to wait to disembark. The brown-out the helicopter had created dissipated quickly in the southerly breeze. Impatient with the wait, Eliana told her security lead to head out as she put on her headscarf. She grimaced at the glaring sun, donning her sunglasses before leaping down from the last stair to both feet, like a happy schoolgirl.

Without hesitation, she took her place in the middle of the Range Rover's back seat and pulled herself forward to get a better look as the vehicle drove away. When they arrived at Doctor Siddiqi's medical site, her security lead told Eliana to hold in the SUV until he confirmed the location via an exchange of pass phrases with the doctor's security team.

Exchange completed, Eliana exited, walking straight into the large tent housing the mobile clinic. She kept out of the way and watched the doctor vaccinate a young woman and her baby while she talked. Finished, Siddiqi nodded to Eliana. She pointed the young patient to an assistant and motioned for Eliana to join her as she strode from the tent.

Both security teams moved with their principals but stayed several meters away from them and from each other. Walking to a white Range Rover, Siddiqi reached into her backpack and took out a pack of cigarettes, offering one to Eliana. Siddiqi lit her cigarette and passed Eliana the lighter before taking a drag and exhaling it, head tilted back into the air. A deep sigh accompanied it.

Eliana gave her the lighter back. "Before we talk about what my company can do for you here in Afghanistan, I have something for you." She motioned to her security lead, who offered a backpack.

"This is for you and your work here with these women and children. Regardless of working together or not, I am moved to make this the first of many donations." Eliana handed the doctor the backpack.

The doctor opened the backpack, eyes first springing wide and then going narrow as she recognized thick bundles of American dollars.

"You are too kind, but I cannot take this. It can be misconstrued as a bribe."

Eliana smiled, putting her hand on the doctor's arm.

"Inside, you will find a note on company letterhead stating it is, in fact, a cash donation that you are free to deposit in accordance with UN and WHO policies. Now, let us discuss how my air and ground logistics organization can reduce your costs, improve the timeliness of your shipments, and as volume grows, see more donations directed to your specific programs."

Satisfied, Siddiqi threw the backpack of money in the SUV's backseat and took Eliana by the arm, walking to the shade of a cluster of palm trees only yards away. As they strolled and talked, Eliana remembered a favorite movie quote her mother had loved from *Casablanca*.

"I think this is the start of a beautiful friendship."

Chapter 31

As the Shadow Tier Deputy for Operations, Gus Morgan pushed himself hard, whether every morning spent on MacDill AFB at the gym, on the roads, or fighting the obstacle course. His goal was to be as good or better in every aspect of Shadow Tier operations as the assaulters and support personnel. It was a heavy burden considering the squadron's manning, which had been designed by Wolf as independent and self-supporting. Once given a mission, the common ask by an operational squadron was for aircraft.

But there were two areas he freely admitted he would never be at an A-plus level—Explosive Ordinance Disposal, and cyber warfare. The one he didn't want to relinquish at the moment was Intelligence. When he joined Shadow Tier, Morgan had three years of college. Just enough for his national and Florida-level paramedic certifications.

As a former 18D special forces medic, many a doctor and officer had pleaded with Morgan to finish college and become an Army doctor, or at least attend the Interservice Physician Assistant Program at Joint Base San Antonio-Fort Sam Houston.

What the special operations forces had missed out on was his unique blend of skills, which permitted him to save a life or take it as circumstances demanded. Morgan was a fast learner, with off-the-charts spatial awareness, and he was as tough as old leather. His teammates called Morgan a one-man A-team.

He inserted his ID badge and punched a six-digit code to enter the SCIF. Scanning the area, he saw the intel team was busy on various tasks, and none of his go-to experts had snuck back into town unannounced. On a normal day, he would have Stewart Portes, the new Charlie Squadron number two and intel lead, to confer with, but Portes was in Germany with Kennedy and the Kid, two of his other go-to people. Even Parker was gone, and he had no idea where she was.

Walking into an empty conference room, Morgan laid out the information folders. The information provided by Colonel Carlos González and his crack intel analysts at *Fuerza Especial de Reaccion*, the Mexican equivalent of the US Army Special Mission Command team, went straight to the point. An informant and a recon team both reported that the Cortes marijuana farms were being razed and plowed up as if to plant new crops.

The reported percent of productive farmland being razed was surprising—upward of twenty-five percent. The DEA report was largely a rewording of González's report, with one odd example which made Morgan laugh.

Laughably, the report said the Sinaloa cartel was possibly "just applying good farming practices to rotate crops and therefore get better yields." What the agriculture contacts and DEA analysts didn't identify were the considerable amount of chemicals the cartel poured into the land to keep their yields up and, sometimes, get any product at all from what was once barren land.

Back in the early Nineties, environmental groups had complained and stupidly gone to protest the chemical use at two farms, only to end up dead in a ditch with a crude sign advising to stay away or suffer a similar fate. The protests ended and the homicides were never solved.

Stuck, and not making sense of the information before him, Morgan signed the folders out and tossed them in his backpack before leaving the SCIF. Walking outside to a picnic table still in the early morning shade, he glanced at his watch, extended the antenna on his satellite phone, and dialed Kennedy.

Kennedy said, "*Guten Morgen*, Herr Doctor."

"*Guten Tag*, Herr Doctor," Morgan laughed at the doctor-doctor joke. "Feeling lonely and need someone to talk to back there?"

"Yes! Ramp-ready to deploy, rockin' on ready with nowhere to go and nothing to break."

Morgan said, "Oh, dear-dear, as the Brits would say. How may I help?"

"I have some data from Colonel González's analysts and the DEA, which say Eliana is razing productive marijuana farms and preparing them for planting. What strikes me as unbelievable is the reports state it's upward of twenty-five percent of her marijuana farms."

"Which seems rather a high level of destruction and disruption of business as to be unsupportable," Morgan- said. "But marijuana has become a commodity business, producing nowhere the profits of meth or cocaine. As you well know, marijuana and cocaine grow in two completely different climates, and meth is a lab product. So, what will they grow if not marijuana?"

Kennedy wondered the same thing. "Exactly my dilemma. Could it be the costs of maintaining productive land have gotten to the tipping point where El Chapo's financial experts are telling him the money is better spent elsewhere? Move the growing to a more cost-effective area, like moving washing machine assembly out of the US to Mexico? Those are some options, right?"

Morgan laughed. "You're thinking like a cartel leader now. Their number one priority is profits. A close second to personal security. Has Eliana reported any of this?"

"No," Kennedy said. "She's been offline for a month. Not even an 'I'm safe' check-in. But Wolf and I have been too busy with the Montana missions, the vice president's push on Afghanistan, and the stand-up of Charlie Squadron to pay attention to Mexico. I suggest you take Harris with you and develop your own intel on what's going on. Wolf will appreciate the initiative. The Kid and I can back you up as needed."

"Agreed. I'll take Harris if LeBlanc will let me have him, and we'll see what El Chapo is up to. If there's one thing I've learned being at Shadow Tier is that El Chapo has an uncanny ability to foresee changes in demand and get ahead of them. He must be planning something big to make such a radical change to a productive business. Thanks for the insight. I'll keep you in the loop."

Morgan ended the call and stared across the runway at the construction taking place. Rumored to be the new home of Naval Special Warfare assets, MacDill AFB was becoming littered with them as the four-star Special Operations Command consolidated its authority and control over SMUs like Shadow Tier.

This will be one not to brag about to the ladies. Covert insertion in Mexico followed by staring at farms. The kind of missions better embellished in thriller novels.

Morgan went in search of Harris.

Chapter 32

Michael Clinton sat in the Shadow Tier trailer reviewing his staffing options. He had asked for help investigating the World Health Organization's lead for medical programs in Afghanistan, and the Kid had immediately volunteered to join the team in Kandahar.

Clinton suspected the Kid was itching to get into the fight. After Shadow Tier's first try at capturing El Chapo, Kennedy had released the Kid to finish his Army intelligence training, finishing at the top of the class. Then, in a *hooah* kind of moment, he'd asked for Ranger school, graduating as honor grad. While his work uniform was civilian clothes, jeans mainly, Clinton was sure the Kid's Ranger tab was talking to him.

Bravo Squadron was the best of Shadow Tier, a team of proven warriors, or so Clinton thought. While his intel lead Devon Lancaster, the SAS officer didn't have access to the systems the Kid was cleared for. As a Brit, he was part of the FIVE EYES intelligence sharing group that included the US, UK, Canada, Australia, and New Zealand. But it ended most of the time at the DIA's secret Stone Ghost network.

The Kid, on the other hand, had or could get access to data from the whole of the intelligence community a few computer keystrokes. With a call, another twenty-plus specialty databases. The PROVIDENCE analytic system he and Kennedy had built rivaled the best of the intelligence community.

So far, Clinton's investigation of Doctor Sima Siddiqi had uncovered an award-winning career of helping other people in need with a particular focus on underserved women and children in the Middle East. The biography he had assembled included her birth in 1974 to a wealthy family. She studied medicine in Kabul and finished her training in Moscow before going to work for the UN and World Health Organization.

After the Soviet occupation, the Taliban had asked her to lead the UN health programs in Afghanistan, which she did. Post-Taliban fall, the new Afghan government had made several requests for Doctor Siddiqi to join the government as minister of health, but she declined, expressing her desire to treat people versus argue about policy and funding.

Her pushing had gotten the UN Population Fund to improve the reproductive health of Afghan women. And she had admirers in the US government, including two congresswomen and a male senator. With their help on the funding side, a logistics contract was awarded to a team led by an Alaskan Super 8A and its subcontractors, Global Air Services and Janus Logistics, for trucking services. The contract was a logical extension of the work the company was providing to the US and NATO military.

Her finances were in order and appropriate for someone in her occupation. There were no indications of misuse of funds or bribe-taking. If that wasn't enough, she had distributed her salary to her workers to ensure their families had food and shelter. And it appeared she did not care about politics or drugs, just the women and children of Afghanistan.

Clinton finished reading the bio and assessment, setting it down to look across the table at the Kid.

"Call me cynical, but in this part of the world, it's all about the deal. Her access to the women and children in Taliban-controlled areas of Helmand province comes at a cost. The Taliban must be getting something for her access."

"She treats the men, too," the Kid said. "Or at least someone on her staff does. Maybe a male nurse? Which means healthier workers tending the opium crops and processing the product."

Clinton stretched his neck, rotating it left then right. "Possible. Another option is for the Taliban to get some use of her trucks and logistics system. It would be a more reliable mode of movement."

"Yes, but World Health's major distribution centers in the area are in Pakistan, the opposite direction of the traditional opium routes to Europe and Russia."

"Good point, but with air transport, who cares if it's out of Afghanistan? What do we know about Global Air Services and Janus Logistics?"

"Not much, except they support US operations and NATO all over the region. Did you hear the SECDEF is on his way to announce the turnover of the Afghan mission to NATO leadership?"

"Yeah, Wolf told me. We're lucky to be the White House's pet. Ever since the prez and vice prez figured out that we close a gap the Joint Chiefs refuse to address, we've been golden. But getting back to our doctor, let's deep-dive her support structure and see if it leads anywhere."

"Roger that. About my request to deploy with the team next

time you head outside the wire. Have you given it any thought?"

Clinton failed to hide his smile. "Sure, Kid, you're good to go if Jocko approves you."

The Kid's smile was about to break his face. "You know I was honor grad of my Ranger class, right?"

Clinton understood the feeling and remembered his first mission. He suspected the Kid saw a chance to prove himself a valued team member in the field, aside from his analytics.

Clinton laughed and thought, *I bet his Ranger tab is itching like a son of a gun right now.*

Chapter 33

Portes stared out the window at the gray German sky. The leaden overcast was what his wife called Seasonal Affective Disorder— SAD, appropriately.

"Is there a playbook for this kind of operation?"

Kennedy joined him at the window. "I'm sure there is at the Agency, but this isn't a normal Shadow Tier operation, is it? Let us talk with our Langley friends and make use of their talents and expertise in backstory and non-official cover building."

"I'm thinking it's akin to Herbert first building out his fictional Dune universe, and then needing to drive a story under it."

"Yeah, I did a little of that for Wolf when we started this fight. Our operation is on another level now. And because we don't know how deep our adversary is connected, our covers and backgrounds will need to endure serious investigation, including by bad actors in German, French, and Turkish law enforcement and intelligence. Even the Taliban's intelligence network is a factor."

Kennedy picked up the encrypted phone on his desk and pushed fourteen buttons. The encryption shook hands with the system, approved the connection, and rang through.

She picked up on the third ring. "Harding."

"Liz, it's Kieran. Do you have a minute?"

"Yes, for you? Of course. How are you recovering?"

"I'm good, thanks for asking. We need your expertise. We're about to head outside our normal mode of operation and start operating in the daylight."

"How many, and do you need banking, tech, or some other company cover?"

"Eight full covers ... and we're going to be a drug cartel."

Harding paused for a moment. "Kieran, your last was garbled. I thought I heard you say you want a drug cartel cover."

"Yes, correct. We're creating a new cartel." He waited a beat, but only got silence. "Liz, are you there?"

"Jesus, Kieran—and they call us cowboys. I can't stress how dangerous this is for your untrained team. My people spend a year at the Farm getting the basics down."

"I hear you and mostly agree. We're lucky to have several members of the new squadron who have extensive undercover time. My plan is to project a military background and act as if we treat everything from that viewpoint, so, typecast. But we will need covers that show criminal rap sheets and forced exits from the services."

"You're not one of the eight cover stories, are you?"

"Ehh, 'fraid so."

"You've been working with Wolf too long. I'd ask you to promise me you won't be a hero, but I know that's a waste of time."

"Not entirely. This is well outside my comfort zone, but it is what it is, right?" He laughed a little expecting her to do the same. She didn't. "So, will you help us?"

"Yes, of course. I'll send two of our best. You will get better re-sults if they're embedded with you for the duration of your op. Where am I sending them?"

"Dulles has direct flights to Frankfurt. We can pick them up there."

"Consider it done. Details to follow on the secure high side. When your operation is over, you owe me dinner with one of those expensive bottles of wine you like to brag about."

"It will be my pleasure, Ms. Harding."

"Okay, then. Later, Kieran. And keep your big water head down."

He hung up the phone and noticed the look on Portes's face—wide eyes and slack-jawed.

"Yes, that was the soon-to-be Deputy Director for the National Clandestine Service, Elizabeth Harding. She can teach us a lot about operating in the light."

"Do we really the Agency's help?"

"Yes, if we want to mature and expand our mission set."

Kennedy called Clinton, arranging for the delivery of fifty kilos of opium gum, the equivalent of ten kilos of heroin, each with a raw value of $300,000 a kilo before the normal cutting process. The Kid worked from the OGA compound in Afghanistan using an inter-preter as he hacked several European banks to create accounts with histories for the team's personal accounts. Each connected to various accounts in Tel Aviv where money laundering was wide-spread and enforcement unlikely.

Taylor and Portes had bought or leased buildings and ware-houses, matching the cover story and growing operations. They also bought lab gear from a major pharmaceutical company.

Only twenty-four hours later, jet-lagged Agency personnel on site, Kennedy introduced them to the team intel cell. He handed the new arrivals a binder the backgrounder team had put together on the cartel organization and the work they had completed.

"Portes," Kennedy said, waving over the analysts. "You are responsible for their health and welfare. Make sure they have everything they need or want. The faster we get this built, the sooner we go operational." He raised a thumb. "Good to go?"

"Yep. Come with me, folks. I have a quiet space for you."

The analyst named Sara sat at a table and opened her laptop, connecting to the encrypted network. "Let's start with this guy. The Kid?"

Portes smiled. "He's forward right now, but we can reach him."

"I see here. It says he is the cartel hacker. He thinks he's a ladies' man. He loves guns and has a pistol collection going back into the American West. He lives in a fancy flat on the north side of Kaiserslautern but does his hacking from a warehouse near Landstuhl. He has close to a million D-marks in offshore accounts. He also has a cocaine habit that he keeps under control most of the time. So, with this, I will start by recording his birth, his mother who gave him up, and his adolescence in the German state-run system. The Kid will have a criminal record but just shy of major crime, which drops to nothing after he meets Herr Merck."

"Merck? Like, the cubic-money-Big-Pharma Merck? "

"Yes," Sara said. "I'm not sure Mr. Kennedy knows, but Harding passed on that she's related to the Merck clan. The tie-in comes from the head of the company in America." She flipped a few pages in her file. "Merck was instrumental in the development of vitamins, sulfas, and antibiotics in World War II. He also led the War Research Service, which initiated the US biological weapons program."

Kennedy was impressed. "How do you know all that?"

"I've got access to a library of secrets," Sara said, suppressing a too-sweet smile. "Don't you?" She tapped the folder cover with her index finger. "By the way, the name we've generated for your new fake cartel is the Angel cartel. It's named after the original Merck family pharmacy."

Chapter 34

At zero-three-hundred, an armored Mercedes sedan led the van into the Shadow Tier safehouse. Taylor and Portes met Charlie Squadron, stored their weapons for them, and took them to their rooms. Taylor suggested resting for the three hours before breakfast and orientation.

A hand went up. "Where's the gym?"

Kennedy and Portes greeted Taylor and two hungrier team members at breakfast. Kennedy put down his fork.

"Where is the rest of your team?"

Taylor smiled and said, "What do you call it in the States? 'Slamming plates,' or some odd thing of that nature?"

Kennedy laughed and Portes jumped in. "Weightlifting, you mean? Probably a bet or two in play, too."

As if on cue, the five missing members of Charlie Squadron appeared and stacked their plates high with food. They were laughing and ribbing each other in the ways of a team who had spent years together. And they didn't spare Taylor or the other team members at the table, all more endurance athletes versus power and strength advocates.

Kennedy sipped his coffee, watching interaction among team members slow as they began to eat. Five minutes later, Taylor stood, and the room fell silent.

"Charlie team. Let me introduce you to the Shadow Tier number two, Kieran Kennedy." Kennedy waved. "And this is our new intelligence lead, Stewart Portes." Portes half-stood awkwardly and offered a two-finger salute.

Kennedy and Portes got respectful nods in return. Kennedy thought he saw Portes and the Swedish female trade more than one glance each other's way.

She's the sniper. I need to learn their names, Kennedy thought.

Taylor sat and Kennedy rose, scanning the assembly and its resolute faces. His furrowed brow and piercing eyes along with animated hand gestures set the tone.

"Charlie Squadron, welcome to what we call a target-rich environment. So far, we've identified opium distribution routes into Germany, which we think includes Ramstein Air Base. We also identified a new element working out of Marseille. Another of our intelligence analysts postulates it is the reincarnation of the French Connection group that distributed heroin into New York City in the seventies. While it was well before we were born, the *Unione Corsa's* legacy of ruthless domination endures, and we see indications of its regeneration at the hands of a new leader."

Kennedy picked up his coffee and moved to where both tables of team members to better see him.

"Why is all this important to Shadow Tier and Charlie Squadron?" Kennedy let the question hang for a beat. "First, our nations have joined under the coalition partners banner to combat the Taliban in Afghanistan. Second, the Taliban generate upward of four hundred million dollars a year in operational funds via the opium trade. And the number continues to grow. Third, much of the opium ends up here in Europe. The fourth reason? Heroin is undergoing a renaissance of sorts. Data suggests it's replacing cocaine as the drug of choice, which indicates demand will continue to grow." Kennedy sat back down.

Taylor stood.

"There's one major difference between our missions and those of the other squadrons—we will operate in the daylight, posing as a drug cartel with raw product to sell and a state-of-the-art processing lab we will appear to operate. Kennedy and the team here have been creating your non-official cover stories. Between now and our green light to operate, we'll focus on the tradecraft necessary to make sure we act and look the part of a new German cartel, known as the Angel cartel, led and staffed by ex-military. Security of our real identities is a primary concern, as many of you well know, having spent time undercover or on missions supporting your intelligence agencies back home. But enough for now." He raised his Breitling watch. "You have thirty minutes to get cleaned up and meet back here to start working on the plan."

The rest of the day was split between working with the analysts to create individualized cover stories and to rehearse using their names and persona. After lunch, they switched to tradecraft, which all the team members already had some training in. Three had excellent skills, and one had spent two years as an undercover insider in a mafia-style organization, helping to bring it down.

Taylor initially broke the team into two-person units, each taking turns to practice surveilling the other, and then split the team in two large groups and went full-surveillance and counter surveillance mode. He played the scenarios out in and around the cartel buildings he and Portes had acquired in Kaiserslautern.

The next morning, Charlie Squadron moved into the buildings and, with the help of the support teams and a Hollywood production designer borrowed from a friend of a friend, dressed them to look like they had history. Then they gamed the ways in and out and how someone might surveil the locations.

The tech team wired the buildings for sound and video, including motion-tracking video in the likely places they would be watched from. Steel plates on swinging hinges were deployed strategically throughout to provide shooting positions in hallways and stairwells. Flash-bangs were hidden in the stairwells and near points of entry to slow down potential attackers. A pattern of life was begun with various team members ordering food and going to the local market.

Back at the safehouse, the analysts had completed their work and briefed Portes on everything and everyone they had created. Dinner was at 1930, and once the aftermath was cleared from the tables, Portes dropped packets in front of each team member, telling them to open their new identities. He gave them five minutes to read through the finished personas, then asked for their attention.

Kennedy stood with arms crossed as the team opened the folders and saw who they were to portray in the production to follow, a different kind of passion play but a passionate one, nonetheless.

"What you are about to hear is a lot of information, and you'll need to be intimately familiar with some of it without thinking. Your NOC is an integral part of our story and history. It's essential to our safety and security." Then a big smile creased his face.

"Welcome to the cartel family, my friends. My name is Allard Merck. I'm the illegitimate grandson of Erwin Merck, a pioneer in the research and production of major life-saving pharmaceuticals.

I think of myself as brave and smart because I am brave and smart. I've created a group of ex-military men and women who were dismissed from the armed forces of several nations, all under questionable circumstances. We are the Angel cartel, and we will rule."

A murmur of whispered conversation rotated around the room as teammates reacted to these theatrics.

"We're in possession of ten grams of China White heroin and twenty kilos of spiked opium gum," Kennedy/Merck continued, "which, as some of you know, is equivalent to two kilos of refined heroin. This has a street value of two to three million dollars. Our supplier is a Pakistani middleman and cutout in our interactions with the Taliban. Our primary enforcement target, the one we believe is connected to the US Army hospital at Landstuhl and Ramstein Air Base, is Jean Paul Croce, a grandson of an original *Unione Corsa* leader. We believe he plans to reconnect with the American mafia in New York and revive old heroin trade routes while creating new ones."

Kennedy let all that sink in for a moment. "Our business profile is low-key while we make new friends and associates with whom we will move our product. Our cover story includes background material, which will ensure anyone checking us out knows we can get nasty when needed. Tonight, I'll call Croce asking for a consultation and his corrupt police connections will check us out. It will be the first test of our cover story, which is full of unproven connections to the Afghan opium trade. I'm certain he will want to take the meeting. He is young, brash, and arrogant, and he will want us owing him favors as soon as possible."

The late-night call went as expected. A weary-sounding Croce had said little other than he would call back once he'd verified Merck's identity. Twenty-four minutes after the call to Croce, the Kid's digital tripwire alerted. He watched as someone in the German

Federal Police accessed the planted files and the carefully crafted information on Merck and his Angel cartel.

The Kid called from Afghanistan, where he was monitoring the interaction, and said the officer or someone using his credentials had elevated his privileges and accessed the attached Confidential Informant file. The officer logged off, but by then the Kid owned his account.

Portes stood startled, with Kennedy behind him.

"Come on, boss. You're not going to start doing that Wolf ninja warrior thing are you?"

"Yes, I am. We are jumping into the deep end of a pool filled with sharks. We're going to need all the skill, talent, and flair we can muster to survive operating in the light. And make no mistake—this is war."

Kennedy grimaced.

"We will shed blood before it's over."

Chapter 35

Evidently, we have passed initial investigation in Germany and France," Kennedy told the assembled team. "We are to meet Croce in Marseille."

To prepare for the meeting with Croce, Kennedy directed an extra level of counter-surveillance. He expected Croce to hunt for him and get surveillance in place as soon as possible. He let the team know he wanted to depict a level of nervous tension at connecting with an unknown drug dealer. So, the team had driven to Frankfurt to fly in Merck's personal jet, a Bombardier Challenger 604 configured to accommodate ten passengers. As the plane taxied to a stop, a large black Mercedes-Benz S-500 sedan stopped alongside, followed by two black Range Rovers.

By the time the crew dropped the stairs, Taylor was standing by the right rear door waiting for Herr Merck to deplane. Kennedy stopped on the stairs and surveyed the area before continuing into the Mercedes's back seat. Taylor joined him, smile in hand.

"How hard was it to find an armored vehicle here?" Kennedy asked.

"Not at all," Taylor said. "They're everywhere, common as bloody Ford pickups in the States. Seems all shootings and kidnappings have the wealthy families driving armored Mercedes, Range Rovers, and even a few of those extra-long Chevrolet Suburbans your Texans like so much."

"Ha, Texans and soccer moms. And the meeting location?"

"At the edge of the city in an industrial area. Acceptable routes in and out. It's an upstairs venue with big glass windows that look into Marseille. We should be able to apply some tech to them for audio. We're headed to the InterContinental Marseille. It's two streets off the old port with a view all the way to Notre Dame and easy access to anywhere in the city."

"Comms survey of the meet location?"

"Some dead spots, looks like. I suggest jamming comms, both radio and cell. Shows we have military tech and it plays well with our ex-military cover story."

Kennedy stared out of the heavily tinted window.

"Agreed. Now that the Kid is back, let's set up his cell tower simulator to capture as many cellphones as we can before shutting down service. Did you detect any countersurveillance?"

"No. Croce has security, but it's not great. I see some of it as arrogance with a lack of training. His close-in protection team has at least two hunters who could be problematic, but the rest are just random gangsters and other subspecies."

Kennedy's entrance at the InterContinental was made with a movie star's flourish. Stepping out of the car, he adjusted his Saville Row suit, wishing his wife Maya could see how great he looked as an executive drug lord.

I will never be more dashing than now, he thought, suppressing a smile. He strode through the lobby like he owned it, walking straight into a waiting elevator that took him nonstop to the presidential suite on the penthouse floor.

Once inside the ornate room, he bellowed at its size and ostentatiousness. Built rather like his Florida home, it was open plan front to back with a full kitchen on his left and master bedroom taking up the whole of the right side. The coffee-table brochure of the layout had two more good-sized rooms behind the kitchen, but he didn't bother checking.

He hung his clothes in the closet and set up his computer kit on a massive desk near an expansive window overlooking the harbor. Kennedy looked in the direction of the industrial area and thought, *I can't believe I get paid to do this job.*

The team spent the rest of the day acting the roles of big shots at the hotel while the overwatch teams and Kid set up in their hides. Kennedy and Taylor gamed last-minute changes to the meeting site, increased security, and batted around other things Croce might throw into the plan to throw them off balance and gain advantage.

Taylor made a joke about having flogged the horse to death, noting Kennedy fidgeting and his gaze darting about. He was about to speak when Kennedy exhaled inside a weak chuckle.

"Yes, I am a perfectionist—one who is nervous about screwing up his first leading role on our first operation in the daylight."

Kennedy's encrypted cell rang. Looking at the screen, he shook his head and accepted the call.

"I'm putting you on speaker, Wolf. I'm with Taylor."

Wolf said, "Good. How you comin' along as the Big Pharma Big Shot, brother? Got your cover persona down pat?"

"We're good, actually," Kennedy said with enthusiasm. "I could convince his mother I'm her son. We're just gaming some alternatives in case Croce changes up the meeting place."

"Yeah, I asked how are you doing? This is your first time role playing, and I know it can be nerve-wracking. Remember, you don't have to be perfect, just good enough. Right, Taylor?"

Taylor half-grinned. "Yes, sir, that's right. I and the other two team members with undercover experience will be with him at the meet. We'll keep him straight all right."

"See, brother, all good. Just focus on being the ruthless, arrogant bastard we all know lurks under the famous Kennedy facade. The rest is adapt and overcome."

"Thanks—but I prefer a bit more planning and control, especially when automatic weapons are in close proximity."

"Taylor. Make sure 'Herr Merck' wears the new gel-based armor. It's unlikely they will have anything heavier than 9mm with them. It shouldn't even mess up that nice Saville Row suit you're wearing, K-man. Okay, gotta go. Out here."

Kennedy stared at the phone, shaking his head. "I have never figured out how he knows when to call. Did you tell him about the suit?"

Taylor coughed, shielding his mouth to hide the smile. "Uhm, no, sir. You do remember me saying the Kid has the suite wired for audio and video?"

"Yes, of course…" Kennedy said, the response trailing off as his gaze circled the room.

Two hours and twenty minutes later the cars were brought to the front door, and once again Kennedy took his place in the right rear of the black Merc. As they rolled out for the meet, he radioed for updates from the Kid and overwatch teams.

The response was "nothing unusual" from the overwatch, and the Kid had collected eight more electronic cellphone IDs that had just appeared, indicating Croce and his entourage had arrived.

Kennedy's black Mercedes stopped several car lengths behind two other Mercedes parked at the restaurant's front door. Taylor stepped out, looking at the two men left behind with the cars, noting their MP5 H&K submachine guns. Two Shadow Tier team members moved forward from the Range Rover to cover "Herr Merck's" exit. A Croce minder and escort stepped out of the restaurant door and nodded, motioning Taylor to follow.

Taylor opened the car door, Kennedy got out, and both heading into the restaurant followed by two team security men. The Shadow Tier drivers covered their principals' sixes until inside, then took up positions parallel to Croce's men, heads on swivels. The opposing security teams nodded acknowledgment to each other in professional courtesy.

Kennedy and Taylor were escorted up a winding stairway to the second floor. At the far end of the dining room, away from the windows, Kennedy saw Jean Paul Croce.

In passable English, their minder said to Taylor, "Please. Only one security with Herr Merck, s'il vous plaît." Taylor nodded and waved their two security men to stay put.

Taylor led Kennedy/Merck to the table. On the way, Taylor pushed the number nine digit on his cellphone, signaling the Kid to start jamming. They both watched Croce's men touch their earpieces as the devices all went dead at once.

Their minder stopped in mid-stride, looking up at the taller Kennedy. He turned and asked, "Monsieur, did you ..."

"Yes," Kennedy said loud enough for Croce to hear. "A regrettable but necessary security precaution."

"It is fine, Lucien," Croce said in French before standing.

Kennedy inhaled to steady himself and extended his hand, speaking English with the fake French accent he'd been rehearsing for days. As accents went, Kennedy's was close enough for government work.

"*Monsieur* Croce, I am Allard Merck. It is a pleasure to make your acquittance at last. I've heard so much about you, of course."

They shook hands and Croce gestured Kennedy to a seat across from him. Taylor stood to the right side, mirroring the positioning of Croce's stone-faced security man.

Croce's face betrayed nothing. "One is never too busy to meet fascinating people for conversation and a good dinner, *ai-je raison?* So, how may I help you, Herr Merck?"

"*Monsieur* Croce, I will be direct. You have a reputation as one who can arrange transportation of sensitive materials throughout Europe and even America. We hope to take advantage of your services. We have secured routes from our production sites to Marseille and another site in Germany. What we lack is intracontinental distribution to other destinations. We are also very interested in options that would put our product in America."

Croce took care to arrange a fine linen napkin across his lap just so before he spoke.

"And what is this sensitive material of which you speak?"

As Kennedy started to reach into his suit, Croce's man swept aside his unbuttoned suit coat to reveal an MP5 on a shoulder sling that he raised to firing position. Taylor, for his part, was well ahead of the guard, who had telegraphed his movement. Taylor drew his pistol and moved to shield Kennedy when Kennedy stopped, raising both flat hands.

"Please. I am quite demonstrably unarmed."

Croce held up his hand and his guard and Taylor moved back to their positions, warily eyeballing each other.

Kennedy brought out a flat golden box lined with velvet. It contained a white powder in a closed plastic bag. "This is for you to verify that we have a product worth your time and effort. We need to move both unprocessed and processed variants of the product."

Croce didn't touch the drugs, but turned to his ever-present aide. "Lucien, test this material and dispose of the box."

The minder took the object and Croce made small talk, asking about the flight from Frankfurt, the hotel, disclosing just enough so that 'Herr Merck' would know the reach of his organization.

Lucien came back several minutes later, a surprised look on his face.

"This is the purest heroin I have seen in eight years."

Kennedy nodded. "Purity is but one element. In our lab, we can provide additives at the buyer's request."

"Lab? And additives. What additives?" Croce said.

"Fentanyl and Ketamine to raise the addictive level of the heroin, as desired," Kennedy said. Croce's eyes closed and his head tilted up slightly, as if he was computing the profits he could reap from the relationship. Croce blinked and leaned forward.

"Let's be honest. We have just met. I need to do more checking before we may even discuss doing business."

"I understand, of course." A sly smile appeared on Kennedy's face. "Allow me leave you with more samples, if I may." Kennedy motioned to Taylor.

Croce nodded, and Taylor put two more large samples on the table. Croce stood, followed by Kennedy.

"I will await your response," Kennedy said. "But please know we require delivery to a UK customer as soon as possible. Our previous partnership was interrupted by agents working with the Joint Narcotics Analysis Center." Kennedy spoke with a hint of exasperation, his lips pressed into slits in fake worry.

Croce gave a slight nod and Kennedy/Merck strode out the way he had entered, followed by Taylor.

Back in the car, Kennedy held up his shaking hands.

"You all right, mister?" Taylor asked. "I mean, you did well."

"Fear, rush of adrenaline, I'm not sure which. Just happy to be out of there."

Their driver shifted into Drive and pulled smoothly away from the curb followed by the security team in a second vehicle.

"All the above, I suspect," Taylor said with a wry grin—then out of nowhere he roared, "Hold on!"

The surveillance team radio screamed, "*Truck on your—*" before a massive impact drove the Mercedes sideways, the vehicle's airbags all exploding open at once with deafening booms. Kennedy and Taylor were tossed violently sideways under their seat belts and into the ceiling as the car spun. The team driver fought to get the car back under control to avoid a second battering-ram truck glimpsed inbound from his left.

He failed.

The second truck collided with the Mercedes, impacting the left rear quarter and spinning it the other way. The left-side airbag was already deflating and Kennedy's head smacked into the thick bullet-resistant door window. The glass didn't crack from the impact but Kennedy's head did, splattering blood across the car door and himself, and knocking him senseless.

As Kennedy felt his consciousness slipping away, the last thing he heard was the unmistakable *thud-thud-thud* of incoming rounds striking the armored car to leave star-shaped impacts in the door glass.

Chapter 36

The security teammates in the follow Range Rover, and two more Rovers that had joined the convoy, watched the dump trucks attack the defenseless Mercedes like starving sharks. Charlie Three drove his SUV up on the right sidewalk to shield the team's exit from potential snipers and take advantage of the parked cars for cover. Charlie Five jumped out and brought his M-249 machine gun to bear, killing the drivers of the dump trucks.

Charlies Four and Six exited the SUV and moved forward, providing each other covering fire while dropping advancing attackers attempting to close on Kennedy's car. Five drew a hail of gunfire as he sprinted across the street to a position on the left side of the crushed Mercedes.

Three radioed, "Charlie Two, status! Status, damn it!"

"Two, she's holding for now."

"Can you move out of the kill zone?"

"Negative. We are inoperable."

Charlie Three was about to transmit again when Five let out a long burst, yelling, "RPG!"

Three followed Five's tracers in time to see the RPG shooter's head explode in a pink mist before he could launch the weapon. Attackers on both sides of the street were falling fast now.

The radio crackled. "Charlie Seven, engaged. Charlie Eight, engaged."

Five on the left with Four and Six on the right pushed forward until they came abreast of the car and cleared the intersection. Business owners, workers, and shoppers unfortunate enough to be in the area huddled in storefronts. Everyone recognized gunfire and no one wanted to be in the middle of it. Down the street a woman was crying out, holding her thigh, a likely from a ricochet wound.

Taylor radioed Three to pull up next to the Mercedes driver's door. They would exfil from it, as the door appeared undamaged and functional. As she pulled up, the team dismounted and closed in to provide a protective shield during the transfer. Kennedy was helped from the vehicle, bleeding and unsteady, but lucid. He scanned over the top of the Mercedes and thought he saw someone who favored Lucien's features standing in a doorway on a cellphone. The man was gone in a flash.

"Radio," Kennedy said to the closest teammate. The man pulled a compact handset from his jacket pocket and handed it over. Kennedy keyed it and spoke.

"Charlie Eight, Charlie One—across the street out of the green doorway. Slender, male, six-feet, black jacket, gray slacks, headed back toward the meeting location. Cell in his left hand at this time."

"Copy, One. Tracking or interdict?"

Kennedy thought for just a beat. "Surveillance only. Copy?"

"Solid copy, One."

Locals were cautiously emerging from storefronts to gawk and see the excitement. Distinctive warbling police sirens started wailing in the distance. Taylor supported Kennedy by the arm. "We have to go, bubba," he said, helping him into a Range Rover.

Four and Six followed Kennedy into the up-armored SUV. Five was the last, closing the rear hatch behind him and kicking out the rear glass as the SUV sped away. After several blocks, Three slowed down so as not to attract police attention.

Taylor ripped open a sterile cloth pack from the vehicle's first-aid kit and swiped blood from Kennedy's head.

"Did you see someone you know back there?" Taylor asked.

Kennedy blinked rapidly, still trying to focus his eyes. When he shook his head, it hurt. A lot.

"I thought I saw Lucien watching the attack, cellphone to his ear like he was talking to someone. Charlie Eight is tracking whoever it was," Kennedy said, rubbing his neck.

Taylor said, "Next time we meet Croce, we should leave the jammers on until we clear the area. It might have disrupted the attacker's coordination."

"Interesting thought. Hold on to that for the after-action debrief. The primary questions we need to answer are who and why. It's unlikely this was solely Croce's doing, if he was involved at all. Even if he didn't bite right now, he knows we're about to make him a lot of money. If the guy I saw was Lucien, maybe he was just going for ice cream when the attack happened and he phoned what he'd witnessed back to his boss, like a good do-bee."

Three said, "Sir, not to presume, but did anyone else notice the attackers had a common undeveloped battle cadence? It was a very jump-out, spray-and-pray, uncoordinated assault. All the men I saw had beards, Adidas tracksuits, and felony shoes. Most had AK rifles." He paused to let that sink in.

"These weren't mafia—they were *jihadis*."

The SUV was silent for a beat before Five nodded. "I agree with Three."

Taylor, Four, and Six each responded one after the other with agreements.

Kennedy said, "It makes sense. I guess I assumed—wrongly, looks like—that the Taliban would be two or three middlemen removed from the business this far up the ratline from Afghanistan."

Three said, "Two minutes out."

"Switch to pistols," Taylor ordered. "Three, see about getting us another Mercedes. BR7-level protection with Kevlar spalling blankets, if possible."

BR7 is the highest workable protection level available within civilian-grade armored vehicles, stopping even high-velocity armor-piercing rounds and sniper fire.

Hard to come by at any time, but here? Three glared at Taylor in the rearview mirror and boiled over.

"You know we're in *France*, right? I got no motor pool here, and I don't think Hertz can help us. So, all I can do is *all I can do*, boss," he said in a tone sharper than intended. Everyone was on edge. Then Three took a big breath and offered a grim smile. "But lemme see."

Taylor nodded and gave him a thumb's-up.

"Hot wash in thirty minutes," Kennedy said. His head was clearing now and at least his eyes focused again. "Taylor, check-in with Eight on the surveillance. I need to call Wolf."

The guests in the lobby stood aside as the disheveled and bleeding Kennedy strode to the elevator. Once back in his room, he took a couple of minutes to check his wounds and wash up. After a change to a polo shirt and jeans, he dropped gently backward on the bed so as not to further rattle his brain case.

The attack replayed in his mind's eye. At the sight of the RPG, he had thought his life was done. His only regret at that moment was the prospect of not seeing his wife and son again. He picked up the room phone and dialed Maya to check in, putting on his nothing-to-see-here face. Fifteen minutes later, reconnected with the loves of his life, he felt better and ready to get back in the game.

Then Kennedy switched on his satellite phone and pushed the numeral one to speed-dial Wolf. He picked up on the second ring.

"K-man, how'd the meet go?"

"Real good. Croce will test our cover from several angles, but I'm sure it will hold. I can tell he already wants to partner with us." He rubbed at his left eye. "But, ah, we've encountered an unforeseen complication."

"What's that? A rival gang? Marseille is like the New York City of Europe."

"I should have seen this beforehand, but to tell the truth, I was surprised. Not another gang—the damned *Taliban*."

"What?"

"They attacked us as we were leaving the meeting with Croce. Wait until you see the bill for a wadded-up armored Mercedes."

"Screw the bill. Is everyone okay?"

"Yes. They caught us in a dump-truck sandwich that was effective in taking us out briefly, but Taylor had prepositioned snipers in overwatch, and they kept the ground forces from getting close. Charlie Seven dropped a guy pointing an RPG my way. Vicious attack, but luckily, they weren't very well trained."

"No luck involved, brother. I knew Taylor was a good choice for Charlie commander. His team selection and their training got you through it. As for the Taliban, the Arab community in France is large and diverse, and not all of it wishes the West well. They can hide in plain sight in larger cities. But I'm as surprised as you are. If they have personnel so far up the line, it means they're serious about locking down their profits and business connections."

"Yeah—and locking us out. It doesn't make sense Croce would attack us, but he might have been infiltrated. As I was moving from the Mercedes crash to the Range Rover, I might have seen one of Croce's lieutenants watching the attack. I have Charlie Eight surveilling him."

"The attack might be a good thing; it locks in your credentials as a serious competitor. Playing Croce against the Taliban is a win-win, like Los Angeles all over again."

Kennedy said, "In-fighting is a solid outcome. But this time, I want to limit collateral damage. The civilians caught in the cross-fire in Los Angeles still weigh on my conscience."

He snapped back to the present. "You will get the AAR later today. I'll make sure Clinton gets a copy, too."

"Good, and since you're about to ask what I'm up to, I'll just say I have unfinished business on the reservation. I'm taking a week's leave, but I'll be reachable if you need me."

"Do some things for me."

"What's that, brother?"

"Do not go to jail, do not get fired, and do not piss off the vice president."

Wolf laughed. "I'll see what I can do, but no promises."

Chapter 37

Wolf loved the country he encountered through the cockpit window of the spanking new Sikorsky S-70, the civilian commercial version of the military Black Hawk helicopter that his friend had sent for him. As the helo flew northwest through Wyoming toward Thermopolis, the diversity of the gorgeous, sun-draped vista reminded Wolf of his beloved reservation. The helo landed in Casper, Wyoming, and Mitchell Jankowski met him in a battered old topless Jeep.

An Air Force veteran, Jankowski had struggled to overcome the loss of his left leg and degraded hearing into a service-disabled, veteran-owned business empire with every possible federal firearms license.

He'd become one of the prime contractors to the Agency and DOD—and the only disadvantaged one, able to sole-source for contracts up $25 million in manufacturing and $20 million in services. He had four to six contracts for various deliverables in fulfillment at any time, all with escalator clauses that allowed automatic compensation increases according to the needs of the government when demands in the field might grow faster than contract mods usually permitted.

Wolf exited the helo and trotted over to the old white elephant, hopping into the passenger seat of a much-altered Jeep.

"What's up, zoomie? How you been out here in God's country?" He and Jankowski slapped hands.

"All good here, brother," Jankowski said with a wide grin. "It's great to see you, man." He pushed the cranky stick left and forward into first gear, and the Jeep took off in a cloud of dust. "Let's go to the house. Patty wants to say hey. Poor woman needs a break. She's negotiating a deal with some Agency contracting noob and she's teaching him his job from the ground up." Jankowski laughed. "If we'd been dishonest, we'd all be millionaires by now."

Going to "the house" was an understatement to Wolf—the prairie palace of thick logs was right out of the movie *Legends of the Fall*. The timber and stone house was stunning against the backdrop of the eleven-thousand-acre "ranch," as Mitch called it. It dwarfed the one-hundred-and-fifty-acre home they kept in northern Michigan near Patty's parents.

As they parked and dismounted the Jeep in front of wide stone steps leading to the open front door, the smell of fresh pie and hot coffee told Wolf that his friend had slipped Patty the word that he was inbound.

Wolf heard Patty disconnecting the Agency contract call as he ambled through the mud room on the way to the kitchen. She greeted Wolf with a tight hug and asked how Elle was, then she proceded to tell Wolf about the kids. She asked how long he was staying and pushed him to stay for dinner. Wolf laughed and accepted; she wasn't taking no for an answer.

While Patty finished cooking, Mitch filled coffee mugs and motioned for Wolf to follow him. They left the house and entered an oversize pole barn that was part man-cave and part high-tech office. There was a large empty space with a moving platform where the helo could be landed and garaged, plus a bar, wood stove, gun-smithing bench, and weightlifting equipment.

And four large gun safes.

Mitch got right to the point. "I have twenty kits for you. The rifles are M4 carbines. One is full auto, it's yours. Each case has six mags. I topped the M4s with a night vision-compatible EOTECH sight and IR illuminator. The NVG case includes the latest generation of dual-tube night vision setup for helmet mounts. There are two kit bags of helmets with extended-life battery packs and glint tape. The other two kit bags have chest rigs with body armor and SAPI plates, which will stop AK and long-gun rounds. I also have two long-gun kits for you, both built to your M-21 sniper weapons system specs with night vision-compatible scope reticules. The pallet has twenty thousand rounds of ball ammo for the M4s and four hundred rounds of match ammo for the long guns."

"Mitch, man, I appreciate the help, but this is too much. I don't want any crap coming back on you and Patty."

"You think I'd give you all this and not cover our butts?" Mitch said, chuckling. "I've worked with too many of you high-speed snake eaters. Have your militiamen sign this paperwork, and we're both covered."

Wolf laughed. "Good. I don't mind bending a few rules, but you'd be date bait in a federal prison."

"Thanks." Jankowski laughed. "You should know. Take one of my trucks; less paper trail. Leave it at the airport in Billings when you're done, and my guys will pick it up when you tell me you're done with it."

Wolf loaded up Mitch's old Silverado crew cab pickup with the offensive treasures, the back seat area stacked with M-4s and sniper rifles in Pelican cases and the ammo boxes secured in the truck bed under tarps secured with bungee cords. He hugged Mitch and Patty goodbye and gratefully accepted the large slice of pie cleverly held for eating in a folded paper plate, and a large Yeti cup filled with coffee. Mounted up in Jankowski's truck, he headed for the reservation.

The more than three-hour drive wound its way through country Wolf could never get enough of. Fifteen minutes after getting to Billy Red Fish's house and unloading into Billy's garage, the space resembled a National Guard armory. Billy was recovering from his attack well enough to help break down the bulk weapons load into individual kits that would be assigned to what Wolf had described as the tribal police civilian support unit. Billy would be the operations officer working under the police chief if Wolf could get him on board. His four combat vets would be squad leaders.

Wolf expected some level of crap about who should lead, but figured the money would reduce the infighting. Wolf had brought along two hundred thousand dollars in cash. Enough to pay the men a hundred bucks a day for three months, plus some contingency funds.

In the early days of Wolf's fight against the Sinaloa cartel, a Mexican police lieutenant had given him a duffel bag with two hundred and fifty thousand dollars of cartel money. It had come from the restaurant where the gunfight killing his parents had occurred, which had started Wolf's war of revenge. He thought it ironic that he was using the cartel's own money to fight them on his reservation.

An hour later, Wolf headed into Billings to do some recruiting. The Veterans of Foreign Wars post sat along State Street across from the rail yard. Behind the red, white, and blue building was a craft brewery and a small casino. Wolf noted the cigarette, cigar, and whiskey odors coming from the canteen. The post president, Jack Miller, had been a Vietnam combat veteran and a friend of his stepfather, greeted him warmly.

Wolf got right to the point, asking for Miller's help identifying able-bodied veterans in need of jobs. They needed to have good health, no substance abuse issues, and be able to run a mile in under ten minutes. Wolf told Miller the pay was twenty-five dollars an hour, and the contract could last up to ninety days.

Miller gave Wolf a sideways glance. "I'll put together a list for you," the post president said. "Pay like that means it's dangerous. Lots of our members are bored and miss the old days, but they ain't stupid and I think they want to keep drawin' breath. What's the activity level, the tempo of work?"

"Very active. Not always on foot, but active," Wolf said, sensing Miller was trying to connect the dots with the little information he had been provided.

Wolf thanked Miller for his help, gave him his contact card, and headed for his next stop, a rural address eight miles outside of town. He reminded himself how on-edge this idea was, and he needed to keep it from slipping over into full-on craziness.

Normally he would never consider approaching a gaggle of nut cases like the leader of the militia he was about to meet with, but these were not normal times.

It wasn't all bad, Wolf tried to tell himself. Several of the militia members he had vetted served honorably in combat. That their societal views seemed a little off-center was a small concern, but he'd rely on their dislike for government oversight, foreign incursion—and their desire to be paid.

Chapter 38

Back on the reservation, Wolf hadn't been in Billy's house in twenty years. He entered through the side door. Inside, the smell of Pine-Sol and Hoppe's No. 9 gun cleaner overpowered all others. The kitchen had been converted into an armorer's workspace, with rifle cartridge and shotgun shell reloading presses bolted directly to the once pretty countertop.

Instead of cans with flour and sugar, there were containers labeled with gunpowders of different classes and grain types. Other containers were filled with Speer bullets and CCI primers. Three green trays with what appeared to be complete 5.56 reloads sat on the table. In typical retired OCD soldier fashion, everything was dressed right and sparkling clean.

Wolf pushed through to the family room to find it kitted out like an operations center, with reservation maps on the walls and multiple handset radios in a charging bank on a makeshift table built from two sawhorses and a door. The windows were blacked out, and an older Kenwood TS-811A UHF/VHF two-meter multi-mode transceiver sat in the corner of the kitchen counter.

This is the reservation rangers command center.

Wolf wanted to have a direct, undistracted, and to-the-point talk with Billy, so he hoped the front room still had some of Billy's deceased wife's charm. It was just as Wolf remembered, with overstuffed chairs and a cozy couch centered around the stone fireplace. It was just as she left it, with one exception. There was a kind of shrine in the corner with pictures of her and Billy. Wolf looked around the room and it clicked what was missing.

Billy entered the room, handing Wolf a cup of coffee doctored up in Wolf's way. "I buried all the wildflowers with my wife six years ago," Billy said with a wan smile. "I can't have them in the house anymore. Too painful."

"I understand." Wolf nodded and sipped the hot, black brew, looking over the top of the cup at his friend. "Sit down, brother. Let's talk."

Billy sat on the sofa and Wolf pulled a chair.

"I'm bringing in help to grow the ranks of our militia," Wolf said. Billy's eyes widened as he moved to the edge of the sofa and Wolf raised a hand. "Hold on, let me finish. Our team needs people with good weapons handling skills and a consistent level of fitness. They'll have some reliability because I'm paying for their services, and for the reservation rangers, too."

Wolf could see Billy was thinking it through, which he took as a good sign. Billy put his coffee down and broke the silence.

"What is it you don't get about bringing in outsiders here? The leadership doesn't trust them, the people don't trust them, and the only reason I would trust them is because I trust you."

"I understand—I do. But I can't see another path forward. Without them, we're outmanned and outgunned."

Billy was getting spun up. "Did you think of asking members of the other tribes? They will come to our aid. We can reciprocate and help push drugs out of all our lands in Montana."

Wolf frowned and stared out the window. He forced himself to return to Billy's gaze.

"I'm embarrassed to say I didn't. For all my big talk about building a coalition, I hadn't thought of asking the other tribes for warriors with experience like ours."

"Forest for the trees, Wolf. You said it yourself—we need to remove this scourge from our lands before it destroys our way of life. Let's check with the other tribes first, and then we can fill in with your VFW and militia wackos if we need them."

Wolf's head snapped up, his gaze hard. "You've been following me?"

"Yes and no. The VFW is an information and gossip sieve. And it wasn't hard to figure out where you were headed after that."

Wolf laughed and shook his head. "Okay, you got me there. Just so you know, Chief Hogan is on board to add outsiders if you and I do the training. My plan has you as his ops officer for civilian support activities. We have no police powers, but in certain circumstances, the teams can detain until a tribal police officer arrives on the scene. If this starts and stays under control, Hogan will consider deputizing members of the force, which will help."

Billy asked, "Do we still have the support of the highway patrol and DEA?"

"Yes, but not full time. So, we need to be smart about their use. Good news is they saw our success and they want in on the fight. For now, let's focus on the other tribes. Who do you know who will help us?"

Billy smiled for the first time since Wolf had shown up with the weapons.

"Many of the greatest warriors are past their prime, but younger generations still serve. I'll reach out to the tribal elders and my friends at the VFWs and American Legion. I think you are in for a surprise."

Chapter 39

Thirty-six hours later, the team had thirteen additional Indian warriors, all under the age of forty and with one or more tours in a combat zone. It meant Wolf only needed one from the VFW, which was okay given the shortlist. The two from the militia had multiple combat tours and could use the work. Wolf had a full team in hand by noon. The following morning at zero seven, Wolf and Billy started the program of training he had agreed to with Chief Hogan.

Hogan had asked a rancher to provide land for training in an isolated section of the reservation. The roads and terrain were similar to where they planned to operate. After being assigned their weapons and gear, the first class was on stop and search. While there were many ways their services had taught the team members when they were in uniform, Wolf emphasized communication and security over individual techniques.

Once agreed to, they were broken down into four-man teams,

and they worked the procedures until noon, when they broke for lunch. Wolf and Billy carried coolers over to the trees letting the team know there were box lunches, sodas, water, and MREs for anyone wanting to partake.

Wolf stood next to Billy as the team grabbed lunch and a spot in the shade. "What do you think of the team pairings?"

"A couple of changes based on who demonstrates leadership, and we're set."

"Good. After seeing them flow better, we can switch to a med refresher this afternoon."

Wolf stepped away, pulling his satellite phone from a cargo pocket. He was holding the phone up to acquire satellites when a flash caught his eye.

"Sniper, three o'clock, four hundred yards!"

Wolf dropped the satphone, spun his slung rifle to his cheek weld, and fired a burst in the direction of the flash. At the same time, the zip of a supersonic round flew by Wolf's right ear, followed by the rifle report. Wolf felt warm blood on his cheek and his ear stung as he ran to cover behind the rear wheel of a car. He heard others yelling to take cover. A second round crashed through the windows, showering Wolf with safety glass.

He peered through the empty window opening and rifles behind him fired. Wolf glanced behind to see three men running together through the trees, looking to flank the sniper. Another round punched through the sheet metal of the fender and trunk, exiting to Wolf's right. The round thudded into a nearby tree, splattering shards of stiff bark into the air.

Shit. That sounds like a big rifle, Wolf thought. Suddenly the sound of four M-4s being fired as fast as possible filled the air. It stopped just as quickly, and one of the team members appeared at the wood line waving his arm in an all clear signal.

"Cease fire, cease fire, cease fire!" Wolf called.

Billy joined him and pointed to the exit hole in the fender just inches from where Wolf had taken cover.

Billy scowled. "Was that a .50 cal?"

Wolf faced into the line of the bullet and pointed at the splintered tree. "I don't think so, but the bullet will tell us. Big though, like .338 Lapua big, I'd guess."

"Anyone ever mention you piss off a lot of bad people? You're a damn trouble magnet, mister."

"Yeah, I may have heard that once or twice," Wolf said, smiling. "Let's gather up the team. I want to commend the guys who took the initiative."

"Okay, but just because you were the target this time doesn't mean they won't be next time. We need to make sure they're mentally prepared for a serious fight. When we clamp down, they're going to come at us hard."

"That's the idea. War of the Flea. Little actions can move big armies. Show them it costs less to give up the reservations and go elsewhere than to stay and fight to keep them. Somewhere in all this, we need to figure out who the cartel has in their pocket. We won't be mission complete until we clean it all out."

Chapter 40

Surrounded by a warm, clear sky with the green-blue Gulf of Mexico below, Morgan had spent an hour sitting strapped in the breeze of the C-130's lowered ramp as they headed southwest to the Mexican special forces base southeast of Mexico City. At the base waiting for Morgan and Harris was Colonel Carlos González, the newly promoted commander of Fuerza Especial de Reaccion the parent unit of his former *Escuadron de Leones*.

The Mexican Army unit had been modeled after elite US units. A captain when he had first met Master Sergeant Lance Wolf, González's friendship had grown until their bond was fused forever through the death of González's brother and his wife along with Wolf's parents at the hand of the Sinaloa cartel.

Wolf considered González a plank owner in Shadow Tier—in the US Navy, the term designates an individual as a member of the crew of a ship when it was placed in commission, and it's a high honor. Such was González's importance to the team's formation.

Both of their organizations had developed in response to the growth and violence of the cartels, in particular the Sinaloa cartel. It had been González's analysts who had ferreted out the change in the cartel business model—marijuana use was in decline compared to the growth of meth and heroin. Recent reports from the Mexican Marine Command, González's sources, and in-country DEA analysts, all pointed to a change in production, with a higher percentage of farms soon to be cultivating opium.

At Kennedy's suggestion, Morgan had taken the initiative and prepared to jump right into the suck, developing his own intelligence. While Afghanistan and its opium were of primary concern to the American president as a Taliban funding source, the primary Shadow Tier charter was still the disruption of the world's largest drug cartel.

Morgan needed to prosecute his mission to determine what impact the crop shift might have on the flow of drugs into the States. Shadow Tier's only informant in the cartel had gone silent, and while disconcerting, it told of additional levels of counterintelligence effort and potentially something new brewing in the fertile imagination of the cartel's leader, El Chapo.

Three hours later, Morgan and Harris, who had slept the entire flight, stepped off the C-130 and shook hands with Colonel Carlos González. Ever since the attack on the colonel's family by the cartel he'd been accompanied by a security detail of four blacked-out, heavily armed troopers with the new experimental 5.56mm FX-05 "Fire Serpent" automatic rifles. They stood in a diamond formation facing outward, and they did not shake hands.

González took the group directly to his operations center and its conference room, where his intelligence analyst waited. After brief introductions, they got right into the update briefing. Ninety minutes of analysis, overhead imagery, and infrared scans of newly planted fields were inconclusive. Like Wolf, Morgan's inclination leaned toward eyes-on-target as the best means of determining your enemy's intent.

Morgan held back his normal toothsome grin, the twinkle in his eyes all the colonel needed to see.

González smiled at Morgan and said, "Thank you, ladies and gentlemen. That will be all for now." The colonel motioned for Morgan and Harris to stay behind. Once the room cleared, González asked for his Sergeant Major Daniel Dominguez to join them. The sergeant major had been with González from the start and was only the second person read into the real story of Eliana Cortes and her placement back into the cartel.

Morgan pointed to a farm on the map display. "Colonel, with your permission, Mr. Harris and I would like to spend a few days on the ground at this site here."

González said, "It is likely some of our analysts will think it odd if you pick a farm out in the middle of nowhere."

Morgan smiled. "Yes, sir. That was cover for action." He pointed to a spot on the map. "We will insert here and surveil this portion of the Cortes ranch where a crop switch appears to be underway."

González said, "That is a remote area. Working it greatly increases your risk."

Harris frowned and Morgan shrugged. "Yes, sir, maybe a bit, but I have a hidden motive. We haven't heard from Eliana in some time, and I need to find out whether she's okay, or scamming us." Morgan frowned. "Too bad for her if it's the latter."

González paced, shaking his head. "Understood. But you know El Chapo has upped his counterintelligence capabilities by hiring three very experienced Cuban intel officers. We have intel suggesting a new level of paranoia from El Chapo. These Cubans are, as you say, no joke. There is so much traffic, all encrypted, between

El Chapo and Cuba as to make us consider there may be some un-known new alliance with the shaky government. Certainly, that would be something Eliana would report, yes?"

"Agreed, unless she feels she is being watched. She knows her phones and computers are tapped. So, the only way to contact her is when she is in route somewhere. A fake robbery, perhaps, where we'd slip her a note, or when she goes for a ride on that stallion of hers."

González was skeptical. "Both high-risk, but we know she rides alone, no security." He scratched his chin. "There is only one way in, and it's HALO. Any other ideas, sergeant major?"

"The coastline is unprotected, so by water—" He traced the blue line of a river with his finger. "—then on foot for about forty-five kilometers. It is far, not enough darkness for a ground approach. Dogs and sentries are very congested for the first fifteen kilome-ters. Yes, HALO is the best option."

"Okay. I'd like to go in tonight," Morgan said. "Is that a prob-lem?"

González laughed. "Just like Wolf, always so impatient. No, no problem. Sergeant major, take them to my personal locker area and have the HALO rigs brought there. The fewer people who know you were here and then left, the better. The cartel has eyes and ears."

At twenty-three thirty, Morgan and Harris were driven up to a CASA C-295 and boarded via the aft ramp. Once inside, the crew chief closed the ramp, and the pilots started the engines. Taking seats on the port side, Morgan and Harris donned noise-canceling helmets with intercoms and buckled in for takeoff on the three-hour flight north to Monterrey, then west toward Los Mochis and the farm on the eastern side of the Cortes ranch.

At zero-two, the crew chief gave Morgan a thirty-minute warning with a hand sign. At ten minutes, they stood and performed their buddy check, which went quickly given the modest jump altitude of fourteen thousand feet.

Standing on the ramp, red light shining, Morgan shifted anxiously from foot to foot, waiting on the drop point. When the light went green, he gave Harris a thumbs up and dove into the night, Harris a step behind.

Morgan stabilized and spun a one-eighty to see Harris through his night vision goggles right where he should be. He held his heading until four thousand feet, then waved off and pulled his ripcord. After the split-second of canopy inflation noise, the quiet of the night consumed them as they flew their square spec-ops parachutes to an opening in a wooded area to land a mile from the target. They rolled up their parachute gear and hid it in a shallow depression, covering it with wood, leaves, and forest debris.

Morgan took a knee and consulted his GPS, oriented himself, and with a knife hand indicated the route of travel. He pushed aside thoughts of seeing Eliana again. It had been a month since their last rendezvous in Miami. He went through a four-count of deep breathing to center himself to the mission and began patrolling to the target.

Chapter 41

The following morning, Wolf stood on the edge of the training area and said, "I don't want to go operational until we practice breaking contact. Most of the team hunkered down and didn't maneuver to improve their position."

"Well, at least they did that," Billy said.

"I know. Not trying to be a hard-ass here, I just want to make sure they live through the next contact. We know the cartel for bringing heat. They're shooting down helicopters in Mexico. If they can do it down there, they sure as heck can do it here, too."

Billy said, "Okay, okay. Point taken, let's work them up. We can fight the teams against each other after we make sure no one is carrying live."

"Good idea, after yesterday I will be. Someone is watching us and knows by now we are building our an army. Which means it can't be long before White Horse finds out and throws a hissy fit."

"I know. I see signs of surveillance. Could it be Amaru?"

"It's possible—but he wouldn't have missed. No, I think it was someone that thinks bigger is better but doesn't have any real sniper training or tradecraft."

Billy said, "As for White Horse, there's nothing he can do to our little club of civilian police supporters," Billy said, switching from serious to a gleam in his eyes.

The rest of the morning was spent practicing break-contact drills. Wolf threw in a couple of unplanned ambushes, and to his surprise, the teams fell back into their ingrained training and assaulted through per Marine Corps and Army doctrine.

Wolf gave a training break and gathered everyone around a cooler of cold water and soft drinks. He had their full attention.

"You are guerillas waging unconventional warfare on a bigger army's logistics lines of transportation. They are slow, we are fast. We fight for our tribes, our families, and this land. Our land." Wolf saw them stir and raise their rifles, yelling out in solidarity.

"Tonight, we take the fight to the evil wanting to take away our way of life, to corrupt our children—tonight, we drive invaders from our land."

Wolf had Billy assigned the teams to their checkpoints. The highway patrol had started health and safety checks fifteen minutes before, at twenty-one hundred. Wolf expected to see rerouting to start within forty-five minutes. Billy sat in the command center with Chief Hogan, listening to the radio reports of trucks diverting away from checkpoints.

Wolf had taken Mitch Jankowski up on his offer of a McDonnell Douglas 500 helicopter, which Wolf had assigned himself and a bear of a man named Steven Johnson, who had been in the 2nd Ranger Battalion as Wolf had, just eight years later. They would be the quick reaction force. Wolf was carrying a belt-fed Mk 48 machine gun that fired the 7.62mm NATO round. Unfortunately, Wolf thought with a frown, he was short on anti-tank rounds, having exactly none to his name.

Billy had put together several teams of watchers whose only job was to report the movement of the vehicles trying to subvert the highway patrol checkpoints. They had two priorities. First, do not get caught. Second, call in the vehicle, roadway, and direction of travel. It was twenty-two-eighteen when the first call came into the command center. Billy relayed the information about a fleeing tractor trailer with a large SUV trailing it.

Wolf went to full alert. He ordered Johnson to get the helicopter spun up. Billy alerted Team Three, and Wolf pushed Team One their way for backup. Wolf sprinted to the helicopter and they surged into the black night.

As they headed for the Team Three location, Wolf calculated they would arrive at the checkpoint just seconds before the tractor-trailer rig. Six minutes later, the pilot slid the little bird over the ridgeline two hundred yards south of the checkpoint.

Johnson came over the intercom. "The tractor is just turning the corner into the checkpoint—oh shit. The SUV has moved forward and is accelerating out in front." He pointed over Wolf's shoulder.

Wolf switched to the team channel and yelled, "Get clear, get clear!" as the SUV rammed a hole between two Tribal police pickup trucks parked in a V formation chokepoint. The SUV spun one truck into the ditch and kept going. Wolf vectored the pilot to come along the left side of the SUV where he could get a shot to the engine block.

A stream of tracer rounds missed high and right over Wolf's position in the right seat of the helicopter. Johnson yanked the collective and quickly took up a position above and behind the SUV.

Over the intercom, Wolf asked him to edge forward to above and just behind the front windshield. Then he said, "Lead the semi on the count of three."

Wolf counted down from three and started firing while the pilot slowed down. When he let off his trigger, the rounds had stitched up the engine compartment, disabling the engine and causing havoc with the bad guys.

Team One arrived and blocked the road to the south, while Team Three raced up just as the helo sat down. The gunmen in the SUV were all wounded, so Team One started treating them and called for two ambulances. The tractor-trailer driver had jack-knifed his rig in the roadway, then jumped out and started running through the scrub into the darkness. It took less than a minute for a Team Three warrior to knock him down and lead him back in flex-cuffs.

"Team Three, you up?" Wolf asked over the radio.

The team leader responded. "Aye-firm. Got a couple banged up vehicles, but we're all good."

Wolf let Billy and Chief Hogan know the outcome and that the bad guys' tractor-trailer rig and SUV were both inoperable. The chief said he would call for a heavy-duty extractor-type tow truck, and he'd be out with officers to help search the trailer in place.

It took a while to find it, but around zero-six thirty, they knew they had the largest heroin seizure in the history of Montana. The broken and dusty TVs in the middle of the truck were the oddity that led a Tribal officer to find their hidden treasure.

There were dozens of boxes marked for eco-friendly recycling. A Tribal police officer opened one box and saw something strange through the air vents in the back of the TVs. He pushed his knife through expecting to hit something metal or electronic and came back with a white powder.

He pulled the TV out of its box and shipping materials. When he turned it over, white powder dust dropped through the vents. Subsequent investigation and testing found the backs of the TVs were filled with White China heroin. The rest of the night had been a bust with no other diversions into the reservation.

Wolf speculated the bad guys had gotten wind of the operation and had rerouted drug transportation away from the reservation at the first call of trouble. A quick tally of the heroin shocked law enforcement all the way back to Washington D.C.—twenty-six million dollars in estimated street value.

Wolf met Billy, Chief Hogan, and the teams at the ranch. They all congratulated the men on a job well done. Then Wolf told them to get some rest and be ready to get back at it at thirteen hundred.

Before heading to his bunk for a few precious hours of sleep, Wolf made sure Billy and Chief Hogan understood what they had just done.

"I did not expect this," Wolf said. "That's a bunch of dope, and someone on the other side will die because of their screw-up. After they take care of that, they will turn to us. We have to be ready for a straight-up punch in the face. Keep your eyes and ears open—even when you sleep."

Wolf couldn't know how right he was.

Chapter 42

The sunny morning was accentuated by a stiff breeze snapping the flags surrounding the podium set up in front of the Crow Tribal Council building. Chief Hogan was bracketed by Frank White Horse, some council members, Montana Highway Patrol, and DEA. In front of the podium was a theatrical stack of heroin in kilo packages laid out on a long table to demonstrate the volume and value of the seizure and, for the cameras, heavily armed uniformed Tribal policemen with M4s standing guard at each end of the evidence table.

Behind the drugs and slightly to the left of the podium was a poster board collage of perp pictures from the dangerous men apprehended during the seizure. Behind the men and women of law enforcement was a semicircle of the cruisers from each of the agencies involved. The press crews included the usual local affiliates and two national-level crews, one from CNN and one from Fox News.

The press conference had started with Frank White Horse

telling the press how proud he was of his police force and their citizen support team, which included warriors from other tribes. He talked about his idea to bring the other tribes in and treat the problem as a statewide issue versus just a Crow issue. He also took advantage of the press conference to call out the governor for funding to continue the fight.

The press conference had been his idea after Chief Hogan got him calmed down. White Horse had first been apoplectic on hearing of the seizure, flopping back and forth like a fish on the bank gasping for air. He jumped from firing Hogan and wanting to kick Billy out of the tribe to wanting a press conference so he could push his agenda.

He immediately had his staff generate a press package, including the media release, perp and drug photos with the statistics on the quality of the heroin, its weight, and estimated street value. He wanted to include pictures of the take-down site, but Hogan convinced him it was still an active crime scene. Hogan told White Horse he could use it later for a follow-up press conference, which would keep him in the national news for another cycle.

White Horse finally left the podium, and the state's top cop presented a message from the governor congratulating the multi-agency team and calling for more federal funding to battle the war against drugs. After the big shots talked, it was Chief Hogan's turn in the hot seat for the thirty-minute Q&A session, and the press did not hold back.

The Fox News reporter started. "Chief Hogan, how long have you been training your civilian support team?"

"One month," Hogan said, stretching the truth.

When the Fox reporter stumbled, the CNN reporter jumped in. "How can it be long enough for such dangerous work, Chief?"

Hogan scanned the crowd, reporters, and cameras trained on

him, taking a beat to formulate his response. "First off, let me say we have trained to police standards. We are not a tribal army or militia. And during training, we focused on policing and police procedures so we would not violate any tribal, state, or federal law. Next question."

The follow-on questions were softballs designed to produce short answers, which worked with the time the story would get on a broadcast.

Unseen on the edge of the press pool, a reporter from the local community newspaper took notes and snapped pictures with her cellphone. Well before the news about the drug bust had gone national, she had reported to the Yellowstone County commissioner. He had, in turn, reported to his contact at the cartel.

From the first call to the cartel to the order given to Amaru, less than thirty minutes had elapsed. Two hours later, he was on a flight from San Francisco to Tampa, mission orders in hand.

"Use Wolf's wife to stop the losses."

Chapter 43

Amaru thought flying into Orlando was a mistake. Good for counter-surveillance if you didn't mind the crush of humanity. The heat and thickness of the air reminded him of flying into Manila in the Philippines, its cloying oppression in contrast to the cool humidity of San Francisco and the northwest cities his work often took him to.

The chaos and multi-lingual jibber-jabber of the airport was disturbing to him and the out-of-control children upset his manufactured balance, though he was adept at hiding his feelings in all aspects of life. His attitude was restored once in the rental car and headed west on I-4 to Tampa.

His cartel orders were simple, as was his plan. One or two days to scout a secure holding location well away from the safehouse. One to three days to observe and record Eleanor Parker's pattern of life, then another three days for the best window to execute the kidnapping. The ninety-minute drive to the safehouse near the

University of South Florida provided ample time to walk through the plan, visualizing each element in detail.

The safehouse was as he had left it. The dart gun was still in place. Logic said it was the perfect place to bring Parker; it was small, easy to manage, with all the right avenues of approach and escape. But he knew others knew of the safehouse. Safe house, it was not.

Amaru waited until after dark to venture out. He wanted to drive to where Wolf and Parker lived to make sure she was even in town. The memory of another predator watching him sent a shiver up his spine. The memory was vivid, as if in a dream where he hunted himself. He took several deep breaths, exhaling slowly. He muttered a chant to instill patience and bring him into balance.

Amaru was sitting in mediation when the face of a wolf appeared out of the void, its jaws wide and dripping saliva as if to swallow him. He snapped out of his mediation and jumped to his feet, cursing. The wolf symbolized ruthlessness and cunning, an enemy of humans.

It can't be. I am the alpha threat.

Amaru made some tea and tried but failed to put Wolf out of his mind. He stormed out of the safehouse in anger and drove south to scout for a site to hold Parker in the decaying industrial area along the backwater of Tampa Bay. It was near midnight when he found it—an abandoned foundry and machine shop at the end of a cul-de-sac, with the Tampa Bay backwater on the south side and entrance on the east. The north side was another abandoned location protected by a high chain-link fence. The west side butted up to train tracks that headed north at the fence line.

Power was out in the dusty office spaces, which sat between the foundry and machine shops. Its only windows to the outside were a couple of dirty and broken skylights. Amaru hiked the perimeter, noting where to cut the fence on the west and north sides in case the need arose for a hasty exit. There was to be a secluded spot just past the railroad tracks perfect for prepositioning a backup get-away car.

Yes, this will work. A quick trip to Home Depot, and it's ready.

Amaru drove north to Kennedy Blvd. The need to put his eyes on Wolf's house was undeniable. He took a left on South Hyde Park Avenue and then pulled over after taking the right leading to Wolf's house. As he drove closer to the likely site for the kidnapping, he switched into fight mode without thought. The only outward appearances of his heightened state were his wide eyes attempting to gather maximum light in the darkness, like a cat, and the tapping of his right index finger on the steering wheel.

A fan of Eighties hard rock, his brain subconsciously linked AC/DC's raucous "Back in Black" to the moment. After several minutes of idling by the curb, Amaru pulled forward and smiled. He didn't sense the other killer. He parked two blocks away and ambled into the alley, where he had a line of sight to the house. He stayed in the shadows until the downstairs light went out. He waited a few more minutes until the master bath window also darkened.

Amaru glanced at his watch: Twenty-three hundred. He smiled at Parker's precise eleven o'clock bedtime and then headed back to the car. There was much to do tomorrow.

Amaru planned out his day on the way back to the safehouse. When he got five miles away, he ran a surveillance detection route that proved he was clear. At the safehouse, he turned down the air conditioning and made a cup of tea, then wrote out a Home Depot shopping list.

Satisfied that he was prepared to maximize his day, he laid down and visualized his wife and family. He had worked hard to get where he was in life, making the kind of money his parents hadn't even dreamed of. That his work involved hurting and killing other people was of no concern. His only thought was for providing for the family he had built, the one he wished he'd had as a child.

Drifting off, he realized the kidnapping could take place as soon as tomorrow.

Amaru permitted himself the luxuries of sleeping in and then a full breakfast. He had eight hours to prepare the holding site, get the backup car in place, and be at Wolf's house ready to execute. Not needing to plan and execute *in extremis* was not something Amaru was accustomed to, so he kept an eye on the time. If he finished his preparations sooner, it would allow more time for surveillance of the area around Wolf's house. Amaru was disappointed in himself when he realized he had no food or water ready at the site, so he went to a Lowe's and bought two coolers, then to a Publix east of Tampa in Sable Park to load up on water, sandwiches, bottled tea, and energy bars.

He was ready. He stood in the office area he would use to hold Parker and determined it too was ready. His route in and routes out were clear. His backup egress was in place. He nodded and left for the Wolf's house.

Amaru thought Wolf must have spent a lot of money and time to landscape around the house and hardscape his back yard. It all made sense for a couple who was often out-of-town, fighting drug traffickers like his boss and their enemy number one, the Sinaloa cartel. What worked in Amaru's favor was the way the hardscape sloped up at the alley in terraced layers with palm trees. Where he sat between the wall and the trash cans, he couldn't be seen by a second-floor neighbor or anyone entering the alley.

The palm trees sported fresh growth, which Amaru used to get a gauge of the wind speed and direction. The hardscape also provided concealment for his approach, but if he went right to shooting, it would still be a ten- to twelve-foot shot with the dart gun. If he was lucky enough to catch Parker at the grill, he might reduce the distance by one or two feet.

Amaru heard the sliding glass doors open and the steps padding across the flagstone. The grill creaked as he peered over the edge with his extended inspection mirror to see Parker turn it on, then go back into the house. He stopped for a beat and heard no one else, so he positioned himself to take the shot. He glanced up at the palms and nodded; the wind was negligible. Squatting in a semi-chair pose with his back to the wall, his legs quivered with the effort and that would affect his accuracy, so he sank to his ankles. Amaru slowed his breathing and waited.

Six long minutes later, the slider opened again, but this time there were two voices, both females. Irritated at the inconvenience of chaos, he worked through his options. Clear in his mind which path to take, he pulled a bandanna over his face cowboy style and stood to find the women with their backs to him.

He shot Parker in the center of her back. When she dropped the platter of food and yelped, reaching for her back, her friend spun. As Parker fell, the friend tried to catch her but missed, so Amaru sprinted forward and landed a left cross to the jaw, putting her lights out, too. He used his backup syringe and jabbed the friend in the arm to ensure she stayed out.

Amaru grabbed Parker's arms and struggled to get her into a fireman's carry, but once over his shoulder and into the alley, he loaded her into the trunk of his car and drove off.

Amaru didn't comprehend the hornet's nest he had just kicked. He would find out shortly, and fear would not be part of Wolf's response—a response that would come faster and harder than any he had experienced before.

Chapter 44

E liana's research consultant had pointed the way, but she decided to seek him out. She enjoyed the international travel, which, unfortunately, had to be kept of short duration and hidden from El Chapo's counterintelligence team. Her personal jet, good food, and lots of water made it tolerable.

Eliana wanted to expand her reach in Iraq and Afghanistan by adding ground-based logistics to her growing list of Global Air Services contracts. As expected, Janus Logistics was already part of the movement of opium into Turkey. With an infusion of cash, she could push Janus to the next level with contracts and routes all the way into mainland Europe and Marseilles. Certain it had to seem to be Jean Paul Croce's plan, she would play to her ability to help him jump forward and upward.

As Eliana's plane taxied to a stop at Marseilles's *Aéroport de Marseille Marignane*, two Mercedes SUVs pulled up. Two large, smartly dressed men exited the second vehicle and stood by the right rear door. Eliana's security lead deplaned first and, after a terse exchange of pass phrases with the men on the ground, waved his okay for her to disembark. Eliana left the plane followed by a security man, and all three sat in the second-row seats with Eliana in the middle.

The sights of the French city flashed past as they drove to the meeting location at a high rate of speed with, Eliana could see, the escort support of motorcycle policemen.

This guy really does think he's mafia, she thought, shaking her head—the new *Unione Corsa.*

They arrived at a nondescript building housing a restaurant and climbed stairs to the second floor. As they headed to the table, a man came forward and, in Castilian Spanish, told Eliana she could only have one security man with her at the meeting. The other would have to wait downstairs with the rest of *Monsieur* Croce's men. Eliana gave her security lead a head tilt and the second man was escorted back downstairs.

She walked around the table to shake hands with Croce as he stood. She stared into his eyes for a long beat, seeing his attempt to hide amazement at the boldness of the woman next to him. Eliana released his hand and took a chair next to Croce, which also surprised him. Apparently, it was not done that way here, and for that reason, Eliana was happy she did it.

She got right to business. "I have been watching you and I like what I see in the way you do business and the plans you seem to have for the future. I am here to propose a partnership that combines the strength of my air services company with your ground logistics so we can mutually expand and profit. But let me be clear, I do not want to buy your business. I want to invest in it."

Croce was dumbfounded. He spun to his number two—or *consigliere,* she wasn't sure which—and saw the advisor nod in return.

A smile broke across Croce's face and he said, "Interesting. But first, may I offer you an espresso or a glass of wine?"

Eliana smiled, knowing she had just rolled right over this small man. She said, "I'll have tequila, with lime and salt."

Croce ordered two. When the tequila came, Eliana licked the side of her fist, applied the salt, and waited on Croce, who must have never before downed a ritual shot of tequila. When he finally paid attention, she licked her hand slowly of salt, downed the shot, and bit the lime, making a humming noise of satisfaction. Croce just stared, but he got the idea at last. He flinched when licking his salt but downed his shot, coughing a little before biting into his lime.

Eliana raised her shot glass with a bit of flourish, slammed it upside down onto the table, and said, eyes blazing, "I look forward to doing business with you."

"As do I with you, Eliana," Croce said. His wide-eyed bobbing head told her they were partners. She was sure he had never met a woman like her before.

Few had.

She had presented herself with the beauty and fierceness of a warrior queen. Her long black hair and eyes were so deep, Croce thought he might fall into them and forgo everything else just to spend a night ...

He stopped himself. She was a potential business partner and one of great value, not a contest or conquest. He had barely caught his breath from the tequila when she'd laid out her plan to become rich beyond the dreams of avarice as his partner. To corner the opium and heroin markets in Europe was his motivation for restarting *Unione Corsa*.

The tequila shot he'd downed had been his first of the disgusting liquor, and he was sure it would be his last. But to close a deal worth millions, he admitted he would have done just about anything. By the time Eliana had slammed down her glass, he already knew he would eagerly accept her offer.

Croce said, "Yes, I would like that indeed."

Eliana's satellite phone rang. She glanced at the number, excused herself, and moved toward the opposite corner of the room. About halfway there, she spun, a momentary blank look on her face. Croce watched as she recovered and came back to the table. She motioned to her security guard and stepped back as he laid his backpack on the table. Croce silently cursed for not having his men check the bag, but a glance showed Eliana was within the blast radius of any bomb. The guard opened the backpack, displaying the stacks of crisp American hundred-dollar bills. Croce started to speak, but Eliana cut him off.

"Please take this one hundred thousand dollars as a down payment on our partnership. A good-faith offering, if you will."

Croce was caught off-guard by the unexpected move and was rendered speechless. *For a captain of the drug industry,* Eliana thought, *he is too easily influenced by minor things. This will go well for me.*

Eliana looked down and laid a gentle hand on Croce's forearm, still buried in the backpack of money. "I must go. My people will be in touch." Eliana looked at him and smiled. "We'll find our own way out."

Croce nodded to his man anyway, who ran ahead of Eliana. He had a decanter of vintage Chateau Petrus brought to him and poured a glass, wanting to rid himself of the vile Tequila residue souring his mouth. *So much to do—close the deal with Herr Merck, and maybe they could take care of the jihadi problem.*

The Taliban attack on Merck and message to him had caused

lost sleep. Then there were the new contacts to be firmed up in New York City, another gold mine in the making. The Big Apple, as they called it, had an enormous appetite for heroin and Croce wanted to satisfy it. And now, his new partner.

I want it all, Croce thought with a smile. *I will have it all.*

Croce stood looking out over the harbor, the wisps of a plan coming into focus. Once Herr Merck was dispensed with, taking over his supply and routes would only be a matter of money. There were a few others who would have to be disposed of and others who would come along for the money, their loyalty to Merck nonexistent.

"The next few weeks will be very interesting," Croce whispered, and took a sip of his expensive wine.

Chapter 45

The following morning at the south Tampa holding site, Amaru checked Parker's pulse. It had been almost fourteen hours since he'd kidnapped her, and he had slept especially well knowing that Wolf probably didn't yet know his wife was missing.

The dart gun syringe had worked for two and a half hours. In that time—after multiple tries—he finally got a good stick with a third IV kit. He checked the flow for the first of the bags prepared for him to keep a subject of Parker's body weight just in twilight. He estimated he had maybe two hours until he would need to replace the sidecar bag.

Now it was time for the first call. Amaru was under no illusion there would be more than one. In this he had been trained, too. Wolf, or whoever would speak for him, would try to get extra time to negotiate. No extra time would be granted.

He remembered his stint working as the department's hostage negotiator, the playbook, and the exhilaration of bringing a bad situation to a peaceful close. Trained by the FBI and San Francisco Police Department, Amaru had been in line for a nice promotion out of uniform with the promise of a bright future until his daughter, Margaret, had come down with leukemia. Like many families do at such times, Amaru and his wife had learned the hard way just how much money specialty treatments cost over and above basic health care.

Without a thought, they burned through all the family savings and every penny their extended family could afford to gift. After a maddening time that saw Margaret's condition worsen in the very face of advanced treatments, the escalating pressure of epic doctor and hospital bills twisted his thinking and, desparate for help, he accepted his first bribe.

Amaru had felt guilty about that, briefly, but in his mind, the cause was just. The corruption soon escalated to overt acts on behalf of the cartel. He'd made a lot of money doing the cartel's dirty business—enough to take care of his daughter's medical bills, with plenty left over. But he'd been careless, and people noticed.

A smart detective and vicious prosecutor ended his law enforcement career. The memory of being arrested and getting the call on the same day that his daughter had died still blackened his soul. Instead of serving as cartel muscle working the edges of the San Francisco, he twisted in his darkness to killing, becoming one of El Gato's top assassins.

In his mind, the top.

Parker secured and stabilized, Amaru crossed the railroad tracks and took the car east to the first Lakeland exit heading south. He found a quiet spot and pulled over to make the call. He pushed number three for the preprogrammed speed dial and waited. The line picked up on the second ring.

"Tribal Police Department, how may I help you?" a desk

sergeant said.

"Put Wolf on the line," Amaru said.

"I'm sorry, but we don't have an Officer Wolf here. Are you sure you have the right number?"

"Yes. Check with Chief Hogan. Tell him it's Amaru."

The desk sergeant replied, "Hold, please."

It was long minutes before the line was picked back up.

"Amaru, I've been waiting for your call," Wolf said, straining to hold back his fury and indignation.

He knows, Amaru thought. "Wolf, my friend. You sound different on the phone. I think stressed is the best way to describe it."

Wolf did know. When Parker had missed a scheduled phone call, Wolf had local assets check on her. They found Maya Kennedy, Kieran Kennedy's wife, unconscious at the scene, and Parker missing, with signs of a struggle.

He wanted to scream in anger at the man but wouldn't give him the satisfaction. "Why don't you come back to Montana, and we can work this out man to man? Amateur move kidnapping my wife. I thought better of you. It's the same move that lost you your job and killed your innocent daughter. Now you've killed the rest of your family, too."

Busted. That was fast. Amaru realized what Wolf was doing. He took a deep breath and exhaled, centering himself. "Let's talk about stupid moves, and you trying to anger the man who has the fate of your wife in his hands." He paused to let that last part sink in. "Here is what you are going to do next. You are going to stop all police and civilian support operations on the Crow reservation and everywhere else in the state of Montana. When we can see you have followed my orders, I will release your wife unharmed." He paused long enough for the words to sink in. "But listen, are you good with puzzles? Because if you don't do as I ask, we will return her to you in pieces."

The rage and venom Wolf howled into the phone then were exactly what Amaru wanted. He held the phone away from his ear for a moment and smiled, then disconnected the call and pointed his vehicle back north. He drove with his knees as he took the battery out of the cellphone and tossed it into the ditch. A moment later, he did the same with the SIM card he had broken in two. Later, after repositioning the car, he would throw the rest of the burner phone into the backwater of Tampa Bay.

Amaru strode with a purpose into the holding site and came up short as he replayed what Wolf had said—Now you've killed the rest of your family, too.

The sudden urge to call his wife bloomed in him. Unable to make the call in order to maintain operational security, he cursed Lance Bear Wolf for putting the worry into his brain. His mind raced through the possibilities as he exhaled in frustration and whispered under his breath.

"Not possible. Only one man knows."

Chapter 46

At the reservation, Wolf relayed the Amaru conversation to Billy Red Fish and Chief Hogan. Both asked why Wolf was not already airborne.

"Look, guys, I appreciate the sentiment, but I can't just leave you without a plan or a way forward."

Hogan took Wolf by the shoulders. "Wolf, you have given us more than a plan—you have awakened the warrior in us, and you have trained us. Until you get back, we will defend our people. No interdiction operations."

Billy nodded grimly and said, "Go get your wife back, brother—and kill that asshole."

Less than thirty minutes later, a highway patrol helicopter touched down just long enough for Wolf to jump in before surging back into the sky, headed for Malmstrom AFB. The forty-five-minute flight permitted Wolf to use his satellite phone to check in with

LeBlanc and the team on their progress in locating Parker.

LeBlanc had no progress to relay other than his enlistment of the Tampa field offices of the FBI and the DEA, Tampa PD, and the Hillsborough County Sheriff's Office. To a person, everyone reached out to street assets and confidential informants and, in several cases, even deep-cover assets.

The deputy director of the FBI, who had tried to send Wolf to prison before the creation of Shadow Tier, was engaged personally, and added resources to the effort.

LeBlanc suggested calling out the Florida National Guard to invoke roadblocks and ID checks. Wolf thanked his friend, who he could sense was frustrated and wanted Parker back as badly as he did. But transforming Tampa into a police state would not help, he said, and in any case, it would be a tough sell to a governor who would likely and rightfully see it as a misuse of state resources to benefit an individual.

"It's simple," Wolf said. "Guaranteed Amaru has Elle at a secure location, with plenty of food and water to last the duration of the event, regardless of how he returns her. The only time he's going to leave is to frustrate geolocation while he make calls, and for that, I've gotten support from our signals intelligence friends. They are deploying as we speak. Keep pushing, brother. I'll be out of pocket in fifteen minutes until I land at MacDill in three hours."

"Wolf, you can't get from the middle of Montana to MacDill in three hours. You mean five, right?"

Wolf allowed himself a chuckle. "Fly high, brother—F-16D Fighting Falcon."

"You *are* the man. See you in three. Out here."

The pilot was briefed on the urgency of the flight and took the Fighting Falcon supersonic. He called up a tanker over Memphis to top off and then sprinted the final leg into MacDill AFB. The pilot got permission to taxi to the Shadow Tier facility ramp, where he was met by a ground crew used to servicing F-16s at the other end of the air base.

Wolf climbed down the ladder and shook hands with the pilot, letting him know his gratitude. He wormed out of the too-small flight suit and the ground crew took Wolf's flight gear as LeBlanc and Alpha Squadron surrounded their boss in a show of solidarity, shaking hands and slapping backs. There was still nothing new to report given the two hours and forty-two minutes elapsed since the last time Wolf and LeBlanc spoke. The teammates piled into a large white passenger van and hustled off to Shadow Tier headquarters. As Wolf entered, everyone stood.

Wolf took a moment to acknowledge them.

"Parker—ah, I mean, Elle and I appreciate every one of you. We will find her and bring her home. I know we can, I you know we will. Thank you all."

One of the whiz kids ran up with an excited look on his face. LeBlanc raised a hand and said, "Easy, kid, easy. Just tell us what you got."

"We know where Amaru called from! It was Lakeland. I alerted the FBI and the Lakeland PD and they're dispatching teams."

"Outstanding. Hook them into the ops center so we can get direct updates. That's where I'll be."

On the way to the operations center, Wolf asked about Maya Kennedy, Kieran Kennedy's wife. She had been at the house for dinner when Parker was abducted.

"She's torn," LeBlanc said, shrugging. "She feels like she should have been able to do more, even though she's not trained to do any-thing. And she feels a little guilty for being left alive when Elle was taken. She's sore from the punch to the jaw, and she's still nursing a headache from the knock-out drug she was administered."

"Anything psychotropic in the compound?"

"The doc didn't mention any. Why?"

"Ah, nothing."

A skilled interrogator with the right drugs could do a lot of damage, Wolf thought for a beat before being jerked back to the present.

An analyst called out and raised a telephone handset into the air. "I've got Tampa PD. They say they have a caller claiming to be Amaru and asking for Wolf."

Chapter 47

Thank you, Sheri," LeBlanc said. "Please route it to my station."

Wolf scanned the Shadow Tier operations center. All eyes were on him, such were the team's feelings for Parker. Wolf exhaled and punched the button connecting the call on speaker.

"Wolf here."

"Wolf? I didn't expect you back in Tampa so soon."

"I have resources you can't imagine. But that's not why we're talking. I'm off the reservation, and operations have stopped. Now keep your side of the deal and tell me where to find my wife."

"Slow down, Wolf. We have plenty of time. I need to check with my people to make sure it is as you say."

"Bullshit—'your people' have been watching the whole time. They saw me board the helicopter and fly out. They've seen Chief Hogan stand down. Tell me right now where I can find my wife."

"No-no-no. That will not do, Wolf. What's to keep you from

restarting operations the second I give your wife back? No, I think I will keep her a bit longer just to confirm that you're a man of your word. I understand your wife is an interesting, extraordinary woman, and I have yet to get to know her." He paused. "Oh, look at the time. It's time to wake her and—"

Wolf clenched the back of the chair he stood behind, his knuckles white, fingers tearing into the leather. In a voice laden with ferocity, he spoke evenly into the phone.

"Amaru, listen carefully. You have no idea what I am capable of in defense of my loved ones. Check in with the Sinaloa cartel. There are many there who wished they'd never crossed that line."

The call disconnected, a dial tone filling the dead air.

Wolf twisted around to LeBlanc, who was low-talking into his headset. LeBlanc looked up and nodded.

"Got him. The intercept teams have his position. FBI and Tampa PD are on the way," LeBlanc said, his excitement contagious.

"Okay, let's settle down and get back to work. Get the location added into PROVIDENCE and start crunching possible hide sites. We'll hear if they got him soon enough."

Wolf marched back to his office and was kitting up when LeBlanc knocked on the open door frame.

"You don't expect they'll catch him, do you?"

"I don't. He's too smart for that."

"What are you going to do?"

"Make him wish he'd never heard my name. I'm getting the FBI files on Amaru. Two can play this game, and I'm playing to win."

Chapter 48

Kennedy sat back in the midday sun as its rays warmed the sitting area of his Intercontinental Hotel suite. Puffy white clouds and blue sky made for a picturesque view over the harbor. While the view was nice, Kennedy admitted he was getting cabin fever. He had risen and was pacing the room when his radio crackled to life.

It had only been a couple days since the meeting with Jean Paul Croce, and now one of the Charlie Squadron members on duty in the hotel lobby radioed Jean Paul Croce's arrival. Croce had not called, and his presence could be for another meeting. But Kennedy changed clothes and put on his Herr Merck persona, just in case.

Kennedy alerted the rest of the team just before the house phone rang. It was the bellman asking if it was okay to send Monsieur Croce up. A minute later, the elevator door opened and Croce stepped out with his *consigliere* Lucien.

"No security, Jean Paul?" Kennedy asked in a curious tone.

"They are downstairs." He waved an index finger in the air. *Is the room clean? Can we talk?*

"Yes, nothing gets in or out without we know it."

"I expected nothing less. After the way you handled the *jihadis*, I feel more than safe in your company."

Kennedy said, "Please sit. What is the reason for your unexpected visit?"

"I have completed my checks, and you come with high recommendations. I would like us to start doing business together."

"Very well. Can you help us with our immediate needs?"

"Yes. I have recently acquired a transportation modality of the utmost integrity and reliability. Along with my ground logistics company, Janus Logistics, and this new air carrier, we can support your needs from the source to destinations throughout Europe and, shortly, even the United States."

"I know you have eyes-on in New York City. Of course, we will need to complete our own checks of your new air carrier, and I will pass on our findings for your review, not that I expect negative ones. What is the company name?"

Kennedy watched Croce stare out the window for a beat.

The money will override his security concerns, Kennedy thought.

Croce said, "Global Air Services. They have American government and United Nations contracts to fly supplies into and distribute them throughout Afghanistan. It gives them unfettered access where others cannot go. As an integrated solution, Global and Janus have the majority of the routes in and out of Afghanistan and Iraq covered."

"So, ground and air redundancy is the foundation of the reliability you speak of?"

"I knew you would understand the beauty of the arrangement."

Kennedy said, "All this planning is making me thirsty. May I offer you something to drink?" Kennedy/Merck gestured to the drink cart crowded with ornate bottles and decanters.

"I see you have a 1999-vintage Chateau Mouton Rothschild," Croche said with approval. "You are a man of exceedingly good taste, *monsieur*. Shall we try that?"

"Yes. I decanted it just yesterday." Kennedy checked his watch. "Thirty hours ago, which is almost perfect for this wine."

Kennedy filled a glass and passed it to Croce, and they both took their time to enjoy the complex mixture of aromas and a luxurious first taste of the world-class wine.

"Smoky notes over a refined berry richness. Excellent balance, with intense but lovely harmony," Kennedy said, suppressing a smirk. He'd practiced his wine banter, but in fact it was so out of his character that it was actually laughable. He changed the subject.

"What else can you tell me about Global Air Services. Evidently, you are highly impressed."

Croce savored a second sip of wine, his eyes closed as if listening to Beethoven. "Yes, I, uh ... I shouldn't say more, but you will know soon enough in any case."

He sipped the wine and closed his eyes, as much to pump up his nerve as to appreciate the vintage.

"Global Air Services is backed by the Sinaloa cartel, and my contact is a personification of beauty and grace, with a wild side like a warrior queen."

Kennedy stopped—breathing, movement, damned near his heartbeat. He willed himself to breathe, slowly and quietly, his brain raced. *The Sinaloa Cartel? 'Like a warrior queen'? It can't be.*

Can it?

Kennedy changed the subject. "So, where do you want us to deliver our product?"

"Lucien will give you the location and time."

Back to the present. Croce downed the rest of his glass. "This will be a profitable partnership." He rose from his seat and Lucien drifted toward the door. "Now, I must prepare to make us rich."

Lucien handed Taylor a slip of paper with a date, time, and address before nodding and opening the elevator doors. Croce entered and spun around with a flourish to bid Herr Merck good-bye. Kennedy caught Lucien's hard stare, which changed to a tight-lipped half-smile as the doors closed.

Kennedy and Taylor waited fifteen seconds to ensure the elevator was gone.

"A 'Sinaloa Cartel warrior queen' can only be one person," Kennedy said.

Taylor shook his head. "It probably cannot be Eliana unless she has El Chapo's approval. And we have no indications of his reaching out to Europe. He has the golden goose in America. It would cost more than he would profit."

"I agree. It doesn't make sense. But whoever it is, Croce is enamored to the point where he believes the magical thinking he has embraced."

Kennedy stood in silence, lost in his thoughts, when his wife's number was displayed on his satellite phone. He sat his wine down. Maya calling the sat phone number was an indicator of trouble.

"Maya. Are you okay, honey?"

"No—I'm not," she choked out between sobs. "I...I was beaten, and someone has kidnapped Elle Parker."

Chapter 49

Two up-armored Chevy Suburbans rolled to a stop, forming a protective barrier around the jet which had just taxied to a stop at the Textron Aviation Center side of Tampa International Airport. This permitted Eliana to deplane quickly and, in three steps, enter the back seat of the lead SUV. The *Tomador de Almas* nodded, and they were off to the safehouse. Eliana stared at her lead assassin for a beat.

"It has been a long time. You are well, *mi buen amigo?*"

"Si, *gracias,*" the Tomador said, nodding his head in respect.

Such a rare and valuable asset. Ten plus years of textbook exemplary service.

El *Tomador de Almas*—the Taker of Souls, as he was known throughout the Sinaloa and other cartels—was a second-generation assassin who had been taught since the age of six how to surveil and target the enemies of the Cortes family. He had taken his first life before becoming a teenager and had served House Cortes for the last ten years, first alongside his father and now solo.

Originally ordered by Eliana's brother to kill Wolf and those close to him, his orders had been changed to maim and hurt everyone in Wolf's circle, inflicting psychological and emotional damage as well as the physical. The campaign of terror was working until the American military had stepped in and saved Wolf by creating Shadow Tier.

After Wolf had saved Eliana and her unborn baby, she had been in his debt. They reinstalled her into the cartel for intel gathering. As part of her repayment, she had the Tomador stand watch over Wolf and Parker without their knowledge. Indeed, they would have demanded no such surveillance if they had known about it.

The Tomador had not stopped Parker's kidnapping, as he had ordered only to watch, not intervene. But he did report the incident, and now Eliana planned to use the event to pay back Wolf in an attempt break free.

Eliana asked, "What do we know?"

"Amaru is a member of *Puma Grande* and is El Chapo's top assassin. He failed to kill Wolf in a complex attack in Montana, ending with the death of his team. The kidnapping was in response to Wolf's creation of what the reservation police chief calls a civil support team. Their first interdiction took a heroin shipment worth over two million. The most recent arrests, while you were en route to your meeting, was twenty-six million."

"So, this Amaru has kidnapped Parker to stop Wolf's operations on the reservation? Can he be that stupid?"

"Yes. His personal feelings about Wolf aside, he appears to be acting on the orders of El Chapo."

"El Chapo has a fascination with Indian reservations," Eliana said. "The kidnapping must have been at El Chapo's direction. Otherwise, he would be waving his gold Beretta in my face."

Eliana gazed out the window in thought and then back at her pet assassin. "Do you know where this Amaru is now?"

"Not yet. But I have indications the LA Kings gave him support."

Eliana cursed for minutes in Spanish and English. When satisfied, she said, "Those idiots are harbingers of the apocalypse. Stupid on a biblical level. You remember what happened when they tried to assassinate Wolf and Parker last time?"

"Yes. They all died. In this case, I think the Kings involvement was for the use of a safehouse. They don't appear to be involved in the kidnapping or holding of Parker. I will know more within the hour. After we get you secured, I will meet a contact who will provide more information."

Eliana nodded and spent the rest of the ride in silence, working out how she could turn this shit show into a positive result that would finally free her from her obligation to Wolf.

In metro traffic it took longer than the Tomador had said, but they were on their way to the safehouse the LA Kings had provided to Amaru. Eliana's team came in from the west and dropped off men to block any escape attempts, and she ordered them to close in on the east entrance to the safehouse.

The SUV with Eliana and the Tomador jumped the curb and slid into the safehouse driveway. The other blocked the entrance and deployed men on the north and south sides. A quick radio check by Eliana, and she was out and moving, the Tomador trying to keep pace and provide backup to his aggressive boss.

Eliana led the team as they cleared the house and garage in what a military onlooker would have called efficient. The only sound during the six minutes it took to ensure the safehouse was empty was *clear*.

Eliana gathered everyone in the garage and sent half of the team back to her safehouse in Parkland Estates. She traced a path around the garage and cursed. The implements of pain and death in the garage gleamed under the fluorescent lights. The stifling fumes from the acid tanks in the closed space screwed up her face in protest and finally drove them all from the building.

"Search this place like a crime scene," Eliana ordered. "Unless he is very good and changed his clothes and shoes before coming back from the location where he has Parker, there is evidence here that will lead us to him. Find out who we can leverage from the police department for some help processing this dump."

"Should we call this place in, get the police to do our work?" Tomador asked. He gestured to the closed front door of the garage.

"No. I must be the one to hand him to Wolf—and to save Wolf's wife. So, find Amaru for me!"

Chapter 50

At his desk in the Shadow Tier headquarters, Wolf had to look up the number before he dialed it. His Secure Terminal Unit phone encryption synced with the distant unit and the call was picked up.

"Deputy Director Andrew Stockwell," the voice said.

"That has a nice ivory tower ring to it."

"Not sleeping much, are you, Wolf?"

"You can hardly blame me."

Wolf hadn't left the building nor slept at all in the last thirty-six hours. Despite his focus on finding some new angle to move along the hunt for his wife, Wolf, a loner by nature, had finally decided to reach out for help. Gallows humor did nothing for the pain, the feeling of helplessness Wolf hid from the team.

"Any changes in the search for Elle?" Stockwell asked.

"No, but this morning it came to me that maybe we can leverage Amaru through his family. Does the FBI have a file on him?"

"Yes. We've been on *Puma Grande* since its beginning, but this Amaru guy has been under the radar. We know he exists, but they use low-level guys to take his heat, even protecting him to the point of admitting to crimes we believe he committed. I suspect a deeper connection between Amaru and his boss than we know."

"Can you send me the *Puma Grande* file?"

"I'll have copies couriered down to MacDill this morning. And, I'll have the section chief coordinate a data dump through your team so your analytics team can have at it. Anything else?"

"We don't have time for a courier. Can you secure-fax me the file? And who should I call in the San Francisco field office if we want more background?"

"Sure, yes. I'll have the file faxed over. Agents Castro and Lopez are the best bet. I can send them your way if it helps."

Wolf considered the offer for a moment, pondering the value of having them at Shadow Tier HQ versus the problems it might cause if Wolf had to step outside of law enforcement guardrails to get his wife back.

I will do anything to save her. The law doesn't play a part in it.

Wolf declined the manpower offer. "Thanks, but phone availability works for now."

"Roger that. Now, if you don't mind, I'm getting some coffee. It's going to be a long day."

"Thanks, brother, I owe you." Wolf set his handset back in the cradle.

The simple act of doing, getting another line of possibilities working, gave Wolf enough relief to finally take a quick nap before hitting the obstacle course Morgan had built patterned after the "Nasty Nick" course at Fort Bragg.

Better at burning out negative thoughts and energy than a run or weights session, the course challenged Wolf and he ran it three times to work up a sweat. The third had brought an internal voice telling him he'd done enough.

He'd heard the voice before, at Ranger School and Special Forces selection. He'd also heard the voice when the FBI had investigated him after corrupt Mexican government officials had labeled him a terrorist. In that time, the Tomador had just missed killing Parker, his finances had been frozen, and he was mentally stuck, not seeing a way out of that predicament.

Wolf pushed forward knowing that doing something positive was all that mattered. He believed a positive attitude led to positive thinking, which led to creativity and new ways to solve problems. While briefly dipping into the darkness of self-pity was to be expected, Wolf quickly vanquished the thoughts and drove on, always striving to move forward to solve the problem.

After a shower and change of clothes, Wolf's rejuvenated body fed extra oxygen to his brain, and he began anew. He was in his office when LeBlanc swung by.

"You're looking bright and ready to go," LeBlanc said. "Did you go home last night?"

"Not yet. I've been working some different angles. PT the team and see me when you're done. I've got a feeling we are going to be busy today."

Chapter 51

The excitement of new data and new taskings filled the air as the whiz kids and Alpha Squadron huddled around the long table in the conference room.

Wolf said, "While we work every angle to find Parker, here is what I need from you. Make a deep dive into the data the FBI has sent us. Look for anything we can leverage via the boss of *Puma Grande* and Amaru himself. The littlest thing could be the key to recovering Parker. Kennedy and the Kid are ready to help from Germany. I want an initial report in two hours; sooner if you find something. Let's go."

While the whiz kids, Kennedy, and the Kid did their magic with PROVIDENCE, Wolf took an approach more suited to his visualization method of data ingest. He called LeBlanc into his office, where printouts, photos, tape, staples, and magnets were his workmates on the walls.

"Impressive," LeBlanc said.

Wolf returned a grim smile. "Take some time, look this over, and tell me where you see any weakness we can leverage."

He sat back in his chair and closed his eyes while LeBlanc paced the room, stopping at a few places and then backtracking.

LeBlanc said, "Do you want a good-cop answer or a cartel-type answer."

"Both."

"Good cop, we bring the *Puma Grande* leader in, this El Gato guy, and tell him we will make his life a holy hell by targeting him and his organization. We tell him to call El Chapo for a recommendation as to our intent and seriousness."

"I like it, but El Gato really has no incentive to give up his guy, this Amaru. And?"

LeBlanc tapped a picture of a young girl. "The cartel answer: We take one or more of his kids and tell him they come back when Parker is released unharmed."

"Take them into protective custody, you mean. For their own good."

LeBlanc said, "Uhm, sure. That. But this option could spiral out of control. And there's no telling what rival factions or even Mr. Murphy might do to take advantage of the situation at any point in the program." He crossed his arms and was lost in thought for a moment. "We could focus Amaru's family. We know he has one, and it has a troubled past we could leverage. It would require a lot more work and time to locate and assess them, though. Time we don't have."

Wolf understood the hesitation. LeBlanc stared at the floor for another few seconds. When he looked up and met Wolf's eyes, he had his war face on. He tapped on the picture again.

"Just my two cents, boss, but we need to make life more interesting for El Gato right now."

Wolf stared into the distance. *I've been down this road, shrouded in darkness. Lost myself last time. Can I let my monster loose and still be myself when it's over?*

A knock on the door brought Wolf present.

Ryan, one of the whiz kids, stood outside looking embarrassed, thinking he had interrupted an important conversation.

"What do you have, Ryan?" Wolf asked.

The poor kid was used to working in isolation behind a SCIF door, not talking to his bosses. He had managers for that.

Ryan stammered, "They told me to tell you we, ahhh, we loaded the FBI's phone records into PROVIDENCE and got some interesting results."

"That's great news. Come on in and tell us about them." Wolf moved around his desk to usher Ryan in before closing the door.

LeBlanc offered him a chair, and the three of them sat around the side table.

Wolf nodded and Ryan said, "We isolated El Gato's calls, which originate in San Francisco and terminate out of state. There has been a high volume of calls to Billings, Montana. Peak times and volume coincide with your travel, Mr. Wolf."

"Just call me Wolf."

"Yes, sir—I mean, Wolf. There are a few calls to Culiacán, Mexico, and four calls to different tribal-operated casino operations, highlighted here," Ryan said, pointing to his report. "He, he is very predictable when calling twice a week to this number—" He traced a finger across a line item on the print-out that was highlighted in bright yellow. "—at a retirement community outside Tucson, Arizona."

He moved to another line highlighted in green.

"And this number in Winter Park."

Wolf furrowed his brow. It didn't make sense. "So, he calls two different retirement communities twice a week?"

"No. The Winter Park number shows up as a condo next to Rollins College."

Wolf said to LeBlanc, "Rollins is an exclusive private college. Can we be so lucky?"

LeBlanc tilted his head. "I'll take lucky," he said. They both had the same thought: El Gato's oldest kid was in the open.

Wolf stood and Ryan and LeBlanc followed. Wolf shook Ryan's hand and, with an arm around his shoulder, led him to the door.

"Excellent work, Ryan. Really good, and we're grateful for it. You may be on the verge of breaking the hunt for Parker wide open. Now get me everything you can on who owns the condo, who is living there, the works. Thank you."

Ryan left, beaming under the praise from the Shadow Tier's leader. Wolf said to LeBlanc, "Spin up your team, brother. We're going to Winter Park."

Fifteen minutes later, Wolf joined Alpha Squadron as they kitted up. While Alpha gave off a visceral feel that they were ready for war, Wolf decided on a low-viz option. He wanted to look like just another middle-aged professor going about his business. But Wolf still slipped on the new lightweight jell body armor Shadow Tier had recently received from a DARPA program.

The program was the work of a small skunk-works body armor shop run in a drafty warehouse by two guys with a coffee pot. Chemical engineers by trade, they had produced a ballistic jell that really did not like fast things like bullets attempting to disrupt its natural state.

In a reaction that Wolf still did not understand, the jell would absorb a bullet, initially slowing it down, and in nanoseconds, transform into a solid, capturing the bullet and transferring its energy across a broad area as heat.

The body armor fit easily under the light blue polo Wolf wore with his khaki pants, looking more like a professor at a community college than a warrior. The team kidded their boss about wanting to take his college classes for an easy A. Wolf appreciated the humor—but it did nothing to keep the darkness at bay.

"On me," Wolf said, standing before a map spread out across a workbench. Alpha clustered around him. "I'm concerned my personal connection to this op might compromise my ability to lead the recovery of Parker ... my wife. As your commander, I want to deny it's even possible, but in truth, I can hardly see for the darkness that consumes me."

He stepped away the front of the group and slowly worked his way through the team to the rear. Wolf saw and sensed his teammates' concern and support. Nods and fist bumps came his way.

LeBlanc spoke for the team. "You got this, Wolf—and we got you." He clapped his hands twice. "Okay, let's get started."

LeBlanc tossed a packet of pictures on the map table. El Gato's daughter was a striking twenty-one-year-old female with long brunette hair and look-right-through-your-soul brown and gold eyes. She was a Rollins junior and marketing major. Slender and athletic at five-ten, she could be any one of young black-legging-clad students on campus.

"So, we're heading out with limited target info into a definitively tough terrain—a college bursting with students all over the place. The whiz kids will update us before we get to our staging area, here. Big trucks and SUVs with blacked-out windows are as fashionable at Rollins as BMWs and Audis, so you don't have to worry about looking out of place. Wolf and I will execute the close-in surveillance, and if we have time to make entry, we will. I want this low-viz and quiet. No one needs to die today. If your life or the high-value individual is in jeopardy, we will disengage and withdraw."

Chapter 52

Eliana had been right. The crime scene tech they'd found discovered drops of machine oil and rust with traces of salt. There were also fingerprints that the tech couldn't find in police or FBI databases. The tech said test results suggested areas of industrial and abandoned buildings around Tampa's Ybor Channel, adding the location might have something to do with heavy equipment. Hence the oil and rusted steel.

Unknowable to Eliana, her team had crossed under I-4 to start their search on the waterfront just as Wolf and Alpha raced east above them on I-4 to Winter Park. Eliana set up a base of operations in a former auto repair shop at the corner of Adamo Drive and North 19th Street. Reluctant to import the LA Kings gangsters for help, Eliana enlisted area locals, enticing them to talk with fifty and one-hundred-dollar bills.

Two hours later they had six locations and three odd sightings to work through. Eliana and her security lead took a beat-up old

Honda Civic and scouted the sightings from south to north, while the Tomador took the body shop pickup and started checking sightings from east to west.

The first was a car no one had seen before parked under the Crosstown Expressway. Eliana and her security lead moved into the area from three blocks out. She had disguised herself with 5.11 cargo pants, Salomon boots, a polo shirt, and a ball cap. Her Ray-Ban aviators and confident walk were easily mistaken for another female contractor from MacDill AFB.

Her security lead advanced across the railroad tracks, staying well away from the tracks he was following. He pointed to the fence and made a cutting motion with his fingers, then stepped away and rejoined Eliana.

The guy whispered, "Someone has cut the fence and staged the car for exfil."

"Did you see anything useful in or around the building?"

"No, but we should look from the other side. Someone could be using the building for a lab or headquarters."

Father said you don't leave fish to find fish, Eliana thought.

"Let's pull back," Eliana said, pulling a map and her cellphone from a thigh pocket.

She called the Tomador, who he said had just finished up clearing the second location.

"I'm sending you the cross streets, meet me at my location."

"On my way. Ten minutes," Tomador said.

Eight minutes later, Eliana nearly jumped out of her skin when the Tomador appeared out of nowhere beside her. She shook her head and poked him in his massive chest.

"Must you do that?" she whispered in anger. "One day you will startle me and you'll get shot." She pointed through the chain-link fence. "See all the rusting steel? The chain link has been cut, and the car to our right, over there in the shadows, appears to be set as a backup getaway."

"Agreed," the Tomador said. "Have you been to the front of the business? Any sounds coming from the building?"

"No. Without knowing what's inside, how many men do you need to assault?"

"I think two back here to stop any runners," Tomador said, then pointed left. "I will provide overwatch from atop that building while you and another seven enter through the front. We should check with the Kings first to see if this is their operation."

"This is one time they might be useful. Call your contact. If it's not their operation, we leave two here. You go high."

They can die for their stupid transgression, Eliana thought.

A four-minute call confirmed it was not an LA Kings operation. The Tomador decided help from the Kings was smart anyway, and a gangster enforcement team was on the way, its cost forty-five thousand dollars. Five thousand for each shooter and ten grand for the contacts facilitation fee. Eliana was surprised when they said they could be on site in twenty-five minutes or less.

Eliana took the Civic around to the front of the building, where she parked just out of the line of sight. She scanned the area around the building, finding no cameras, and crept over to where she could see the front of the building. She saw the briefest flash of movement as the rear security faded into the shadows. She moved back to the Civic and leaned against the car to wait for backup from the Kings.

Two black Ford Expeditions with yellow pin stripes, blacked out windows, and oversized spinner wheels rolled up, and seven men exited. Their leader slid up next to Eliana when she waved.

"Who are you? Where is the Tomador?"

"He is here. I am Eliana Cortes—ah, yes, I see you know the name. I learned to shoot, field strip, and clean an AK at six. Give me a rifle before there are only five of you."

The leader slowly handed Eliana his AK, and his men lowered theirs. "Do you have another to use?" Eliana asked.

The Kingsman said, "Yes, TEC-9. Fully automatic. Unbeatable for close-in work."

"Good. Take this back and get me one of your TEC-9s."

The leader nodded, and one of his men retrieved the weapon and four extra magazines for Eliana.

"Here is the plan. Just beyond our line of sight is an old foundry and machine shop. We are going to assault through the front. I have two men out back, and the Tomador is in position on a nearby rooftop, but he can't see into the building. We believe there are only two people in the building, a hostile, and the woman he kidnapped. The hostile is not the primary mission. If you safely exfil the woman, there is a five-thousand-dollar bonus for each of you."

The Kings nodded their understanding.

"I am not sure how the building is laid out, but expect offices up front with the machine shop and foundry out back. We have to move fast, or he may try to kill the woman."

She looked around at the faces for understanding.

"Good to go?"

The Kings nodded and the leader said, "Si, *comandante!*"

Eliana smiled in approval. "Okay, gear check." Eliana gawked when the men didn't move.

Amateurs, she thought, wishing for one of her German or Israeli-trained teams. She proceeded to walk them through a thorough weapons check and hit the speed dial on her cellphone for the Tomador. "We go in three."

She dropped the call and stuffed the phone into her cargo pocket. She held up three fingers and counted down. "Three–two–one. Go, *go, go.*"

She followed behind the men as they closed on the front of the building, moving in a semi-tactical formation. At the front door, one of the men used his AK buttstock to break the glass, reach through the gap and open the door. The Kings broke into two-man teams and started clearing rooms quickly and efficiently. Just as a door was opening to another hallway, an explosion tore the door off its hinges. Before the smoke cleared, one of the Kings started shooting blindly through the gap.

Eliana yelled for him to stop shooting over the din of the full-auto AK-74, and when he didn't, she shot him in the back of the head. He dropped and Eliana cleared the last room herself.

She cursed the unreliable Kingsmen and wished she hadn't mentioned the bonus. She cleared the room and, in a tactical crouch, moved past the dead gangster and back into the hallway. Bullets zinged over her head as she dove into a break area for cover. The sound differed from the AKs, reminding her of the M4s Wolf liked to use.

There was more gunfire in the building but not directed her way. The Kings were yelling to each other in Spanish to coordinate their moves. A King screamed at being shot, then went silent. Another minute of relative quiet was followed by another large explosion. The King's leader called out and got no response.

Eliana switched out her partially used magazine for a fresh one and dropped the bolt to ready the weapon. She was moving forward when she saw the muzzle flash of an AK on full auto. The Kings leader was running toward the machine shop, rifle blazing away. *The idiot is going kill Parker.* Before Eliana could react, shots rang out again from the mystery rifle and the AK went silent.

She crouched and snuck a peek around the door frame to find the King's leader's body crashed against a wall and slowly sliding to the floor, leaving a streaky bloodstain behind. Eliana thought she heard someone running, then the report of a large-caliber rifle quickly followed by another shot. She kept moving forward, careful to scan for tripwires and booby traps. There were more shots from out back, then the squeal of tires.

Eliana inhaled a deep breath and swung in, kneeling to stay low. As she swept the room, her muzzle crossed over the chair where Parker sat. She finished clearing the room and closed the door behind her before moving to check Parker. She was unconscious but unharmed. Eliana wasn't sure how Parker had remained unscathed, considering all the uncontrolled shooting by the idiot LA King gangsters.

A side door creaked and Eliana stepped in front of Parker, her weapon pointed forward and ready.

"Black!" she said loudly.

"Stallion," the voice replied.

The Tomador opened the door, and Eliana set the TEC-9 down to cut Parker's restraints. She went to the table where the drugs were kept but could identify nothing to help Parker.

The Tomador said, "I hit Amaru and knocked him down, but the shot did not kill him. With your permission, I will dispose of the men who died."

"Okay. I will let Wolf know where to find his woman and meet you at the plane."

Fifteen minutes later, Eliana stood toe-to-toe with two Shadow Tier operators. The Tomador was at her side as she briefed them on what had occurred and the safehouse Amaru had used. She also mentioned the safehouse might include a clue to what drug had been used to sedate Parker.

"Tell Wolf he *owes* me," Eliana said before she and the Tomador drove away.

At her plane, she strapped in for takeoff, satisfied knowing she had just taken another important step on the road to freedom. Her mind switched back to the French playboy who thought he was God's Gift, and the Germans who supposedly had direct access to Afghanistan's richest crop. In her mind, all the pieces were falling in place.

She didn't know they weren't going to fall into the places she wanted.

Chapter 53

The Winter Park condo was outwardly indistinguishable from any of the dozens of others. Its recessed entrance doorway provided a little concealment for Wolf and LeBlanc, and relief from the midday sun that felt millions of miles closer. Wolf's shirt was wet seconds after they had left the Suburban, combining the heat and stress he felt.

His cellphone vibrated but Wolf let the call go unanswered, focusing on the door lock he was picking. The simple construction-grade lock slipped easily and he and LeBlanc stepped inside the condo, listening for any movement by an occupant. His cell started vibrating against his leg and again he let it go.

He hand signaled to start clearing the rooms when his cell buzzed a unique vibration indicating a text message. Irritated, he motioned to LeBlanc to hold. He pulled the phone from his back pocket and stopped breathing.

The text from Eliana Cortes said I have your wife & she is safe.

Wolf made a cutting motion across his throat and held the phone for LeBlanc to see. LeBlanc nodded and placed a small black box on the kitchen countertop. They left hurriedly, relocking the door behind them. Clear of the target location, Wolf radioed the team to close on the rally point. Then he listened to his voicemail. Surprised to hear her voice, Wolf relayed the location and told the drivers to hit the emergency lights as they raced back to Tampa.

Wolf spun in his seat and said, "LeBlanc, who's at headquarters that we can send right now?"

"LaMorte, our EOD team leader, and Doc Wilson, our surgeon."

Wolf said, "Both are SF and solid with a rifle—they can be there in fifteen minutes. Send them, we still have forty until we reach the location."

Wolf called Steve Gates, the Shadow Tier JAG. In the heat of the moment, he had forgotten Gates was a combat-tabbed Ranger.

"Steve, yeah, it's me. We have a lead on Elle. No, it's a location in Tampa. We're on our way via ground, but I need you to kit up and go with LaMorte and Doc Wilson to respond and secure her right now. Yes, Tampa SWAT is a good idea, but don't let them keep you from entry as soon as you get to the site. Eliana—yes, *our* Eliana— says the site is clear of hostiles, but watch out for booby traps. Call me back with a SITREP as soon as possible."

Thirty-five minutes later, the convoy with Wolf and Alpha was still minutes away when Gates's text rang in to Wolf's work cell. The SITREP was simple and profound. *Parker was drugged but unharmed, now lucid & stable. Doc says she'll be okay.*

When the Shadow Tier teammates pulled into the parking lot, Wolf jumped out of the Suburban while it was still moving. He sprinted to the ambulance where his wife was being lifted in.

Doc Wilson said, "Give him a second," to the ambulance crew.

"She is twilight sedated, Wolf," Doc Wilson said. "It's possible she can hear you but probably can't respond coherently."

Wolf took Parker's hand and leaned in to kiss her forehead. He turned to whisper in her ear.

"It's me, honey. You're safe now."

She didn't respond, but Wolf thought perhaps he'd felt Parker offer a weak squeeze of his hand. Or maybe he'd just imagined it in his despair.

He saw the bandages around her wrists and ankles. She had fought hard at some point. The rage boiled up in Wolf again at the injustice and he resolved all over again to find Amaru and make him pay. Dearly.

"Wolf," Doc Wilson said, "we gotta go, boss. I need to get her cleaned up, treat her wounds, and get some IV antibiotics on board."

Wolf nodded and stepped back.

"Thanks, Doc," Wolf said, gripping the man's hand. "Take care of my girl, okay?"

"I'm on it, brother," Doc Wilson said. He handed off his M4 rifle to LeBlanc and hopped up into the back of the ambulance. The doors closed, and the lights and siren ignited as it headed out hot for Tampa General.

Wolf turned to find Gates and LaMorte. He shook hands and backslapped them. "I can't thank you guys enough."

LaMorte said, "Anything for a teammate."

Gates placed his hand on Wolf's forearm and said, "We need to talk."

"Of course." Wolf nodded and asked LeBlanc to join them. They stepped to the grimy concrete seawall as LaMorte led the Tampa EOD and police crime scene teams into the building.

Gates said, "I had a five-minute data dump from Eliana when I got here."

Wolf interrupted. "She stayed on site to talk with you?"

"Yeah—she led us in, around the booby traps and dead bodies. There was one other guy with her. He wore a mask and carried an H&K PSG-1. Scary, lifeless eyes. He said he thinks he shot Amaru and knocked him down but didn't kill him. She also said the LA Kings rented Amaru a safehouse up by USF. I sent Tampa PD the location."

He leaned against the sea wall.

"The Kings thought it was El Chapo asking for assistance so they complied, but they claimed they didn't know what for. Eliana had gotten word Parker had been taken and started her own hunt, finding evidence at the safehouse pointing to this area. A few thousand bucks of enticement and the normally closed-mouthed people who live around here gave her some leads. Her surveillance found physical evidence of coming and going, so Eliana hired a Kings hit squad and assaulted the place. All the onsite dead are Kings—booby traps tore them up badly."

"I don't mind that so much," Wolf said with a grim smile.

"Right? By the way, LaMorte must have some Indian in him, too. He tracked what we believe was Amaru's path as he ran away. Looks like the lucky bastard tripped over some rusty pipe and rebar. He left a big chunk of his shin that I imagine the police can process for DNA, and there is a good blood trail heading through the fence and across the railroad tracks to a prepositioned bug-out car. Anyway, tripping evidently saved him from catching the sniper's bullet, though the sniper tried. Sniper says he also put a couple of rounds in the car."

Wolf shook his head. He wanted to say, *Gates, you were just feet away from El Tomador de Almas, the Taker of Souls. The guy who killed your father and nearly took Parker and Maya from us.*

LeBlanc said, "So how does Eliana 'get word' of Parker's kidnapping? Does she have you guys under surveillance, Wolf?"

Glad for the distraction, Wolf said, "Good question, and why help? What does she want?"

"Easy. She wants to pay you back for saving her and her unborn child. And she wants her freedom," LeBlanc offered.

"If I were the paranoid kind, I'd also wonder if she manufactured the kidnapping for this exact purpose," Gates said.

Wolf made a skeptical face. "Maybe. I guess it's possible. We know Eliana doesn't do anything out of the kindness of her heart. She always has a motive and will play the long game when it aligns with the outcome she is seeking. The question, gentlemen, is what the hell is she trying to do?"

Chapter 54

After the unannounced visit by Croce, Kennedy ordered the team back to their headquarters in Kaiserslautern, Germany. He had gotten word of Parker's kidnapping. Kennedy and the Kid had spent thirty hours nonstop on a open line with the whiz kids as they crunched data in the hunt for her.

As happy as they were at Parker's recovery, Kennedy had told Wolf it concerned him that the rescue had been Eliana's initiative. Kennedy relayed the story Croce had told him about meeting a potential partner with the point-of-origin access to Afghanistan opium processing locations, that the female contact carried herself as if a warrior queen. That she claimed operational connection to the Sinaloa cartel had thrown them for a loop.

Taylor made use of the Taliban attack after-action report to put a fine edge on Charlie Squadron. They had come together in an extreme situation, proving their combat effectiveness. Taylor told

Kennedy he was going to run a couple of days of scenario training focused on soft skills, intelligence collection, and gray-man tactics.

Somehow the Kid had found time to research other German drug cartels and gangs connections they could use to make to bolster their story with Croce and against any probing by the new partner.

The briefing he gave was based on all source intelligence that the Kid, an analyst from the JNAC, and PROVIDENCE had created. Number one on his list was the new incarnation of the 36 Boys. Originally, the 36 Boys, mostly of Turkish descent, had run themselves like an American mafia. They ran drugs, prostitution, marijuana, and cocaine. They had broken up in the late Nineties, but an element remained. And like the resurgence of the *Unione Corsa* in Marseille—who thought of themselves as the new French Connection—this new crew called themselves the 63 Boys. So much for originality.

Next on the list was the Temmo family. Notorious for their gold and valuable jewels heists, they also owned most of the cocaine and heroin business in Berlin. Their reach stretched east to Poland and south to the Czech Republic.

The final name on the German list was the Siris family, who focused on drug trafficking, extortion, prostitution, and had a working connection to the European branch of the Mongols Motorcycle Club. They worked the port areas around Bremerhaven and Hamburg and were distributing into the UK and Ireland.

The plan put forward by the Kid was to contact all three and push the quality of product from the Angel cartel lab, just small amounts to seed their curiosity and build the backstory.

Tagged products could be tracked to gain an understanding of their paths to market and the people involved, who then, at the right time, would be handed over to the German police. Kennedy approved the basic plan and told the Kid to coordinate with Taylor for the resources and detailed planning around each connection.

After lunch, Kennedy called Clinton to brief him on an idea he called Project Joshua. The short version was to put Croce's ground and new air assets to a test. As the partnership was new, each package would be escorted by one of Kennedy/Merck's Afghanistan-based men. Ten kilos each, twenty-two pounds of morphine base ready for lab processing into street-level heroin cut with the buyer's dilutant of choice.

As previously agreed, Clinton assigned JNAC's Lancaster the role of Pakistani middleman. His story was that direct contact with the Taliban was too risky; Herr Merck had lost good men learning the hard way, the story held.

Jeff Nash, the team's British demo/blaster, would provide security for the air route, and Ernst Mallard, the team's French medic, for the land route. The air route would take hours and the ground route four to five days.

The critical part of the ground crossing would be the transit of Iran versus the traditional route around Iran, through Turkmenistan and across the Caspian Sea.

Mallard's excellent command of the Persian language was the deciding factor. They'd go out of Afghanistan to Mashhad Iran, then around Tehran north to the Turkish border south of Armenia. Once in Turkey and relative safety, the rest of the trip would pretty boring, by comparison, as they crossed the Bosporus at Istanbul on their way up the eastern Adriatic to the top of Italy and into Marseilles.

With Clinton and Bravo team read in, Kennedy grabbed one of the burner cellphones and dialed Croce. He picked up on the second ring.

"It is time to test your logistics capabilities, Mister Janus,"

Kennedy/Merck said, using the agreed-upon codename for Croce.

"Yes, I am ready."

"Both ground and air options."

"Yes. It will cost you three hundred thousand dollars for the test, and you can transport up to thirty kilos on either route."

"No, no, this is too much, Jean Paul. I will pay one hundred fifty thousand, an appropriate percentage for unprocessed product."

"Two hundred thousand, and we are ready when you are."

Kennedy paused for a moment, doing the math. "This is a deal. Where do we meet your teams?"

"I will have Lucien send the date, time, and coordinates within the hour."

"Excellent. To a successful test."

"Herr Merck, here is to a profitable partnership. I know the test will be successful."

Chapter 55

This time at the hospital, Elle didn't look like a sci-fi movie science project. The doctor had employed a single IV and a pulse ox monitor, which stood in stark contrast to the machines and devices at work the last time she had been at Tampa General fighting for her life.

Severely dehydrated and sore from fighting against Amaru's restraints, Parker rested peacefully while Wolf gazed at her.

Wolf was still amazed she had chosen a life with him. He wasn't sure he would have made the same choice if their positions were reversed. She had lost her career as an Army officer; gained a new one; been shot by an assassin sniper; supported his and Shadow Tier's growth into a top tier unit; survived an attack on the reservation; and now had been kidnapped and drugged as part of a scheme to stop Wolf from executing Shadow Tier's charter. Any one of those would be enough for a woman with an inkling of self-preservation to throw in the towel.

Why is she still with me?

Wolf's cell buzzed. He checked the Caller ID and left the room, touching Accept.

"Herr Merck, what's the good word?"

"How is she, brother?"

"Good. She's cleaned up and sleeping. They've got fluids and nutrients on board. The last of the drugs are out of her system."

"Any long-term effects?"

"Unknown."

"Got time for a quick SITREP?"

Wolf took a seat in the hallway. "Yes, of course. Go."

"We're expanding our German cartel footprint. The rest of the backstory is complete. The agency analysts have asked to stay on; they like the action and per diem with hazard pay. Project Joshua is a day or two from kick-off, and Croce is coordinating the link-up locations. We've crafted up fake morphine blocks with embedded slices of the real product in case we need to prove its authenticity. Clinton's guys are ready to go. It's going to be interesting to see whether our UN target is involved, and how much."

"Sounds like you're moving forward," Wolf said. "Keep an eye out for Taliban surveillance. After you crushed them during their attempted hit, they're going to try to locate you and finish what they started. As for the lady doc from the UN, that still baffles me. Why risk the bad press, potential loss of donors—and jail time?"

"It could be she's just open to taking money wherever it comes from to improve the lives of the people she cares about. But let's explore that another time," Kennedy said. He paused and fidgeted, like he often did before broaching a tough subject. "I need to switch topics while I have you."

"Talk to me, brother," Wolf said.

"I have read the SITREP from Gates. I need you to tell me he was not feet away from the Tomador. Tell me we did not have armed Shadow Tier troopers within feet of the guy *who tried to kill our wives*," Kennedy said, just short of shouting.

Wolf felt Kennedy's pain and frustration. "I can't, brother. And I didn't bring it up with Gates as nothing good would come from it. Imagine finding out you were feet from your father's killer, and you didn't shoot him in the face. No, my questions are, why did Eliana bring the Tomador to Tampa to help with the rescue, and why did Eliana go against the cartel? Morgan thinks it's to pay us back and stop being our informant."

"I don't care about that! Tell me we'll get another chance at him," Kennedy said, the pleading coming through loud and clear.

"Hell, yes. Count on it," Wolf said with authority he didn't feel.

Kennedy said, "And Morgan is probably right, too. Eliana has wanted to get out from under our deal the moment her son was born. Other questions to add to the growing pile are, was the Tomador already in Tampa, and how did Eliana know Parker was kidnapped? I suspect something more than she's telling is going on. When Croce described his new partner as a 'warrior queen' and connected to the Sinaloa cartel, she's the only person I thought of."

Wolf saw a nurse and doctor enter Parker's room. "Okay, gotta go, doc's here. Let me know when Joshua gets underway. Thanks, bro. Out here." He disconnected the call.

Wolf entered the room to see the doctor stimulating Parker to wake up, and she was groggy. She motioned to the nurse and croaked out, "Water, please."

She closed her eyes and drank hungrily from the bendy straw, and Wolf heard a moan of what he recognized as satisfaction. She raised a hand at him and he took it.

"We got to quit meeting like this," she whispered.

The doctor said, "Okay, Ms. Parker. Let's do a couple of quick checks, and then I'll get out of your way." He examined her and, after looking at the bandages, asked the nurse to refresh them. "Ms. Parker. Do you remember struggling against your restraints?"

"No. Is that what these are?" Parker said, pointing to the bandages.

The doctor nodded. "Yes. Reviewing your records, I don't see any medication for seizures, correct?"

"Correct. I've never had seizures."

"I see. Well, we may have to address that issue before your discharge."

Wolf frowned and asked, "Doc, is it possible she struggled but doesn't remember it?"

"Possible. Ms. Parker. Do you remember anything else?"

"Yes, actually. I remember a man talking, and then later a woman talking. I couldn't see, but I could hear."

"And what did you hear?" The doctor asked.

Wolf raised his hand. "Sorry, Doc, that's part of our ongoing investigation." His gaze lingered on the doctor. *Do we need to worry about whose side do you play for, doc?* Wolf thought automatically. He trusted only Parker and Shadow Tier now.

The doc showed no concern at the admonishment. "All right, understood. I'm ordering up a couple of tests this morning. If you feel up to it by this afternoon, let us know and we'll get you discharged and headed home. You'll be on antibiotics for another ten days to make sure the wounds don't get infected. Do you have a PCP?"

"No," Parker whispered. Her last personal care physician had been back home, long before she even moved to Tampa. "But I know where to find one."

"All right. Take the antibiotics for the ten days and then I recommend you go see your local doc for follow up. He can request your medical records for background. I'd like you on light duty for a few weeks, minimum."

The doctor wished her well and left, and the nurse changed Parker's new bandages. Wolf said nothing, staring into the eyes of the woman he loved when not watching the nurse's hands and scrutinizing her work. The nurse then departed too and Parker fell asleep, so Wolf stepped outside the room again, this time calling Chief Hogan at the reservation.

He picked up on the third ring. "Wolf, let me put you on speaker. Billy's here with me. Your wife, is she okay?"

"Yes, thank you, Chief. She is. What's your status there?"

"All quiet right now. Waiting for *Sinaloato* to cross us again."

"Let me know as soon as you see any indication. We deep-dived the *Puma Grande* leader El Gato. One of his daughters is at a private Florida college an hour from Tampa. I left a message that she has likely passed on to her father by now."

Billy said, "The fight's not over by a long shot. Nature abhors a vacuum, right?"

"Agreed. If Sinaloa stays away, then someone else will likely make a play," Wolf said somberly.

Hogan said, "We're keeping training on the down-low and making use of some wireless camera technology a Marine Corps buddy of mine sells to extend our surveillance footprint."

"Good plan. Is White Horse okay with the civil support team under your control, Chief?"

"Yes, so far. He's gotten a lot of positive press from the seizure, so that feeds his ego. I expect he'll sour if we suffer more losses."

Wolf said, "Roger that. Keep after it, and we'll immediately pass along any intel about activities on or around the reservations. I believe we will get two weeks' reprieve at most before we need to repel the next wave of attacks."

Chapter 56

The rings of sentries tiered outside the Cortes ranch gave Eliana plenty of advanced notice of El Chapo's pending arrival. His barely constrained anger on their last call had been all the warning she needed to plan for his eventual visit. Which, in her case, always happened sooner than later.

Over the years, she recognized that the sooner he showed up, the angrier he was, and the more likely violence would ensue.

If he's not careful, he's going to set a pattern for a visit from an American Hellfire missile, Eliana thought, shaking her head.

Twenty-two minutes from the first notification, El Chapo rolled up into a courtyard. The security contingent was larger now, dressed in camo uniforms, and appearing like they had gotten some serious training.

"He must have hired a Cuban to do some training," Eliana said to herself. Then Eliana did something she had never done before and laid her personal MP5 on her desk where she could reach it. In a play on one of El Chapo's beloved tactics, she was wiping down her Sig P226 pistol when El Chapo's security men barged in and flowed around the room to the windows. El Chapo was right on their heels, yelling at them to put their guns away before his favorite lieutenant killed them all.

El Chapo laughed, pointing at the MP5. "Very nice, Eliana. I see you haven't lost your penchant for drama."

"As you have taught me, it is a tool we must use more often now that we are assaulted from every corner by the government, military, and rival cartels. We are strong. We do not back down. We are Sinaloa." She smiled. "Expect us."

"Yes. You understand we must fight to stay on top."

It worked. He's here on business, not anger.

El Chapo sat in her front her desk and plopped his boots on top. A flat cake of dried mud flaked off the sole of his boot and dropped on the pristine desktop, cracking apart. At least, she hoped it was mud.

"Tell me about your crop transition progress."

"It is proceeding as reported. I have dispersed the opium grows so they are less obvious to overhead surveillance, and an attack on one does not account for a large percentage of a harvest. Just as we do not keep all our money in one bank, I will ensure we maintain an appropriate level of product decentralization."

"You heard of the loss the *Puma Grande* suffered at the hands of Wolf?" El Chapo asked.

"Yes. They are stupid. Too much product in a single load."

"My experiment with contracting in Montana has not produced favorable results. Send in more of our people."

"I encourage the expansion in Montana, but we should avoid the Indian reservations. The state is so big we don't need them. The reservations are so comparatively small that they are easy to defend. To resist us." Her tone was supportive and conciliatory, but what she was doing was cautioning El Chapo to not be stupid.

"No!" he interrupted. "I want it all. We do not run from Wolf or anyone else."

"*Jefe, escucha*, hear me out. While *Puma Grande* has been getting robbed by Wolf, I have co-opted the Yellowstone county commissioner. He is the governor's best friend and a trusted confidant. We get everything we want with less risk of loss or interruption. We can slide in unseen and maximize the value of your investment. And heroin demand in the American Northwest and mountain states is skyrocketing. All those rich internet kids and the partiers are bored with cocaine and moving to heroin."

El Chapo considered Eliana's argument. She had made excellent points. And though he would never admit it to the woman, he knew her to be very smart and well-reasoned. She had calmed considerably since the birth of her child.

"All right, we shall risk it. I will give you sixty days to show me profits from your plan for the Northwest." He pulled his boots from the desktop to the carpet and pointed a finger in her face. "But understand me—I do not fear Wolf."

El Chapo stood and turned to depart, his security scrambling to prepare for his exit. He was just about to clear the doorway on the way out when he said, "Eliana, one more thing. That's a very nice plane you bought. Lots of trips to Miami, too. I guess *hombres Mexicanos* are no longer worth your time?"

Eliana worked to keep her laughing reply light and free of the fear she felt rising in her chest to grip her heart.

"El Chapo knows all and sees all," she said, extending her hands and bowing in comical fealty. "*Jefe*, you are not the only one with Cuban connections, although mine is a second-generation American botanist with a receding hairline. I will share with you the tests he is running on a new method of opium production when the results are confirmed. It holds the promise of doubling and possibly tripling our output. I just wish I could surprise you one time."

"Ha! I am allergic to surprises. They often lead to prisons," El Chapo said darkly as he left.

Eliana waited until all the SUVs and trucks had headed back for the mountains before standing to shake off the fear that had gripped her. She picked up her Sig, dropped the magazine and racked the round out of the chamber, catching it mid-air. Then she slammed the magazine home, racked a round into the pistol, and put it on safe. She dropped the magazine again and put the spare round back in the stack before double tapping it to ensure it was seated. The whole process was completed in seconds, semi-mindless and therapeutic in its flow.

Eliana brought the pistol up, aligning the sights center mass in her mind's eye on El Chapo's face.

"My surprise will come soon enough," she said to the face.

Chapter 57

The searing heat, a hallmark of the Kandahar province, made leaning against the truck a risky proposition without a burn kit. After being dropped off by a beat-up old Toyota Hilux, Mallard had been led to the fifth truck in the convoy bookended by two trucks, one at the front and one at the back, painted white and clearly displaying the large blue UN logo on the doors. He had been standing around with nothing to do as the thirty drivers, evidently leaderless, argued over trivial issues for the last ninety minutes.

His driver had tried to toss his backpack in the back of the truck, claiming there was no space in the front with the three of them, but just one hard stare and flash of a dagger dissuaded the man from further attempts.

Two hours and thirty-five minutes later, the load-up command was given and trucks started a raucous harmony of diesel power-plants in various states of tune. A low cloud of black smoke chuffed from exhaust pipes and stacks to drift lazily toward the sky.

The first leg of the journey was but one of several, as this convoy would eventually go as far as the Turkish border. It would be inspected and controlled by Qods Force assets through Iran, clearly the most dangerous portion of the six-day journey. With Wolf's help, Mallard and Clinton believed the risk was manageable.

The UN convoy designation would do next to nothing for their security while in Afghanistan. Intelligence reports suggested a new hardline group of *jihadis* led by Abu Musab al Zarqawi was flexing its muscles along their route, near the border area with Iran. Bravo Squadron's intel support cell had said this new group, who were calling themselves The Islamic State, were hardcore, nasty, and unpredictable.

Unconfirmed reports, but believed by many in US and NATO intelligence, said the group was a collection of leftovers after the crushing blow al Qaeda in Iraq had taken. From Mallard's point of view, the backstory mattered little as convoy security would come down to the situation on the ground at a given moment and how generous a rebel commander was feeling that day.

Mallard had found in his many years in the region that some commanders wanted nothing to do with outsiders, even if what outsiders brought was for the good of their people. Others accepted that aid could indeed be received within Sharia law for the betterment of the Afghan people.

As the convoy rolled on, the drone of the cross-country drive was superseded by the stark beauty of Afghanistan, which changed from the lush greens of Lashkar Gah to the mountain roads heading northwest to Herat.

With fourteen more hours to the border, Mallard did what soldiers around the world all do when being transported longer distances—he went to sleep, backpack between his legs, the insulated bottom protecting the morphine bricks from the vehicle's heat.

Nash had been covertly exfiltrated from the OGA compound in the back of an unmarked pickup, drugs in hand, via a circuitous surveillance detection route to Kandahar airport and a C-130 with a logo for Global Air Services on the nose and the tail. The UN logo was placed above the GAS logo and it was five times larger.

Nash noticed the UN logo was also on the underside of the aircraft's wings on both sides in the hope it would keep the Taliban from shooting at the planes bringing humanitarian aid to the Afghan people.

Nash walked up to the UN C-130J and approached a jumpsuited crewman holding a clipboard standing at the ramp. His coverall said JAKE SLATON on one side and LOADMASTER on the other.

"Hi," Nash said, extending his hand and cover name. "Jeremy Thornton. I'm your cargo for the trip back to Ramstein."

Slaton shook Nash's hand with a friendly smile. "Welcome aboard, cargo," he said. He gestured to Nash's small backpack. "That all you got?"

"Yeah. I travel light," Nash said. He pointed under the left wing. "Has the addition of the logos done us any good with managing small arms fire from the ground?"

Slaton grinned. "Sure—forty percent of the time they work every time," Slaton said, laughing. "But you know, it is what it is, right? Hell, if it stopped completely, we wouldn't get that sweet hazard pay. My beach house ain't gonna pay for itself."

Just what I need, crazy flyboys zooming through ground fire to make sure they get paid extra, Nash thought.

Nash hefted the backpack.

"I'm supposed to give this to the pilot."

"There you go," Slaton said, pointing. Nash groaned to himself as a youngish pilot sauntered over. The guy studied his passenger over Ray-Ban shades and held out his hand.

"Fencer," the pilot said with a single upward head nod and a half-grin, introducing himself by his former Air Force callsign. "Like the sword fighter."

Nash instantly thought the moniker must rather have been awarded because the man must have once landed a jet through the fence at the end of an airport runway, not because he knew how to use a thin sport sword.

"Pleasure. Nash. Like the Rambler sedan."

Nash offered Fencer the backpack with the dope. He slung it over one shoulder by a strap and headed for the flight deck.

"Find a seat and strap in, man. We're wheels up in fifteen," the pilot said over his shoulder.

The first thing Nash noticed as he walked up the ramp was a palletized lavatory. He'd used them before, and they were better than nothing. This one was relatively opulent as military accommodations go. The pallet held two airline-style restrooms and a hand washing station. *Very civilized*, Nash thought.

The pilot ducked into the left-most door, glanced back at Nash, and reached back in the door to post a metallic placard that let you know the lavatory was out of order.

Nash shook his head: *Of course it was.* At least there was one left.

He selected a canvas seat beneath the wing root near the oval window. He leaned back against the webbed backrest and fastened a lap belt like you'd find in a car before shoulder belts.

The smell of diesel fuel powering the Auxiliary Power Unit and the exhaust of its combustion wafted around the tarmac on the hot breeze of the day and the familiar aromas filled the cargo hold.

The aircraft was leaving Kandahar slick—with no cargo— which felt odd to Nash. He'd spent most of his C-130 time stuffed into such airplanes alongside vehicles or pallets of gear chained to the deck. The smells and the gritty feel of the casual seats was well known to him and, he would admit, reassuring. He was asleep before the Allison turboprop engines started.

Nash was jolted awake when the taxiing plane stood on its nose gear in a near instant stop. He would find out later the maneuver was to avert a ground collision with a Russian Antonov aircraft piloted by a drunken Polish crew on the wrong taxiway.

Once on the active runway, the pilots held the brakes as the Allison engines powered up and stabilized. Brakes released, the plane surged forward, picking up speed fast owing to the empty cargo bay. Seconds later, the plane rotated and climbed steeply into the cloudless blue sky.

Nash looked out the window as the C-130J banked hard around to the south, standing on the wing, red tracer rounds attempting to follow the plane as it climbed out.

Bloody hell. Some idiot is serious about becoming a Taliban legend by bringing down a C-130.

The plane leveled off at what Nash thought might be about ten thousand feet and reduced its speed to cruise. A bit jacked and no longer sleepy after seeing the tracer rounds so close, Nash pulled from his cargo pants pocket *The Da Vinci Code* paperback he had gotten from Clinton.

Loadmaster Slaton ambled over to Nash and extended his hand for a fist bump. Nash obliged, and Slaton bent and yelled over the turboprops.

"See what I gotta deal with? Tali-man wants to be a hero. He never got over not being selected for F-16s."

"Get me safely to Ramstein and this aircrew will all be my heroes," Nash said, playing along.

"No problem, will do. In a few minutes we'll be in Turkmenistan airspace and then the pressure's off. We run this route so often the plane damn near flies itself. We'll be at Ramstein in about eight hours, no sweat." He pointed forward to a row of seats next to the bulkhead. "I'm up there, bro. Let me know if you need anything. I got sammiches and drinks if you get hungry. Some books 'n stuff."

Nash nodded. "Thanks!" was all he said.

Just tell me where you guys hide the dope, he thought, staring at the lavatory pallet.

Chapter 58

So, where *are* they hiding the dope, Jeff?" Kennedy asked over dinner at the safehouse.

"Damned if I know. There are lots of places on a C-130 to hide dope," Nash said, "but I didn't notice anything out of place. The crew didn't act out of character. But I do have a question."

"Okay, what's that?"

"What was on the manifest for the flight to Kandahar? Troops and gear?"

Kennedy gestured to the Kid.

"Medical supplies. No people other than crew," the Kid said.

"Then why the lavatory pallet? I mean, crew comfort and stuff, okay, good, but it takes up cargo space. Lots of good places in something like that to hide dope."

Kennedy and the Kid nodded as Taylor arrived, slapping Nash on the back.

"How you doin', mate?" Taylor said.

"Good, sir, thanks. Bravo isn't lacking for opportunities."

"So we hear. At 2300 tonight, I'm meeting a contact to collect our drugs. You are coming with me. Are his clothes ready?"

Kennedy said, "Your school clothes are waiting in the bunk house, Tom. Get yourself cleaned up. You'll be in a suit tonight."

The Kid offered to show Nash around the compound before he headed to the bunk house and they departed. Taylor poured himself some tea, sat down, and he took a tentative sip of the hot liquid. "Any word from Mallard?" Taylor asked.

Kennedy said, "No, but his beacon is working and they're about to cross into Iran. Let's hope Wolf's contact can take control of the convoy. If Qods Force goons start searching for contraband, it could get dicey."

"Agreed. That drive is thirty-plus hours on what Iranians call Route 2. All we can do is wait."

Kennedy massaged his neck and asked Taylor, "Is the Swiss banker NOC you used on your last visit to Tehran still intact?"

"Yes. In fact, I reached out to my Central Bank of Iran contact just last week to stay in touch."

"Good. We may need it."

Six thousand kilometers to the south, Mallard watched four MI-8 helicopters fly in low led by two MI-24 gunships. The gunships broke left and right, gained altitude, and circled the checkpoint. The MI-8s landed and disgorged well-armed men wearing green berets. Mallard suppressed a smile. Wolf's contact had come through: The men belonged to the Iranian 65th Airborne Special Forces Brigade, also known as the NOHED Brigade.

Mallard watched as a colonel demanded to see the IRGC commander of the checkpoint. The officer, a major, didn't salute the colonel and the tone of his voice was improbably insolent. The major told the colonel he had taken charge of the border crossing after intelligence had reported contraband on board the convoy. He claimed it to be foreign interference and deviant movement of banned substances.

The colonel reminded the major of the Army's role to guard Iran's borders and maintain internal order, and when the major was insolent again, the colonel drew his pistol and shot him dead in the chest. The Special Forces soldiers and IRGC troops raised their weapons at each other, each screaming at the other to drop their weapons.

The colonel holstered his pistol and barked an order for the IRGC to disarm. When they did not, he raised his hands as if pleading with his brother Iranians, but it was a signal. Mallard ducked.

The chain gun of a helicopter gunship moaned and rounds tore into the IRGC soldiers, who had unknowingly clustered themselves into a tidy target package. Spent chain gun shell casings and links pinged on the concrete road just before an MI-24 roared by overhead.

Mallard peered over the dash and scanned where the men had once stood, the dead bodies ripped into unrecognizable pieces of flesh and cloth. The surviving IRGC troops were disarmed and made to clear the mess of their colleagues off the road.

Two young officers each with two NCOs broke into teams and started stamping documents and passports. Within the hour, the convoy was back on its way, escorted by three teams of Special Forces driving the IRGC's liberated Range Rovers.

Mallard laughed. "How much longer?" he asked the driver.

In broken English, the man said, "Thirty-six hours, no breakdown, no attacks."

Mallard whispered to himself. "No breakdown, no attacks. Thirty-six hours just to transit Iran."

He couldn't know the storm the colonel had caused, nor what was brewing up ahead as they rolled closer to Tehran with every mile traveled.

Chapter 59

W e meet our contact on Ramstein?" Nash asked.

Taylor said, "Yes. I know what you're thinking. I'm thinking the same thing. Where else does Juno Services Incorporated provide cleaning and maintenance services?"

A quick ID check at the gate and they were on base, headed to the warehouse where JSI was housed. They had an aircraft cleaning and maintenance contract and, interestingly, a contract for hospital services at Landstuhl Regional Medical Center.

The drive took another eighteen minutes at the base speed of twenty-five miles per hour. The lights in the warehouse were on and a roller door stood open. Taylor parked in the shadows next to the building and they entered through a side door whose placard read JSI *Contractor Maintenance Services.*

When they stepped inside they were met by an attractive woman in a starched white shirt, form-fitting black skirt, and high heels. Taylor estimated her age in the mid-thirties. Her short blonde hair and blue eyes projected an air of confidence and control.

"Gentlemen, how may I help you?"

"Fraulein Skorzeny, I am Danny Ocean, and this is Sam Harmon," Taylor said. Nash nodded a curt greeting.

Skorzeny said, "I know everything that goes on in my hotels." She parroted dialogue from Andy Garcia's character in the *Ocean's Twelve* film right back at them.

"So, I should put the towels back?" Taylor asked with a grin.

Bloody stupid using movie characters and lines for bona fides, Taylor thought.

Skorzeny was unfazed. She was accustomed to fake names and awkward codename exchanges, and just nodded and motioned for Taylor and Nash to follow. She stopped at a door with a cipher lock and keyed in a six-digit code, then held her hand up to a reader. Several electric deadbolts clunked as they released their hold on the door.

The three stepped inside, moved around a stainless-steel workbench to a wall of classified materials safes, and Skorzeny spun the dial on one. A beat later it was open, and she laid Nash's backpack with its fake morphine blocks on the workbench.

Nash inspected the blocks to see if they had been tampered with. They looked fine to him.

Skorzeny said, "You will not find any tampering. If you ever do, we eliminate the problem in real time. Our leader commits to on-time delivery without any worry of intervention. This is what you get every time you use our services."

Taylor nodded. "Are you our contact if we want to move product from here to other locations, like the UK and America?"

"Yes. But you must contract through headquarters in Marseilles first. We are field operations, not corporate."

"Understood," Taylor said. Then, playing it as if an afterthought, he asked, "Operations in Afghanistan?"

"Yes. We provide services and drop locations at Kandahar airport and the NATO compound. And in Kabul at the International Security Assistance Force headquarters."

The mention of NATO and ISAF as a drop location caught Taylor short, but he didn't react outwardly. "Okay then, good. I think that's all for now." He strode around the workbench to offer his hand. Skorzeny took the offer, shaking hands with a firm grip and a direct look into his eyes.

"Perhaps we will see you again," Skorzeny said with a dazzling smile.

In the car and headed off base, Taylor said, "Well, that was short and sweet. And educational. Thoughts?"

"Did you notice the palletized lavatories in the warehouse? Looks like they service them there."

"Yeah, your intuition appears to be on point. They do provide a secure means of transport and likely not discoverable during a search of an aircraft, even with dogs. I mean, the mess, the smells. What else?"

Nash chuckled. "Fraulein Skorzeny is a looker, mate. I could see you struggling not to drop into your famously effective James Bond persona. And I was surprised at how easily she offered more information about their operations."

Taylor shook his head. "An effective, long-living operator stays on mission and doesn't break cover for a beautiful woman." They both laughed. "Plus, "Taylor said, "women trust me."

"I think the openness must have been ordered by Croce. He sees large profits working with us. A smart cartel would have multiple methods and providers helping them get to market. I'm of the opinion Croce thinks he can be our exclusive logistics provider.

Especially now when he has ground and air assets not only from Afghanistan to Europe, but beyond. The big hit tonight was the confirmation of his capabilities to move product to America."

"So, the combination of Janus Logistics, Juno Services, and Global Air Services has created the world's first Heroin Parcel Service, HPS—the underworld cousin of UPS," Nash said.

Taylor chuckled. "Yeah, they most likely think in those terms, too. I wouldn't be surprised if Fraulein Skorzeny has experience at FedEx or DHL. She mentioned drop locations, and running a janitorial contract is not heavy lifting. Bid at a cost to win the business and set up shop on base. Coordinate with your air partner who has contacts making use of the same bases, and you have a secret pipeline pumping gold-plated kilos of dope."

"They make use of American military infrastructure but not the military itself, and that removes a breadcrumb that could lead back to them. You said Kennedy was given a task to investigate the possible use of Air Force aircraft to transport opium out of Afghanistan. Good news is it's not happening via Air Force C-130s and C-17s. Bad news is it's happening on Air Force bases through contract services."

Taylor said, "You know we have enough information to act now and take down Croce and his accomplices. But it's often just what our Joint Narcotics Analysis Center and the American DEA do not want. They tend to want to prosecute the whole system end to end. Once we update Kennedy and Wolf, you watch—we'll get more resources and direction to take all three parts down."

"Our governments will let Shadow Tier lead the effort?"

"I think so. The politicians will want someone to insulate them from blame if this all goes sideways. And Wolf is already known as a rogue actor and terrorist, so. Natural scapegoat."

Chapter 60

C linton was reading the report from Taylor outside their trailer in the Kandahar OGA complex when the alarm sounded. Training alarms are often considered a nuisance, but Clinton made sure Bravo took each alarm seriously.

Enemy rockets and mortars were sometimes fired from hastily set up rails and tubes and just as quickly thrown into the back of vehicles after firing and dispersed. If the Taliban took more than a couple of minutes to tear down a mortar, their sloth invited a fast counter-battery calculation and a returned mortar or artillery round back on their location, with a one hundred percent chance of ruining their lives.

Early in the war, soldiers who didn't take the alarm seriously had paid the ultimate price. Clinton's advice was to be pissed if they wanted to be, but to get their butts in the bunker.

Instead of timbers over a hole in the ground, some enterprising Marine Corps gunny sergeant had field-engineered up a plan with concrete culverts. Surrounded by sandbags on all sides, they did the protective job admirably.

But incoming enemy rounds are indiscriminate in their attack on human flesh. They collected Devon Lancaster and Robert Baskins, who got caught in the open, but lived. Clinton watched Lancaster run for the bunker and he was blown off his feet when the mortars started falling. He grabbed his leg as he fell into the dirt, swearing so professionally one would be forgiven for thinking he was a sailor.

Clinton ran out and dragged him to safety. Baskins had been right behind Lancaster and was slammed to the ground when he was collected by the same blast. Clinton turned Lancaster over to Jocko and sprinted to fetch Baskins, now struggling to his feet. Back in the safety of the bunker, Jocko gave a thumbs up at the *all clear* signal and Clinton said he was going to grab a vehicle.

When Clinton returned with a pickup, he saw Lancaster bandaged and squirming against the pain. Baskins just sat with a dazed look. They were loaded up and driven the quarter mile to the hospital that abutted the taxiway. It had direct access to the flight line for the short air evacuation of critical patients to Landstuhl.

Jocko flew with Lancaster and Clinton with Baskins. When Jocko found Clinton in the Landstuhl emergency department he relayed the physician's assistant's intake triage. The cleanup and stitches were standard expectations, but the blast had caused a greenstick fracture in Lancaster's tibia that also had to be addressed.

Another doctor took his time checking Baskins because his injuries were less obvious: He confirmed Baskins had a serious concussion, potentially a traumatic brain injury. The hospital staff were keeping a watch for internal bleeding and had him on a TBI protocol.

Now with two of his people stable in the Air Force hospital,

Clinton and Jocko headed back to the compound. Once there, Clinton used the information provided by Taylor to make some calls. He soon found that figuring out who was doing the contracting for the various military compounds and hospitals was like trying to decipher the Pentagon phone book. He quit that idea and took a dirt bike around the side of the base to the hospital.

Inside he stopped a nurse and asked for the administrator's office. The response he got back was clearly shy of admiration for the lieutenant colonel's office he was pointed to. Clinton took a few steps across the lobby, knocked on the door, and waited.

A beat later, a female voice bellowed. "What is it?"

Clinton stepped inside, presenting his best smile.

"Excuse me, colonel. Major Mike Clinton. I wonder if you can tell me whether Juno Services is a contractor here."

"Why are you asking?"

"It's not really formal business. I got to know a few of their staff at Landstuhl and heard some of them had taken positions here. They were very nice to my wife when I was recovering."

"Yes, good people, hard-working. Excellent contractor. They are here. Is there anyone in particular we can help you find?"

"Yes, Elisa Skorzeny?"

"I've heard her name before, but she's not here. The manager here is Siena Woods."

"Well, thank you, ma'am. I appreciate your help," Clinton said.

"You're welcome, major," she said, and Clinton turned to leave.

Clinton stepped outside about fifty feet away to a covered pavilion that served as the smoker's area and punched the number two on his satellite phone for Kennedy. He picked up on the first ring.

"How are Lancaster and Baskins doing?"

Clinton exhaled audibly. "Lancaster will be out in a few days, operational in two or three weeks, probably. Baskins, it's hard to tell. I don't think the doctors know yet. His bell got rung pretty good."

Kennedy said, "Think about putting Baskins on a flight back to Bethesda. They have the best TBI specialist in the world and they're on the cutting edge of new therapies." He paused and his lips got thin in a grimace. "They get enough damned practice."

"That they do. I'll look into Bethesda. As concerns your French partner, Juno Services does have a contract at the hospital here. I'll check, but it seems likely they are also working the military side of the airport, too."

"Agreed. I've got one of Parker's stateside analysts looking into the contracts held by Juno and Janus Logistics."

"How is Parker, anyway?" Clinton asked.

"You know. She's Parker. She's as stubborn as Wolf when it comes to pulling her weight. She's checking into Global Air Services. Says she has a feeling about who might be behind the company, but no facts just yet."

"Did she say who she thinks it is?"

"Not yet. She wants to be sure it's not someone pirating the Sinaloa brand to win business."

Clinton laughed into the phone. "Good brand, though, right? Any news from Mallard?"

"Not yet. They should be nearing Tehran about now, for the ultimate test of Wolf's contact's power to control the Qods Force. Do me a favor and get to know the Juno Services manager? I see a pattern playing out here, with women occupying interesting positions in our mapping of Croce's organization. It could be that Croce is just an asshat who thinks he's a player. Or maybe he's just a front man, and someone else is in the shadows pulling the strings."

"I thought we were the ones pulling the strings from the shadows," Clinton said.

"Sometimes. Mostly we just bring the hurt. No, my gut says it's someone else even Croce doesn't realize is in play."

"So, the question is, who controls Croce?"

"Yep. We need to figure that out in real time before we can't fight our way out of the next ambush."

Chapter 61

Elle, that's not what I'm saying," Wolf said. "No one would fault you or question your commitment if you stayed home and took some more time off, that's all."

"You are my husband, right? You love and trust me, right?"

"Yes, of course. Without hesitation."

"Then quit acting like my mother and trust me like my husband does. I'm good, and as they asked, I've scheduled time with the Agency shrink to talk."

"Like your husband does?" Wolf said, smiling.

"Yes..." She fake-pouted, extending her bottom lip in a passable boo-boo face.

Wolf grabbed Parker and held her tight, kissing her neck. "Still love me?"

Parker squeezed his hands around her waist. "Till death plus two weeks. Now let go of me. We need to get to work."

"Yes, boss," Wolf said, smiling as he released her and grabbed his coffee and backpack.

First thing on the day's agenda was a squadron report via international video teleconference. The tech nerd in Wolf took over, playing with the Polycom for twenty minutes until he and the Kid in Germany got the configuration they wanted.

When the call started, everyone's first comments were directed to Parker. The family aspect of Shadow Tier's culture was something Wolf had driven from its inception. Now the norm, it still made Wolf proud about what they had built.

He could also see the effect the genuine love and respect for her leadership had on Parker. Her tight-lipped smile, nods of appreciation, and whispered thank yous were all she could muster on her first day back.

Once all the pleasantries had been exchanged, Wolf started the meeting.

"All right, let's begin. Taylor, bring us up to date."

"Bloody busy here. 'Herr Merck's' men successfully tested the air route and pickup through Juno Services at Ramstein. The test of the ground route is ongoing. Bit of a testy situation at the border and near Tehran yesterday, but your contact came through."

"Our master of understatement," Kennedy said. "Seventeen dead Qods Force at the border and another five outside of Tehran. Could have been a lot more until the Supreme Leader demanded the IRGC and their Qods Force goons to operate within the Iranian constitution. Strangely enough, we might have set the conditions for uninterrupted drug transportation through Iran, where before it was hit or miss depending on the Qods Force commander's need to plus-up his revolutionary support fund. Sorry for taking us off task. Back to you, Taylor."

"Thank you, 'Herr Merck,'" Taylor said, trying to keep a straight face. "Mister Kennedy and the Kid are working with Ryan from your whiz kids to run down the ownership trail and contracts for Janus Logistics and Juno Services. We request Parker do the same for Global Air Services. We have expanded our cover footprint in Germany, and the word is getting out about our secret lab and the quality of its product. The Kid reports growing interest in our activities from German and French counternarcotics units, a reliable sign of authenticity that will also help our cover. And finally, we're working on a plan to exercise Croce's ability to move products to the UK and America. More on that as we flush out the operation."

"Any indications Croce is in contact with the New York mafia?"

The Kid jumped in. "Yes. He's pinging contacts and coordinating a visit. His use of unencrypted cellphones makes tracking him and listening to his calls absurdly easy. He thinks hopping between burner phones protects him from surveillance. Nine times out of ten, he initiates a call from his latest burner from his headquarters at the restaurant. He doesn't realize we are the reason he went from three-bar signal strength to five."

Wolf said, "Good work, team. Kennedy, how is our relationship with the JNAC?"

"Could not be better. They have become the collection and analysis organization for Europe right down to Afghanistan. They have tripled in size and doubled their collection sources, so we coordinated the biggest network pipe we could covertly get to their database. We get near real-time updates."

"Okay. Well done. Clinton, over to you."

"Important news first. Lancaster will be operational in two weeks or less. Docs loaded him up with antibiotics, he'll be out tomorrow. I'm sending Baskins to Bethesda for TBI treatment. The docs think he'll recover, it will just take longer. I know you're in touch with his wife, Beth. If you could coordinate getting her to the hospital to see him, that would be helpful to his recovery."

"I'm on it," Parker said. "I have a friend ready to meet her when she arrives at National. She's offered to let Beth stay with her at her place, less than a mile from the hospital."

"Perfect! I'll let him know. It will take a load off, for sure. On the ops side, the word is the Marines here are confused about what their mission is. They are tasked for counterinsurgency but are getting dragged into counterdrug ops by the DEA, who have figured out they can get extra resources when they add hit-list terrorist sightings to their reports. Personally, I think it's bullshit. The DEA is playing the system, and it's about to go sideways with the Marine commander and ISAF, who are one hundred percent against spending time in opium fields doing the DEA's bidding."

"How is your relationship with the Marines?"

"Good enough," Clinton said, but he made a cynical face. "We pass them intel and targets they can prosecute, and they're responsive enough. If we called, they'd answer, but subtle they ain't. Mostly they're just door kickers and trigger pullers, and we don't have a lot of call for that just yet."

He flipped a few PowerPoint slides of stats and maps on a screen inset.

"We continue to identify labs," he said. Red circles appeared around a succession of locations. "The last two we flattened with airstrikes tasked from Carrier Air Wing Eight on TR. I've spoken to Navy Captain Tom Sizemore a couple times, the CVW-8 skipper, and he can't be more eager to help. They're flying the last F-14s and he said his people like the break from flying *Operation Iraqi Freedom* missions."

USS Theodore Roosevelt was spending much of its recent deployment in the Med, and it was always in range for sorties of any kind, from mild to wild.

"I've got a team going in on an objective tonight. We think

there's a clandestine lab along the Pakistani border that we can't get a good view of, even with drones. It's in ugly terrain, and we believe the operators have taken a page from El Chapo's playbook and built the lab underground. Tonight's op is a sneak and peak."

"Will you have air on station in case you can target the location?"

"You bet. No chance we would waste an opportunity to bring the hurt. Also HH-60G Pave Hawks with Air Force PJs on station in case we need any pilot recoveries."

"Good deal. Anything else?"

"Nope, that's it from here."

"All right, good to go. LeBlanc, you're up."

A green outline identified LeBlanc's screen when he spoke. "Yeah, besides training, we're working with DARPA, thanks to the Kid. They've developed an enhanced ground penetrating radar and imaging platform small enough to be operated by two privates, with a graphical interface to match. The operations and intel guys at Special Operations Command-Korea have been playing with it at General Nathan Tally's request. Now we have a copy too, and I have four Alphas down at EPIC figuring out where to test it along the border. A single high-energy pulse can see sixty feet below the surface. My demo guys want to target tunnels they find with those big-ass shaped charges the combat engineers have, but the EPIC director is concerned about the press coverage if we start cratering streets."

Wolf and the others on the call laughed. "You know if you find a tunnel, you'll be in the tunnel, right?"

"Yeah, no one's favorite, unless your name is Morgan. And where has he been lately?"

Wolf smiled. "You got anything else Alpha related?"

"Yeah, just one. The device we left behind in El Gato's daughter's condo is working. Just like you thought, she freaked out and immediately texted daddy. We attached our code to a picture of the device and your message she texted him, and now we own his iPhone and Apple laptop. The cyber team is working to cascade the code to his associates."

"Good. And as for Morgan, he's on assignment. If you see him, remember he's undercover. Thanks for the update, everyone. I do read your reports, but it's great for me to see your smiling mugs now and again. Kennedy, Taylor, and Kid stay on. The rest of you bums get back to work."

There was a chorus of Bye, Later, and See ya, and several screens went dark and then disappeared. After the room emptied, Wolf said, "I'm getting pressure from the vice president for results. Bravo's activities have kept her happy so far, but now she's looking for headlines. How long are we talking to learn Croce's UK and US routes?"

Kennedy looked thoughtful for a moment before answering. "If we push, show some cash, a week. Maybe two."

Taylor and the Kid agreed.

Wolf crossed his arms and sat back in his uncomfortable chair. "Okay, push. Whatever you need, I'll get it. Kennedy's report to the Air Force chief of staff has made him happy, but the SECDEF and joint chiefs are now asking, if not the Air Force, who and how. And someone on one of those staffs in the Building leaked the information to the vice president's chief of staff. We need to close this out before government leaks get us killed."

Chapter 62

Wolf departed the office to stretch and exchange indoor lighting for the white storm clouds of a typical Tampa Bay afternoon. He moved fluidly in the heat of the afternoon sun and humidity, stretching in a tai chi-like flow.

He stopped stretching to call Hogan at the reservation for an update. "Chief, what's the good word?"

"All quiet here as far as we can tell, just the usual reports of pot sales and a call for service to what looks to be a meth overdose, but no serious cartel activity."

"Good news," Wolf said. "Hey, I think I've figured out how to get you more coverage not attributable to me, and White Horse is unlikely to find out about it. I've contracted with a company that primarily does airborne infrared mapping and analysis for logging companies, large farms, and ranches. You will have a small aircraft with an IR pod at your disposal. She's going to fly out of the Laurel airport. I suggest having her fly the border of the reservation first. As we learned in California, the cartels and drug gangs like to set up operations on the edges of reservations and the national forests. It's good, proactive press for you even if they don't find anything."

"Well, that will help. We can't get near there without attracting attention. When can she start?"

"Tomorrow. I'll have the pilot contact you today to coordinate her flight pattern. Sound good?"

"Yeah. Thanks, brother. Like you, I don't think Sinaloa will give up this easy."

"Chief, hold on a sec. Parker's here." Wolf put him on mute.

Parker whispered, "You're talking to Hogan?"

"Yeah, why?"

Parker smiled. "I just tried to call him. His phone is busy, and you're here."

"What's so important you had to find me?"

"Put the chief on. He needs to hear this, too."

Wolf took the phone off mute. "Chief, Parker wants to talk to us both. We're on speaker."

"Chief, it's Elle. You and your family good?"

"Yes, thank you. You have something for me?"

"Yes, and I'm afraid it's not good. Motivated by your report of Sinaloa member marriages, I investigated the Yellowstone County records."

She pulled her cellphone from a pocket and thumbed it live to read from its screen.

"There have been twenty-three marriages out of one hundred and sixty-seven where one of the couples hits our system with association to the Sinaloa cartel or one of its affiliates. I fear the promise of a new life and lifestyle funded by the cartel is luring a younger generation away from the reservation."

Wolf said, "I fear a long-term play to gain control of the executive council and its power over the police force."

"Agreed," Hogan said, "but what can we do? It's not against the law to marry a dope gangster."

"True enough, but we need to think of something to kill the virus before it kills the host," Wolf said.

Chapter 63

Amaru didn't dare visit or even talk to his family. He knew he was a hunted man. He'd driven until nearly crashing from fatigue, but finally got stopped in a darkened rest area for a few hours of uncomfortable but sorely needed shut eye. He woke up when his watch alarm sounded and walked a lap of the rest area to refresh his senses, finally relieving himself in some bushes, then drove on until exhaustion made him pull over again. On the third leg, he crossed the bay bridge into San Francisco.

The Israeli bandage had done its job stopping the bleeding, but he didn't like the smell he found when checking his wound in the depths of an underground parking garage. He had resorted to an off-book doctor who had spent an hour cleaning, debriding, and partially closing the wound.

Amaru had complained he wanted the wound sown up, but the doctor explained it wouldn't heal that way; he would sew it up after the swelling had reduced and the antibiotics kept infection at bay.

He was having trouble sleeping. In his dreams, he didn't trip as he ran away, and the sniper didn't miss. He was waking up from the last wisps of his dream where he stared into the exit wound in his chest pouring out his life's blood like the water fountain at Mission San Juan Capistrano.

In his arrogance, he had convinced himself he was the apex predator. And it was true until he met Wolf and whomever had tracked and shot him in Tampa. He was lucky to be alive, as much as it hurt, and it fueled his hate and paranoia. Had his people given him up? Was it the L.A. Kings? Had he seen a Kings tattoo on one of the gunmen who died in one of his booby traps? *Will my arm ever work again?* The bone and muscle damage was extensive. Wolf and the other assassin would have to wait until he was whole again for the inevitable rematch.

Dealing with them would take all his skill and commitment. The stupid militia at the reservation, though, they were easy targets by comparison.

Setting a trap for them would be child's play, and he could watch that unfold from afar.

"They can't turn down a meth lab, can they?" Amaru muttered to himself.

Chapter 64

From his headquarters in Marseille, Croce listened to a voice on the speaker as it snarled, saying things Croce did not understand. The accusation he had leveled at the lack of quality and exorbitant price for the caller's product had not gotten the result Croce expected. But then, what could he expect from the savages who had brutally attacked his new partner? One-minute level-headed businessmen, the next, *jihadis* who cursed your infidel soul.

Until Herr Merck came on the scene, the Arabs had been the best source of raw opium. Now he had a partner in Herr Merck, and he had a lab where custom formulations of highly addictive heroin could be designed.

He no longer needed the old partners.

Abbas, as he called himself, began to threaten Croce, saying he would stop selling him product and leak his operation to the police. Croce let him speak for a second longer, knowing he was fire-walled off from the Taliban, then interrupted.

Croce tried to sound menacing but the act was thin. "Abbas, if that's your real name, listen to me. Marseille is *my* city, and I decide what is best for *Unione Corsa*, not you or your boss, me—only me. Everyone who has threatened *Unione Corsa* has ended up dead. If you cross me, I will have my people kill you all, including your women and children. If more of you come, we will kill them too. If you expose our former relationship to the police, I will give them your routes, which we know so well. Go find another buyer. The cost to do anything else is higher than you can afford."

Abbas had switched from French to his native language with an occasional French curse word sprinkled in. When Croce ended the call, he slammed the burner phone on the table, cracking its screen.

Lucien, his *consigliere*, whispered over his shoulder. "I will increase security here and at your penthouse."

Croce nodded assent but was lost in thought. *I can use a war with the jihadis to create the final alliances I need to own the south of France.*

Croce disassembled the broken burner phone. He used a wire cutter to break apart the SIM card, the pieces put into two different burn bags along with pieces of the phone. He opened a drawer and selected another prepaid burner. He trotted over to the stairs and took them up two at a time, slowing as he burst through the door onto the roof and dialed a number.

He ignored the sprawling urban vista before him, urgency driving him to focus. He considered himself a celebrity worthy of presidential-level protection such as the United States Secret Service provided to the American president, both physical and technical, and he had striven to create a similar organization for himself. The crew leader he called could best be described as his counter assault team leader. The crew was also tasked as his final extremist recovery team.

His call complete and personal protection set, Croce focused on the issue at hand, one that had been growing clearer as he evolved his relationship with Herr Merck. Lucien had first shown his true intentions after the initial meeting.

One of his security team had seen Lucien follow Merck as he drove away. The report was that he had been on his phone and watching from a storefront's shadows when the *jihadi* attack had occurred.

Now the look on Lucien's face during Croce's call with Abbas had cemented his suspicion that his *consigliere* was secretly working with or for the Taliban. His loyalties were divided, in any case. Croce dialed a tech and set an intercept on Lucien's phones. He had been a trusted partner to the family for a long time, and now it was all suspect.

Has he been radicalized? I want to trust him.

At the sound of footsteps, Croce turned to find Lucien.

"Herr Merck's man is requesting another meeting. They are interested in distribution to England and the United States. I suggest we wait until the land route is proven. It gives us more time to check their story and connections. There must be something in their past we can use as leverage."

Croce decided on a tight-lipped frown and a curt nod of his head to feign concern.

"Your suspicions are well-founded, and the considerable money they are giving us to get preferential treatment seems too eager. We must balance security with growing our organization. This is essential in order to be seen by the New York mafia as a viable partner in the way my grandfather and *Unione Corsa* were seen. The partnership with Herr Merck will see us grow in Europe and England. The mafia will do the same for us in America. I will take the meeting and set it up for dinner at the penthouse."

A brief flash of disgust on Lucien's face flared just before his nod of acceptance. Lucien turned and left the roof and Croce took one more look at his beloved Marseille. The city stretched out before him. The storm front in the distance over the Mediterranean created an image of dark forces consuming the light.

He shivered at the cool breeze, not comprehending a forewarning of death that had just caressed his soul.

Chapter 65

Kennedy sat back in the aircraft seat he'd just reclined. Across the aisle Taylor was engrossed in a copy of *The Economist*. A smart and capable operator, Taylor was a good foil for Kennedy and the Kid's machinations. Unlike Wolf, Taylor saw what was in front of them and, from time to time, a ring or two out.

Actively in the center of Croce's communications networks had given Kennedy and the Kid a bird's-eye view of Croce's actions, but more importantly, his thinking. Kennedy considered he was on the ragged edge of pushing the partnership too fast, but time was not on their side. He opened the aircraft's window shade and took in the French countryside as the plane hummed through the sky at four hundred miles per hour. The speed and altitude reminded him of a crazy saying Wolf had once uttered.

Go fast, take chances, and leave a good-looking corpse.

They were certainly going fast and taking chances, but he doubted he would live up to the last part. At tonight's meeting with

Croce, Kennedy/Merck would spread some fear, uncertainty, and distrust. After the *jihadi* attack he'd assigned one of the Agency analysts the job of uncovering exactly who Lucien was and which side he played for. The report Kennedy would hand Croce would be filled with circumstantial information the analysts had high confidence was true. Kennedy admitted he could not care less.

He was sure Lucien had set up the attack in Marseilles. Croce would see "Herr Merck" had reached back into several countries' intelligence apparatus for incriminating information, and that likely would seal Lucien's fate. The consigliere was dirty, Kennedy knew, but even he had been surprised at the man who sat at the top of that corruption.

An hour and twenty-one minutes later, "Herr Merck" and his security team arrived at the stylish penthouse. Kennedy/Merck and Taylor were escorted into a lavish living room. The bold colors and lights illuminated cubist paintings, one which Kennedy thought might be an original Picasso. They framed the Italian leather pit sofa and gave the room a vibrant, 1960s-throwback feel.

The rest of the team was shown the security ready room, which provided video coverage of every part of the penthouse except for the bedroom. It also served as out-of-sight access to the wrap-around deck and stairwell to the rooftop helo pad.

Kennedy stood at the wall-to-wall windows and reminded himself that Croce wasn't to be trusted any more than his consigliere. Using the Roman god Janus as his logistics company namesake was likely a subconscious idea Croce mistakenly thought funny in a droll way. Normally depicted as two-faced, representing a host of elements, Janus was thought of as time, duality, doorways, and beginnings and endings, to name a few. Kennedy took a drink of wine to hide his smile.

A few minutes later Croce made his grand entrance, with an

impressive women on each arm who Kennedy thought might be actual runway models. Croce bade him take a seat and when he did, Croce sent one of the models to sit next to him.

Croce smiled and waved his hand. "I understand you are not married, Herr Merck. She is yours for the night."

"Thank you," Kennedy/Merck said, "but this is unnecessary."

"Oh ... perhaps you prefer a young man, then?"

"No, no, I have someone. I admit to being old-fashioned in this way."

"As you please. Do you want her to leave?" Croce waved at the woman.

He put on a genuinely wistful half-grin. "Regrettably, yes, both if you please, so we may talk business."

"Ha! You Germans—always business first," Croce said, nodding to the ladies who were ushered away.

"Short-term pleasure deferred for long-term gains. There will be time to party, as the younger generation calls it, after we conclude the next step of our partnership," Kennedy/Merck said. "The test of your air services was end-to-end perfection. The worrisome section of the ground services test is past, and we await our security officer and product. We consider the test successful, barring any last-minute issues. Now we'd like your services to England and Canada as well."

Croce smiled and spread his arms. "Yes, of course. If you accept my seven percent fee, we can do business."

Kennedy stood. "A five percent fee. Our volume will more than pay your cost, cover your risk, and make you wealthy."

Kennedy offered his hand and Croce shook, beaming. "Agreed, *mon frère*. Let us drink to the next step in our success, Herr Merck, and in expanding our partnership."

"Once again, your taste in wines is exceptional, *Monsieur* Croce.

Domaine Laroche 96, I believe. Exquisite."

"I get hungry when concluding profitable business," Croce said with a grin. "Lucien, have the ladies join us. I hope you like bouillabaisse, Herr Merck. It was invented here in Marseilles, you know. I have paired a 2000-vintage Domaine Tempier Bandol Rose and Champagne with the meal. I hope it is to your liking," Croce said, leading the way to the dining room.

The conversation during the meal was casual as Kennedy interacted easily with Croce, the topics light and unchallenging. Finally, Kennedy/Merck stood and raised a glass of champagne to his host.

"Here's to an excellent host, a great meal, engaging company—" He raised his wine glass to the women, then back to Croce. "—and profitable partnership."

Kennedy stopped mid-sentence at the clunking sound of the power shutting off. A few battery-powered emergency lights illuminated, surprising Kennedy with their red lenses.

"My apologies," Croce said. "This storm is violent; the generator should start in seconds."

The dim red glow was broken, but not by the generator. Instead, it was by muzzle flashes from AKs firing on fully automatic.

Chapter 66

Taylor grabbed the model seated next to him and Kennedy by the collar and pushed them low as he moved them at a crouch toward the security ready room. The other model stood reflexively to run away screaming, then fell silent with a grunt when bullets stitched across her bare back. Croce barked orders to his bodyguards but they were already firing back blindly at shadows.

Taylor radioed the penthouse team for a SITREP. Their response was punctuated by background gunfire.

"We are engaging attackers attempting to breach."

He switched to the frequency for the ground team at the vehicles and found more of the same. They were in a firefight in the parking garage. Charlie Two relayed, "The attackers must have been here waiting for us to arrive."

A high-pitched flash and bang of light outside a nearby window told Taylor the team was taking control of the immediate situation. He cleared a hallway and took Kennedy and the model to a door on the left. He entered and cleared the studio apartment, only to find the chef and a female servant hiding in the bathroom. Kennedy moved inside with the model and took her to the bathroom as Taylor motioned them over.

Taylor nodded and, in French, told the chef and servant to stay quiet. They nodded vigorously in the affirmative. Outside, they could hear Croce calling for his men but not getting a response.

"We have to save him," Kennedy said to Taylor.

"Bloody hell."

Taylor radioed the penthouse team to move down to his position, then cracked the door for a peek. Croce was there cursing his attackers, evidently *jihadis*, telling them there would be no virgins waiting for them when they were dead, only demons.

Kennedy squeezed Taylor's shoulder and whispered in his ear. "*Jihadis*. Same group who attacked us?"

Taylor kept his eyes focused over his pistol sights and whispered back. "Maybe. If we're going to save Croce, we need to go now."

"Charlie Two, Charlie Four entering your six."

Taylor whispered. "Copy inbound my six."

Kennedy spun at the sound of the door at the end of the hallway and nodded as Charlies Four, Five, and Eight huddled up with them. Charlie Eight passed Kennedy and Taylor their H&K submachine guns.

"What's the plan, boss," Charlie Four said.

"Is the deck clear?"

"The south was when we left it. The north is where the attackers are concentrated."

"Four," Taylor said, "go through the kitchen to the deck and come in from their nine o'clock. Five, do the same from their three. Eight and I will get Croce." He turned to Kennedy. "You stay here and protect these folks. Once Eight and I have Croce, we all fall back here and work our way down the south stairwell. Alert me when you are in position. Copy?"

The head nods acknowledged the plan and they took off for their assignments. Twenty long seconds later, Four and Five called in position. Taylor counted down from three.

"Execute, execute, execute."

The volume of gunfire rose dramatically, as did the yelling in what Kennedy recognized as Pashtun. Cries and prayers of the dying followed the multiple explosions of the team's mini-frag grenades.

Taylor radioed he had Croce and Lucien. When they got back to Kennedy, he had Eight disarm the consigliere and flex-cuff him. Lucien's struggle was wasted against Four's knee in his back. Croce protested Lucien's treatment.

Kennedy said, "We can discuss this later—for now, your traitor stays in restraints."

Taylor said. "Four and Five, lead us out. Then staff and *Monsieur* Croce, *Herr* Merck and I, followed by Eight. Copy all?"

Charlie Four led the way as Eight threw two more mini-frags down the hallway to discourage anyone still able to follow them down.

Taylor radioed the ground team for a SITREP.

"All clear."

They had descended eight of the twenty-five floors when gunfire erupted from above. Kennedy and Taylor pushed Croce and the staff against the wall. Eight returned fire, yelling. "Grenade!" A small object bounced down the stairs and landed at Eight's feet.

Kennedy watched wide-eyed as Eight calmly picked up the grenade and tossed it underhand back up the stairwell against the wall. There was a moment of shouting in Pashtun before the grenade exploded and *jihadis* screamed. Taylor used their pain and confusion to get the team moving down again.

They were on fifteen, moving down as quickly as the staff could go. When the consigliere broke free, still in restraints, and started hopping down the stairs two at a time, Taylor laughed and shook his head.

"Let him go. The lads will pick him up at the bottom if he makes it that far."

Chapter 67

A beat later, a massive explosion shook the stairwell. Dust and smoke filled the air. Four moved forward slowly until out of sight. Taylor put a hand to his earpiece for a moment and then said, "The stairs and the *consigliere* are gone."

"Eight, we're coming back up—hold at the door to fourteen."

"Charlie One, Charlie Three. Police and fire are inbound. Ready to assist."

"Charlie Three, copy. Can you tell if the power is back on?"

"Generator power. The elevator is operational."

"Roger that, send the elevator to fifteen with a surprise for our friends. We will move to the north side stairwell."

Croce interrupted. "No, there is a better way. There is an apartment on thirteen with access to the office building next door."

"There is no thirteenth floor," Kennedy said.

Croce said, "Not in the stairwells, only the core of the building. We can access it from fourteen on the north side."

Taylor looked at Kennedy, who thought about it for a moment, his hard stare drilling into Croce, and then nodded. He radioed the ground team to the new pick-up location.

"Eight and Four, lead us out. Speed is our defense," Taylor said before translating for the staff.

They passed the elevator bank and were closing in on the north side when an old woman stuck her head out into the hallway and shrieked at the sight of dirty, heavily armed men. Croce told her in French that there was a situation being handled and to lock herself in because the police were on the way. She slammed the door, and Croce joked about how many of the owners in the building were the oddball black sheep of old-money families.

The blast from the explosive surprise sent to the fifteenth floor rattled Kennedy's teeth.

Holy shit, that was big, he thought.

The last door on the right was locked.

"Do you have the key for this?" Taylor asked.

"No," Croce said. "It was in my office."

Four and Five stood and kicked together. The door flew open to bang against the inside wall. Eight closed the door behind them and followed the pack into the master bedroom, then down a narrow hallway to a bathroom. Kennedy stood dumbstruck as Croce pulled a narrow linen closet on hidden hinges away from the wall to expose stairs leading down a dimly lit corridor.

Eight heard yelling in the hallway and moved to a position with a sightline to the front door. Five kneeled beside him, aiming at the door. Taylor looked their way and nodded before getting Croce down the stairs with Four.

The staff followed with Kennedy bringing up the tail end. He was just stepping onto the first step when rounds started punching holes in the walls. Eight and Five returned fire, shooting through the front door and walls on either side.

Taylor yelled for them to break contact. Eight and Five both fired until their H&Ks locked open as they ran for the bathroom. Eight closed the bathroom door behind while Five reloaded, then wedged a mini-frag between the door handle and wall. He sprinted to the closet and closed it behind him, following Five to the bottom of the stairs.

At the sound of the grenade exploding in the bathroom, he ran down the corridor and threw open the door before rejoining the pack at the office building elevators. Less than a minute later, they were loaded up and driving toward the airport and safety.

On the way, Croce used "Herr Merck's" cellphone to call his counter-assault team. The CAT was waiting at the airport and they surrounded Croce as one of their team ushered the staff into a vehicle, which departed immediately.

Croce told the leader to give him a minute with Herr Merck. He marched over, hugged Kennedy/Merck, and shook Taylor's hand with both of his.

"You saved my life, and I will not forget. I am in your debt."

Taylor pulled his hand back from the extra-grateful Croce. "It was what we found on your consigliere that made us extra vigilant tonight. Your man was Persian. What you didn't see is he's been working for the Iranian Revolutionary Guard since your parents found him not long after the fall of the Shah."

Croce's eyes widened in shock. He was used to being better informed than this, but he'd been taken in by his closest advisor.

"What?"

"It was they who tried to intercept your ground team twice in Iran. Once at the border with Afghanistan and again outside Tehran. Talk to your convoy leader, he will confirm what I'm telling you. We used our contacts to stop the intercept and ensure free movement for you in the future. I find sometimes it's good business to help a partner maintain their value."

"*Thank you.*" Croce nodded. "I will contact you. We have much business before us and profits to make."

"Yes, agreed, my friend. Much business!" Kennedy/Merck said, climbing the stairs into the aircraft.

After the plane leveled out, Kennedy moved aft to thank the Charlie team for saving his backside, the staff, and Croce.

"I've operated with Alpha and Bravo, who are terrific, but you guys may be the best we have, especially considering how little time you've had together." Kennedy smiled. The team smiled back and fist-bumped each other.

"For an common intel nerd, you were surprisingly calm," Taylor responded. "And effective."

Kennedy grinned. "I know I can count on our operators to make sure I do not, as Wolf says, get dead. I had a mission to do while you were moving us out of danger. We both did our jobs, and now we are tight with Croce. Well done, Charlie."

Taylor went forward when Kennedy left, his curiosity piqued, and plopped into the aisle seat.

"What mission were you referring to back there?"

Kennedy's mischievous childlike grin was the tell.

"I planted a cellphone we registered to Lucien with one number on speed dial—Colonel Khorram of the IRGC, his Iranian handler. The colonel and several of his staff, who we know are supplying ISIS, will be implicated in a major drug ring run by the *Unione Corsa* and Jean Paul Croce. The Taliban bodies will implicate him in terrorism on French soil. After he's sent to prison or likely hanged, it will remove an antagonist from the field who's been blocking Wolf's contact from moving into a more senior position in the Iranian armed forces."

He poked Taylor in the shoulder with an index finger.

"And it will end his attempt to control the drug route through Iran, which would cause us problems. When the dominoes fall, we'll be there to shore up our partner, including in New York City, where our actions tonight will surely be seen with cynical eyes."

Kennedy looked out of the aircraft window at the setting sun.

"Now we need to be flawless in our execution to survive taking down this transnational heroin cabal."

Chapter 68

Parker crossed her arms and frowned.

"Are the daily reports enough for you?"

Daily reports from Chief Hogan were Wolf's connection to the reservation and his people. He lied to himself knowing he'd have to live with only the reports while focusing on Afghanistan. In reality, he hated the administrative side of his job.

Wolf smiled. "No. But they have to be if I'm going to keep from getting fired."

No matter the weather or physical threat, outside was a better day than in the office with one exception, and she was standing in the doorway. She seemed as normal as the next person, but Wolf had a hard time accepting all was well with his wife.

Time would tell.

Maybe she had worked it out or talked it through with the shrink. Kennedy had suggested Parker talk with an alienist, as Wolf's CIA ground branch friend had called her psychiatrist, Janet

Winter. Winter had come down to MacDill for other business and she and Parker had spent a couple hours together, talking and getting to know one another. Afterward, Parker had been relaxed and calm. Wolf had sensed her old self coming back.

Parker stared at him and he laughed. "What is it?"

"Your eyes give you away, knucklehead, and the smoke from your ears. You're thinking again, and we know that leads to no good," Parker said.

Wolf shook his head. This was the old Elle Parker.

"Excuse me. That's Director Knucklehead to you, Miss Spook. What have you learned Global Air Services?"

"Not much yet. I do know it's a Tribal 8A, also known as a Super 8A. Easy to contract with, high contract ceiling, and so on. Standard stuff. I have the folks at Treasury's Financial Crimes Enforcement Network helping me sift through all the layers of contracts, business entities, and bank accounts. Mapping them out is a bit like filling in the people and businesses of the Sinaloa cartel, except they seem to follow Securities and Exchange Commission and state rules for corporations. I sense a connection between Global Air Services and Juno Services. Contracts at the same places for the same customers seem a logical extension that I think is hidden in the corporate filings. The folks at FINCEN understand all this stuff better than I will ever want to. I should hear something by the end of the day."

"Is it a corrupt company, or are the bad actors just an element within? How deep does the collusion go?"

She pointed at him. "Exactly. I have work to do. If you'll excuse me, Director Knucklehead, I'll get back to it."

Wolf gave Parker a halfhearted salute. "Roger that. Carry on."

After lunch, Wolf was reading the SITREP Clinton had sent from seven thousand miles east of MacDill. The Marines were pissed at being assigned drug missions instead of hunting terror-ists, as their original mission statement had directed. The DEA's focus on building out the Counter Narcotics Police of Afghanistan was just starting using Marines as cadre and trainers for what amounted to basic and advanced combat training.

In the DEA's push to plus-up three thousand Afghan counter-narcotics police, the training pipeline had consumed people and critical air resources essential to Bravo Squadron. Clinton hinted at the fact that they were operating on their own with little to no support.

The one positive note was the training consumed none of the Marines' excellent human intelligence resources and very little of the technical collection capabilities of the unit. Clinton had rec-ognized their availability and willingness to work with Shadow Tier, even if it was one with a counter-drug focus. At least it was real operations that ran parallel to the terrorist hunt, and some-times aligned with it.

The Taliban were terrorists and drug producers at the same time. Clinton had told Wolf he was open to taking down terror suspects if Bravo was available and the Agency requested. It had happened twice in their deployment, and he was sure it would happen again.

Wolf's personal cellphone buzzed, but the number wasn't one he recognized. He walked out into the unclassified reception area and accepted the call. "Hello."

He recognized the smirking voice. "Wolf, your friend Billy had a bad heart. Did you know? He didn't last as long as I thought he would."

Amaru.

Wolf stood growling as his cellphone rang with another call.

"That should be Chief Hogan with bad news, I'm afraid. You

should take his call. We'll talk again." Amaru ended the call.

The second call had ended before Wolf could change to it, so he called it back.

Chief Hogan said, "Wolf, it's all gone to hell here. They shot the plane out of the sky. And when Billy went to take down a meth lab we identified, it was a trap. There are eight dead, including Billy. Amaru carved him up and left a message, blaming you for everything. White Horse has seen the message and called an emergency council. Ah, shit—White Horse is here now, I need to go. I'll call when I have more."

Wolf's hand dropped to his side as he walked out of the building. Visions slammed into his mind's eye of Amaru torturing Billy.

Wolf felt like his life's mission was spinning out of control.

Chapter 69

Y ou okay, brother?" LeBlanc asked, as he walked by Wolf on his way into the building. At the lack of response as Wolf walked away, LeBlanc grabbed the reception phone and dialed Parker's office in the SCIF.

"Parker, something's going on and it probably is bad. I've seen Wolf like this before. Meet me outside?"

Parker caught up with LeBlanc, who was just outside the front door, radio in hand. The responses he was getting about Wolf's whereabouts were all negative until Jerry, the rangemaster at the shoot house, responded.

"He's here."

She grabbed LeBlanc's sleeve, and asked, "What's going on? What do you mean you've seen Wolf like that before?"

"Last time I saw Wolf behaving like this, he was on his way to kill El Chapo."

When they found him, it was via the overhead video playback

system. The bang of the multiple shots Wolf was putting into each target hammered their ears. The rangemaster handed them Peltor headsets.

Parker counted the pistol magazines on the chest rig and war belt Wolf was wearing. She pushed a chair over to LeBlanc and took one for herself.

"You're going to want to get comfortable."

Heart in her throat, Parker watched as Wolf kept going, moving from one lane to another. She saw tears coursing down his cheeks. It took a full eighteen minutes for Wolf to run through all three lanes. At the end of the third, he cleared and holstered his pistol before kneeling, head down, hands on his thighs. A moment later, he was up and walking back to the control center.

Wolf stuck his head in the control room and told Jerry thanks, then motioned to Parker and LeBlanc to follow him outside.

Wolf was leaning against a picnic table when Parker and LeBlanc got outside. She moved toward him and stopped—his body language screamed rage.

"What's happened?" Parker said.

Parker was stunned as Wolf relayed the calls from Amaru and Hogan in a cold, flat tone.

"That's all he had time to say."

LeBlanc swore for colorful seconds. The fury Parker felt from them was palpable.

LeBlanc said, "Want me to get the team ready?"

Parker held her words, willing Wolf to keep his emotions in check.

"Chief Hogan hasn't asked for help. And I'm not welcome."

Parker realized she had been holding her breath, which she let go hidden in a cough. Her cellphone buzzed.

"Parker," she said, listening. "Okay, put it through," she said, holding the phone out for Wolf. "It's Frank White Horse for you."

"Wolf here. You can't—my bloodline can't be in question. Harm to the tribe? That's not true."

Wolf handed the cellphone back to Parker. "Now I know what the emergency council meeting was about. I've been dis-enrolled."

LeBlanc beat Parker to the question. "What does it mean?"

"I'm no longer an official member of the Crow Tribe."

Wolf started walking west on the service road toward the end of the runway.

Parker held LeBlanc's arm and said, "Let him go. He needs to talk."

"Talk to who?"

"His mother and his ancestors."

Chapter 70

Wolf eased off the country road through the gate to the classi-fied facility called Pinecastle, north of Altoona, Florida. Run by Micanopy Enterprises on behalf of the Navy, the little-known facility was a training and mission prep site for Agency and special operations units headed to Central and South America. Wolf had, at various times in his Army career, flown from the site to Ecuador, Colombia, and Peru.

At the second gate, there was an armed guard and a friendly face. Wolf stopped and stepped out to shake hands with his friend.

"Istonko, Wolf," Wade Micanopy said in his native Seminole.

"Kehee, Wade," Wolf said in Crow.

"Got your message. You're all set up. How long?"

"Three to five days. Is that okay?"

"Sure. Put you in a restricted area. No one will bother you. And the interactive stuff is clearly labeled. Here's a map to your lodge."

Wolf bro-hugged Wade, then jumped in his truck and drove

north on the service road between the Navy property to the west and Wade's to the east. Wolf knew from experience Wade's property was four times bigger, and the total was just short of one thousand acres.

Seven miles later, he took a right and used numbers written on the map in black Sharpie to unlock the gate. Another four miles east and a left back north for half a mile, and he saw it on his left in the fading light.

Wolf stoked the fire outside the sweat lodge and entered to do the same to his frame of mind. The smell of the freshly cut branches and old animal hides, which had been used for this exact purpose many times before, brought Wolf an instant sense of peace with resolve.

He stripped down to running shorts and entered the lodge. It was already warm and getting hotter as he stoked the fire to begin his journey.

Chapter 71

Parker sat in the Shadow Tier headquarters SCIF staring at the virtual pile of documentation and filings for the one hundred and forty-seven different entities the Alaskan Native Corporation had created. All of them were part of direct bids and partnerships with companies as large as SAIC and Lockheed, to as small as a five-person service-disabled veteran-owned business from Manassas, Virginia.

"I know you're in there," Parker said to herself.

The whiteboard in her office slowly became a visual representation of the Indian conglomerate in all its many colors. She took a page from Kennedy's playbook and investigated each of the organizations and their subcontractors to ensure she understood all the direct and indirect connections. As a veteran of Bosnia and the first Gulf War, Parker was aware of the profitability of seemingly low-end services in war zones.

The Alaskan Native Corporation had created a brilliant web

of self-dealing and interconnected services for logistics, maintenance, and cleaning throughout Europe and the Pacific. The lower cost of employees added to its enormous profitability.

An analyst friend she called in from Defense Security Service (DSS) for a second opinion suggested that many of the ANC workers might be undocumented, and thus paid even less than US citizens, further boosting the bottom line.

But the big money makers were the services the corporation provided in the war zones of Afghanistan and Iraq, a natural extension of its European presence. Hidden in the companies and partnerships of the European division was the connection to Janus Logistics.

Parker's other target, Global Air Services, had been a recent partnership formed just four months ago. It was already under contract with the US Air Force, US Army, the German Air Force, even the United Nations.

Parker stopped to take in her whiteboard. She huffed as she noted her visualization had started to look like a train route map with interconnects. The glaring dead-end spur track with question marks had the label *Global Air Services*.

At the side table she was using to sort all the documentation and filings, she picked up the intelligence summary Kennedy had provided in his conversation with Croce. She had put the thought aside as it didn't fit their intel on the subject and her known pattern of life.

Then she reread the details from Croce's description of his meeting and agreement to partner with Global Air, she thought of the saying attributed to Sherlock Holmes.

When you have eliminated all that is impossible, whatever remains, however improbable, must be the truth.

Parker wrote out her questions.

1.   *Can Eliana travel internationally without El Chapo knowing or*

    giving his permission?
2.   *If Eliana is behind Global Air, what does she gain?*
3.   *If El Chapo is behind this, what does he gain?*
4.   *Are her trips to Miami related?*

Parker picked up her phone and dialed the FINCEN supervisory agent working the money side of her investigation. FINCEN and the intelligence agencies had become very good at following money trails to identify paymasters and thus top-tier leaders of terrorist organizations.

While the phone rang, she mumbled a quick prayer for the analyst working her tasking.

"DeFranco," the FINCEN agent answered.

"Parker here, Danny. Anything new on your end?"

The excitement in the supervisor's voice was contagious.

"Miss Parker, yes, there sure is. The corporation is registered in Panama. It uses a Miami-based private bank to buy and lease aircraft. A Swiss bank is used for European and Middle Eastern operations. An Australian bank account is set up but hasn't been used yet. There is also a cash account at the National Bank of Cuba. These accounts have been funded from BBVA Bancomer and its primary location and headquarters in Mexico City."

Parker asked, "How much longer will it take to identify any signatories of the original account?"

"From our experience with Mexican accounts, I'd say we have another couple of days of work to push through the remaining shell companies to get to your origin-account owner. Frankly, I would be surprised if it's who you're looking for."

"Okay, thanks," Parker said. "Keep me apprised?"

"You bet. More as I know it."

She ended the call and punched the button for the whiz kids.

"Ryan," the voice answered.

"Time to give PROVIDENCE a workout. Come to my office."

"On the way."

Parker placed the handset back in the cradle. She closed her eyes and breathed deeply. A vision of Wolf meditating in the sweat lodge was clear in her mind's eye.

She whispered to herself.

"You are more than your birthright to me, mister. Don't let the darkness take your soul."

Chapter 72

G ray rain clouds were low over JFK Airport, unsure whether to rain one more time or blow away. Morgan had flown up from Miami and was happy for his hoodie's protection against the damp, and he appreciated its anonymizing effect. He suppressed a laugh watching Croce, who stopped and looked around to see if he was in the right place as if trying to hit his mark on a stage.

He wore sunglasses and had a copy of *The New York Times* in his left hand. Morgan wondered if it was a test to see if he could follow orders or some old-school tradecraft prank.

"Herr Merck" had pushed Croce to make the trip, as it was too important for both their businesses, and Kennedy/Merck's men would provide *Unione Corsa* their protection until he could regroup.

Croce had finally agreed, telling Merck the trip was to make connections and show off his distribution capabilities. Croce's concept was to set the stage and prove he was worthy of the New York mafia's trust.

A man addressed Croce and they spoke briefly, then headed for the parking garage. Morgan followed and called the surveillance team, giving them a description of the vehicle as it headed toward the exit. Then he trotted back to the passenger pick-up area to be driven into the city, and a meeting with the undercover FBI agent Croce was on his way to meet.

Morgan's cover was as a heroin and cocaine supplier out of Miami with connections to the Sinaloa cartel. If needed, he could be vetted by Eliana Cortes and El Chapo's east coast operations chief. The FBI agent, undercover name Frank Sarti, had infiltrated the Genovese family, and his deal with Morgan, as directed by the Genovese's number two, would cement his takeover of Anthony Tostas position running firearms and narcotics.

Morgan was dropped off at the Pierre Hotel, where the young lady at reception gushed over him even as he stayed hidden in the hoodie. An assistant manager guided him to his grand suite on the thirty-eighth floor overlooking New York City's Central Park.

Morgan paced the suite admiring the finer things in life he could only get on mission. The suite's Parisian sensibility was to his liking, but for two grand a night, the Pierre's sumptuous two-bedroom suite was well beyond his Motel Six reality.

Morgan used his satellite phone to text Kennedy that he was in play. Then he left a coded voicemail for Wolf through their Telmex message exchange. A quick shower and change into his suit saw him ready for his eight-thirty dinner with Sarti and Croce.

Sarti was sure to have his crew there, which included not only muscle but a tech who would sweep the location in the hour prior to dinner for listening devices. As they had for many previous meetings, Sarti said his tech would also place white noise generators on the windows to defeat high-tech listening via laser and microwave.

In a move that made Morgan smile at its genius, the FBI had

gotten an undercover to replace the white noise generators with modified units. There would be hell to pay if the tech ever cracked open one of his devices. In the meantime, the FBI had hundreds of hours of digitally recorded conversations, more than enough to put away his crew for a long time.

But the special agent in charge of the New York office, and leadership down in Washington DC, wanted more. They wanted *capo*-level family members or higher at the very least. In a non-FBI manner, they were playing the long game, betting on better days of catching bigger fish.

Morgan thought it too bad the FBI's not-invented-here-so-it-can't-be-any-good mentality was keeping them from getting the latest tech. Like the Laser Imaging, Detection, And Ranging the Kid was testing against Croce in Marseilles. LIDAR's standoff capabilities would make risky moves like replacing the white noise generators obsolete.

The government-cops-in-nice-suits gang have never been bleeding edge.

The ringing phone took Morgan out of his musings. The voice on the other end told him a car was waiting downstairs. Morgan placed his push dagger inside his belt on his right flank and his 9 mm Sig on his left. His jell-based body armor was built into a black V-neck T-shirt. He covered that with a black silk shirt, double-breasted suit, and black slip-on shoes, no socks. He added a Heuer Monaco square watch and silver ring with the Corsican coat of arms on his right hand. Then a multi-strand silver chain surrounding a miniature dagger on his left wrist completed his costume for the night.

Morgan stopped in front of the full-length mirror as his cover identity was likely to do for a last once-over. Satisfied that he was ready, he dropped into character and headed to the elevators specifically assigned to the guests in the grand suites.

From the back seat, Morgan noted the drive started down the east side of Manhattan, then back west into Little Italy, taking about twenty-seven minutes. The car stopped in front of Ballato, and the driver told Morgan to go inside and ask for Frank.

The driver said, "Get the *Costolette d'Agnello al Rosemario*, it's the best in the city."

"Ehh," the fat driver's associate said. "It's okay. But get the *vongole*."

"Thanks," Morgan said, jumping out of the car.

The hostess evidently was expecting him. She nodded and touched finger to her temple. The maître d' appeared and led Morgan back to a private dining room. Inside the door, Morgan wondered how many mob meetings had been held in this very room. Its dark wood had an old-world feel, the lighting diffused. The chairs were wrapped in leather and studded with brass, adding to the old-world formality of the setting.

Morgan was immediately blocked by another large guy who said he was going to pat him down. Morgan nodded and let the man take his pistol and dagger.

Sarti stood from across the room and said, "Marco!"

Morgan held his hands up as he approached.

"Sorry, Frank. Can't be too careful in the city."

"Not to worry. We are all among friends here, right?" Sarti gestured to a second man. "This is Jean Paul Croce, from Marseilles."

Morgan moved around the table to introduce himself as Croce stood. "Marco Defendini, *Monsieur* Croce. *Enchanté—ravi de vous rencontrer*." Nice to meet you, Morgan said in French.

Croce's eyes widened as he took in the crest on Morgan's ring. "You are Corsican?"

"Yes. My family immigrated to Cuba, then America."

Croce nodded in approval and sat down. Morgan took his seat, and when Sarti raised a glass of wine, Morgan and Croce did too. "A toast to the forming of a profitable relationship lasting many years. *Salute!*"

"*Salute.*"

Sarti got right to the point of the meeting. "Jean Paul. Marco supplies me with my product now. Why should I buy yours, and how can you ensure secure and reliable delivery of your product?"

The next twenty-three minutes was a well-rehearsed explanation of the quality of his product and the secure distribution routes Croce had at his disposal. With one exception.

"You are ready to provide proof of quality?" Sarti asked.

"Yes." Croce nodded, beaming with what Morgan guessed was pride. "Yes, I am."

"No sample?" Morgan asked, adding fake disappointment in his voice and eyes.

Croce smiled and reached into his inner right suit pocket for a pair of glasses. Clunky black glasses like Morgan's straight-A nerd brother used to wear in high school. The military calls them BCGs—birth-control glasses.

First, he carefully popped out a lens and set it on the table. Then he broke both earpieces, emptying their powdery contents on the lens. Croce pointed at the lens and said, "Et *voila*—sample. I can have volume product for you in forty-eight hours. If you prefer a formulation to your specifications, it will take only one week from the time my scientists confirm the validity of your chemistry."

Sarti nodded to the big security guy who had done a good job of becoming invisible. He stepped forward and used a thin stainless tool to put some of the powder into a miniature test tube that already contained a reagent. He shook the tube vigorously and held it up to a white-light penlight pulled from his pocket.

He grinned modestly. "High level of purity, boss."

"Mister Croce, you impress. Tell him, Marco."

"The quality of the product and reliability of its delivery has become a problem using our Mexican supplier. You have reached out at the right time. We are looking at alternatives. How soon can we begin doing business?" Morgan pushed a small piece of paper to Croce.

Croce read the note, his eyes going wide. The note said **25 kilos**.

"I can have this amount in ten days or less," Croce said before writing on the flip side of the note Your cost $750,000 on delivery and pushed it back to Morgan, who showed it to Sarti.

Sarti looked at Morgan and then Croce while raising his glass, beaming.

"Condordato. Now, let's eat."

Chapter 73

K ennedy grabbed the Kid and they flew to London. The plan was to update Andrew Cavendish and select members of his Joint Narcotics Analysis Center at its new headquarters in Thames House. Just upriver from Horseferry Road and the Lambeth Bridge across the Thames, the facility was originally built as the primary headquarters of MI-5, Britain's internal security service.

The JNAC, and the newly formed Joint Terrorism Analysis Center, were its recent additions. Some in leadership positions at American intelligence agencies and the military services saw the formation of the JNAC as self-serving, but Kennedy understood the UK prime minister's desire and willingness to support his partner, the United States, with his greatest capabilities.

The JNAC mission illustrated support without committing more troops. It also provided much needed expertise and analysis to MI-5 and the multitude of police organizations combating illegal narcotics in the UK.

Kennedy smiled as he drove into London. It was the Kid's first time in the UK and the shock of driving on the wrong side of the road wasn't for first-time UK drivers like him. Nevertheless, he was giddy at setting foot in the historic city.

"Don't get too excited, bubb," Kennedy said, but he smiled. "We may get to carve out some personal time for you to see some things, but first things first. We'll spend most of our time in a drab government building, not at all different from DC," Kennedy said, seeing he wasn't eroding the Kid's enthusiasm.

"Is the traffic always this bad?"

"Oh, no—many times it's much worse. Ten million people live in and around London. The estimates are eight hundred thousand people commute into the city every workday."

The rest of the ride was in silence, the Kid seeing the expertise of a London cabby firsthand as he took several side streets to get them efficiently to Thames House. Cavendish met them at a covered private side entrance and whisked them inside to an office where RFID wrist bands were affixed to them by unsmiling security men.

A tech told them they wouldn't need escorts, but Cavendish would be with them during their visit through unknown hallways anyway, and their badges limited them to the JNAC and its British version of SCIF.

Cavendish took them out a back door to an elevator that he summoned with an eight-digit keypad code and retina scan. The lift had just one stop: the JNAC. Built to provide cover for confidential informants and undercover staff, it opened to a light blue hallway. The ceiling, walls, and floor tile were all the same odd shade of blue from the fluorescent lighting. As they moved down the corridor, Kennedy observed that the blue was mildly disorienting, with each featureless door outfitted with the same keypad and retina scanner like an optical illusion that went on forever.

Kennedy looked up and recognized the shape of a nozzle, then a series of them.

Gas dispersal—immobilizer? Seems extreme.

Cavendish stopped at the fifth door on the right, entered a code, and leaned forward into the retina scanner. The magnetic locks clicked open for access to a room also painted in a light blue. A large table stood in the center and workstations at another table on the right side. There were two people at the table and one person at a workstation.

Cavendish said, "Ladies and gentlemen, this is Kieran Kennedy. Full disclosure, he is my American cousin, but I accept no responsibility for any bad behavior by a colonist." He grinned at Kennedy and the other Brits in the room chuckled respectfully. "And this is, ah…"

"This is Jack Wayne," Kennedy offered. "We just call him the Kid." The Kid waved and said nothing.

"Right, then." Cavendish gestured to his people for introductions. "This is Mr. Staunton on the left, Miss Truxton on the right, and over there—" He pointed across the room. "—Mr. Drury at the terminal." He pointed back to the Americans. "These gentlemen are from the American Shadow Tier organization. Our goal is to support their ability to disrupt the flow of heroin from Afghanistan and its resultant funding of the Taliban. A matter our brothers and sisters at the JTAC are very interested in. Before we begin, Kieran, I should point out that Mr. Drury has been responsible for the data feed you have been receiving from us."

Drury said, "Thank you, director." He stood and shook the Americans' hands. "You can call me Timothy. Kid, it's good to finally put a face with the name."

"Thank you, Timothy," Kennedy said. "Your data brings context and depth to activities we are just starting to understand. Andrew, if you don't mind, I'd like to jump right in." Kennedy paused to scan the room. What he was about to say was audacious, bold, and one hundred percent cowboy, as the Brits like to say.

"Lady and gentlemen, at the order of the President of the United States, we've been working to fill the gap between the combat units left in Afghanistan and the DEA—the same DEA who's stalled in attempting to build out an organic Afghan counter-narcotics capability. To date, we have successfully penetrated several distribution modalities feeding Taliban opium into Marseilles. The French connection is important, as it's the central operations hub for the movement of opium into Europe. And now, we know, out of Germany to Britain and America."

Truxton raised her hand.

"Pardon me, please. You just used the term French Connection. Are you suggesting *Unione Corsa* is reborn?"

"Miss Truxton, you know your history. Yes—in fact, Jean Paul Croce has resurrected *Unione Corsa*. We have a partnership with him to distribute our faux opium from Afghanistan into Marseilles and Germany. We're on the cusp of testing routes to Britain and America, in particular to New York City. And he has secured an initial deal to supply one of the five New York City mafia families with twenty-five kilos of heroin."

Kennedy let that information sit for a beat and stole a glance at the Kid, who was smiling like the Cheshire cat.

Cavendish asked, "How do you know all this?"

Kennedy nodded to the Kid. "We have become the Angel drug cartel," the Kid said, pointing at Kennedy. "This is 'Herr Merck,' leader of the cartel. Separately, we just saved *Monsieur* Croce's life when the Taliban attacked his home in Marseilles. I'm sure you've seen the reports and TV news about it. And last night, one of our men was at the meeting in New York with the mob. So, you can see we've infiltrated every step of the path opium takes from Afghanistan to Europe and beyond. What we need is your help here in Britain when we close the noose. What we're looking at is a multi-national effort that will deny the Taliban tens of millions of dollars in funding. And in the process, we'll roll up hundreds of drug traffickers. The severe damage to the opium trade should last for a year, maybe two."

Cavendish began clapping and his team joined in.

"Bloody amazing, a real operation. Count us in. I didn't come here just to provide intelligence. When can we start?"

"You already have," Kennedy said.

They spent the rest of the day planning and agreed, for now, *Operation Lionheart* would be kept close hold.

As they headed out for dinner, the Kid said, "You know, for an operation that was intended to clear the Air Force connection, this has grown into something else, boss."

"Yes. Things are starting to get fun again."

Chapter 74

"This can't wait?" Wade Micanopy asked. "I know he's your husband, but he does have a day job right now."

Parker half-grinned and said, "I know he wanted more time, but the request came from an old friend, and just the fact that the friend contacted me says it's urgent."

What she didn't say was how shaken she was that an Iranian general officer had her new phone number, and had begged her to give a message to Wolf.

"Okay, okay. I'll have him call you ASAP."

A diesel truck headed his way filtered through Wolf's meditations, the bear root and sage smoke gritty in his eyes as he opened them. The truck stopped and Wolf knew instantly it was Wade, the keys for the various gates and buildings clinking as he ambled over. He stopped before the closed flap of the sweat lodge and called out.

"Wolf, man. It's me. Sorry, brother, but we need to talk. Elle asked me to come out."

At the mention of his wife, Wolf crawled out of the lodge and looked up at Micanopy from the ground.

"Is she okay? What's happened?"

"She's okay, brother. She said to tell you an old friend called asking for your help."

"Did she say who?"

"No, but she said it's urgent."

"Thanks. There's a drying rattlesnake skin in the lodge for you if you want it," Wolf said. He headed to his truck and wiped down his glistening body with a terrycloth hand towel, then dressed.

Wade smiled. "Rattlesnake. Thanks. Did he talk to you?"

"Yes, he did," Wolf said, grabbing his cellphone and pressing the speed dial for Parker. "But I don't believe him." He walked a few paces away for privacy.

Parker apologized for interrupting his personal time and told of getting the call for Wolf at the end of an eight-mile run. And how it scared her—the general seemed to know she had just finished.

"He's been trying to find you and it sounds urgent. He wants you to meet him in Islamabad. There's a meeting the Pakistani Ministry of Narcotics Control is hosting that he'll attend. It's called the Triangular Initiatives Senior Officials Meeting. It's the counter-narcotics leadership from Pakistan, Iran, and Afghanistan. I checked with Clinton, and no one at DEA or the Agency has mentioned the meeting."

"Sounds like something the Agency might keep close hold. I'm sure the person sent from Afghanistan will be one of their assets. Did he say why he wants me to meet him there?"

"No. Just that it's important to your mission. You have forty-eight hours to get to the Islamabad Marriott."

Wolf rotated his wrist to look at his watch. "Okay, I'll drop by the house and pack. I'll see you before I leave."

"Did you find what you were looking for?" Parker asked. She didn't fully understand Wolf's Indian traditions and wasn't sure she even believed in them, but she knew her husband did, and if it worked for him it worked for her.

"Answers no, but paths to them, yes."

Wolf saw Wade standing by his truck as he walked back. "Do me a favor, Wade?" He pointed to the lodge. "Don't tear it down just yet. I have a feeling I'll be back."

"You got it, brother. Be safe. And if you can't be safe, be violent."

Of the three travel cover stories Parker had waiting for him, Wolf chose the pretense of economics professor from the University of Mexico. He could easily talk about drug policy and the problems Mexico was facing while trying to control an illegal fifty-billion-dollar portion of the economy. The documents section had his new passport, university photo ID, and driver's license ready along with pocket litter and school papers, meeting notes, and other random essentials in a worn leather messenger bag.

LeBlanc joined them for an update as Parker joked about Wolf getting more Marriott points.

"I'll be okay. There's no chance any of the other attendees will know me except General Ahmad. And as far as the Agency knows, the ISI does not have a file on me."

"How does an Iranian general know you by name?"

"Long story short, I met him when he was a new lieutenant before the fall of the Shah. We kept in touch at first through an archaeology bulletin board, and then through various websites describing digs and finds in Native American and Persian history. Just last week, it was his people who interdicted Qods Force at the Afghan border, making sure the UN convoy with Mallard and the opium could pass. He hates what illegal drugs do to his country as much as we do ours, and he thinks the Qods Force is out of control. They work with ISIS, sending EFPs into Iraq and supplying the Taliban chemicals it needs to process its opium. So, he must have some info too sensitive to risk sending electronically."

"I should go along as your grad-student assistant," LeBlanc said.

"I appreciate it, brother, but this is a solo mission. It's Islamabad, so not much risk there."

"Can we get Clinton and Bravo to Jalalabad, just in case?"

"Decent idea, but they wouldn't get clearance to enter Pakistan. No, there's a large and active Agency contingent in Islamabad I'll rely on if this goes sideways."

Parker's phone rang and she raised the cell to her ear. "Got it. Thanks." She disconnected the call. "The Gulfstream is waiting. They'll take you to Doha, and from there you fly Qatar Airways. Give me your sat phone."

"Why?"

"I have a new one the Agency sent for you. It appears commercial and works as such, but it has encrypted voice, text, and data, and it interfaces with these remote button cameras—" She handed him a small booklet and two black dots the size of pencil erasers in tiny zip-locked plastic bags. "—that stream video, tested and configured to the system. You can read the manual in the plane."

There was a growing moment of uncomfortable silence. "Okay, understood," Wolf said. Looking to LeBlanc, he asked, "Give us a moment, brother, please?"

"Absolutely." LeBlanc clapped him on the shoulder. "*Bon chance*, my man." He nodded and left the room.

Together for the first time in three days, Wolf hugged his wife, lingering in the scent of the woman who understood him, whom he loved with every fiber of his being. Wolf relaxed his hold and

Parker pushed him away, her smile replacing her angry grimace.

"You will always be my husband and an honorable and fierce Crow warrior, regardless of what that idiot White Horse or the council says."

Wolf grinned. She would always be his best cheerleader. "This is why I love you. You and I know no one can take it from me. But I have to fight for my family and my ancestors and I will at the right time, just not now when we're so close to taking down this transnational collection of traffickers. And if we can help General Ahmad hurt the Qods Force and the Taliban in the process, well, that's found money. There is almost nothing I wouldn't do to get these people."

"I know," Parker breathed softly. "It's your passion for the job and the loathing of the cartels that keeps you focused. But I worry about the darkness. It's always right there, within you. In reach."

"I'm the Cherokee story of the two wolves. One black and evil, full of hatred and vengeance. The other white and good, driven by love, family, and community, always helping. Every day is a fight, a choice. Most days, I admit to being some of both in thought, but white in action. I hold my darkness close, so it's ready to protect you and our Shadow Tier family. I choose the time and place for its release, which is not something I take lightly. I'm in a good place now. I'm looking forward to our taking the fight to our enemies."

"Okay," she said. Even though Parker was tall, she had to stand on her toes to kiss Wolf on the lips. "Just come back to me."

Chapter 75

"Here's what I need you to do," Parker said to the whiz kids she had asked to her office in the Shadow Tier SCIF. "Wolf thinks the gang we're fighting at the Crow reservation has influence over the tribal executive, a man named Frank White Horse. When Wolf has a feeling, he's usually right. So, I want you to deep-dive him, the Crow tribal council, and the Yellowstone county commissioner. See if there are any dots that connect, and how. You know what to look for."

Parker used her mouse to drag a Zip file of information into a yellow Top Secret folder on the shared computer drive. "I just sent you what we have on the people in question. It should be in your high-side transfer folder. Questions, comments, concerns?"

Ryan half-raised a hand and asked, "What do you want us to do with pop-up leads outside the cluster of people we've discussed?"

"Work them, too. I want to identify any corruption or links to Sinaloa you find, no matter where they go and who is at the receiving end. We're talking politics here with the reservation, at least, so it's probably going to be messy. SITREPs at thirteen and seventeen hundred. Clear?"

The chorus of *Yes, ma'am* responses were what she was looking for. As the whiz kids filed out of her office, Parker grimaced. The thought that she was no closer to figuring out who was behind Global Air Services bothered her. And even more so was waiting on FINCEN and their expertise to uncover the original account holder. She was agitated that she had to rely on others to solve the mystery for her, but she was not above asking for help.

She picked up her handset and dialed Kennedy's satellite phone. It took a couple of seconds for the encryption to handshake and sync. He picked up on the second ring.

"Fraulein Parker! To what do I owe the pleasure of this call," Kennedy said in his passable "Herr Merck" German accent.

Parker laughed. "Herr Merck, I need your wisdom, *mein herr*."

"Hopefully, it isn't about women, as I admit to being proven worthless on the subject time after time," Kennedy said playfully.

"I'm sure Maya would disagree. But no, this is about a specific woman with whom you have a comfortable level of expertise— Eliana Cortes."

"What is she up to now?" Kennedy asked with fake exasperation.

"That is the sixty-four-million-dollar question, isn't it. Do we have any ongoing surveillance?"

Kennedy said, "At a technical level, yes. PROVIDENCE is set up to monitor her bank accounts, and Colonel González has someone on the inside at her son's private school in Mexico. He's the trip wire. From experience, we know she will scoop her son up and bolt at the first whisper of danger. Why are you asking?"

"You've always told me to go with my gut," Parker said, "and not ignore what my subconscious is trying to poke me with. Well, my gut is telling me Eliana is behind Global Air. I don't have any proof yet, but I think I'm close." Parker stopped and examined her glorious fingernails, always perfectly polished. The act often helped her think more clearly, somehow. "One of my many unanswered questions is why would she invest in cargo planes?"

"I can think of a few," Kennedy said. "One, she can launder her money and make a nice profit at the same time. The price the US government pays to have contracted flights into war zones is measured in cubic hectares of money. Two, if I'm Eliana, maybe it's time I set myself up for a profitable life outside of Sinaloa. And the obvious third item is access to the world's largest source of opium and, therefore heroin, via cargo planes. We created a decent paper and digital cartel with smoke and mirrors. What if she wants to create a real one—one she leads, making the decisions and reaping the profits?"

Parker thought about that for a minute and it made more sense by the second. "A cartel that uses American, NATO, and UN infrastructure for distribution. With access to a worldwide network of drug producers in a market with growing demand."

"No one else, not El Chapo or Croce, is thinking this big. I mean, they don't have megawatts of brainpower anyway, but you see my point. They already have too much to deal with in their relatively limited markets. It's more likely she thinks she can become the FedEx or UPS of illegal narcotics. And even then, it's a bold and risky move. Eliana is El Chapo's number one producer, regardless of what we and Colonel González's team do. If she tried to leave him, I believe it wouldn't end well, right?"

"Agreed," Parker said.

"Leave yourself open to other possibilities. This might point to Eliana, but don't stop there."

"Right, I hear you."

"Ha! You do listen."

"Seldom, actually. Deniability is my game. I'll talk to you later, mate—I have more detective work to do."

"Roger that. Out here."

Parker scanned her whiteboards and the pile of files on the side table, and decided it was a good time for a gym visit. She usually worked out with heavy weights that required focusing on form and breathing, a welcome break from the grind of basic intel work and sifting through reams of information. She grabbed her gym bag and headed out, determined to be back in time for the thirteen hundred SITREP.

Workout completed, Parker dug into a Cuban sandwich. Her post-workout hunger was always raging, unlike her friends who had to nearly force food down after seventy minutes of heavy lifting. She drank sweet tea through a straw to help stave off the inevitable brain freeze from drinking too fast. She reminded herself there was no reason to rush.

She followed the knock on the door with a quick, "It's open," and took another bite. The whiz kids tumbled in amid hushed comments about how easy it was.

Parker asked, "What was so easy, Ryan?"

"Our ability to defeat the Montana Department of Justice Criminal Investigations system."

"I beat your time by twenty seconds," said Jennifer Lynn, one of the newest analysts. She turned to Parker. "Do you want a copy of the DOJ files?"

"Wait. You spent the morning hacking Montana and the Department of Justice?"

Ryan frowned. "Well, yes, ma'am. It falls under our charter to investigate illegal narcotics activities and associated persons. We fed the data into PROVIDENCE, and she's connecting the dots as we speak on a second, more-focused run against the data."

The whiz kids all nodded and bumped fists.

"What did you find?"

Ryan nodded to Jennifer, who took the lead. "A bunch. I think the Yellowstone County commissioner is dirty. He has financial accounts and amounts in places a man at his level of government doesn't even think about. One interesting indicator is his oldest son is getting a full scholarship to the Colorado School of Mines. Yet there is nothing in his grades or SAT scores to suggest he warrants the treatment."

"Is there a family endowment to the school, possibly another hook? A legacy?"

Ryan shrugged. "There could be, but we don't see any old or new money being obviously gifted. It could be repayment for something that happened or was taken care of long ago. It would be hard to find unless it's in county records somewhere. He was the county sheriff at one time, so the paper records were likely destroyed. We did find interesting donations and payments out of his political action committee, including substantial donations from organizations in San Francisco and Seattle. The PAC uses the donations to take out advertising against the current governor. And they're pushing the commissioner as 'the people's man' in a run-up to the governor's office. And guess who is listed as a consultant to the PAC?"

"Frank White Horse?"

"Bingo. So far, it seems legit. He's listed as consultant for Native American affairs."

"This is amazing work team. Keep after it. Let's see if we can't stop Sinaloa's influence, and get Wolf his family back."

Chapter 76

Security had already been high at the Islamabad airport, and while driving to the Marriott, Wolf saw it had sustained a dramatic increase. The few civilians at two security checkpoints likely were agents of the Inter-Services Intelligence. The checkpoints were fully kitted out as if they were a military forward operating base in Afghanistan, each with four well-armed guards and scowling, turn-around-go-away attitudes.

One checkpoint was at the start of a traffic-throttling concrete barrier switchback and the other was at the end. Twelve minutes later, and Wolf was at the entrance to the hotel. He paid for the taxi and was greeted by a young man whose nametag, thankfully, had an English translation.

In lightly accented English he said, "Welcome to the Marriott, Professor Acuna. If you will follow me, we have already taken care of your registration for the hotel and conference. I will have your bag taken to the room."

"Thank you. Can you show me to the restaurant, please?"

"Of course. This way, please."

Wolf had no idea when he might eat next, and eating something now would help him sleep better after the twenty-plus hours of flying he'd just endured. He took an outside table and he hoped he was in plain view of the officer who would take him to his meeting. He was finishing a glass of orange juice when a man interrupted.

"Professor Acuna?"

Wolf spun to see a young man. His beard was trimmed close and he was in a suit, but his eyes gave him away as a predator. Relaxed but scanning, classifying everyone in sight as friend or foe.

"Yes. I am Professor Acuna. And you are?"

"I am Major Al-Hashimi of the Iranian Army counternarcotics team."

"Ah, major, of course. Please join me. Coffee?"

Wolf signaled the waiter and asked for coffee as he scanned the area.

"Congratulations on the promotion," Wolf whispered. "I know your father must be proud."

"Thank you," Al-Hashimi said, nodding. "You have been busy, as the saying goes. A new squadron, based in Britain?"

"Yes. Very busy. Was it you at the border?" Wolf asked, knowing the answer.

"No. My next assignment will be a battalion command." The waiter brought a coffee cup and a fresh carafe of strong Iranian coffee, clearing away the old one. The major poured the dark fluid into his cup and sipped it. "I only have a few minutes, sir. You have traveled far and should get some sleep. My father will want you focused for his meeting."

"And when will that be?"

"Not until tonight, at the earliest. You will be notified in plenty of time and transportation will be provided." The Iranian officer placed his coffee cup back on its saucer and stood. "In the meantime, please get some rest and enjoy the conference, Professor Acuna."

Wolf nodded and watched Al-Hashimi walk away, wondering if they might meet over gunsights on a battlefield one day. Today a friend, tomorrow a target. It was the way of warriors.

Wolf huffed. *He's probably thinking the same thing.*

Wolf signed the bill and headed to his room on the second floor. He called the front desk for a wake-up at thirteen hundred, took a quick shower, and slid between the sheets naked and barely dried off. Sleep came easy.

Wolf woke groggy and jet-lagged when the hotel phone rang and he squinted at his watch: His time asleep had seemed no more than an eye-blink. He swung his legs over the edge of the bed and answered the wake-up call, ordering an urn of coffee and some pastries.

Somewhere in the darkened room was his suitcase. He flicked on the bedside lamp and its warm incandescent glow made the foreign room almost homey. He seriously considered laying his head back on the incredibly soft pillow for just a few moments, but he feared he would drop back into a sleep the room service knocking wouldn't penetrate. Instead, he rose to his feet and pulled gray sweatpants and a black T-shirt from his suitcase just as room service tapped lightly on his door.

The server rolled in a narrow cart laden with his order. Wolf tipped him modestly, consistent with his academic's persona, and poured coffee into a ceramic mug. He savored the coffee's aroma for just a moment and then drank it like his life depended on it. He grabbed a particularly gooey cinnamon pastry slathered with tan frosting and took a huge bite, chewing hungrily and then washing it down with more coffee. At that moment, Wolf thought his life was complete.

The combination of caffeine and sugar made him feel normal for the moment. The rest of the afternoon he spent on the laptop using his university account and access to securely tunnel through to Parker and the Shadow Tier covert communications system. She provided an update lifting his spirits and souring his stomach at the same time.

Like Parker, he too had hoped White Horse was on Team Good Guys, but it was looking like he wasn't. To stand at odds with his tribe and, by association, his extended family, bothered Wolf more than he let on. He told himself that in time the full truth would reveal itself. The question dogging him was when to take revenge on Amaru.

Revenge. There, I said it. I can feel the darkness growing. How long can I let it be?

At the conference reception, Wolf worked the room, focused on name and face pairing. Some attendees Wolf recognized from the briefing folder Parker had supplied. A striking young lady spoke to him in Russian, asking what he thought of the conference so far. Caught by surprise, Wolf automatically responded in Russian, cursing himself at the slip.

"Professor Acuna, your Russian is as good as mine, though I was born in St. Petersburg. Where did you learn it, if I may ask?" the woman asked in Spanish.

Wolf smiled and looked straight into her deep blue eyes. "I was privileged to spend time in Cuba in my early years as a revolutionary, when Russian soldiers and scientists were still commonplace. This was before I came to understand how illegal narcotics were eating our children as if a ravenous monster, tearing at the core of our revolution. And you, miss? Where did you study Spanish? At the academy?"

"Svetlána Pavlova," she offered, extending her hand. "What is the academy? I studied at Lomonosov Moscow State University. It is the number one university in Russia, of course you must know of it."

Wolf kept his expression neutral and focused on her smiling face. It was a challenging task in that the deep scoop neck of her form-fitting dress showcased her ample curves in a profound way.

Her slight eye movement away indicated deception. Wolf was about to ask another leading question when they were called in for dinner. Pavlova sat next to Wolf and the other six seats taken by Pakistani and Afghan officials of different levels. After the wait staff asked for their food choices, Wolf smiled at the young woman and asked if she had ever studied birds.

"My favorite are sparrows," Wolf said, using the term for female spies trained to lure men into compromising situations.

She blushed slightly and said, "Mine is crows. They are smart and make clever use of tools. Always learning and adapting."

Wolf smiled and changed the subject to the food, which was presented to the diners with a flourish of silver cloches removed all at once. After dinner, Wolf finished his coffee and was taking his leave. Pavlova squeezed his leg and, with the slightest of smiles, asked if he would escort her to her room.

"Of course. It's been a long day. I am terribly jet-lagged and need much more sleep before the morning sessions."

One of the younger men at the table nodded his approval with a knowing half-smile as they rose. The rest were too engaged with their self-importance to notice. They took the elevator to the fourth floor and, at her door, Wolf kept his distance until she whispered.

"We must talk, Professor Wolf. Come inside."

Chapter 77

Wolf checked the hallway to his right then left before following her in. He slipped the push dagger from its sheath. She closed the door behind them and came close.

"You do not need your dagger. I am here to pass a message. The Taliban is in attendance here for the conference, with the support of the Pakistani ISI. They know who you are. One of the women you saved during the SAS raid on the processing plant took a picture of you with the little girl who died, and she blamed it on you. There is a three-man hit team here in the hotel waiting for the green light, as you Americans say, to take you out."

"How do you know me this and why are you telling me?"

"There is someone in my leadership who sees you as a friend."

"Let's say I believe you. What now? I don't have any weapons besides my dagger, and I prefer not to bring a knife to a gunfight."

"I have this B&T MP9 and two extra magazines," Pavlova said, opening the closet to reveal the black weapon hanging from a coat hook by its sling. The Brügger & Thomet 9mm was marketed as a submachine gun but, all things considered, it was a polymer-framed, striker-fired, full-size pistol much like the Glock 17. And this one had a big honking suppressor on it.

"Will that work for you?"

Wolf grinned and stepped forward to lift the gun from its coat hook. "That's a good start, thank you." He examined the weapon. It seemed fully functional and was graced with thirty-round extended magazines. "Any idea when they will come for me?"

"No, but it will not be tonight. They want to make a public spectacle of your killing during the middle of the conference."

"Great." He pulled a decorative cloth from the back of the sofa in her room and wrapped it around the gun as best as he could and grabbed a pillow to hold over it next to his body. It would have to do, and he didn't have to go far to reach his own room.

"Is there anything else I need to know?"

"I think so ..." she said, grabbing his hand with both of hers and pulling it tightly against her full chest. "Stay with me." She moved in close and the look on her upturned face was clear. "You were right with your clever talk at dinner. I was trained as a sparrow ... but I am also just a woman. I am told I am a good lover," she said, and paused. Was she blushing? "It's because I so enjoy my work ..."

Wolf slowly withdrew his hand and felt his face flush red.

"Thank you, Sveta. You are *very* kind," Wolf said in Russian, "but I am very happily married." He kissed her on the cheek. "In another place, another time ..." he said. He lingered just seconds at the door, his eyes appreciating the sight but utterly not tempted to indulge, then headed to the backup room on the sixth floor.

The special activities folks from the Agency had reserved another room for him under an alias. It looked like laying that on had been a smart call.

How do I let General Ahmad know I'm here?

Wolf had just enough time to put the question mark on his thought when there was a knock at the door. MP9 held at low ready, he peered through the peephole to find the Iranian general himself, dressed in a dark business suit with an Iranian flag lapel pin. He opened the door and stepped back as the man entered and stopped in the middle of the room. Wolf let the MP9 hang from its sling.

"It would be nice to meet just once more like we did when we first met," Wolf said, finishing with a smile.

"I'm afraid those times are gone now, my friend, and meetings with you often bring unwanted excitement. But tonight, we will interrupt those plans. I have a team ready for you to lead. Strike now and end these threats before us."

"I appreciate the offer, but I'm not here to start a war. My only reason for coming is your request. Tell me why you needed me to come all this way, and I can fly out tonight."

"Very well. I hope you do not come to regret this decision."

"Sometimes, the shots you don't take have the most impact."

General Ahmad nodded. "Indeed. But I have news: I am being promoted to chief of staff for the Joint Staff of the Islamic Republic of Iran Army. This will move me out of the tactical hierarchy, but my 65th Airborne Special Forces Brigade commander is a good officer. He will continue to protect the UN convoys as long as he is needed."

"Well done, and congratulations." Wolf stepped forward and shook Ahmad's hand. "That's a third star for you, isn't it? It won't be long before you command the whole of the Iranian army."

"Thank you. Indeed it is. But such increased responsibilities come with increased scrutiny." The general leaned closer and lowered his voice. "Now, to the reason I asked you to come. I want you alone to be my contact henceforth. I will report through you and only you."

Wolf stepped back, mind racing. "I'm not trained for that. I'm afraid I might get you hurt. Would you consider someone I recommend? Someone I trust with my life?"

The general paused before responding. "Yes, I might. But know at the first sign of incompetence, or if for any reason I lack trust in your recommendation, I will terminate the connection. I think you want me to stay connected, though."

He looked out of the hotel room window at the glittering downtown tableau. Cars choked the city streets, and the sidewalks were full of life. You'd hardly know from this vantage point that this was such a repressive regime.

"We live in perilous times, my friend. We must keep open all channels of communication."

Wolf said, "I agree. But you must protect yourself and your family at all costs."

Ahmad nodded. "One more issue for you and Mister Kennedy. The Taliban have infiltrated Janus Logistics and Juno Services. Sympathetic Pakistani and Yemeni workers are their ears and eyes. They have placed a bounty of one hundred thousand American dollars on your head, dead or alive. That's real money even in your country—in mine, it exceeds the dreams of avarice. Directing your Shadow Tier operations from MacDill for a time would be a good strategy for an extended life. Personally—" He laid a hand on Wolf's shoulder. "—I do not want you dead."

Wolf frowned. "It's not my style to run from trouble, you know."

"I know. But at least you can try to side-step it. Let us see if we can continue our relationship another decade or two."

General Ahmad slapped Wolf on his back and handed him a card for a freight forwarding company. "My retirement plan and alternate comms. Until we meet again, my brother."

They embraced.

"*Salamat bashid*," Wolf said in Farsi. May you be healthy.

Wolf waited fifteen minutes before calling the Shadow Tier duty officer on his secure satellite phone. After they exchanged code words, she put Wolf on hold for only a minute.

"An SUV will be waiting downstairs in three minutes. You have a first-class ticket on the twenty-one hundred Qatar Airways flight. Go now."

Wolf said, "Roger that. Thanks. On the way."

There was nothing he needed in the abandoned second-floor room. The Agency would send a cleaning crew who would gather up everything from his room and provide Professor Acuna's apologies for his emergency departure due to a family emergency.

Wolf saw three SUVs in the hotel circle drive and entered the back seat of the second in line, scooting across the seat and slipping out the door to a sedan with desert-grade darkly tinted windows parked alongside. The sedan took off with Wolf on the floor and the three black SUVs departed in different directions. When Wolf glanced back, there was a gaggle of bearded men scurrying to their cars to follow the SUVs that would take them on a grand tour of metro Islamabad.

On the way to the airport, Wolf called Kennedy. Once the encryption synchronized, Kennedy said in a fake German accent.

"*Herr Professor Doktor Acuna!* How nice of you to call."

"I'm clear. Headed to the airport after an interesting meeting. Check the text app for the details."

Kennedy could be heard pushing buttons on the phone. "Shit."

"Yep. I know how to use them to our advantage. I'll have the plan ready to execute by the time I get back. Headed into the terminal shortly, so I'll catch up with you later."

Chapter 78

Where is the Kid?" Kennedy asked, looking around the dining facility full of people.

One of the Agency intel analysts said, "He's on the phone with Army medical at Fort Detrick."

Except for the Kid and one new guy watching the security cameras they had placed around the property, everyone from Charlie Squadron and the support teams were assembled in the DFAC.

"Okay, listen up. This is important," Kennedy said. "We're in the final stages of setting the table for an end-to-end takedown of the French Connection and its distribution apparatus. We need to be on our A-games and ready to respond to threats as they appear. I just got word that the Taliban have infiltrated Croce's organizations, including Janus Logistics and Juno Services. As we saw with the attack on Croce himself, they do not respond well to change."

Kennedy let the laughs purge the tension from the room.

"They would rather burn Croce and us to the ground and party with our remains than let us take their downstream business. And if they must, they will destroy valuable assets like Global Air Services and Janus Logistics for the greater cause."

He paused as someone entered the room in the back to as not to disrupt the proceedings. "Ah, Kid," Kennedy said. "Good of you to join us."

The Kid waved shyly and took his seat.

"So, back to the Taliban and their sympathizers. I know I don't have to say this, but I'm an intel nerd so I will. I want everyone's head on a swivel and watching each other's back. Intel team stay for a minute please. Everyone else, dismissed."

When it was just the intel team and Taylor, the Kid walked up from the back of the room and said, "I was on the phone with Army medical and the bioweapons folks up at Fort Detrick. It was the Army cancer researchers who provided the means to track Monsieur Croce's shipments of our product. They're sending us a dozen iridium tracers with half-lives of seventy-three days. Sixty of those we can detect via the scanners I'll pick up later today at Ramstein. When does Croce want the product?"

"Unknown," Kennedy admitted, "but we're rockin' on ready for the call. Taylor, head to Marseilles and show Croce some love. Tell him we're excited to hear how his meetings went and find out how much product he needs for his date with the New York mob."

Kennedy's sense of pressure to perform was growing. Their crazy plan to create the Angel cartel and engage in the drug business was costing upwards of a million dollars. General Davidson was reporting up the Shadow Tier's actions and planning through the SECDEF to the President of the United States—and the front office, as they say, was getting nervous.

Kennedy took a deep breath and exhaled slowly. *What's the next right thing to do?*

At eight-thirty that evening, Taylor caught up with Croce at *Le Petit Nice*, Marseilles only Michelin three-star restaurant. On the ocean with a spectacular view of the Mediterranean, Croce had a private room to himself, and he invited Taylor to partake with him. They dined on the chef's delectable selection of seafood appetizers, then sea bass, with wine pairings for each of the ten courses.

Croce's security team, what was left of it, was discrete but on edge. Back at Croce's headquarters, Taylor found his suggested upgrades had been implemented. Steel barricades on large hinges had been installed to give defenders some level of protection while keeping them out of sight behind plants and fake walls. The viewing and gun ports were professionally designed with Kevlar blankets holding extra magazines, fragmentation, and smoke grenades. Taylor had taken the idea from a design he had seen in the hallways of a British embassy on the floor housing MI-6.

On the second floor, Taylor shook hands with the leader of the men. The team leader and another of his men were in full battle rattle, body armor, H&K 416 rifles, pistols, and grenades. Taylor took a note to ask the techs if they had intercepted radio comms. A few surreptitious cellphone camera shots later, Taylor sent his imagery to the Kid to identify.

Taylor saw Croce end a call and used the break to address him.

"It looks like you've taken some smart steps with your physical security, *Monsieur* Croce."

"*Merci.* I have implemented all your suggestions. My combat action team is good but not as good as yours. Your people are very professional and focused. I have not once seen your snipers. They are out there, no?"

Taylor smiled.

"Yes, they are. Which means they are doing their job. Pardon my need to switch topics, but Herr Merck expects your meetings went well and is looking forward to your request for product." He handed Croce a new satellite phone. "This is a new military-level encrypted phone you can use to call him directly without concern of interception. Two-zero-three-one is the unlock code. If you need to clear the device, just dial six-six-six and press Enter. All data and calls will be wiped."

Croce chuckled.

"You are addicted to the latest high-tech like it is a badge of importance."

"You are right, of course, but in this case, it's all about our mutual security. And speaking of security beyond your personal safety here in Marseilles, there's the issue of staff in Janus Logistics. We have confirmation that Janus has been infiltrated by the Taliban."

"It is to be expected, no? They were my main supplier until I found your product."

"Yes—and when you switched to us, they attacked you. They dislike change, especially when it costs them tens of millions in profits. They will attack again, most likely, during a convoy or a perhaps a flight. You have given them enough justification to martyr themselves. They will not stop."

Croce stood and looked out of the window. Over his shoulder, Taylor could see he was gazing over the harbor. His reflection in the window was a look of concern, but not fear.

"What do you suggest?"

"We have counterintelligence experts we can insert covertly to see how bad the problem is. Then you can choose how to deal with it once we understand the scope of the problem. We believe investigating without interrupting business is smart, and I know you didn't get this far without being a smart man."

"What will it cost?"

"No charge—security is part of the service. We do this to make you more secure and therefore make us more secure, too."

"Okay, do it. There is too much at stake to let the Taliban interfere in our partnership."

Chapter 79

Wolf and Parker took his truck to MacDill AFB. Leaving the house at zero-five-thirty, they headed straight to the gym and their LSD run. The long-slow-distance method was Wolf's way of getting the stiffness out of his body after being on airplanes for forty hours in the last three days. Out of the house and on the Air Force base, Wolf felt secure enough to talk with Parker about the trip. By forty-five minutes into the run, Wolf had covered the whole nine yards.

"I think that's it. There might be more after the cobwebs clear," Wolf joked.

He watched his wife take it all in, her relaxed stride hiding the processing she was doing about the meetings and close-in-hand threat. She was a long-experienced intel pro, and he respected her sensibilities. He wanted to know what she thought.

"The Agency is going to pee itself when you tell them you have admirers—*friends*—in Russian intelligence. And it's going to be fun the next time you get hooked up to the liar's box. But the part of your story that concerns me is the Taliban had a hit squad on site. That means they knew you were coming. If we assume it didn't come from someone inside our organization, it means it was someone inside Russian intelligence or on General Ahmad's team."

They trotted to a stop at a park bench near a public water fountain and stopped for a drink and a moment's rest.

"There have been plenty of Russians gunning for you over the years," Parker said. She ran her hand across the beads of sweat clinging to her forehead. "The leak could have come from a Bratva asset inside Russian intel, but those Russian mafia assets have mostly been rolled up, I heard.

"I just don't accept that it was the general," Wolf protested. "I mean, Ahmad said he wants to work closer with me, so why would he get me killed?"

Parker said, "Who knows? The general didn't mention this. He seems a careful man who, like you, can see connections the rest of us can't. It's likely his ranks are jam-packed with Taliban and ISIS sympathizers. And how the hell did the Taliban identify you when we were in full battle gear, camo, and eye protection?"

Parker furrowed her brow and stared ahead before placing her hand on Wolf arm.

"Let's walk for a minute. Hear me out. I'm thinking Pakistani ISI. They helped identify you and cross-matched their facial recognition against all the attendees to their little counter-narc party."

"Yeah, our good partners, the Pakistanis."

"The Agency has a love-hate relationship with them."

"I hate to say this," Wolf said, "but I'm a threat to everything Kennedy and Charlie Squadron have accomplished so far. Likely Bravo Squadron, too. I don't like running from a fight, and that's what it feels like I'm doing. But I need to focus on this side of the pond where there is less chance I'll blow the Croce operation."

Parker hid her joy at Wolf's realization. He was thinking bigger than himself, and now he wasn't going into the hit team's backyard. That was priceless. And she'd have him home with her, besides. She had never known anyone with so many enemies actively tracking them. Sinaloa, Amaru, and the Taliban. At least she could strike the Russians from the list. For now.

"It's the smart move," Parker said. "Lots to do here supporting Kennedy and Morgan. And I know you haven't forgotten about your buddy Amaru. What are we gonna to do?"

"To be honest. I want to hunt him down and remove him from the gene pool. But Croce is the more important target. So, I'm going to ignore Amaru. It'll drive him nuts. More than likely make him do something stupid, and then we can deny him breath."

"We are not chartered to target American citizens, right?"

"No, of course not. Our Rules of Engagement allow us to defend ourselves, but capture is the first plan and let the judicial system punish him." Wolf's grim smiled was punctuated by a heavy sigh. "But how all that works out in real time is up to him."

Parker believed Wolf wouldn't lie to her—or he wouldn't have included the Svetlana Pavlova event in his mission recap—but she did wonder if Wolf would lie to himself.

They had made the turn at the beach and started running again when Wolf's cell rang. Parker started to slow, but Wolf kept running, taking the call without stopping.

"What's up?"

"The vice president wants to talk," LeBlanc said.

"Tell them I'll be available in about forty minutes. I'm disarming a nuke at the moment and a little busy. She'll understand."

"You're *what*?"

"Kidding, bro. Forty minutes."

"Yep, got it. Nukes. You're crazy. Out."

"The president wants to talk to mister big shot?"

"No, second team this time. The vice."

Just before Parker took off sprinting the last hundred yards to the gym, she said, "Second string is right, loser."

Wolf laughed and took off after her. He was just able to touch her back when they reached the gym parking lot.

Out of breath, they laughed and hustled into the gym to shower; at home, they would have gotten into their oversized shower together, but the second most powerful person in the nation was waiting for them to rinse off the salty sweat so they had to hustle.

Sweating anew out of the shower, Wolf and Parker entered the climate-controlled SCIF conference room where the moisture quickly evaporated. The secure video conference system connected and the encryption took a few seconds to sync before the large LED monitor flickered to show an empty blue screen that flipped to black.

"One moment please," a voice said.

The screen flipped again and this time the vice president looked back from the White House Situation Room.

Wolf said, "Madam Vice President, good morning. Let me introduce our head of intelligence."

"No need, Mr. Wolf. I know who she is. Good morning, Ms. Parker. Good to see you up and around again."

The vice president smiled her warmest fake smile. It was almost convincing, and Parker appreciated the extra effort it must have taken for her.

"Thank you, Madam Vice President," Parker said with a smile.

"I'll get to the point of this call. The president needs the *Joshua* operation wrapped up in two weeks or less. Mid-term elections are next month, and we want to demonstrate to the American people that we're tough on drugs, not just terrorism. Can you do it for us, Lance?"

She'd used his first name, which she never did unless she was simulating sincerity. He looked down and paused before answering. He knew the answer, of course, but he wanted the V-P to see him as thoughtful and not just a trigger puller.

"It's possible. We're close, but there are some activities needing attention to ensure we take down the operation from end to end. I can confidently commit to three weeks."

The V-P's tone turned harder. "Mr. Wolf, do not mistake discussion for negotiation. You have two weeks, period-dot. Less if you can do it. Take down as much as you can, make sure it includes the New York mafia element—and then you're out. At least until after the elections." Wolf and Parker both recognized her power move of leaning just slightly forward to emphasize her point. "Am I clear?"

"As a bell, Madam Vice President."

"And Wolf, your report got a double fist-pump out of the Agency director. Well done. I wasn't sure he even had a heartbeat until then. Keep the updates coming." The screen went black, and the link was disconnected. Wolf and Parker sat in silence for a minute.

Wolf spoke first. "Well, she awarded us a 'well done,' so in human terms, that's like a big pat on the back, right?" They high-fived and he laughed. "We should play the lottery on the way home."

Parker chuckled. "Well, the director didn't pee himself, but hey. Close enough for government work," she said.

"Shit, two weeks or less. I need to reach Kennedy right now."

Chapter 80

Two weeks or less? Friggin' politicians. If she wasn't our biggest fan and funding source, I'd ..." Kennedy said.

Wolf chuckled. The lighting in the Shadow Tier SCIF framed Kennedy's video visage with a blue tint. "You'd what, brother?"

"Never mind, damn it," Kennedy growled. "The Agency will sniff my bitching from the air and I'll be on the beach with newspaper help-wanted ads in forty-eight hours. Two weeks can work, I guess. We just need to make sure Croce stays on task, and he sometimes has a short attention span. Another attack by the Taliban, though, and all bets are off. Taylor has convinced him to focus on the deal, and we will take care of security."

"Right. I have confidence you'll make it happen for us." Wolf raised a positive thumb at the camera.

"Hard to believe, isn't it? From where we started to now providing security for a drug trafficker who is about to import twenty-five kilos of heroin into the United States."

"Hell, I never would have thought I'd be a member of the Angel drug cartel," Wolf said. "Are there any retirement bennies with this side hustle?"

Kennedy laughed. "Yeah, there are retirement benefits for us all if we don't do this correctly. Not the condo-in-Boca kind."

"Copy that," Wolf said. "So, here's what we have planned. There are two drug flights. One specifically for Herr Merck, which will leave Ramstein and then stop in Gander. There it will offload a package that will be taken via Canada across the river to the New York Indian casino. You and Parker are the pick-up team. Anyone handling the package will carry residual radiation, which we can identify with scanners Ft. Detrick sent us. Besides the pick-up, it's your job to blueprint the delivery process and mechanisms.

"The second flight is for Croce and will fly from Ramstein to McGuire Air Force Base in New Jersey. Morgan will be given credentials as part of the Juno maintenance and cleaning crew. Once he has the package, he will drive it into the city for delivery to Croce and the mafia. I'm coordinating with the FBI on the timing of their raid. Morgan wasn't happy about dying. He says the squibs and submunitions hurt. I called him a big fat baby. I don't think he liked it."

Kennedy said, "No, probably not. Next time he sees you, he'll tie you in a knot, but he won't kill you."

"Yeah, so we changed the plan, and it works better. Morgan slips out, and it's a contact in the Agency who owes him a favor getting him out of town. What do you think, Parker?"

"Y'know, I don't know. You can never be sure with him. The dude is certifiable. He'll probably still tie you in a knot."

"Very funny, you two," Kennedy said, but he was smiling. "So, listen. When we take down Croce, we need to make sure he can't communicate. It will give us a bigger window to take out his crew in Marseilles and have the appropriate authorities raid the distribution businesses. What we're looking at is nearly simultaneous ops in Afghanistan, France, Germany, Canada, New Jersey, and multiple sites in New York."

Wolf crossed his arms. "At the Indian casino in New York, I want their tribal police to get the credit for the busts."

"Understood. The credit goes to tribal police, with support from the FBI and DEA. I have the Agency analysts here working on your cover. Professor Acuna will transform into a wealthy Mexican big shot. You will be gambling in the high-zoot VIP area and staying on the high-roller floor in a penthouse, befitting your status. We'll change the tail number of our Gulfstream, and the flight plan will show you originated in Acapulco."

"You know, I could get used to the high life, jetting around, gambling, eating well, and lots of hot babes."

Parker punched Wolf in the arm. "Second day, you'd be bored to tears."

"Ow, stop hitting me with those bony knuckles."

"You deserved it," Kennedy said. "This is serious. Stay on point."

"You know me, when it gets serious, I start making bad jokes."

Parker shook her head. "Yeah, we know."

"Right. Okay, so, you should get your cover packages tomorrow. The analysts will coordinate with the document folks on your side. Learn your cover stories and standby. I will let you know when the product is in transit."

"Roger that, and thanks. You're doing an amazing job, brother," Wolf said.

"Agreed. This is going to be epic," Parker said.

Kennedy furrowed brow and tight-lipped smile belied what he said. "Thanks. I appreciate that. Out here." His screen went blank.

Wolf pushed back from the table and stood, stretching. "While we have a minute, let me bring you into what I've been having Morgan working on in Miami."

Parker stood as well. "This should be interesting."

"Yeah. Interesting is an understatement. The Agency has reports from Cuba that El Chapo has been over for meetings with the head of the *Direccion de Inteligencia*, their version of a combined Agency and FBI. Somehow a Miami-based narco informant named Luis Cardoza heard about this, and the Agency inserted Morgan undercover as a consultant with ties into the DGI and the communist party. Morgan has been working out of Miami and traveling to Cuba via Venezuela. Two weeks ago, Eliana reached out and wanted to talk to Morgan. She flew to Miami and Morgan took her to Cuba by boat. She claims she's trying to understand the sudden interest in Cuba given their harsh treatment of drug traffickers and abusers. Morgan and I think it's El Chapo proposing to switch out some of the sugar cane for something more profitable. And it appears there is interest in the shit-ton of money to be made. I agree with the Agency on this one. It's worth continuing to investigate."

Parker said, "Wow. If Cuba got into opium production as a national program, it might rival Afghanistan if they were serious."

"I've got a feeling we will be headed to Cuba soon. In the meantime, let's blow up Croce's future and deny the Taliban millions of dollars."

Chapter 81

Parker sat in her office and read through her cover package, amazed at how complete her fake persona was. She wanted to go deeper, but her whiteboards and the pile of printouts on her side desk mocked her. The grind of the hunt for the majority owner of Global Air Services was easily left behind for more exciting and rewarding efforts. Even going for a second cup of coffee was a relief.

Parker told herself she wasn't a quitter, but hoping the FINCEN analysts would come through was not a strategy. Second cup of coffee in hand, she opened a new spreadsheet and labeled it GAS *Investigation Steps to Closure*. Her secure phone rang, and she picked it up on the second ring. The phone chirped as the encryption synced.

"Miss Parker, it's Tony Jackson from FINCEN, ma'am. How are you doing?"

"I'm well, thank you. Do you have news?"

"Yes. This is a little odd. We've not seen this before. The origin account is in the name of Alejandro Cortes."

"What? That can't be. He's in—"

Jackson interrupted. "Yes. He's in WITSEC, the US Marshal's witness protection program."

Parker started pacing, dragging the phone with her back and forth across her desk. "Is there anyone else listed on the account?"

"Yes, his wife, Eliana."

Parker stopped abruptly grabbing the edge of her desk, She held back from telling the supervisor from FINCEN the real relationship between Alejandro and Eliana. The phone conversation continued, sometimes talking, sometimes listening.

"Thank you, Tony—thank you. You and your team have been very helpful. Here is my high-side email." She recited the electronic address. "Yes, that's it. Please send me all the details. Thank you."

Parker placed the handset back in the cradle and whistled soft and low. She pushed the I-knew-it feeling down and basked for a beat in the glow of confirmation. She glanced at her whiteboard and was reminded of her questions.

Alejandro. Is he back in the game operating under the protection of US Marshals? Or is it just a way for Eliana to hide her connection to the Alaskan Native company and Global Air Services?

Parker headed to Wolf's office, rapping on the door frame to get his attention. Wolf waved her to the chair next to his gray institutional office desk while he finished his call.

"Budget pukes at SOCOM."

"Alejandro and Eliana are the majority owners of Global Air Services."

Wolf head snapped up so fast he risked a cervical injury.

"Alejandro?"

"Yep. He's primary on the account."

Wolf moved around his desk, rotating his neck, and stared at the ceiling for a moment before turning back to Parker. "He's building a drug trafficking business while in WITSEC. He can't be that stupid, can he?"

"My money's on Eliana. Somehow, she figured out how to hide money inside a WITSEC-protected account. It's brilliant when you think about it. You hide your purchases and profits inside a US government-protected account while using US military infrastructure and contracts to run your business. She's built the narco's version of UPS right under our noses. If it weren't for the chief of the staff of the Air Force asking Kennedy to investigate drug transportation on Air Force flights, we wouldn't know any of this."

Wolf nodded. "What's your plan?"

"I'm going to scoot up to Alaska and get the cooperation of the parent organization. Need to figure out how deep the corruption is on their side. I'll couch it as an investigation into illegal arms trafficking. No mention of drugs, so I don't blow up our current ops. Then I'll head to DC and have a discussion with a friend at the Marshals Service. Marie Mount runs their counterintelligence program, and I trust her."

"Okay, make it fast. We need to be available when the flights take off from Ramstein."

"Got it, high roller."

Seven hours later, Parker met with FBI agents Sloan and Voss at the Anchorage field office. Deputy FBI Director Stockwell had called ahead and cleared the way, saying it was a national security matter.

Parker told them the illegal arms story, and they drove across town to the headquarters of the Alaskan native corporation. It took a few minutes to convince the CEO, and his legal counsel, just who was being investigated—their subcontractor, Global Air Services. With his okay, they were given access to the documents relevant to the formation and operation of the GAS partnership.

Parker exhaled quietly, there was Eliana's signature on the partnership paperwork laid out in front of her, and right below it was Alejandro's.

"Were you there when the documents were signed?"

The corporate lawyer said, "Yes, of course. Mister Cortes, his wife, I, and our CEO signed these documents in the CEO's office."

"Is this the woman claiming to be Eliana Cortes?" Parker asked, displaying a picture of Eliana on her phone.

The lawyer squinted at the cellphone. "Yes. Her hair was different, but that's her."

"What about this man?" Parker said, displaying a picture of Alejandro.

"No. Same build, similar eyes, but his nose and cheeks were different."

"Thank you. We'll need these Global documents for a time."

"I would need a warrant to relinquish them," the lawyer sniffed. "They're proprietary."

Agent Voss stepped forward. "Not a problem. Here you go." She handed the lawyer the warrant with a knowing grin.

"Good," Parker said. We appreciate your cooperation. One more thing, though: We'll need the names of all the staff on contract at Kandahar, Ramstein, and McGuire Air Force Bases."

"Yes, ma'am," the lawyer said, now in whatever-the-feds-want mode. "Let's head over to human resources. They can compile that information for you."

Parker smiled and followed the lawyer, followed by Voss and Sloan. *Taking Eliana out of play once and for all is something we should have done a long time ago.*

Chapter 82

Compared to the pace of a Tampa Florida rush hour, The Fashion Centre at Pentagon City was madness. A multi-level mall and Ritz Carlton Hotel combination, the atrium amplified the sounds from its ground floor up through its four floors. Thousands of workers exit the Metro station in streams, stopping to grab coffee and breakfast in the food court.

Only ten minutes from downtown DC and walking distance to the Pentagon and US Marshals Service headquarters, Parker knew from experience this was how weekdays went. She had wisely chosen the Ritz Carlton restaurant for the initial meeting, as it was close, quiet, and discrete. The restaurant was filled with military, contractors, and lobbyists. And more than likely, an intelligence operative or two. It was the way of Washington DC and the surrounding Virginia and Maryland centers of power.

Parker recognized Marie Mount at the doorway, waved and smiled. She stood when Mount approached.

"It's been a few days," Marie said, giving Parker a warm hug and an approving smile. "You look good, Elle."

"Yes, it has! Thank you—you, too. This job suits you. How do you like working for the Marshals Service?"

"I wasn't expecting a job interview." Marie said with a wry grin. "Are you trying to recruit me already?"

Parker laughed. "No, not yet, at least. But you know what it's like to work in a pool of testosterone and self-admiration."

"I do," Mount said with a chuckle. "I like it, though. The job. It took some pushing and shoving to get some respect. A couple of early wins didn't hurt. How was it for you? I hear through the grapevine you are the intel chief now."

"After siding with Wolf and then being on the verge of losing everything, the unit was a gift. Then it was just hard work and sleeping with the director of operations," Parker said, smiling.

"I can see you're happy, and that's what matters." She unfurled the cloth napkin, placed the cutlery on the table, and spread the napkin over her lap. "So then, why are we here?"

Elle covered her mouth with her hand, and whispered, "I need help with a potential WITSEC problem."

Marie placed the napkin on the table and pulled back. "All right. Finish your coffee, and we can walk over to the office."

Fifteen minutes later they were at the Marshal Service headquarters reception desk getting Parker a badge that read ESCORT in large red letters. In another five, they were in Marie's SCIF.

"If we're missing lunch for this," Mount said, "it has to be good. What's this all about?"

"Back in ninety-eight, we put two Sinaloa senior leaders into WITSEC. Six years later, I have evidence pointing to one of them setting up a drug trafficking business with an Alaskan Native organization. And to top it off, they have won government contracts with the Air Force and Special Operations Command."

"There have been a few cases where the people we protect have reverted to old ways, but nothing at this level—nothing involving big fed orgs." She crossed her arms and tried not to look as skeptical as she felt. "Are you sure?"

"No, I'm not. That's why I'm here. We have information pointing to the gentlemen in the program, but one of them has a sister, and they didn't part on good terms. It was Wolf who saved her from her brother's death squad of *sicarios*."

"Cartel drama. Hard to compete with that level of crazy."

"Truly. I'm thinking a few minutes with the WITSEC team, and we can figure this out."

"Probably, but we'll need permission from the director."

"Not a problem." Parker grinned. "Will a call from the vice president work?"

"Yeah. The vice president put the director on the job." Mount grinned back. "It will definitely work."

"Mind if I use your STE?"

"Go ahead. The techs were in the process of an update yesterday of all the secure telephone equipment, so it's a fifty-fifty chance it works."

Parker picked up the handset and dialed. The call to the V-P's office was picked up on the third ring and took a beat to sync. Parker told Shirley Chisum, the vice president's chief of staff, what she was after and Chisum asked her to please wait. When she came back, the answer was "twenty-five minutes." Parker thanked Chisum and ended the call.

"Maybe a half hour," Parker said to Mount, raising a thumb in approval.

"Must be nice. You are dancing in high cotton, Miss Parker."

"The president and vice president are fans, for now. But it's politics, so it can change with the wind. You know, you live here."

Mount grinned. "Well, in the meantime, why don't you fill me in, and we can continue the recruiting process."

Parker laughed. It was fifteen minutes later when the knock at the SCIF door stopped Parker's recounting of what she'd uncovered. Mount opened the door to find the Assistant Director for WITSEC, Todd Wilkins, standing there.

Wilkins said, "The director has requested we extend all courtesies and access to your friend, Miss Parker." He turned. "Please follow me."

Parker smirked. It usually was the counterintelligence team who were banished to the basement, hidden away from the normal staff of an agency. By the time the elevator stopped, Parker had figured they were forty to fifty feet below the Potomac River, less than a mile away. As they walked through the WITSEC operations area, she saw the same desktop technology Shadow Tier used to connect to multiple classified networks like the encrypted DOD Secret and Top Secret networks. These systems had different colors for their classifications and a host of strange names for the networks they accessed. Parker couldn't help but stare at the systems she wasn't meant to see.

Wilkins said, "Miss Parker. In here, please."

Shaken out of her natural need to collect data, Parker followed Marie into a room with no windows and no electronics of any kind. Just recessed lighting, a table, and four chairs.

Wilkins closed the door. "Please, have a seat. Ms. Mount, consider yourself read on. You are the service's liaison to Miss Parker and her organization per the order of the director."

"Yes, sir," Mount said.

"Miss Parker," Wilkins said. "Outsiders are not normally welcome here. Classification aside, we run one of the most sensitive operations in the US government. But when the director gets a call from the vice president and she invokes national security concerns, well, we're all on the same team." Wilkins pushed a piece of paper and pen across the table. "This is the Classified Information Non-Disclosure Agreement I need you to sign before we go any further."

Parker scanned the SF-312 and signed.

Wilkins countersigned on behalf of the government and nodded once. "Good. Now, how may we help you?"

"Thank you, sir. The bottom line is I believe Alejandro Cortes, who we put in your program in 1998, has with his sister Eliana Cortes built an international drug trafficking business behind the anonymity of WITSEC. Their business, which is a partnership with an Alaskan Native organization, has won government contracts for air cargo services. They are simultaneously moving soldiers, military cargo, and dope from Afghanistan to Europe and the United States. I've been working with FINCEN to identify the owner of this account."

Parker showed Wayne the account information and he took a moment to scan several pages.

"I need to determine if Alejandro is actually involved, or if Eliana is just using the account to hide her activities."

"This a new one on me," Wilkins said. I expect Miss Mount has told you we've had a few instances of WITSEC members trying some of their old tricks over the years. In most cases, it got them killed." Wilkins looked thoughtful for a moment and then stood. "I'll be right back."

He left the room and returned in two minutes with a young man. He closed the door behind them and introduced the new addition.

"Steve Nutter here is our financial analyst." Parker and Mount said their hellos, and all shook hands. "Steve, tell them our process."

"Yes, sir. We monitor all our protectees' financial accounts and those of close family members, which we flag, looking for standard indicators. We also make the stipend payments and any others agreed to by the courts to those accounts."

"What about international accounts?" Parker asked.

"We don't monitor those unless they're disclosed in the proceedings leading up to their entry into the program."

"Do you monitor their travel out of the country?"

Wilkins nodded. "Yes, to the extent we're able, but only through feedback report we get from Customs and Border Patrol."

Parker asked, "Can we get someone to check if Alejandro Cortes—that's his pre-WITSEC name—has traveled to Mexico since entering the program? The other question is, have any indicators popped on any of his accounts? And just one more thing. Can you check the same for a Martin Amaro? He was to enter the program at the same time but died before we could get him to you."

Nutter said, "Give me fifteen minutes."

"Who was Martin Amaro?" Wilkins asked after Nutter left.

"He was Alejandro's operations chief. Alejandro was the west coast lieutenant for the Sinaloa cartel. Amaro was a former *Sendero Luminoso* guerilla who Alejandro found as he was growing his drug business under El Chapo. We took them hostage as part of a prisoner exchange that got spicy. Amaro died in the gunfight."

Mount said with a dry smile, "Spicy is an interesting word for a protracted gunfight with El Chapo's top assassins and contractors with heavy weapons."

Wilkins shook his head.

"You run in dangerous circles, Miss Parker."

She shrugged. "Nature of the beast, sir."

Nutter rushed in, slamming the door behind him. "No travel or financial pops on Alejandro's accounts, but this other guy rings both bells. Travel to Mexico City and a subtle, just-below-indicator-levels increase in monthly payments to his account from an investment firm in Mexico."

Mount said, "Looks like someone is posing as the dead Mister Amaro. Could it be Alejandro?"

"Maybe. But I suspect Eliana Cortes has someone else playing the role for her benefit. She could easily sign his name. It appears she is trying to leave the Sinaloa cartel and her connection to us behind. The irony is, when we take her down, she'll immediately come back to us and ask for WITSEC claiming the threat of El Chapo's wrath."

Chapter 83

With Charlie Squadron operating out of Britain and Germany and Bravo in Afghanistan, the morning calls across global time zones were becoming a standard cadence for the Shadow Tier leadership. Today it was headquarters, Alpha, and Charlie. Clinton had not dialed in.

"Any idea when the drugs get to Global Air?" Parker asked.

On the other end of the video conference, Kennedy and the Kid shook their heads.

"Not yet," Kennedy said.

The Kid chimed in. "He'll use most of the time he told Sarti he needed to get his crew back together. He lost a lot of senior guys in the attack."

"Can you push him? Get him to understand it's just as important?" Wolf asked.

"Not my first choice," Kennedy said. "He committed to a date and Sarti agreed to it. It would look suspicious if it was changed.

What did you find on Global Air Services?"

Parker said, "Looks like Eliana and someone posing as Martin are working together. We think Alejandro is unaware she created an account in his name. There are nine layers of partnerships and cutouts. Hard to believe FINCEN can weed through all of it to find the origin account. I still can't figure out why they're doing it this way; there are easier ways to launder money. Just send it to Israel and pay the Russian mob a small fee. It's what Russian intelligence does with their Columbian cocaine profits."

The Kid said, "If it's easy, there must be something else going on. Like wanting to create her own empire and get out from under El Chapo. As you said before, become the UPS of the multi-billion-dollar illegal drug business."

Parker could see Wolf was in an analytic mood. His chin was resting on his interlaced figures. He said, "I think you're both right. She is or has been looking for a way out from under her deal for some time. The Mexican government has taken a harder stance on the cartels, using the Marines and Colonel González's unit to hit them when they get out of line. Not to mention the attacks from other cartels like the Zetas. She hasn't suffered as badly as El Chapo's other lieutenants, but she fears every day for her son. He is her key motivator in all things. She could just come to us and we would put her in WITSEC, but that's not the life she wants. She has a warped image of living the high life, but somehow remaining safe from retribution."

Kennedy said, "I think you're on to something here. All she needs to do is distribute drugs for a short period, combined with the profits of contracts in combat zones, and she will have replaced the millions Alejandro squirreled away that we never found. That's serious, generational, screw-you money. I never mentioned this before as it wasn't relevant, but she was almost penniless when we put her back into the game. She must be putting her profits into the account you found, at least initially, knowing it will be hard to take the money she made working for El Chapo."

"So, why don't we just grab her son?" the Kid asked. "She'll do anything for him."

Parker said, "Because kidnapping a six-year-old will not sit well with a judge—or me. If Eliana was labeled a terrorist, maybe, on the grounds that it's a rescue, not a kidnapping or abduction. No, it's time to set a trap. I can get her to Ramstein and take her down with any aircrews who happen to be there, plus the Juno Services deception."

"She's right," Wolf said. "Kidnapping is a bad idea. So, how do you get Eliana to Ramstein?"

A devious grin spread across Parker's face.

"*Mo money, mo money, mo money.*"

Wolf said, "Okay, Parker will coordinate with you guys on timing. Let's change subjects: What's the deal with Mallard?"

Kennedy said, "After he got back, we put him right back in, but this time as a close protection specialist assigned to Doctor Siddiqi's security team. He transformed our concern about the Legionnaires into an old-buddy-back-slapping fest. They're headed back to Kandahar with more medical supplies for the clinics the doctor set up. Mallard will get us an inside look at operations and where the doc stands in all this."

The conversation stopped when the red light started rotating on the ceiling at Parker and Wolf's end of the SCIF. The door opened, and the duty operations manager told Wolf that Clinton was on a secure line. "Sounds important."

Wolf thanked the ops manager and told him to add Clinton to the conference call. Door closed, and the flashing light stopped.

"We are all here, brother, what's up?"

Clinton said, "Do you have Devon on a mission you haven't mentioned to me?"

"No. Why?"

"He's missing, and the hospital doesn't know when he left. I've got the team checking into it. Got to tell you, I have a bad feeling he might have been taken."

"Taken? Who would take him?"

"If the Taliban has infiltrated Juno, it could have been directed by someone here or in Marseilles. Devon's last mission before joining our team was to infiltrate a nasty Taliban cell. He helped to identify leadership two levels up, which the Agency eliminated with extreme prejudice. Wait one ..."

There were voices on the other end, muted but clear enough to hear their agitation. "The hospital administrator just confirmed Devon was put on a medevac flight to Landstuhl."

"Clinton. This is Kennedy. I will send a team to the base to intercept, and another to the hospital."

"Why send him to Germany?" Parker asked.

Wolf said, "Yeah, why Germany? Do we know if one of our German competitors is working directly with Juno or Croce?"

Kennedy said, "No. What do you think, Kid?"

"We've been wondering who might be pulling Croce's strings besides us. I think we're seeing indications of a new player, one with the reach to snatch a service member from a military hospital." He took a deep breath. "This stinks. I don't like any of it."

Wolf said, "Whoever it is, they are a serious threat to our plans for Croce. We need to know who it is before our work unravels." His face hardened.

"And we're going to recover Clinton."

Chapter 84

The automotive repair shop in the suburbs of Landstuhl was drab, bearing the crust of three generations of mechanics and sixty years accumulation of oil, sweat, car parts, and poor lighting.

Croce said, "Why did I come here? What was so important we had to talk face-to-face?"

"Because your new partner, Herr Merck, employs agents of the Pakistani ISI and Central Intelligence Agency," his swarthy *bratva* contact said. The Russian mafia enforcer stared down at a bloody man, a black sack over his head, industrial earmuffs blocking him from hearing the conversation.

Croce said, "What is so odd about that? Many Pakistan and Afghans do it, and more."

"True, but they are not British SAS. This man is. His real name is Devon Lancaster. Born in Pakistan but adopted by a couple in the British diplomatic service at the embassy in Islamabad."

"How do you know all this?"

"The *bratva* has many connections to Russian intelligence. SVR, GRU, FSB. We are mindful of potential infiltration of our ranks, and we take measures to ensure it does not happen unless we allow it to for our own purposes."

Croce stood and walked around the captive. "It is exactly what Merck's security lead told me to look out for after the Taliban attack. Are we being played? Or is Herr Merck being played?"

"Possibly both, certainly Merck."

"What do you suggest?"

"A simple test. Bring them here and ask what they want to do. If they want to take him away, you have a problem. If they take care of the problem, your business is safe. We can afford to briefly expose this location for our mutual security."

"Agreed. I will make the call."

Croce went outside and leaned against a Mercedes, punching numbers into his cellphone.

"Herr Merck. Good morning. Yes, we are recovering from the storm damage, but we have an issue we need to deal with. How long will it take for you to drive down from Frankfurt to Landstuhl? Yes, I am in Landstuhl now. It seems key equipment damaged in the storm requires some special attention. I am here with the technicians right now and need your opinion. The address is in your text. Yes, one hour works. I will be waiting."

The *bratva* man said, "Good. There is nothing to be gained by revealing our relationship to Merck, however. We will be across the street should you need us."

Fifty-six minutes later, after deploying Charlie Squadron at the only viable exfil choke point and snipers to a nearby building, Kennedy and Taylor stopped in front of the automotive shop's open roll-up industrial door. Croce waved them inside from the shadows. As soon as they were out of view, Croce's men frisked them, making a show of the weapons retrieved.

"Why are you taking our weapons, Jean Paul?"

"Precautions, *mein Freund*. We are not at my restaurant. Come, I'd like to show you the problem we have encountered."

Croce strode down a hallway and knocked on the left side door, speaking French. When the door opened, Croce stood just inside and focused on catching the looks on Herr Merck and his security man's faces.

Seeing confusion, not fear, is good, he thought.

Croce faced the two men, and said, "It seems your man is not who you think he is. This man is British SAS, most likely working for British or American intelligence."

Herr Merck said, "You are sure of this, Monsieur Croce? I hired this man to be our go-between with the Taliban. If he is an agent of British or American intelligence, it is my fault. I had him vetted."

"Let me have him," Taylor said in a menacing growl, stepping forward.

"No time for that. This must stop immediately," Herr Merck said.

Croce watched Merck step to the bound man and rip the bag from his head, his eyes wide and telegraphing fear. Merck grabbed the prisoner by the hair, screaming curses, his angry spittle showering the prisoner. He let go of the prisoner's hair, stepped back, and drew a pistol the security team had missed. Croce was reaching for his own gun when Merck raised his weapon and shot the prisoner in the forehead. His head snapped back and stayed, blood dripping into the hairline. Croce jumped at the gunshot in the confined space, and his security lead cursed.

Merck threw the bag back over the dead man's head. "Problem solved. We will dispose of this pig. I suggest you leave at once, *Monsieur* Croce. I am very sorry for this inconvenience. We certainly will make sure any loose ends are taken care of here. But yes, you must go now. A gunshot may summon the authorities even in this dingy neighborhood. Please leave our weapons on the bench outside the door and we will take this from here."

Shaken, Croce holstered his pistol, took a last look at the dead man, and headed for the door with his security people.

Once Croce and his people were outside, the roll-up industrial garage door began lowering with metallic creaks and steel-on-steel moans. Croce took a deep breath and exhaled. Evidently Herr Merck could be vicious if prompted, which was an important note for the future. When Merck and his people had saved his life during the attack, their work had seemed clinical and in line with their military backgrounds. This, on the other hand, was a ruthless, cold-blooded side of the methodical businessman he hadn't seen before but was glad to know existed.

Croce called his *bratva* contact. "It is done. The spy is dead. I am in your debt for this." There was no immediate response, and he listened for several seconds as the silence began to draw out. Then a simple response.

"*Da.*"

Croce told his driver to take him to back to his plane.

Inside the shop, Kennedy had Taylor call for the van and then massaged the prisoner's neck, a low groan bubbling from him. The black bag had been removed and he was sipping from a bottle of water.

"Bloody hell, that hurt," Lancaster said in a hoarse whisper, very much alive. He raised the water bottle. "Nothing a little extra to put in this then, I suppose?"

Kennedy whispered his response. "Better outcome than the real thing, though, mate."

"Indeed it is. But damned spy-acting is going to get a man killed one day. It shan't be me, I trust. How did you know to bring the squib gun?"

"I didn't, but with you reported missing, then suspecting you had been brought to Landstuhl, I thought we might need it."

Kennedy said to Taylor, "Check the door. See if they're gone."

Taylor said, "Yes, they have departed. Charlie Eight reports a team she IDs as *bratva* watching the repair shop from across the street. Were they involved, Devon?"

"It's not a language I know but they could have been Russian."

Kennedy used his secure phone messaging app to tell Charlie Five to back the van in. He said to Lancaster, "We want to show just enough dead body to convince the guys across the street but not suffocate you."

"I appreciate that, sir."

Three minutes later, Taylor cracked the door. "The van is here. Let's use this tarp to roll you up."

Kennedy and Five rolled Lancaster in the tarp and helped hoist him over Taylor's shoulder. Herr Merck took the passenger seat as Lancaster was dumped in the back. Taylor closed the van cargo door behind him, and they drove away.

Inside the van, they unrolled Lancaster and filled the tarp with inflated trash bags and plastic milk containers, wrapping it tightly to give it a mummy look. Then it was wrapped it in chain. Working the problem on the fly, Kennedy called the Kid and asked if there were any abandoned quarries in the area. The Kid sent a location and Kennedy handed Five his phone. Five's radio chirped and Kennedy switched channels.

The countersurveillance team reported there was a Range Rover with three large men following them.

Arriving twenty-six minutes later at the quarry, Taylor jumped out and defeated the cheap gate lock with a pry bar. Inside they motored past the former office and rusting trucks and cranes. Near the back of the property they found the quarry, filled with water as still and dark as a moonless night. They took their time removing the fake body and made a show of struggling with it as they threw it over the rocky edge into the water.

Taylor displayed theatrical caution pretending to look around to see if they had been followed. They jumped back into the van and they drove to the airport where the rest of the group was already on board their aircraft. Five drove into the darkness at the back of the hangar to hide their boarding of the plane just as its engines started up and taxied to the runway. As the plane rotated and took to the sky, the radio call from the countersurveillance team confirmed the Russian team had broken off.

Kennedy put a hand on Taylor's shoulder and shook his head.

"First the Taliban, then Iranians, and now the Russians. Is there anyone who doesn't have a piece of Croce's operation?"

Chapter 85

M organ griped on the cellphone with Kennedy. "I don't know, man. Seems he's getting twitchy, Croce. His telling us an hour out the drugs are on the way is bullshit. Even though it was handled well, that Lancaster thing has put a dent in his trust."

Kennedy said, "I hear you, but nothing trumps his hunger for money and power. Nothing. Stick to the plan, pick up the dope at McGuire, and get back to New York for the handoff."

"Roger that, heading on base now. I'll let you know when I'm headed back to the city."

Croce and crew had been told Morgan carried several identities, one of which was as a private military contractor employee. Desert-tan cargo pants and a Janus logo polo was Morgan's cover story. He handed his retired NCO ID card to the Air Force security NCO who scanned its bar code with a handheld device, cleared him, and Morgan rolled onto McGuire AFB headed for the Juno facility.

Sandwiched between the 6th Airlift Squadron and the Boeing maintenance facility just off the flight line, Morgan took a manager's parking spot at the Janus facility and sat in the quiet, the only sound the ticking of the black Escalade's engine as it cooled. Wanting to be seen by as few people as possible, Morgan scanned the area for foot traffic. It was light.

As was normal for this time of day, most airmen and contractors were in their offices pushing through what Morgan expected was piles of paperwork and operations orders for overseas flights. Satisfied with the small number of people out and about, Morgan left the SUV for the building and grabbed the first person he saw.

"Can you point me to Linda Tilden's office, please?"

"You bet. In the back," the guy said, pointing. "Straight to the wall and turn right."

Morgan followed his instructions and was reaching for the door knob when the door opened and a distracted Linda Tilden emerged looking at papers in her hand. She was a short woman on tall heels and she crashed into Morgan, who caught her. He watched the color rise in her cheeks as she looked at him for a beat, then she asked, "Can I help you?"

Miss Tilden, if it was her real name, was Morgan's type. Broad shoulders, a tattoo telling those in the know she had trained in martial arts, and legs that comprised more than half of her entire body. Morgan willed himself to stay cool but he could feel his agitated hormones reddening his face as well.

"Uhm, yes, ma'am. I'm here to pick up a Janus delivery. Medical equipment I'm to take to the manufacturer for repair."

"The GE equipment from Germany?" she asked, starting the bona fides process.

"No. I'm here for the Phillips equipment from Afghanistan," Morgan said in response.

She looked him up and down and her face returned a small smile. "All right. Please follow me."

Morgan followed Tilden through a door to another section of the building and into a warehouse with cages along one side and work areas and benches filling the rest of the space. In the end, there was another door, solid steel by the look of it, with a keypad and iris scanner.

At a secure interior door, Tilden keyed in an eight-digit code and bent slightly at the waist for a retina scan. That returned a green light and clunking sounds from the door locks as they released, and they were in.

Inside the room was a safe, weapons lockers, and a table with two chairs. The walls and ceiling were painted in government gray to match the institutional table and chairs. Lifeless and simple to maintain by the lowest bidder. On the table were two hard plastic Pelican cases.

"Can you check that everything is in order?" Tilden asked.

"I can."

Morgan opened the first case and lifted out large, tightly wrapped bundles from the surrounding foam insert that secured them. He pretended to examine each block of heroin, then put them back before counting to three and closing the case.

"All good."

In truth, he had no idea other than he was able to verify the count of packages while recognizing the test ports the team had built in case someone wanted to test or sample the product. While each looked like a full kilo of heroin, there was, in fact, less than a gram, and that was located in the test port.

When Tilden held out a transfer receipt for the medical equipment, Morgan took a moment to place his hand over hers. When she didn't reject the move and pull back, he smiled and signed the document. She escorted Morgan to the door, where he handed her his business card.

Tilden smiled, read the card, and said, "Mmm, Miami. I love warm weather. Why are you here?"

"I'm helping a friend. I'd like to see you again. Let me know when you're free and I'll send my plane for you."

Morgan glanced back her way as he left and Tilden was biting her lip.

Shadow Tier was the best decision of my life, he thought, walking to his SUV.

Morgan pulled over just off base and changed polo shirts to one with no logo. Ninety minutes later, after collecting the tail he expected, Morgan was back in New York City and the valet at the Pierre was parking his Escalade. Morgan took the VIP elevator to his suite and waited.

If their idea went as planned, Croce would take possession of the dope just long enough to make the handoff and seal his fate.

Chapter 86

Three hundred and seventy-five miles to the north, Wolf and Parker were landing at the Massena New York International Airport in upstate New York. The setting sun with its golden rays lay in long stripes around the hangars, and fully in character, they kept their sunglasses on as the airstair lowered to the asphalt at the FBO where the jet was to refuel. The black limo had been brought up from the city just to take them the twelve miles to the casino.

Though small by Las Vegas or even Reno standards, the casino was world-renowned for its invitation-only poker tournaments and special pampering of high rollers.

On an Indian reservation, the services aren't regulated like those in Las Vegas. A select few players connected through the dark net and knew, much like a TV Fantasy Island, there wasn't anything here you couldn't have here.

Wolf was dressed in a dark gray suit with a black shirt without tie, black Italian shoes, gold chains on both wrists, and the

Blancpain Fifty Fathoms watch on his left. The watch was the only example ever made and had been borrowed from Harry Winston—"Hollywood Jeweler to the Stars"—who famously provides the biggest movie stars with hideously expensive baubles to wear to the Academy Awards and so on.

On his left hand was a chunky King Baby special-order gold skull ring with a viper curled through the mouth and eyes. Parker was sheathed in form-fitting black, long stiletto-heel boots with silver spike chains at the ankle running into black leggings and a Cheongsam goth dress. Her hair had been dyed black and her lipstick and nails had chalky black dead looks.

Kennedy had the Kid deposited a hundred thousand dollars into Wolf's casino account. After checking in, Wolf went straight to the no-limit poker table in the VIP room. He quickly lost twenty-five thousand on bad bets and faked a lack of interest before telling Parker he was hungry.

Parker whispered. "You know what they say ... unlucky in gambling means you're lucky in love.'"

Wolf gave Parker a tight-lipped smile and nodded. "Is that what they say? I don't recall seeing that in the casino's TV ads." He looked around casually to see who was noticing them and then announced, "Let's go eat. The chef in the Chop House is waiting."

Wolf spoke just loud enough to make sure whoever was watching understood they would not be going to their hotel suite for at least an hour.

Wolf and Parker sat next to each other in a private section of the dining room, drinking a second round of adult beverages when their bone-in ribeye steaks were delivered hot and sizzling with the quiet fanfare befitting the restaurant's status.

Wolf leaned into Parker and whispered.

"I like taking you on high-end date nights with drug money.

Maybe we should set aside a slush fund."

Wolf had to take another bite of his steak to keep from smiling at the change in Parker's look. From surly goth *I-do-not-give-a-damn* to *bullshit* and back in a flash.

The maître d' appeared and handed Wolf a note. "Your suits and shirts have been cleaned, per your orders, Mister Beltran."

Wolf and Parker took their time finishing the dinner, then strolled arm-in-arm through the casino and a few high-end shops before heading up to their suite. Wolf used the wrist band he'd been given at check-in to open the door to a suite tastefully appointed with modern Italian furniture in blond woods and white leather.

The ceiling-to-floor windows started halfway down the right side of the room and rounded the corner to include the whole of the north-facing wall. Meant to highlight what surely would be a spectacular sunrise, the darkness muted the effect.

The professional-level kitchen was to their left and could be closed off if desired. They reached the master bedroom that Wolf estimated had to be a thousand square feet. He went to the walk-in closet and found his dry cleaning, which, in fact, was not his but could have been. Inside the second suit he checked, he found a coat check ticket and a small flip phone.

Wolf set the note and claim check on a side table and made small talk while pointing at the numbers. They had been briefed that the note from the maître d' included the combination. The claim check ticket was at the numbered vault. The cellphone had one programmed number, a local call.

The casino was testing an anonymous equivalent to a bank security deposit box. In this case, though, there was no need for a second person with a second key. The system was built to require something you have and two things you know. Its third security factor was a preregistered phone number to start the sequence to unlock the so-called vault.

Wolf had heard the FBI, DEA, and ATF were not happy with the new service, for the reason Wolf would access it in the morning.

He handed the cellphone to Parker and hid the note and claim check in a zippered pocket hidden under his belt. Parker slipped the cellphone into her inner left sleeve, where it was held in place by the dress. They went back downstairs, where over the next three hours Wolf lost another twenty thousand dollars and Parker ended up eight thousand in the black.

Convinced they had played their roles well, they headed to the vault and picked up the product, which was in two Pelican cases that had undamaged tamper tape over the latches.

Back in their hotel room, Wolf put the cases next to the nightstand and sat on the bed to unstrap the ankle holster he had been wearing with its Walter PPK. He dropped it into his roller bag and removed his Browning High Power from his inside the belt clip, putting it on the nightstand. Parker took off her thigh holster and caught Wolf looking. Wolf's low whistle let her know he still found her more beautiful than he could explain, and he always would.

Wolf pushed the power button for the TV and upped the volume. They sat side-by-side on the bed and he said, "Your idea to install a scanner on a Predator was genius. Now we know the route the drugs took from Gander to here."

"Croce's met with Morgan and Sarti by now, right?"

"Croce is old school at heart. I'd bet his money that it's a quick exchange between now and midnight, followed by a meal to talk about the future."

Parker stared into Wolf eyes. "It feels like we are making progress, at last. Putting a dent in the system."

Wolf smiled. "If we pull this off, it will be much more than a dent. The level of distrust alone will be worth all the effort."

Chapter 87

The following morning Wolf and Parker took the limo south about fifteen minutes where they changed over to a staged Suburban that Parker drove to the meeting. The FBI-provided safehouse was surrounded by a working farm and thick stands of trees, making it invisible from all but airborne eyes.

It appeared to be every bit a part of the farming community outside of Middletown and was a perfect pick for the multi-agency meeting. The attendees arrived at different times via different routes, each running surveillance detection patterns well before closing in on the safehouse area.

An FBI tech had set up a video conferencing system that Wolf planned to use at the outset of the meeting. Wolf needed to set the tone for the teamwork required to take down Croce and his partners, and everyone would get their share of the glory if it went right.

If it went sideways, it would all be on Shadow Tier.

Wolf and Parker had dropped character after switching to the

SUV and they relaxed in polo shirts and jeans. The majority of the men and women joining them were similarly dressed, with a few in tan-colored tactical cargo pants indicating the wearer had been in the Middle East, or at least knew the location of a 5.11 tactical clothing outlet.

Wolf had been on his satellite phone and ended his call.

"All right everyone, let's begin." The room lights dimmed and a familiar face hove into view on the video screen. "Ladies and gentlemen, I give you the vice president of the United States."

Hushed conversation stopped cold as the screen bloomed to life, displaying the vice president sitting in her West Wing office.

"Good morning. I'm excited to speak with you today. The hard work of Shadow Tier has brought us to this point of inflection. A time when together we will bring down an international conspiracy to import large quantities of Taliban-grown opium and heroin into the United States. You will be the face of the largest drug bust in the history of this long drug war. Good luck, team!"

The speech was so short and bereft of two-way communication that the pep talk might well have been prerecorded. Wolf suspected that it had. The screen went blank and Wolf stepped up.

"We are callsign Joshua-Actual," Wolf said. "We're responsible for the takedown of Jean Paul Croce, head of *Unione Corsa* and the reformulated French Connection." Parker put Croce's photo on the screen. "A Shadow Tier team will support the takedown and hand off Croce to the FBI."

Parker put a picture of Morgan on the screen.

"This man, who goes by the alias Marco Defendini, is our insider. He will make sure Croce is at his Pierre Hotel suite tonight at twenty-two hundred. FBI and DEA lead that raid. My team and I will follow." Heads around the room nodded their acknowledgments in the dim light of the video screen. "I will have personnel posted at

the other possible exfil routes. Marco will make sure Croce doesn't
go loud. Try not to shoot him, please," Wolf said smiling. There was
a chuckle in the room.

These folks are pros, Wolf thought. Still ...

"About an hour after the subjects are processed and out of the
building, my tech will provide you with copies of all the bodycam
and helmetcam video and audio recordings. Any questions?"

"What's the haul?" a DEA agent said.

"Twenty-five kilos of hyper-pure heroin laced with fentanyl. A
wrong dose drops you like a bullet to the head," Wolf said.

What Larry Quinn—jokingly nicknamed Q at the Agency—
had synthesized for the fake-dope program was the equivalent of
fentanyl-laced heroin with all the markers of the real thing, but
without the homicidal high. The Agency was considering a large-
scale trial of the formula to see if a non-active compound could
be used to destroy a cartel's reputation, like counterfeit currency
could disrupt an economy.

"Is this Croce dirtbag a violent type?" asked a voice in the back.

"Not generally. He did fight back when the Taliban attacked him
at home."

"How'd he survive?" an FBI agent asked.

"We saved his butt for him."

"You saved him? Why didn't you give him to the Taliban?" the
FBI agent asked.

"It would have been a temporary fix to a much larger problem.
Tonight in New York City, Landstuhl, Germany, Marseilles, France,
and Kandahar, we destroy not only Jean Paul Croce's trafficking
routes to the US but also cut off routes from Afghanistan to Europe,
which funds the Taliban's fight against America and our NATO
partners. All in, well north of a hundred million bucks of impact."

"So, that's what the veep meant," the lead FBI agent said.

Chapter 88

P arker was wearing a blond wig and dressed in a baggy aircrew flight suit with the rank of major. She exited the aircraft with the pilots and was taken to the flight operations center. Inside the building she encountered Kennedy, who snapped to attention with clicked heels and a snappy salute.

"Stop it, you knucklehead."

"Follow me," he said, grinning, and headed toward a Mercedes SUV.

As they drove off base Parker said, "The CEO told me she's not happy, but we know Eliana, and she's coin driven. She'll come for the contract of a lifetime," Parker said.

Kennedy agreed. "From cartel dirtbag to international capitalist—not a far stretch given how El Chapo runs things now with his first real chief financial officer, and a new target for us."

Thirty minutes later they wove through the last of the checkpoints at the safehouse. Parker got out of the Mercedes and leaned across the hood. "You're taking security seriously. I caught a glimpse of det cord wrapped around the base of a couple of trees lining the driveway. Is it to keep bad guys out or trap them in once the shooting starts?"

"Yes," Kennedy said with a wry smile. "A walk through our woods is not conducive to a long life at this time. Come inside and meet the team supporting you at Ramstein."

The next ninety minutes were spent in meet and greet, walking the grounds, and having lunch. After lunch, Kennedy assembled the team. Parker saw the Kid and gave him a warm hug. The team immediately played up his reddened face and calls suggesting it was the best squeeze he was likely to get for a long time.

Parker said, "Will you guys a get hobby? Goes to prove gun monkeys are the same all over the world. What would you gals and guys do without us giving you stuff to tease us about, besides shoot each other for fun?"

Parker watched the teammates laugh and poke at each other. A classic sign of a bonded team who'd do anything for the woman or man on their left and right. Parker had to admit Kennedy and Taylor had done an amazing job recruiting the right folks, from the selection process to their early trials by fire, to now, right at the bloody tip of the spear. How they had jelled and accomplished so much in such little time was all Kennedy, although Parker was sure he'd give all the credit to Taylor.

Parker took thirty-five minutes to brief the overall plan. She answered questions and took in the squadron's thoughts, incorporating two, which made the plan safer to execute. The first was to have Charlie team members pose as the team servicing Eliana's jet; the second was to have the drivers played by Charlie personnel too.

Parker studied her buzzing cellphone.

"The Alaskan company CEO has landed. Eliana should be behind her by two hours. Let's gear up and head for our staging areas."

An hour and forty-five minutes later, Parker was monitoring the tower frequency and heard the pilot of Eliana's plane call into the pattern. Cameras installed on a nearby hangar zoomed in on the plane as it was guided into its parking spot. Parker counted the men exiting the plane.

Just two. Good.

Ten seconds went by, then another thirty. Parker unclenched her hands and reached for her radio, freezing as Eliana Cortes stepped out of the plane and marched down the stairs to the waiting car. Parker flushed with excitement, the danger flowing through her, readying her body for a fight. The hand on her shoulder light and comforting.

"Breathe. You've got this," Kennedy said.

Parker responded with a tight-lipped smile.

The first to report Eliana's movement via code word to the contracting officer was the Charlie Squadron female sniper. "Panther Actual, Panther Eight, package passing Texas."

"Panther Eight, copy," Parker said.

Four minutes later, Panther Six, with Panther Nine in a car on the route, called out passing Arizona.

The car stopped at the front of the building. Playing the role of assistant to the CEO, the Kid met Eliana and escorted her and her security team inside. Parker and Kennedy watched the video feed as they were given preassigned badges and led into the main conference room.

Parker coughed, her throat dry as she stared at her shaking hands. She pressed them into her thighs hoping Kennedy didn't notice. She heard the Kid say, "Mister Eaglak will be here momentarily. Can I get you anything?"

Eliana took a seat and said, "No, thank you. I just want to sign the papers and leave. I am very busy."

"As you wish," the Kid said. The side and front doors to the conference room opened then and the Kid said, "I believe you know our management team."

Eliana stood and cursed. On seeing Parker, she spun to seek escape but found Kennedy and two members of Charlie's Squadron in full battle kit, M-4 rifles raised.

Parker took a deep breath and tried to keep the excitement from her voice.

"Hello, Eliana. We finally meet. I've heard so much about you."

"Elenore Helen Parker. Wolf's bitch. I know you, too—and your *hijo de puta*," Eliana said, turning to Kennedy. "He likes to keep the yoke of oppression tight around my neck. Not caring what danger my son and I face."

Kennedy's calm demeanor belied his inner turmoil.

"Bullshit, Eliana. Against our better judgment, we have permitted you to run your business with little interference compared to actions we have taken against the other parts of the Sinaloa cartel. You know our goal has always been to cut the head off the snake, but you never took us there. And so, today, we take away your plan to escape. We take away your plan to create the first global drug distribution and trafficking airline. And by the way, Jean Paul Croce is either in handcuffs or dead by now, his operations closed permanently. Now your view will not be as pretty. You will never ride your stallion again."

Kennedy stood right in her face.

"And unless you comply with us, you will never see your son again."

Chapter 89

E liana contorted and she screamed, charging at Kennedy. Parker drew her Beretta and, before Eliana could strike, pushed the barrel into Eliana's forehead. She stopped in her tracks, but the hatred on her face was unabated.

"Listen to me very carefully. Here is what will happen," Eliana snarled, forcefully leaning her head into Parker's pistol. "I am getting back on my plane and going home. If you have taken or even just frightened my son, I will use all my money to hire every *sicario* in North America to kill all three of you."

Eliana turned to leave but Parker grabbed her by the shoulder and tore open her black blouse. Parker gasped and heard curses from her team member as Eliana's security lead ripped away his own loose-fitting shirt. Time stopped for Parker, the fine hair on her arms and back of her neck standing up as a chill coursed over her body.

Suicide vests.

Eliana saw Parker's frozen face and laughed. "Even this dumb bitch understands. A trick I have learned watching you fight the wars in Afghanistan and Iraq. As I said, I am leaving."

She's bluffing. Her son means too much, Parker thought.

Eliana held out her hand. "Pistol."

Parker hesitated.

Eliana growled, "Now, damn you!"

Parker handed over her Beretta.

Eliana said to Parker, "Have my car brought back around." She nodded to her bodyguard. "My security lead will stay here and you join me on the trip home to ensure we do not have any regrettable accidents. Once I am safely out of German airspace, my security lead will render his vest safe and surrender to your people. Call my plane to prepare for immediate departure."

Parker glared at Eliana for a moment, but she didn't see a way out just yet. She nodded to the Kid, who called the driver and then the tower to contact Eliana's pilots.

Eliana donned and buttoned her suit jacket to cover the explosive vest and pushed Parker to the car. Outside, Parker saw the driver signal readiness, and she responded, "Another gray day in Germany."

The code phrase to stand down.

Eliana said, "This is an ugly country. You will like my ranch. It is a very comfortable place to be a hostage."

Outside the civilian-side Ramstein executive terminal, the car pulled up to the cartel's jet, its engines already hot and running. Eliana stayed tight to Parker to ensure a sniper's shot would kill them both. Small consolation, but an effective countermeasure. They boarded the plane and were the only passengers.

"Depart immediately!" Eliana said to the pilots. "You," she said, turning to Parker and gesturing with the Beretta to a wide seat, "sit here and buckle your seatbelt. Do not move."

As the airstairs retracted and the door closed behind them, Eliana took a seat across the wide aisle from Parker and buckled her own seatbelt without looking away from her captive.

With immediate departure priority, the plane taxied to the runway. The pilot went to full power and took off, quickly gaining altitude and distance from Ramstein. When the pilot reduced power and began his climb to cruising altitude, Eliana dropped the magazine from the pistol and cleared the round from the chamber. Then she stripped the rounds from the magazine and threw them all into the seat across the aisle. Stretching, she unfastened the plastic buckles securing her suicide vest and slipped it off, letting it slide to the floor.

Parker snorted and offered a half smile. "Nice play back there. But we both know you wouldn't dare blow yourself up. You would never leave your son like that."

"This is quite true. This vest is not real. So why did you not act?"

"You could be crazy enough, and I couldn't count on your security lead's vest being fake, too."

"Wise choice. His is live, but it was all for show. Now we can report the plane lost over the Atlantic, and I can join my brother in WITSEC."

"Wait—*what?*"

"Yes, Parker. Your husband and I collaborated on this part of the plan to give my son and me a clean break. El Chapo has become even more unhinged and unpredictable. His paranoia grows by the hour. Yet, somehow in moments of lucid thought, he continues to grow and adapt to the demands of American drug users. Those users are pushing heroin upscale, so he pushed me to switch crops. You were right—Global Air Services was part of my attempt to break free. When I got reports of your investigation—by the way, using FINCEN was a brilliant idea—I knew my plan was done. Wolf offered my son and me a way out. I am grateful, and it's good to see you have recovered from your time with Amaru."

"How do you know about that?" Parker's normally unflappable calm was fraying at the edges.

Eliana raised both hands and shrugged.

"Not to worry," she said. "You do not have a leak. I was there. I hired the LA Kings to assault the foundry while the Tomador and I waited for Amaru to run. The Tomador apologizes for not killing him before now."

"Why would you do that?"

"A life for a life. Payback for saving me and my unborn son."

Chapter 90

R oger that," Kennedy said. "We're in position outside Croce's Marseille home, at the *Unione Corsa* HQ, Janus Logistics, and Juno Services in Kandahar, and Ramstein. French and German police with Interpol and JNAC agents are standing by. The DEA and their new Afghan team have been told they're on a simple sweep of a suspected trafficking waypoint in the ratline. And there are SMU teams assigned to the two Taliban cells we located. They're launching as we speak."

"Good. We'll go first in." Wolf glanced at his watch. "Twenty-three minutes, and we cut the head off the snake. You'll get the 999 text to execute the *Unione Corsa* site, then Bravo and Charlie can execute at will."

Wolf ended the call and asked his tech. "Good to go?"

"Yes, sir. They're talking about fast women and fast cars. Croce took a hit from the sample into the bathroom. The audio indicates he's cooking it up."

"You didn't put a camera in the bathroom?"

"Sorry, sir, but negative. I didn't have time given all the other priorities."

"Noted." *From now on, two techs all the time,* Wolf thought.

The tech pointed to the screen. Morgan was walking to the bathroom. "Croce just told Morgan to come and take a hit."

Wolf slipped on a headset and heard Croce getting belligerent. Morgan was telling him his fear of needles kept him to cocaine. Croce continued to rant, getting hotter and hotter.

"We have to go now. The target is getting agitated."

Wolf led the lead takedown team to the service elevator and they headed up. En route, the tech came over the team radio net.

"Croce has called for backup. He's accusing Morgan of being a plant from a rival family. His paranoia is getting worse. There are four heavily armed men moving up from the floor below. They will get there before you do."

Wolf willed the elevator to move faster. He sent the 999 to Kennedy, triggering the other assaults, and spun to face the team in the elevator. "The target has lost it and called for backup. There are four heavily armed men who will get to the suite ahead of us. Get tight, we are going in hard."

Wolf scanned the four men and two women and got only confident nods in return. As the service elevator door opened, Wolf saw the door to the suite closing.

No better time to bust up the party, Wolf thought.

Wolf sprinted across the foyer and threw his shoulder into the door before it latched, knocking the guy behind it to the floor. Wolf rolled in, came up to a knee, and shot the guy twice in the face, his dumbfounded look quickly melting away. Wolf spun to engage the other men, just focusing his way as the rest of the team flowed in. Shots rang out and Wolf heard another man hit the floor. He spun and saw an angry and confused Jean Paul Croce. Croce's face was twisted into an eyes-wide look of pure manic evil—and he had a Scorpion machine pistol in each hand.

Wolf dove for the floor and yelled, "Cover!" as brought his H&K around.

Croce sprayed gunfire across the room, not caring who he hit. He kept firing until they ran dry. Wolf fired back a stream of lead tearing up the wall where Croce and Morgan had been. Croce ran into the master bedroom slamming the door behind him.

Wolf stopped and scanned the room, then pointed his weapon at Morgan. He shouted extra loud so that any Croce men could hear him. "Drop the weapon, dumbass, before I end you."

Morgan made a show of cursing and dropped his pistol with a thud on the floor.

Wolf pointed to Morgan and said to LeBlanc, "Cuff this dirtbag. I'm going after Croce."

Wolf ran to the master bedroom door and kicked it open to find it clear. He heard a thumping noise and saw the emergency exit door ajar. Wolf ran past the agents and his team cuffing Croce's team and treating the wounded. At the elevator he punched the Express and Staff Only buttons together. He keyed his mic as the doors closed, he radioed.

"All stations, Joshua-Actual, our target is in the wind. Anyone got him?"

Twenty-five seconds later, after multiple negative responses, Wolf was with his tech watching the video streams.

"Where is he?" Wolf demanded.

The tech pointed at a camera feed.

"There he is," he said, adjusting the zoom as the camera tracked Croce across the street.

Wolf jumped from the loading dock and sprinted around the

building, across the street and into the subway. A bullet zipped past Wolf's head at the same time as a loud *boom*. The wall tile behind him splintered, showering him with razor-sharp ceramic shards.

Late-night subway riders screamed and ran up at Wolf as he worked to push through them and down the escalator. At the platform, he glanced right then left, just catching a man running into the tunnel. Wolf stopped for a beat to radio his position but the radio only returned static. He ran down the platform, switched to his cellphone and called the surveillance tech with his status and location.

"And call the MTA and stop the trains on this track at my pos. Position a team here and one stop to the south. Copy?"

"Yes sir, good copy."

He jumped down to the track bed, making sure he oriented himself to the high-voltage rail. It had a cover, but in his aversion to electrocution, he wanted it spatially imprinted so as to not have to think about it in the middle of the coming fight.

This has all the makings of a bad movie where everyone gets shot, Wolf thought.

Wolf sang his death song as he hugged the left side wall, moving into the dark along the way Croce had fled.

Across the Atlantic in Marseille, Kennedy gave the execute order. There were three senior members of *Unione Corsa* still in the restaurant, which was not unusual given their propensity to party until sunrise. Three guards were killed in the assault, but the senior guys surrendered to the police without incident; they figured their expensive on-call lawyers would have them released from police custody soon enough. With few exceptions, the night shift workers at Janus and Juno also gave up meekly.

One suspect at Ramstein tried to make a run for it. He had

impressive speed, the Air Force Security dog handler reported, but it was eclipsed by a German Shepard hair missile named Thor.

In Kandahar, Clinton all but led the lead an Afghan counter-narcotics team to the opium waiting to be shipped out, but kept a low profile. The DEA agents made a big deal of the find and took pictures of the smiling Afghans narcs surrounding the bust, all with their weapons held in the air.

Chapter 91

As Wolf moved forward in the dimly lit New York City subway tunnel, his subconscious categorized each sound and light as friend or foe. Before he had jumped to the track bed, his mind had already made the switch to kill or be killed. He was in predator mode, and he was at peace with himself. He would emerge from this pursuit alive or dead.

Croce would be served the justice he so richly deserved.

Wolf stepped into a shadow and took deep breaths, exhaling slowly to still his mind. As he stepped out, a rusted piece of cyclone fencing he stepped on grated against the track bed. Then, boom-boom-boom, three muzzle flashes in rapid succession from about fifty meters down and across the tracks.

Wolf leaned back into the shadow for a moment to settle, then ran forward, shooting where he had seen the flashes. He stopped after only a few meters, taking cover in a maintenance alcove.

"Jean Paul, do not fight the inevitable," Wolf said, dropping the magazine from his pistol to reload a fresh one. "You leave here in handcuffs or a body bag. That choice is yours alone, *mon ami*. There are no other options."

Wolf took off after the footfalls he heard when Croce ran farther into the tunnel. He heard a creaking noise ahead and then cursing. Wolf slowed, his pistol up. Croce shot again, the muzzle flash low this time. The sound of the ricochet was immediately followed by pain as Wolf's pistol was ripped from his left hand. The sting numbed his hand, and he dropped to find his pistol. He grabbed it with his non-dominate right hand and tried several times to rack a fresh round into the chamber by running it against his leg. He tore his pants, but the slide did not move.

Shit—it's jammed.

Wolf tried slamming the front sight into the brick wall, but it didn't budge.

Wolf went flat as Croce unloaded. Five, six, seven shots.

Croce yelled.

"Stupid Belgian pistols. Always breaking down when you need them. Unlike the Glock I have. As a Frenchman, I am happy to use a Bosch weapon to kill you. Superior engineering and reliability."

Eleven shots. Sounds like 40 cal. One more before he's out or has to mag change. I need a visual.

Wolf stole a quick look up the track. There was a transformer box up ahead. Muscles tensed, Wolf bolted for the box, diving low into a roll, and coming up behind it as round after round slammed in the box.

Great, extended mag. Shit.

Just then he heard Croce running toward him, shooting. One shot then another. Wolf heard Croce's pistol run dry just as a transformer inside electrical box exploded with a *whummp*, blowing its door open and illuminating the black tunnel in white-hot light.

Wolf shielded his eyes from the bright sparks lighting the tunnel like mortar parachute illumination rounds. Croce cried out a curse, hands to his eyes, just as Wolf came around the burning transformer and slammed into him.

Croce was surprisingly nimble and quick for a man who had done a hit of heroin. He took the collision with Wolf and rolled to the gravelly surface of the tunnel. Wolf jumped to his feet in time to block a side kick to the head and countered with a sweeping kick to Croce's planted knee. Croce grunted and stepped back, reversing his lead, a four-inch blade glinting in his right hand. Wolf feinted a right cross, and as Croce defended, Wolf used a Karambit knife pulled from his belt to slash across Croce's right forearm. The deep gash made Croce switch hands with his knife.

As Wolf and Croce circled each other, Wolf pulled a second Karambit from his belt.

"You know my people like to take scalps," Wolf said with a wide grin, "and you don't even have to be dead. Yours will look good in my collection."

Croce screamed and attacked in a flurry of Jus Marseilles-style Savate kicks and strikes. Wolf blocked most of the assault, his razor-sharp knife lacerating Croce in the process. Wolf grunted as a fake head kick snapped into his left-side ribcage, the sudden excruciating pain an indication of fractures. But Wolf saw Croce was getting tired. Blood loss and the energy needed to repel Wolf's attacks was wearing him down fast.

Wolf lunged as if with a sword, the Karambit in his right hand opening a deep gash through Croce's shirt between his ribs. Bright red blood bubbled out. Croce laughed as they struck at each other, first on the offense and then defense as Wolf took his place as the attacker. Wolf was bleeding from both arms. If not for the finger hole in the Karambit, he would have lost his grip on both knives long ago. His hands were as slick from his own blood as with Croce's.

Croce attacked again, his eyes wide, fear and desperation in his scream. As he swung his knife in a downward wood-chopping motion, Wolf stepped into his space, pivoting to align his body with Croce's. Croce's energy did most of the work as Wolf punched him in the chest with his knife. Wolf dropped to a knee, throwing Croce across the tracks. Sprawled out on his back, Croce grunted as tried to stop the bright red blood bubbling out his chest. He rolled to his side and reached out, seemingly to get up.

What Wolf saw next would stay with him for the rest of his life. "No!" he yelled.

Croce's outstretched hand touched the high voltage rail. A lightning-like pulse of high-voltage electricity arced out of his rigid body where his chest lay, completing the connection to the track. Frozen in agony, Croce died instantly. Smoke drifted off his charred hand where his fingers used to be, and the fist-size hole in his chest oozed a black coagulated jell of fried lung and other flesh.

Wolf sat against the tunnel wall and lay back. His spirit guide called him. He closed his eyes as the warm light around him grew. All-enveloping and peaceful, Wolf felt his body relax. Unsure how long he'd been in the spirit's presence, Wolf felt the pain return. Someone was yelling. The slap was too much. Wolf growled back in fight mode.

"Wolf, Wolf! Damn it, wake up."

He sensed the stick, the rush of fluid into his system.

Wolf opened his eyes and said through gritted teeth, "You're an ugly-ass angel, Morgan."

Chapter 92

The mood in Shadow Tier headquarters was a combination of back-slapping hugs and fist bumps with nods from the knowing. Wolf's overnight stay in the hospital had been just a precaution. He had skipped PT and had garnered some getting-old jokes. Each of the squadron commanders had held their own hot washes and after-action report meetings. This morning's meeting was the time-honored leadership review.

Wolf had always been a supporter of deep and direct reviews of missions and outcomes. Not meant to demean anyone's performance, but to focus on continuous improvement. In Wolf's mind, it meant his people coming home alive, the bad guys not so much.

Wolf smiled as his warrior family was with him in person, and not over video conference. Kennedy, Taylor, and the Kid from Germany; Clinton from Afghanistan; Parker and LeBlanc. All were with him now.

Wolf asked LeBlanc, "Where are we?"

"Eliana Cortes and her son are in-processing to WITSEC. She's given us a massive data dump. Her dope networks have collapsed, and we will make El Chapo and his leadership's lives hell."

Clinton said, "The exact amount of monetary damage we have done to the Taliban is hard to pinpoint with certainty, but the nerds at DEA think it's on the order of many tens of millions. As Wolf mentioned before, the psych job on the paranoid Taliban leadership is priceless—I'll give it a twelve on a scale of ten. And believe it or not, the DEA has become friendly."

"Any fallout for the mafia?" Kennedy asked.

Wolf said, "The FBI's guy Morgan worked with was just the middleman in the transaction for a family member and that has kept him insulated. There will be hell to pay when their distributors and street sellers get feedback that the powder doesn't get you high, but bonus: It isn't going to kill you anymore either. They will test and test, and it will always test as high-grade heroin. It's brilliant. More to come as we watch it unfold."

"What else?" Parker asked.

The Kid said, "Well, we got you back."

The conference room went silent. You could hear a pin drop. Wolf glanced Parker's way and she was staring at her boots. Wolf knew it was likely to hide the flush of water to her eyes. These people were her family, too.

Wolf smiled. "You know, maybe we should make it part of the Shadow Tier load-out plan. Item number one, make sure you have your Parker," he said, and smiled. Parker gave him a *you-will-pay-later* look, but followed by a smile.

Wolf asked, "What are our unanswered questions?"

"Amaru. What are we going to do about him?" Kennedy said.

"El Gato has dropped kicked him. He's an assassin without a home, a Ronin. Our not responding is getting to him and he wants a fight. He thinks he can end me and looks forward to trying to do so. Therefore, I am purposely not giving him the opportunity. I'm demeaning his self-appointed stature and place in the hierarchy of predators. A couple of weeks from now, he may start making mistakes. If he does, we'll take advantage of it."

"What about El Chapo's plan for Indian reservations?" Parker asked.

"To be honest, all we did was push the problem out to other parts of Montana," Wolf said. "But there haven't been any reports of activity indicating that Sinaloa is moving back in. Dismantling Eliana's network helped with that. We need to keep watch on it."

Morgan said, "Eliana told me El Chapo had been pushing her to replant with opium. He mentioned looking into Cuba as a distribution partner and even farming for him there. We need to keep an eye on it. Our friends at the Agency see it as a possible path to turn Cuba into another Mexico dope center."

"I'd like an analysis of the opportunity from El Chapo's point of view."

Parker nodded. "Yeah. Ninety miles from Florida, easy access to the Gulf of Mexico states, shipping lanes, the whole deal."

Wolf let the silence hang. A beat later, he said, "Okay, if there's nothing else, let's get back to work. El Chapo and his switch to a higher percentage of opium has me worried. We live in an opportunity-rich environment, so let's do what Shadow Tier does best. Orient, observe, decide—and act."

Acknowledgments

This novel, as with *Shadow Tier* before it, would not have been written but for the inspiration to read instilled by my mother, and with the support of my wife. Add to that the lessons I've learned and insights gained in courses with Jerry Jenkins and Career Authors, and at conferences like International Thriller Writer's ThrillerFest and Rocky Mountain Fiction Writers' Colorado Gold Conference.

I keep learning through reading this rich genre and I pick up something to make my craft better every time I read a Brad Taylor, Mark Greaney, Jack Carr, or Don Bentley novel, to name just a few.

To the authors whose works brought substance and concepts to this story: They include *Rainbow Six* by Tom Clancy; *War of the Flea* by Robert Taber; *Counting Coup* by Joseph Medicine Crow; *Myths and Traditions of the Crow Indians* by Robert H. Lowie; *Narconomics* by Tom Wainwright; *Seeds of Terror* by Gretchen Peters; *The Politics of Heroin* by Alfred W. McCoy; *Indian Gaming and Tribal Sovereignty* by Steven Andrew Light and Kathryn R. L. Rand; and *Money Laundering and Illicit Financial Flows* by John A. Cassara.

Thanks to Jeffery J. Higgins, author and retired DEA supervisory special agent, for his on-the-ground insights to the early days of setting up shop in Afghanistan and hunting the kingpin of opium.

To my crack team of beta readers: Brad Seal, Mark Elliott, Chris Minchin, and Elle Pope.

To my ITW critique partners: Millie Hast and Traci Abramson, Jack Stewart, Ann Feinstein, and Michael Niemann.

To my writing family that continues to provide insight, advice, and support: Brian Andrews, Chris Hauty, Eric Bishop, David Temple, and a host of others. You know who you are, and you are appreciated.

To the hosts of the podcasts and radio shows who graciously allow me to join their shows: KOA 850 AM/94.1 FM *The Ross Kaminsky Show* with Ross Kaminsky; *The Team House* with David Parke and Jack Murphy; DTD with Dustin Kelly; *Forward Observer* with Mike Shelby; *Course of Action* with Jeff Clark; *The Thriller Zone* with David Temple; *American Warrior Radio* with Ben Buehler-Garcia; *The Kit Cage* with Dan Brocklebank; and *The Protectors* with Dr. Jason Piccolo.

And to the past and present men and women of the US Army Special Forces Regiment, *Free the Oppressed!*

"The views expressed in this publication are those of the author
and do not necessarily reflect the official policy or position
of the Department of Defense or the US government.
The public release clearance of this publication by the
Department of Defense does not imply
Department of Defense endorsement
or factual accuracy of the material."

This narrative is a work of fiction. Nothing in this work con-
stitutes an official release of US Government information. Any
discussions or depictions of methods, tactics, equipment, fact
or opinion are solely the product of the author's imagination.

Nothing in this work reflects nor should be construed as any
official position or view of the US Government, nor any of its
departments, policies, or personnel.

Nothing in this work of fiction should be construed as asserting
or implying a US Government authentication or confirmation
of information presented herein, nor any endorsement what-
soever of the author's views, which are and remain his own.

This material was reviewed for classification by the Defense
Office of Prepublication and Security Review and was cleared
as amended for public release.

About the author

S teve Stratton started his US Army career at the White House Communications Agency, where his work took him around the world. The jump from WHCA to the US Secret Service was an easy transition, but after several years, Steve left for the commercial sector and joined the National Guard and its 20th Special Forces Group.

He was awarded his Green Beret in 1986, and from the 1980s through 2000 he deployed with 20th SFGA on counter-drug and training missions in the SOUTHCOM region. During this time his civilian work included supporting CENTCOM, SOCOM, and DIA. Today he develops cyber security products that support the DOD and Intelligence Community.

When not writing or working, Steve splits his time between Aurora, Colorado and his cabin in the Tarryall mountain range west of Denver for mountain biking, hiking, and hunting.

For more information on this and other exciting new authors, please see ForcePoseidon.com
contact@ForcePoseidon.com

Made in United States
Troutdale, OR
09/02/2023

12549179R00278